Bittersweet Memories

CATHARINA MAURA

This one is for the dreamers, the ones who create Pinterest boards of their dream life and then fight to make those dreams come true.

You've got this.

Per aspera ad astra.

Contents

PART ONE
The Past

Chapter One

Silas

My heart wrenches as I stare at my father's casket, the pain so great it nearly brings me to my knees. Every breath of air I suck in *hurts*, and my throat is burning from the screams and tears I'm keeping within. Helplessness and a great sense of injustice claw at me. Why my father? How could it possibly have been his time? He was far healthier than I ever have been, and he stuck to his workout routines and his healthy diet without ever missing a day. It makes no sense to me. I sit up in my seat at the front of the cemetery, my eyes roaming over the crowd that has gathered to bid my father farewell. Do these people feel the same injustice I feel?

Over the last few days, I've felt like I've been witnessing everything from a distance, as though I wasn't there at all when we were told my father had a sudden heart attack. I recall going to the hospital and holding his hand, not comprehending what the doctors were trying to say. To me, it looked like Dad was simply asleep. His hand was still warm in mine, and unlike what I'd read about death, he wasn't stiff at all. I was so certain they'd made a mistake, or that, perhaps, this was all an elaborate joke. My father always had a morbid sense of humor, and I hoped that's all it was.

It wasn't.

My stepmother rises from her seat opposite me and disgust settles at the pit of my stomach, uncurling and spreading through my body until I can barely stand to look at her. She's wearing a black hat with a black dress that's far too short to be appropriate. Matching black heels with bottoms the same red color as her lips complete her outfit. While I understand everyone deals with grief differently, I can't help but resent the perfect smile on her make-up riddled face. I could barely get myself into the shower this morning, and even as I sit here, I'm shaking from the force of my suppressed tears. How does she smile like that when she just lost her husband?

Mona's gaze roams over the sizeable crowd that has gathered at the cemetery to say their last goodbyes to my father. It's almost as though she suddenly realizes that all eyes are on her, because she freezes for a split-second before she sniffs as tears gather in her eyes.

"Thank you all for being here today to honor my late husband, Jacob Sinclair," she says, her voice trembling ever so slightly. "He leaves behind two beautiful boys, both of whom are evidence of the great man he was. In them, he instilled love, honor, kindness, and a moral compass stronger than any other. While we may have lost Jacob, I take solace in knowing that I'll see him in the eyes of my sons every day."

I glance at my younger half-brother, who is seated next to his mother's empty seat. Ryan is looking down at his lap, his hands clenched and his head bowed. I see the tears that fall from his eyes, the pain he tries to hide. Unlike my stepmother, Ryan is drowning in the same pain I feel, and regret hits me hard. Several times, he's come to my room to tell me about his memories of Dad, as though he needed someone to remember him with, someone who would truly understand.

Each time, I turned him away, unable to face the fact that our father is truly gone. Being five years older, I should've known how much my thirteen-year-old brother needed me, and I failed him. Instead of pushing him away, I should've hugged him the way his mother won't. I should've done what Dad would've expected of me. Instead, I lost myself in my own selfish sorrows.

I inhale shakily and rub my hand over my face as I try to keep it together. I can barely even focus on my stepmother's speech. All I can hear is the sound of my own beating heart. I focus on the steady thumping throughout the rest of the eulogy, wishing I could just get out of here. I don't want to watch my father's casket close, and I can't stand the thought of him being cremated, no part of him remaining on this earth. Somehow, I always assumed he'd want to be buried, just like my mother. I assumed there'd be a place I could go visit him, the way he and I used to visit Mom. Until this morning, I didn't even realize that I'd never be able to do that.

Mona takes a step away, and one by one, people approach Dad's casket, saying their final goodbyes. I don't have it in me to do the same. I've seen Dad several times at the funeral home since he passed away, but it still doesn't feel real to me.

My gaze shifts to Ryan, whose eyes are on Dad. I can tell he wants to approach him and say his own last farewell, but he doesn't dare to. Once again, hatred for my stepmother overwhelms me, blinding me as I rise to my feet. Before I even realize what I'm doing, I've got my hand on Ryan's shoulder. "Come on," I murmur. "Let's go together."

He looks up at me through teary eyes, so much faith and relief in his expression. Sometimes it gets hard to remember that Ryan isn't his mother. It's no secret that Mona and I don't get along, but our feud never should have touched Ryan.

I lead him toward Dad, his entire body shaking with each step we take. By the time we pause in front of the casket, Ryan is barely containing his sobs. "*Dad*," he whispers, his voice breaking.

Our father looks so serene, lying there in his favorite suit. His thick dark hair is neatly combed, and his hands are laid on top of each other. It's strange to see him like this, because it's clearly him, yet it also feels like it isn't him at all. I don't believe in souls and such, but watching my father lying there truly makes me feel like he's no longer here with us.

I wrap my arm around Ryan fully and swallow hard, struggling to keep my own tears at bay. "We were blessed to have had him, Ryan. You and I… we'll carry forward Dad's legacy."

He nods and leans into me, and I squeeze his shoulder reassuringly. "Is there anything you still want to tell Dad?" I ask, my voice soft.

He hesitates for a moment. "Thank you, Dad," he whispers, his voice so soft I wouldn't have heard him if I weren't standing right next to him. "For giving me Silas, and for always loving us. You always told us to be brave, and I will try to be. I… I'll be the b-best brother and son I can be, so you will n-never have to worry about Silas or Mom."

My heart shatters and I bite down on my lip harshly. My sweet young brother is a better person than I'll ever be, and I need to work harder at being the person he thinks I am.

"Come on," Mona says from behind us. "They're going to take him away now."

Ryan nods and turns at the sound of his mother's voice, but I don't follow him. I can't. I stand there, frozen, taking one last look at my father.

I love you, Dad, I think to myself. *I always will. I'll make you proud, I promise. I'll be everything you ever wanted me to be. I swear to you that I'll do better from today onward. I'll take care of Ryan as if he were my own. To this day, I'm not sure if you saw her true colors, but I'll shield him from Mona nonetheless. I'll do everything I know you'd expect of me. This is the very last promise I get to make you, and I swear I'll keep it. I'll ensure you can rest in peace, knowing I'll be there to protect him in your stead. I promise, Dad.*

I take a step away when the funeral director smiles at me apologetically, his hands on the casket's lid. This is it. This is the last time I'll ever see my father again.

I walk away, needing a moment to myself before I'm forced to face the countless guests that came to see us. As if on autopilot, I walk the path that leads to the graves I know are behind this building. It's a path I've walked countless times with my father.

Just as I'm about to round the corner that leads to my mother's grave, the sound of soft sobbing stops me in my tracks. On the ground by the trees along the road sits a girl dressed in black, her knees drawn up and her face hidden, the force of her sobs shaking her body.

Before I know what I'm doing, I'm kneeling in front of her, the handkerchief my mother embroidered for me in hand. "Here," I tell her.

The girl looks up, and the expression in her honey brown eyes hits me right in the chest. She is sorrow personified, and in her, I see myself.

Chapter Two

Alanna

I look up into the most beautiful dark green eyes I've ever seen, surprised to find no pity in them... there's only understanding.

I take the handkerchief with trembling hands and sniff as I wipe away my tears. "Thank you," I tell him, my voice hoarse. My heart is aching so badly that I think I might be sick, and I clench the fabric in my hands, as though I'm hoping it'll give me the strength I need today.

"What's your name?" he asks.

I look into his eyes, and something about his gaze takes the edge off my pain. He's kneeling in front of me, no doubt ruining his suit pants, yet his entire focus is on me. "Alanna," I whisper before looking down again.

I trace over the embroidery on his handkerchief absentmindedly, feeling numb. "*Psi*?" I ask, referring to the greek letter on the fabric.

He nods. "You're a clever one, aren't you? I'm surprised you know what letter that is."

I look up at him indignantly. It's clear he thinks I'm a child, and it annoys me. "Why Psi?"

He smiles, but it doesn't reach his eyes. "It's my name. Or, well, it's a nickname. It's interesting that you pronounced it the same as *sigh*. Most people pronounce the *P* too."

Psi. What is that short for? Simon, I assume. It's a bit of an old-fashioned name, so I'm not surprised he'd abbreviate it.

"It's Ancient Greek," I murmur. "None of us truly know how it's pronounced, right? As far as I'm aware, both pronunciations are considered correct."

Si sits down next to me and smiles, startling me. Until now, I hadn't even realized just how handsome he is. "Now, where did you learn that, little girl?"

I narrow my eyes at him. "I'm *thirteen*, I'm *not* a little girl. I'll be fourteen next week."

He chuckles and shakes his head. "Yeah, I remember being your age and feeling the same way. I'd tell you to enjoy being so young, but I always hated it when people said that to me. All I wanted to do was grow up already. But let me tell you a secret: even when you get to my age, you'll still feel like a child."

I roll my eyes at him, my previous grief melting away. "Okay, Grandpa. How old are you?"

He crosses his legs and smiles. "I'm eighteen. Much older than you."

I shake my head and huff. "Five years, or probably more like four and a half years. You act like you're ancient, but you can't even buy a drink yet."

Si bursts out laughing, startling me once again. He's so handsome that he could fit right into every single one of my favorite boy bands. That thick dark hair that's in the same style as a few of my favorite Korean actors, and those cheekbones should be in magazines... he's the kind of guy I'd never dare speak to at school.

"You're clever *and* sassy, huh?"

I smirk at him, and he stares at me for a moment.

"I'm glad you're smiling now, Alanna. Considering where we

are, I can only imagine how much pain you must be in. I'm sure you found yourself sitting here because it was all too much and you didn't want anyone to see you fall apart. It's how I feel too... but don't forget that sometimes, letting others be there for us is a way of offering consolation too. Whoever you ran away from might need you more than you think. Sometimes, having someone who shares your grief makes it more bearable."

I look into his eyes, recognizing the pain in them. "Do you have someone who you can share your grief with?"

He shakes his head and looks away. "Not anymore."

I reach for him without thinking and grab his hand, my grip tight. "You've got me now, Si."

He chuckles and tightens his grip on my hand. "Has no one ever warned you about strange men?"

I pout and look away. "You're hardly a man."

Si coughs, and I look back at him to find him looking at me with an outraged expression.

"Little girl," he says. "If you weren't so young, I'd feel inclined to defend my honor."

I burst out laughing, my hand still in his. "*Defend your honor*... honestly, it's like you stepped out of one of my tv shows."

He smiles and leans in, tenderly brushing my hair behind my ear in an almost brotherly way. "I'm serious, though, Alanna. Please be careful around people you don't know, okay? It's when we're hurting most that people are most likely to take advantage of us. Keep that in mind, okay?"

I nod, my smile melting away. "Does that mean I should be worried about you speaking to me?"

He shakes his head. "Never me, sweet girl."

Si pulls his hand out of mine and looks away. "I need to head back, and you should, too. Your family is probably looking for you. Today must feel incredibly hard for you, and I can tell you from experience that the pain never truly fades, but you'll learn to live with it, Alanna. Each day, it'll get a little easier to breathe, until one day, you find yourself smiling at the same memories that once made you cry."

He rises to his feet and offers me his hand. I take it, and he pulls me up, making me stumble forward. Si catches me and steadies me, his hands on my shoulders.

"Thank you," I murmur, feeling oddly flustered. I've never had a crush on anyone other than celebrities, but I think I might be developing one now.

I stare at Si's handkerchief for a moment, unsure whether I should give it back to him or not. It's filthy now, and I'm too embarrassed to hand it to him.

"Keep it," he says, his voice soft. "If we ever meet again, you can return it to me."

I nod and fold the fabric carefully. "Thank you, Si. Not just for the handkerchief, but also for sitting here and talking to me without asking me who I lost or what happened. It's... it just..."

"I know," he says, a cute smirk on his face. "I know, because I'm in just as much pain, and I definitely don't want to talk about it either. Remember what I said, okay? Don't lose yourself in your grief. Let the people who love you be there for you."

"Yes," I murmur, nodding. I hadn't really thought of it that way before, and he's probably right. Dad must be hurting too, and maybe the two of us will get through this together.

Si turns and walks away, looking back at me once he's a few steps away. I don't want him to leave, but I don't know how to ask him to stay. "See you around, Alanna."

I bite down on my lip and wave at him before he walks in the opposite direction of where I need to be. I stare at his back for a few moments as I try to gather my courage.

Normally it'd be Mom I'd turn to when I'm as upset as I am today. But how can I, when it's her I lost?

I'm absentminded as I walk back to her grave, not wanting to face the fact that we're burying her today. I wish I could just go home and pretend this isn't happening, but I can't.

"Alanna!" Dad rushes up to me, his eyes red from the endless tears he's shed, his expression worried. "Are you okay, sweetheart?"

Dad wraps his arms around me, hugging me tightly, and I hug him back with all my strength. "No," I admit. "I'm not okay, Dad. It feels like I'll never be okay again."

He rests his chin on top of my head, his body trembling just as mine is. "I know, sweetie. I feel the same way, but we *will* be fine. So long as we've got each other, we'll be okay, won't we?"

I nod. "Yeah," I whisper. "I just don't understand. Why weren't we enough, Dad? Why would she... why didn't she stay for me? Didn't Mom love me? Why wasn't I enough?"

Dad tightens his grip on me. "She did, Alanna. Mom was just very sick, and the medication never made her better. It just... It just made her more depressed. It isn't anything you did, my love. It isn't your fault at all, okay?"

I nod, but I can't help but wonder what I could've done to prevent my mother's death. If I'd told her that I love her more often, would that have prevented her from taking her own life?

Chapter Three

Silas

This can't be right. I look up from the document in my hand, barely comprehending what I just read.

"I'm sorry, Silas," Michael, my father's lawyer, says. "Your father left everything to your stepmother. Neither you nor your brother inherited anything at all."

I rise from my seat and place the document on his desk with trembling hands. "Is this real, Michael? You were there when he signed this?"

He nods, his expression apologetic. When the will was read, I assumed my stepmother was pulling a trick of some sort, but this entire document is in my father's own handwriting. He's leaving his entire estate worth millions to *Mona*.

"Why would he do this? Why would he cut Ryan and me out like that?"

I bite down on my lip, my thoughts reeling. Of course Mona would take care of her own son, but Dad must have known that she'd never do the same for me. It's no secret that she and I haven't been on good terms in recent years.

Not since I found out that she'd been cheating with the gardener and told my father about it. That was over three years ago, and though it didn't seem to affect my father and Mona, my bond with her was severed the moment my father confronted her.

"I don't know, Silas. I asked him whether he was sure when he came in with this will, and he was. Perhaps he assumed your stepmother would continue to care for you as she has for the last thirteen years."

I shake my head in disbelief. How could he possibly have believed that? The older I get, the more I see Mona for who she really is. She's a vicious little bitch, and I thought my father was finally starting to realize it too.

I'm certain he never even would've married her if she hadn't shown up on our doorstep, six months pregnant with Ryan. I know how much my father loved my mother, and at the time I was far too young to understand, but I see it now.

She was just a rebound fling, someone to help ease the broken heart my mother's passing left Dad with. She was barely twenty at the time and half my father's age. The older Dad got, the more the age difference worked against them. They had nothing in common, and in the last two years, all they'd ever done was argue. If she'd truly loved him, it'd been a different story, but I don't think she ever did.

"Can I contest this?"

Michael sighs. "No, Silas. Your father was of sound state of mind when he signed this, and two witnesses were present, including myself. I wish I could give you a different answer, but I can't."

I nod and sink back into the seat opposite his desk. Why would Dad do this to me? How could he have trusted his wife to this extent, when the two of them could barely stand each other in recent months?

"I'm sorry, Silas."

I force a smile onto my face and shake my head. "Thank you for your time," I tell Michael as I rise to my feet, feeling more lost than ever before. Losing Dad so unexpectedly was hard enough, but this document will ensure that my father isn't all I'll lose.

I'm filled with dread as I make my way home, a dozen different scenarios playing through my mind. Mona and I haven't spoken to each other at all since Dad passed away, and I have no doubt that it won't take her long to act on her newfound power and wealth.

The house is quiet when I walk in and I almost breathe a sigh of relief, but then I hear the telltale sound of Mona's heels on our marble floor. She smirks when she sees me and pauses, leaning back against the wall as her eyes roam over my body, her gaze unsettling.

"I take it you have by now verified that you have no claim on any of the Sinclair assets?"

I stare at her, my words caught in my throat. Mona chuckles, and the knowing look in her eyes grates on me.

"Cat got your tongue? I didn't think I'd ever see the day you don't talk back to me."

I sigh and run a hand through my hair, annoyed by her mere presence. Everything about her annoys me. The skimpy clothes, the excessive makeup and jewelry, the sound of her voice. I hate everything about her.

"I'm going to my room," I say, walking past her.

"No, you're not." Her voice is soft, but it's got an edge to it. "You're going to pack your bags and get the hell out of my house."

I turn around to face her, confused. "What?"

"You heard me. You never liked me anyway, and I have no intention of putting up with your moody ass for a moment longer. Pack your bags and get out of my house."

"*Your house*?" I repeat. "This is the home I grew up in. We buried my father three days ago, Mona. You can't be serious."

She smiles, her expression venomous. "I'm dead serious. This is a new start for us, for *Ryan*. I want you gone by the time Ryan gets home from soccer practice, or I'll have security escort you out for trespassing. Don't try me, Silas. You won't like the consequences."

"Dad would never want you to do this. Is this how you honor your marriage with him? By evicting his son days after his funeral?"

Mona smiles and crosses her arms. "Your father is dead, just like our marriage was. I want you gone. Consider this your last warning."

She walks away, and I stare after her. I know her well enough to know that she isn't joking, but where does that leave me? With nothing to my name, I won't even be able to afford to go to college. How could she do this to me when I've barely even recovered from losing Dad?

It's strange how disappointed I am in her. I never had high expectations, so why does it hurt so much that she proved me right? Part of me wanted to believe that she truly loved my father, even though I knew better.

It only takes me an hour to pack my bags, and before I know it, I'm pulling up in front of my best friend's house. At least I still have some cash in my bank account, and I've got my car.

I lean back in my seat and stare at Lucas's front door, unsure what my next steps should be. Can I even afford to attend college? Am I better off not going at all?

I'm filled with heartache and shame as I get out of my car, the backseat filled with my belongings. Even as I press the doorbell, I'm second-guessing coming here, but I have nowhere else to go. I have no family, and though I know many people, Lucas is my only real friend.

He opens the door before I have a chance to change my mind, and I smile at him nervously. "Hey," I murmur. "I really need a place to stay."

CHAPTER 4
Two Years Later

Alanna

"Dad, are we seriously doing this?" I ask, staring up at the building that houses a homeless shelter. When he told me he'd take me out on Saturday, I assumed he'd be taking me somewhere nice to make up for having to work on my sixteenth birthday.

Instead, I find myself staring up at a place that seems incredibly detached from our usual lives. Why would he bring me here?

Dad leans back against his beloved truck, a pensive look on his face. It's almost like he isn't even here with me at all, as though he's lost in memories I know nothing of. Lately, he's been like this often. When we lost Mom, Dad and I didn't fall apart like we both thought we would. We just got closer. We learned to lean on each other. He was the one I'd turn to if anything interesting happened during my day, and he'd tell me about boring work stuff that I'd barely comprehend. We'd have dinner together, and we'd act as though Mom didn't leave a gaping hole in both of our hearts.

In the last couple of weeks, things have been different. He doesn't come home until I'm fast asleep, and on the odd occasion that he does, he's buried in work, barely present when I try to talk to him. I miss him, and I was really hoping to spend some quality time together. I don't understand why he'd take me to a homeless shelter on the first day off he's taken in weeks.

"*Dad*," I complain, my tone whiny.

He sighs and runs a hand through his hair, his gaze lowering. "I used to live here," he says eventually, his voice soft.

I look up sharply, shocked. "*What*?"

Dad nods, a melancholic smile on his face. "Come on. It's about time I came back here. This place was instrumental in getting me back on my feet, and it's about time I pay it forward."

I'm in a daze as I follow Dad into the building, feeling somewhat on edge. The facility is well-maintained, and the entrance looks like an office building that they've tried to turn into a home, complete with pictures of frequent visitors and notable people that have tried to make a difference.

"Robert!" I look up at the sound of my father's name. A tall, friendly looking man with the kindest smile walks up to us, his eyes roaming over my father. "Look at you! I once said I never wanted to see you here again, but you're a sight for sore eyes. I can't thank you enough for everything you've done for the shelter."

"Ricardo," Dad says, an equally radiant smile on his face. There's something more in Dad's expression, though. He usually looks proud and stands tall, but today he looks humble and grateful. Whoever this man is, my father values him endlessly. "I'm here to show my daughter around today. Donating is one thing, but I thought it was about time that I visit."

Ricardo offers me his hand, and I shake it the way my dad taught me, my grip firm and confident. "It's good to meet you, Alanna."

I nod. "Likewise." I'm curious about the man in front of me. I never knew that my dad was homeless once upon a time, and I'm curious... not just about this place, but about that time in my father's life. He's a well-known and prominent businessman, and though we don't discuss finances often, I'm certain he's worth millions. I know his company is, for sure. He started as a general worker in construction, learning the trade and working his way up before he was offered investment opportunities that led him to where he is today, becoming one of the biggest property development contractors. I never thought much about where he started, and he's never volunteered any information before.

"Let me show you around," Dad says. "It looks like not much has changed in the years since I left."

I follow him quietly, my heart filled with a type of sorrow I've never felt before as I take in the people around us. Many of them look just like us, and not at all what I'd consider stereotypical homeless people. They look clean, their clothes tidy.

"You'd be surprised just how easy it is to lose everything," Dad says softly. "Sometimes all it takes is losing your job. The bills pile up, and one thing leads to another. Often, people are only here for a few days or a few weeks. Those are the lucky ones."

"How long were you here?" I ask, part of me fearing his answer.

Dad looks at me and sighs. "Over a year. Far longer than I should have been. Ricardo helped me find a job, and he made sure I always looked presentable. He kept us all fed and as healthy as we could be. Many of the guys that work for me today are people I met right here, people who just needed a chance, someone to believe in them."

Dad leads me to what appears to be a large sitting room, filled with books and one television that a dozen people are sitting in front of. "You said you wanted some more pocket money, didn't you?"

I nod, and Dad turns to me. "Come volunteer here once a week, and I'll pay you for the time you spend helping others. I know you're upset that I've barely spent any time with you lately, and I think it'll be good for you to spend some time *here*. We're blessed, Alanna, but things could have been very different for us.

It's important to me that you remember that, that you realize what I work so hard for."

I blink in surprise. Work here? This isn't at all close to our house. It'd take me ages to come here and then travel back home.

"Think about it, sweetheart. If you agree to volunteer here, I'll pay you twice the rate you'd get working in retail. Go walk around for a bit while you decide. I'll be right here."

I nod and look around me hesitantly, but Dad smiles encouragingly and tips his head toward the door behind us. I sigh as I turn around and walk away, doing as he asks.

My heart sinks when I walk into a large room filled with more bunk beds than I can count. I could fit ten of these beds into my bedroom, and it instantly makes me feel guilty for having as much as I do, and still wanting more of Dad's time. I suppose that's exactly why he brought me here today, to help me realize what the cost of everything we have is, what his success stemmed from.

"*Alanna*?"

I look to my side and I'm met with familiar dark green eyes. "Simon?"

He smiles, and my heart skips a beat. He looks older, rougher, but every bit as handsome. Simon is wearing jeans and a plain black t-shirt, but he looks good. What is he doing here? That day I saw him at the cemetery, it was clear he wasn't poor in the slightest. I still remember the watch he was wearing then. It was identical to my dad's in everything but the color. Simon's watch was gold, while Dad's is silver.

"That's what you think Si is short for?"

I nod, feeling oddly flustered. "What are you doing here?"

His smile drops, and he cups the back of his neck, his expression vulnerable. "I live here," he says, his voice soft. "What brings you here?" His eyes roam over my body, and I wonder if he still thinks I'm a little girl.

"I... my dad told me to, um, to volunteer. Here." My cheeks heat rapidly and I bite down on my lip. Why am I being so awkward all of a sudden?

He nods, his expression on the wall behind me. "I'm not sure that's a good idea, Alanna. It isn't that safe here. I'll admit that this is definitely one of the better shelters, and they care a lot more than they do in other places. They guarantee a spot for months at a time if you can prove you need it, and that you're working hard to reverse your circumstances, but we still have many people with mental health concerns, and it's not uncommon for them to lash out. Theft is common too. You won't last a day."

"Why not?" I ask, indignantly.

He smiles then, disarming me. "You're too pretty, Alanna. You look too sweet, too easy to take advantage of."

I cross my arms, and for a moment, Si's eyes drop to my chest before he looks away. "I think you underestimate me," I tell him.

Si shakes his head. "It's not a challenge, Alanna. I'm serious. This is no place for you."

I bite down on my lip as I consider his words, but my mind is made up.

"We'll see about that," I tell Si, before walking away to meet my father. I'll tell Dad I'll do it. I'll volunteer here.

Chapter Five

Alanna

I'm second-guessing myself as I pause in the doorway of the shelter. Being here without Dad makes me feel out of place and uncertain. I've never really volunteered before, and I'm worried I won't do a good job. It's clear to me that this place means a lot to Dad, and I'm afraid to let him down.

"Alanna!" Ricardo walks up to me with the kindest smile on his face, and I smile back instinctively. There are some people that just truly resonate positivity and hope, and Ricardo is definitely one of those people. "Come in, come in!"

He leads me to a small office near the entrance and offers to make me a cup of tea, which I decline. "I'll do my best," I promise him, as soon as we sit down. "You don't have to look after me or babysit me. I'm not here to be a burden to you."

He chuckles and shakes his head. "You really are your father's daughter, aren't you? When he first walked in here needing a place to stay, he also promised me that he wouldn't be a burden to me."

My heart aches for Dad and everything he must have gone through. There's so much I never knew about him. He's always been my hero, and Dad has always seemed larger than life to me. When we lost Mom, he took on her role in addition to his own with such ease that he's always seemed like a superhero to me.

"Dad said that?"

Ricardo nods. "You definitely take after him, but you've got your mother's smile."

My eyes widen and my heart skips a beat. "You knew my mom?"

Ricardo nods. "Do a good job today, and I'll tell you a story about your parents, okay?"

I grin. "I was always going to do a great job, but I won't say no to this."

"Come on. Let me show you what you'll be doing today. Our needs shift daily, so the work you'll do here will never be exactly the same. Today, I'll have you help with inventorying our canned foods. Lately we have, unfortunately, had some thefts in the facility. We're switching to a more secure storage system, and we want to create a better ordering system, so we can order more food at better prices further ahead of time. To do that, we first need to know exactly how much we have of everything after the recent theft incidences."

I follow him through the building, trying my hardest not to stare at the people in the various rooms. The last thing I want to do is make anyone uncomfortable. Dad told me to remember that he often had to sacrifice his pride and dignity when he was homeless, and that it hurt each and every time. He specifically asked me to keep that in mind, and to be careful with my actions and expressions. *Just a single pitiful gaze can hurt, Alanna*, he said.

The job Ricardo gave me is easy enough, and though it's slow and boring work, it at least makes me feel like I'm doing something meaningful. As I count the various cans of food they've got, my mind keeps drifting to the people that live here... in particular, *Si*.

How does a guy like him end up here? I know Dad said that it's easy to lose everything, but it just seems impossible. I may have been young when we first met, but I'm not blind. Just his watch was worth several thousand dollars, unless it was fake, but Si doesn't seem like he'd bother with fake goods.

I'm still thinking about him as I lock the storage room. I know I need to return the key to Ricardo and go home, but I'm curious about Si. It doesn't take me long to find him sitting in the corner of a room with a book in his hands.

I smile as I approach him, my heart pounding wildly. "Si!"

He looks up, but instead of the smile I expected, he's frowning at me, a hint of annoyance in his gaze. My heart sinks, and I draw my shoulders up defensively.

I sit down next to him, despite the fact that he ignores me and continues to read his book. The rejection stings, but I don't let it discourage me.

"Hey, I... I've been meaning to return this to you." I take his handkerchief out of my pocket and hand it to him with both hands, not really wanting to let it go.

Silas stares at it in surprise and then looks up at me, the ice in his eyes melting away to reveal the same caring expression he wore when we first met. "You kept it all this time?"

I nod. "I'm not too sure why, but it just helped me stay brave when the pain became too much. Every time I found myself lashing out, I'd hold it tightly and remember you telling me to share my pain, so I'd talk to my dad instead of crying myself to sleep. Before I knew it, I'd come to consider this handkerchief as somewhat of a lucky token, so I carry it everywhere I go."

A small part of me also hoped I'd run into Si one day, and I'd be able to return it to him. He has no idea how that one small act of kindness kept me from drowning in my sorrows.

He wraps his hand over mine, hesitating for a moment before curling his fingers closed over mine. "Keep it," he says, his voice soft. "It seems like you valued it the way I always have, so I'll leave it in your hands."

"Are you sure?" The look in his eyes tells me this handkerchief means a lot to him, so I'm surprised he's letting me keep it. I'm sure there's a story behind it.

"I'm sure."

I nod and rise to my feet, not wanting to leave, yet not wanting to disturb him unnecessarily either. It's clear my company isn't welcome, and I'm feeling awkward enough as it is.

I smile at him as I walk away, trying my hardest not to look back as I walk to the door. I'm stopped in my tracks when he wraps his hand around my wrist once I'm halfway through the room and pulls me against him suddenly. My head bumps against his chest and he wraps his arm around me, but it isn't me he's looking at.

"Jonathan," he says, his tone admonishing. "How about you return her keys, and I'll pretend I didn't see what you just did? You know as well as I did that this will get you kicked out of the shelter."

I turn in his embrace, and Si's arm moves to my shoulder. He's holding me so protectively, his gaze so fierce that my heart can't help but skip a beat.

A lanky blonde guy groans and takes both the storage key and my car keys out of his pocket, holding his hand up. Si snatches the keys out of his hand and shakes his head as Jonathan rushes off, an annoyed expression on his face. I stare at his retreating back in shock. I never even felt him lift my keys.

Si takes my hand and holds it in his, putting the keys into my palm with the other before curling my fingers closed again. "I told you this was no place for you. Don't put yourself into dangerous situations unnecessarily, Alanna. This isn't a place you should come to voluntarily."

He takes a step away from me and walks away, leaving me staring at him, my heart racing. "Thank you, Simon! I'll be more careful next time!"

He turns around to face me, a cute smirk on his face, and butterflies erupt in my stomach. "You'd better."

Si walks away, and I'm pretty sure he takes my heart with him.

Chapter Six

SILAS

I can't believe this dude paid me two hundred bucks to trail his boring wife for a week. The woman is so dull, I can't imagine where she'd meet anyone who she could possibly cheat on him with. She goes for a run every single morning, and then she heads to the grocery store downtown. Next she goes home, prepares food in front of the large kitchen window, after which she watches TV, again by a large window. Some days, this woman doesn't even go to the grocery store and just has her groceries delivered.

Honestly, this guy would've been better off buying a home security system. He'd quickly realize that she rarely leaves the house. It's the easiest job I've ever taken, and I kind of wish it wasn't so easy, because he promised me he'd pay me five hundred bucks if I could find proof of her cheating on him.

I sigh and stretch my legs, ready for the run she'll be going on any minute now. This lady leaves the house at exactly ten in the morning, every single day. She's not much of an early riser, but she sticks to her schedules. I snap a pic of her when she walks out of the house and text it to her husband, letting her get a head start before I run after her.

She runs the exact same trail every single day, but today she deviates, and it doesn't sit well with me. I started taking on these kinds of jobs a year ago, and word quickly spread about how good I am at remaining invisible as I trail people, how easy it is for me to get to the core of clients' requests. The more I do this, the quicker I can tell when something is wrong. Today, something is definitely wrong. If I'm lucky, this deviation is going to earn me the big bucks.

She slows her pace and waves at a man seated on one of the benches in the park, and I smile to myself as I disappear between the trees, my phone ready to take photos. She sits down next to him, and he hands her a paper coffee cup. In return, she leans in and kisses him.

I snap a picture, equal parts happy and annoyed at this new development. Is nothing sacred anymore these days? Why get married if you're just going to cheat on each other? I sigh as I snap a few more photos of the couple, part of me wishing she'd turned out to be just as boring as I thought she was. I send the photos to her husband, and he replies almost instantly, promising to wire me the money before the day is over.

I'm in a shit mood as I walk back through the park, reminded of my stepmother. I rarely think of her these days, but these types of cases always bring her to mind. She'd been cheating on my father throughout the last few years of his life, and he knew it. It still doesn't make sense that he cut me out of his will and left everything to her, and I'm determined to get to the bottom of it. I may not have the resources that I need right now, but eventually I will. One day, I'll take back everything that I lost. Every single thing.

"No!"

My head snaps up at the sound of a familiar voice, and I frown when I see Alanna with a boy her age. What is she doing at the park on a weekday? Shouldn't she be at school?

I've been avoiding her lately. Against my advice, she started volunteering once a week, and from what I understand, Ricardo is doing a good job keeping her safe. She's sought me out a few times, and each time, I've made up an excuse not to spend any time with her. Something about her just reminds me of everything I lost. The day I met her was also the day my life changed.

The boy leans into her, and she backs away, her body language conveying her reluctance. "Come on," the boy coaxes her. "It's just one kiss, and it's just the two of us here."

I walk up to them, but in her distress, she doesn't even notice me. Not until I place my hand on her shoulder. "Don't touch her," I warn, my tone harsh.

She tenses and looks up at me, the stiffness in her body draining away when her eyes meet mine. She melts into me, and I wrap my arm around her fully.

The boy looks at me, his eyes flashing with anger. I'm all too familiar with guys like him. Entitled, snobby and bratty. I used to be him. I can pretty much guess what happened here. The two of them must have been hanging out, they might even have been seeing each other, but he's asking more of her than she's willing to give. It's a good thing she's finding out he's such a pig sooner than later.

"Who the fuck are you? Get your hands off her." Pretty Boy straightens his shoulders and puffs his chest, as though he's actually readying himself to fight me. I wouldn't put it past him. His ego is clearly bigger than his brains are.

"He's my boyfriend," Alanna says, pressing herself against me. I nod and tighten my grip on her, playing along.

"Stay the fuck away from my girl, or I'll break every part of you that touches her," I snap, the words tumbling out of my mouth before I even have any idea what I'm saying. I generally try to stay away from trouble, but I can't today.

He looks at Alanna, but she turns away and tucks her face into my chest. I wrap my arms around her fully, covering her in my embrace. She's shaking, and I have no doubt she's feeling vulnerable right now. What the fuck was she thinking, finding herself alone with such a fleabag? Why the fuck does she keep putting herself in unsafe situations?

The boy looks at us one more time before he grits his teeth and walks away, stopping a few paces away. "This isn't over, you slut."

I tense, but Alanna fists my shirt and clenches tightly. I watch him walk away and cup the back of her head, holding her protectively. She's so fucking small that the top of her head barely reaches my chin. How was she going to protect herself against this guy?

"Are you okay?" I ask when Pretty Boy disappears from sight.

She nods and takes a step back, but I keep my arms wrapped around her, unwilling to let her go just yet. In the last couple of years I've taken to caring only about myself, and nothing and no one else. Alanna awakens a protective instinct in me that I thought I'd lost.

"I'm fine," she says, but she's still trembling.

"We need to talk about your propensity for putting yourself in dangerous situations," I warn her, my tone harsh.

She looks up at me, her expression so deceptively innocent yet alluring. Does she realize how beautiful she is? She's only sixteen, and she already looks like a vixen. She's got curves most girls her age could only dream of, and those lips of hers have me looking away, because she's far too young for me to be thinking about that way. Then there's her eyes. She's got the most beautiful hazel eyes I've ever seen. I can only imagine what boys her age must think of her, what they'd want from her. The thought of her kissing Pretty Boy fills me with a sense of dread, and it leaves me feeling uncomfortable.

"What would you have done if he'd forced that kiss? What if he forced you to do more than that? This park is mostly deserted, Alanna. What were you thinking?"

I tighten my grip on her shoulders, resisting the urge to shake some sense into her. I get being young and reckless, but this just isn't right. I need her to understand how wrong this could've gone.

"I'd have kneed him in the balls, Si."

She's only just about stopped shaking. Maybe she would have gathered her courage, maybe adrenaline would've kicked in, but what if it hadn't?

"Try it. Try kneeing me in the balls."

"What?"

I nod, my gaze provocative. "Try kneeing me in the balls, Alanna. Try getting away from me." I tighten my grip on her, and she frowns.

"Remember, you asked for this," she warns, and I smirk.

She moves her leg, trying to knee me quickly and with a sufficient amount of force, but she isn't quite fast enough for me. Before she realizes what's going on, I've twisted my body and have the leg she tried to kick me with wrapped high around my waist, my hand on her thigh. She gasps and loses her balance, but I pull her into me, her body crashing into mine.

"You can't protect yourself against me," I tell her. "If I wanted to kiss you right now, there's nothing you could do about it. If I wanted to take advantage of you, my hand over your mouth to silence your screams, there's nothing you could do about it."

She swallows hard, her eyes on mine, our bodies far closer than I should allow. "Caleb isn't you. I'd be able to get away from him."

I tighten my grip on her thigh and bury my other hand in her hair, barely able to restrain my anger. "Damn right, he ain't me. That still doesn't excuse what happened today. You shouldn't have to defend yourself at all, I know that, but the world isn't as pretty as we'd like it to be, no matter how unfair that might be. Don't put yourself in this kind of situation ever again, you hear me?"

She nods, and I let go of her. Alanna takes a step away from me and looks away. "Thank you," she murmurs, her voice so soft I nearly missed it.

"What the fuck do you see in that asshole, anyway? Who is he?" I shouldn't ask, but I can't help myself. I'm irrationally angry at the thought of her being with him. She's too good for him, whether she sees it or not.

"I... it isn't really like that. We aren't dating or anything. We both had a free period, and we're supposed to write a paper together. He suggested we go for a walk to talk it over and divide our tasks, and I didn't think much of it."

I sigh and shake my head. "Promise me, okay? Don't put yourself in dangerous situations. I don't agree with you volunteering at the shelter, but I definitely don't agree with you doing this kind of stupid shit."

She nods and falls into step with me as we head back to the park's entrance. "Yes, Si," she says, her voice filled with defeat. "I promise."

I pause and take my phone from my pocket. "If you ever do find yourself in trouble, you call me, okay? No matter when or where. If I can help you, I will."

I hand her my phone, and she gives me her number, letting it ring once, so she's got mine too. "Why are you so good to me? First at the cemetery, and now too."

I look into her eyes for a moment, wondering the same thing. "I don't know," I whisper. The years I've spent homeless have hardened me, but I have a soft spot for her.

"Let me walk you back to school."

She nods, a small smile on her face. Each time I speak to her, I'm left feeling unsettled. There's something about her that tugs at my heartstrings, and I hate it.

I hate it, yet I keep finding myself entangled with her.

Chapter Seven

ALANNA

I'm nervous as I make my way to the shelter. I've been working there for a few weeks now, and usually Si just ignores me, clearly going out of his way to avoid me. I wonder if he'll do the same today. I'm not sure why he purposely keeps me at a distance, but I love catching glimpses of the boy he used to be.

I haven't been able to stop thinking about the way he helped me in the park last week, and the strength with which he held my body against his. I'm not blind. I've noticed his muscles and the few faint scars on his face that weren't there before. I can't help but wonder what his story is. How does a guy like him end up in a homeless shelter?

Each night, I wonder if I should text him, perhaps to thank him for his help. I find myself curious about him, and I won't deny that I find him attractive. I suspect that he still sees me as the little girl from the cemetery, and I can't help but want to change that.

Ricardo waves at me when I walk in, a warm smile on his face. Over the last couple of weeks, I've come to understand why my father values him so much. I've never met a person as genuinely good and caring as Ricardo, and he makes me want to be a better person, too.

"Hi!" I tell him.

"I've got a boring job for you today."

"What is it? Packaging food?"

Ricardo grins and nods. "How did you know?"

I shake my head. "I *have been* coming here for a while, you know? Usually when you tell me it'll be a boring day, it means packaging food to distribute. Boring days are my favorite, because that's when you tell me stories about my dad while we work."

Ricardo looks down, his expression regretful. "Unfortunately, I can't accompany you today. I've asked someone else to help you, and I trust him fully. He'll keep you safe."

I frown, and Ricardo tips his head toward the doorway behind me. "*Si*?"

"You've met Silas before?" Ricardo asks, his tone carrying a hint of curiosity.

Silas. His name is Silas, not Simon. "Yeah. We first met each other years ago."

Ricardo looks between the two of us, an unreadable expression on his face. "I see," he says, his voice soft. He turns to Silas and nods. "I'll leave Alanna in your care for the rest of the day. Please walk her out once she's done, will you?"

Silas nods, and Ricardo claps him on the back before walking away, leaving the two of us standing in front of his office.

"*Silas*," I say.

He looks up sharply, his gaze dark. Something about his expression has my heart beating a little faster, and I can feel heat spread across my cheeks.

"Your name is Silas... not Simon."

"I never said it was."

"But you also didn't tell me your full name, nor did you ever correct me."

He looks away and leads the way to the storage room, where

Ricardo and I usually prepare the food packages that we hand out outside of the facility. "There was no need for you to know my name."

I bite down on my lip and push down the indignation I feel. "Surely we're at least on a first name basis?"

"We shouldn't be."

He takes a key from his pocket and unlocks the storage room, holding it open for me before locking us inside the way Ricardo always used to. From what I understand, it's to prevent anyone from coming in here to steal the food gathered here, but it feels different being in here with Silas.

"Does this count as putting myself in a dangerous situation?"

Silas leans back against the door, his gaze roaming over my body, before settling on my lips. Perhaps he no longer sees me as a little girl, after all. I did have my entire body pressed against his just a week ago.

"No," he answers, his voice soft. "I will never knowingly harm you, Alanna. I do appreciate you being aware of the situation. If it had been anyone other than me, you should've declined to help out today. Who knows what could happen when you're locked into a room with a man for hours?"

I smirk and cross my arms. "You're hardly a man," I say, repeating the words I said years ago.

Silas chuckles and runs a hand through his hair. "Little girl," he says. "If you weren't so young, I'd feel inclined to defend my honor."

He remembers. He remembers the words he said to me back then. I'm not sure why I care so much, but I do.

"I'm not so young anymore," I murmur.

Silas's smile melts off his face, and he looks away. "You are, Alanna. If I recall correctly, you're about sixteen now. You're still a baby, little girl."

He should be twenty or twenty-one now, yet he acts like he's thirty, just like he did back then. I'm about to argue with him, but he holds his hand up and shakes his head. "Let's get to work, shall we? There's a lot to do."

I nod and join him at the table, the two of us working harmoniously for a little while. There's something equal parts soothing and unsettling about his presence. I feel at peace, yet my heart won't stop racing.

"That boy," he says eventually, an edge to his tone. "Did he do or say anything to you?"

I hesitate, unsure of what to say. Ever since I boldly claimed that Silas is my boyfriend, Caleb has been spreading rumors about me, saying I'm a slut, and that I did things with him I've definitely never done before. No matter how much I dispute it, most people just believe him anyway.

"No," I tell Silas, forcing a smile on my face. "He hasn't said anything at all."

I pick up another cardboard box to fill with food, my heart racing. I hate lying, I always have.

"Tell me the truth."

I look up to find his gorgeous emerald eyes narrowed, a hint of annoyance in them. "I did."

Silas takes the box from me and puts it down on the table before reaching for my hand. He holds my hand between both of his and shakes his head. "Tell me," he repeats, his tone pleading, sweet even.

"I..." Silas tightens his grip, his thumb caressing the back of my hand. "He's been spreading some lies about me, but it's okay. I can handle it, Si."

Silas looks into my eyes, as though he's assessing my words, and then he sighs. "What has he been saying?"

I bite down on my lip nervously and look away. "Silas," I whisper. "It's nothing."

"If that's the case, then you'll have no problem telling me all about it."

The look in his eyes tells me he won't let this go, and I look down in defeat. "He said that I... I... sucked, um, that I—"

"That you sucked his dick?"

Heat rushes to my cheeks, no doubt turning them rosy. "Yeah," I whisper.

"Did you?"

I look up, shocked. "No, of course not!"

Silas chuckles, his thumb drawing circles on the back of my hand. Does he realize he's still holding my hand? "Have you ever sucked dick, sweet girl?"

I swallow hard, unable to calm my racing heart. I'm so flustered, and I have no idea how to answer. For some irrational reason, I want to lie and say yes, so I don't seem as young and naïve as Silas seems to think I am.

"I didn't think so," he murmurs, his eyes briefly dropping to my lips before he looks away.

"What makes you think I've never done that before?"

Silas smiles before facing me. "Besides the fact that you can't even say the words?"

There's something different in his gaze now, and it makes him look sexier than he ever has before. Something about the way he looks at me has my heart thumping loudly.

"I… I…"

"Don't be in such a rush to grow up, Alanna. Take your time. Firsts are important, whether that be your first kiss, or the first time you do anything sexual. You'll remember every one of those instances for the rest of your life. Make them count."

I pull my hand out of his, unable to suppress my annoyance. He's treating me like a child again, and I hate it, but that's not all. My annoyance is fueled by the irrational anger I feel at the thought of him remembering some other girl that he had his firsts with. Knowing that there's someone who will always have that place in his memories irritates me.

"What's wrong?" he asks, his voice soft.

I shake my head and wrap my arms around myself. "So you remember all of those firsts?"

Silas smiles at me and nods. "Yep. I had most of my firsts on the same night, with a girl I'd met at a house party. *Linda*." He smiles when he says her name, and my heart squeezes painfully. "Girl had a sinfully wonderful mouth and an even hungrier—" he stops talking abruptly and shakes his head. "Anyway, my firsts were rushed and not with anyone special. If I could go back in time, I'd have saved them for someone I actually wanted to share those memories with, you know?"

I nod, but my mood is entirely ruined. I know he sees me as a child, and I know he isn't someone I should be interested in, but I can't help myself. I hate that his firsts are all gone, that they'll never be mine.

I bite down on my lip and focus on adding cartons of fruit juice to our food packets, trying my hardest to keep my attention off Silas, but I can't. I keep wondering what he might be like with a woman. What would it be like to date him?

"You're quiet," he murmurs eventually, and I look up at him. "Penny for your thoughts?"

I chuckle and shake my head. "My thoughts are worth a whole lot more than that."

He takes a penny out of his pocket and pushes it toward me. "Penny is all I've got, my love."

My eyes widen as realization dawns. I never should've said that... not when I know he's homeless. It was thoughtless and insensitive, and I should've known better. "I was joking," I whisper, pushing the coin back to him. I force a smile onto my face and lean against the table that separates us. "My thoughts can't be purchased, Silas. They have to be exchanged. I'll give you mine if you give me yours."

He looks into my eyes for a moment, and I worry that he's seeing straight through me, that he can see the embarrassment I'm trying to hide. He nods, and I exhale shakily.

"Very well. What is it going to cost me?"

I smirk, relief rushing over me. "One question, and you have to answer honestly."

He pauses, as though he's going to decline my request, but

then he smiles, his dimples making an appearance. "Okay. Tell me what you were thinking just now, Alanna."

I look into his emerald eyes, taking in that intense look of his. "I was thinking of *you*, and how unfair it is that every one of your firsts was taken by someone who won't cherish them." It isn't the full truth, and the way he smiles tells me he knows it. He stares me down and lifts his brow, indicating for me to continue. I sigh as I drag my gaze away. "I want them for myself, Silas. I want your firsts. I want to be someone you'll always remember. I don't know why, okay? I just do."

He nods and pulls a hand through his thick, dark hair. "You're young," he murmurs. "It's only—"

"Don't," I cut him off. "Don't dismiss my feelings by bringing up my age. You asked me for my thoughts, and I gave them to you. Take them for what they are, without trying to distort them into something you find easier to handle. If you can't do that, then *don't* ask me what I'm thinking."

He looks thrown-aback, and I regret my words instantly. I shouldn't have lashed out at him. Why is it that I'm always making a fool of myself in front of him?

"You're right," he says, surprising me. "I apologize, Alanna."

I nod and pick up a six-pack of fruit juice to tear off the plastic holding the small cartons together. I'm flustered, and I hate feeling this way. I was excited to be spending the day with him, but I shouldn't have been. Every time we're together, he makes it clear he doesn't actually want to be around me. I suppose it's about time I accept that.

"Ask your question," he tells me.

I shake my head, dismissing him. "It's fine."

Silas reaches over the table and takes the juice cartons from me, placing his hand in mine. "I'm sorry, Alanna. You're right. I have been treating you the way I would others your age, but it's undeserved and unwarranted. I won't do it again, okay?" I nod, and he squeezes my hand. "So ask me your question."

I look into his eyes and inhale deeply as I gather the courage to ask the one question I've been wanting to ask him ever since I ran into him again. "Why are you here?"

Silas pulls his hand off mine and looks away, his smile melting away. "It's a long story," he says, his voice soft.

"You don't have to tell me," I whisper. I'm being intrusive, and I know it, but I can't help but be curious about him. He was clearly well off when I first met him, so how did he find himself in this situation?

"The day I first met you? That was also the day that I lost everything. That's why I avoided you when you first started volunteering here. You were just a reminder of my past, of the person I used to be."

He falls silent for a moment, his gaze apologetic.

"That day? It was my father's funeral. I'd just turned eighteen, and it hit me hard. My father was my last remaining family. I have a stepmother and a half-brother, but it always felt different with them. My stepmother and I never got along, you know? Even when I was little, I could feel that she never really liked me."

He runs a hand through his hair and sighs, seemingly lost in thought for a moment.

"When my father passed away, he left everything to my stepmother. Days after the funeral, she kicked me out, leaving me with nothing but my car and whatever cash I had in my account. I couch surfed for a while, staying with friends and acquaintances, but once it became clear that I'd lost everything and would be of no further use to them, they all cast me aside. None of the friendships I thought I had were real, and that realization paired with the loss of everything I'd ever known sent me spiraling down a path I wish I'd never embarked on. If not for Ricardo finding me one day, I'm not sure where I'd be. It's taking me some time, but I'm putting myself through college. I have every intention of regaining everything I've lost. I'll turn my life back around, one step at a time. When my father passed away, I made him a promise, and it's one I still want to keep. I'm in no position to do so right now, but I *will* keep that promise."

I nod at him, a strange sense of pride washing over me. "I didn't know you were in college."

Silas smirks at me. "Where did you think I go most days? I attend classes in the morning and help out around here afterward. Ricardo and I came to an agreement when he first found me. He told me he'd let me have a bed here if I could get into college, and in return for a guaranteed place to stay, I help as much as I can. My student loans are outrageous as it is, so this arrangement has been a blessing to me. I can't afford to rent a room. I know it's not ideal, but it works for me. This place is more of a rehabilitation centre than a shelter. They really want you to never come back here once you leave, and they really do support you until you're ready to stand on your own two feet. It's a strange thing to say, but in a way, I'm lucky I found myself here."

"And it won't be forever," I tell him. "I have no doubt you've got an amazing future ahead of you, Si."

He smiles at me. "You really believe that, don't you?"

"I do." I've known it from the moment I met him. Silas is going to leave his mark, and it'll be a sight to behold.

Chapter Eight

ALANNA

"*Slut*," some girl murmurs behind my back as her friends giggle beside her. They've been daring her to say something to me, and I'll admit I was betting against her. I didn't think she had the guts.

I slam my locker closed and turn around, my jaw clenched. Her eyes widen, and she turns around, her cheeks crimson.

"*You*," I snap. "What did you just say to me?"

She rushes off, and her friends send me taunting looks as they follow her, their giggles grating on me.

"It's not like they're wrong." Pure violence rushes through me at the sound of Caleb's voice. "I saw how that guy held you. There's no way he ain't screwing you." I turn toward him angrily, and he chuckles. "Should've just kissed me when I gave you a chance. If you want this to stop, I can make that happen. Just go on a date with me, Alanna."

I cross my arms over my chest, but all that does is draw his gaze to my breasts. "You need to stop harassing me," I warn him. "I've been lenient so far because I'm not into drama, but I *will* sue you for slander. It's clear you're not used to hearing the word no, so read my damn lips, Caleb. *No*. I will *never* date you."

I walk past him, barely able to contain my temper. I'm trying my hardest to pretend that words can't hurt me, but they do. Every time I'm called a slut or a whore, my heart breaks. I'm a virgin, for God's sake. It's unfair that this is happening to me because I wouldn't let Caleb take advantage of me.

He's hot on my heels as I walk to the exit, and I'm so tempted to turn around and punch him in the face. I've never truly hated someone before, but I can honestly say that I *hate* this guy. I hate everything about him. His stupid hair, his entitlement, the way his stupid friends fall in line, the fact that no one will stand up to him.

"It's just one date, Alanna," he says, his tone coaxing.

"Are you dumb?" I ask, pausing in the hallway. "What makes you think that harassing a girl will make her want to go out with you? We aren't in kindergarten anymore, Caleb. I get that your emotional intelligence hasn't caught up yet, so allow me to enlighten you. Bullying a girl whose attention you want is childish, and it's ineffective. Leave me alone, or I'm submitting a formal complaint."

I walk out of the building, relieved he isn't following me. I head toward my car in a rush, but before I reach it, I'm yanked back. Caleb has his hand around my wrist, impatience flashing through his eyes. He opens his mouth, but before he can speak, we're interrupted by a voice I know all too well.

"I highly recommend that you let go of my girl."

The tension flows out of my body at the sound of Silas's voice. I turn around to see him walking up to us, his eyes on mine. He wraps his arm around my waist and leans over me, roughly yanking Caleb's fingers away.

"I've warned you once. I won't warn you again," he says, his voice soft. It looks like he's holding Caleb's hand with considerable force before he pushes it away, and I notice the way Caleb clenches and unclenches his fist, as though his hand is hurting.

Caleb looks at me, distraught. "You're not seriously dating this guy, are you?"

I nod and turn in Silas's embrace, pressing my body against his. I rise to my tiptoes and press a quick, nervous kiss to the edge of his mouth, not quite on his cheek, yet not on his lips either. "You're late," I say, my voice trembling just a little. What is he doing here?

Silas looks into my eyes, his intense gaze making my heart skip a beat. I almost stop breathing when his free hand slides up my back and into my hair. He cups the back of my head, his touch possessive. "I'm sorry, baby. My seminar ran longer than it should have." He tips his head toward Caleb, a questioning look in his eyes. "Is this guy giving you any trouble?"

I hesitate, wanting to say yes, but knowing that I can't. Silas has so much on his plate already. There's no way I can add to it. Besides, I don't want to be the kind of girl that needs help from a guy. I can deal with this myself. "Not at all."

He nods and glances back at Caleb. I follow his gaze to find Caleb staring at the two of us, his eyes dark with jealousy. He throws me a venomous look before he turns and walks away, his demeanor spelling trouble. I sigh and drop my forehead to Silas's chest, enjoying the way he's holding me.

It's insane, and I know this is all fake, but Caleb's behavior is granting me moments with Silas I'd otherwise never have. "What are you doing here?" I murmur against his hoodie.

"Something about our conversation yesterday didn't sit well with me, and I wanted to come see you at school, just to make sure you really were okay. As expected, that guy is still pursuing you, and it doesn't look like he's going to give up anytime soon. I thought being seen with your alleged boyfriend might make him back off."

He smiles at me in a way he never has before, and I can't help but smile back. "You didn't need to do that for me," I murmur. My school is really far from the shelter, and I can't imagine how long it must've taken him to get here.

"It's okay," he says, the back of his fingers brushing over my cheek tenderly. I swallow hard at his touch. It's strangely intimate. I know I should step out of his embrace, but I want more of this. I'm not ready to let go of this fantasy. "Your school is pretty close to Astor College."

I gasp, my eyes widening. "You go to *Astor College?*" It's the best school in this state, and it's my dream college. It's not easy to get into Astor College, and because it's a prestigious private school, it's insanely expensive too. I can't even imagine how high his student loans must be.

"I do. I study Computer Science. Their programme is among the best in the country, and I've always wanted to go there. Some days it's still surreal to me, to be honest."

Silas lets go of me and takes a step back. I sigh, missing his touch already. The way he smirks at me makes me suspect that he realizes how I feel about him, but thankfully he isn't teasing me.

"Let me drive you back," I murmur, suddenly feeling self-conscious. Silas glances at the car behind me and nods. My dad bought me a Porsche for my sixteenth birthday, and at the time I loved the car, but now that I'm standing in front of Silas, it seems pretentious and shameful. I hesitate for a moment, and then I hand him the keys. "Actually, why don't you drive?"

He looks at me the way he does sometimes. Over the last couple of weeks, I've managed to decipher the looks he throws my way. He's trying to figure out if this is a pity move or not. "Si," I murmur. "I've only been driving for a couple of months, and I don't want you to judge my driving. You just drive."

He smiles then, and I breathe a sigh of relief when his fingers curl around the keys. He walks around the car and holds the passenger door open for me, surprising me. I don't think anyone has ever done that for me before.

I'm nervous as he gets behind the wheel. It's silly, but I've never been in a car with a guy I like. I frown when he adjusts the seat and mirrors with ease. It took me ages to figure out what all the buttons did, and where they even were. "You seem really familiar with my car," I murmur, surprised.

He smiles at me. "I used to have a Porsche 911 myself. It's a good car."

I blink in surprise. "What?"

Silas glances at me as he reverses out. "Alanna... I grew up really rich. My father was the founder of a popular hedge fund."

I nod, surprised. "I see... but then how... I mean..."

"I don't know," he says, his tone strained. "I'm sure something dodgy went down when my father passed away. There's no way he wouldn't have had a proper estate plan. He wouldn't have cut both my brother and me out of his will, and his will couldn't have been as simple as it was, but I can't prove that. I couldn't then, and I still can't now. One day, I'll regain everything I lost, but until then, I'm biding my time, studying as hard as I can and working my way up the only way I can. I'm in no position to forcibly take back what's mine, but one day I will be."

I nod at him. "I have no doubt," I tell him. "You're going to do amazing things, Silas."

He smiles at me. "So will you, Alanna. I know it probably isn't easy for you right now. You may not have said much, but I was sixteen just a few years ago, and I have a pretty good idea how much of an asshole that kid must be. Always remember the bigger picture, okay? Don't get into silly fights, and don't let him get to you. If you need help, just ask me, all right?"

I nod, refusing to voice the words. I can't promise him anything. I don't want to rely on Silas. I don't want to be another burden to him. I'll take care of Caleb myself.

Chapter Nine

ALANNA

I frown when my card is declined at the online dress store I've been using for years. I spent weeks picking the dress I want to wear for dinner on my seventeenth birthday, only for the transaction to be declined. My birthday is still several weeks away, but Dad promised to spend all day with me, so I've started planning way ahead.

I sigh as I try my card one more time, only for it to be declined again. "That's weird," I whisper to myself. Something about this doesn't sit well with me. I haven't said anything to Dad, but I've noticed the overdue bill notices we get in the post, the one he keeps trying to hide. Each time I make any kind of remark, he shuts me down and tells me not to worry. It's clear he doesn't want me to know, but it looks like something might be wrong. Surely the business isn't in trouble?

I bite down on my lip as I close my laptop and pick up my phone. Should I call Dad and ask him about my credit card? If something truly is wrong, then that'd just add to his worries. I can't do that. It's probably better that I bring it up in person.

I check the time and sigh. It's nearly nine in the evening, and he still isn't home. When was the last time we even had dinner together? He's been working far harder than he ever has before, and I can't help but worry.

I inhale deeply and tighten my grip on my phone as I move from my desk to my bed. On nights like these, I always feel lonely, and I find myself second-guessing my decision to ostracize Caleb. Because I rejected him publicly, *multiple* times, I've found myself becoming a social pariah. No one talks to me unless they're talking shit about me. I've always been a bit of a loner, so I've never really had any friends, but now my chances of ever making any are gone.

I glance back at my phone, my mind drifting to Silas. I wouldn't say we're friends, per se... but he's the closest thing I've got.

I bite down on my lip, hesitating for a moment as I scroll through my contacts. He gave me his phone number so I could call him if I'm ever in trouble, and I'm not sure he'd be okay with me calling him out of the blue for no real reason. I'm worried that he just sees me as an obligation, someone he has to be nice to because Ricardo values my dad.

I thought we were getting a little closer after we spent an afternoon packaging food together, but I've barely even seen him in the last couple of months. I'm not sure if he's avoiding me, or if he's just busy with school, but he hasn't been at the shelter during my weekly visits. When I ask about him, Ricardo always tells me he's fine and that he's doing well, but that's as much as he'll tell me.

My heart races as I press the dial button, and my eyes widen as I listen to the dial tone. I can't tell whether I even want him to pick up or not. Part of me wants to just end the call and pretend I butt-dialed him if he ever asks about it, but a larger part of me wants to hear his voice. Maybe it's silly, but every time I go to the shelter, I secretly hope to catch a glimpse of him. There's something about him that's insanely addictive, and in my mind I keep replaying moments I've shared with him. When I can't sleep, I think of the way he held me each time Caleb was around, the way he pulled me against him when he told me to knee him in the balls, the way he sometimes looks at me. I know he isn't interested in me, but part of me is hoping to change his mind someday.

"Alanna?"

I swallow hard at the sound of his voice and clench my phone tightly. "Silas, hi!"

I let my eyes fall closed and suppress a groan. I'm so awkward, and I'm grateful he can't see me right now.

Silas chuckles, and the sound of it makes my heart skip a beat. "What's up?" he asks. "Is everything okay?"

"Yes!" I clear my throat awkwardly and fall back onto my bed. What was I thinking, calling him? "Nothing is wrong... I just, well, I just haven't seen you in a couple of weeks, and I wanted to know how you are, that's all."

"Question for your thoughts?"

I smile to myself, surprised he remembers the conversation we had when we were packing food together.

"My thoughts? I'm not sure there's all that much on my mind, Si."

"I'm sure there is," he says, his tone different to usual. He sounds more relaxed, and even through the phone, he does to me what no one else can... he makes me feel like I've got his full attention, like no one but me matters. "What was on your mind before you called me?"

I fall silent, surprised he realizes anything is wrong at all. "How did you know?" I ask, my voice soft.

"Alanna," he murmurs. "I just do. Tell me."

"My mind is a scary place, Si. You have no idea what you're asking for."

He chuckles, and I grin, imagining what he must look like with that smile on his face. "Shock me, Alanna."

I turn to my side and stare at the wall for a moment. "There's a lot on my mind, Si. I think my father's company might be in trouble. Dad is always working, and I miss him. I hate being home alone all the time. I hate that I don't have any friends, and I blame Caleb for it. But then I also blame myself for being such a bitch to him. Maybe if I hadn't rejected him the way I did, school wouldn't have gotten as bad as it is now. No one talks to me. My entire life is just homework, studying, volunteering at the shelter, and spending my evenings eating dinner by myself."

"Sweetheart," Silas says, and my heart starts to race. Every once in a while, he'll call me sweetheart or baby, and I doubt he even realizes it. "That's a lot you're carrying. Do you want my advice, or do you want to vent?"

I hesitate for a moment, surprised he's even giving me those two options. "I think I want your advice," I whisper.

"Tell your dad that you miss him, Alanna. I buried my dad on the day we met, and if I could go back in time, I'd make sure I spend more time with him, even if it means hanging out at his office with him. You could do your homework at his office, right? I'm sure you can think of some ways to spend more time around him without him feeling like his work would suffer for it. If his company truly is in trouble, he can't take time off right now, but you can silently support him by being around him. Do you think that might work?"

I nod to myself. "To be honest, that hadn't actually occurred to me before. It's a good idea. Back in the day, Dad never wanted me around, because there were so many construction guys, and the sites he used to work on weren't that safe, but these days Dad has his own office, so I think it'd be fine."

"As for Caleb," he says. "I honestly don't know what to say. I truly thought he'd get over it, you know? I guess he really likes you."

I bite down on my lip nervously. "About that..."

"What?" he says, his tone rougher. "Don't tell me you actually went on a date with him?"

Something about his tone has my heart beating a little faster. I know he isn't jealous, but this is exactly how I imagine he'd sound if he were. "No, of course not. Three weeks ago, I spray painted a message onto his car, and I'm pretty sure he knows it was me. It kind of took our feud to a different level."

"What did you do?"

"I used a can of graffiti to spray-paint *My Owner is a Prime Example of Fragile Masculinity* all over the hood of his car. In pink."

Silas bursts out laughing, and the sound of it makes me smile too. "Alanna, you beautiful soul. Every time I talk to you, I'm reminded that someday, you're going to drive one lucky man completely crazy in the very best way. Caleb hasn't been able to pin it on you, has he?"

I shake my head, even though he can't see me. "No, of course not. I found out where he lives and went to his house at night. No one saw me, and he can't pin it on me at all. I guess that's why he's so mad, but it's fine. It accomplished what I wanted it to. He's stopped pursuing me."

"Good," Silas says, his voice low and... *possessive.* Every once in a while, I wonder if he might like me a little too, but then I remind myself that he wouldn't be going out of his way to avoid me at the shelter if he did.

"Anyway," I murmur. "How are you? I haven't spoken to you in so long."

"I'm fine, sweet girl. Ricardo has officially hired me to become a part-time house manager. He wants to retire soon, and he's giving me the job until I graduate in two years. He's made it clear that he expects me to find a well-paying corporate job then, but in the meantime, this is a good gig. It'll give them time to find the perfect long-term candidate too."

"What will the job entail?" I ask, curious. I've never really asked Ricardo what his exact job is, because he seems to do *everything*. Surely Silas doesn't have time to be studying at Astor College and do Ricardo's job on top of it?

"It's mostly monitoring and implementing house rules, screening everyone's belongings when they come in, conducting facility searches for drugs and weapons, keeping track of different kinds of inventory, and a whole lot of admin work. It's a lot of stuff that I'm already doing anyway, except they'll pay me for it now, and I'll get my own bedroom with its own shower, so I won't have to sleep in the big hall anymore. I'm never going to spend another night in any of those bunk beds. Not ever again."

I'm not sure what to say to him. "It's definitely better than sleeping in the big hall, but remember what you told me, okay? Never lose sight of the big picture. You can't stay there, Silas."

"I know," he murmurs. "I know, and I won't. I have big plans for the future, Alanna. I won't give up on them, but this is a step forward, even if it doesn't sound that way. None of my belongings are ever safe in the shelter, no matter how hard Ricardo tries to make this place more of a home than a shelter. I have to carry a backpack with me wherever I go, and I'm dying to finally have a space of my own again. Having my own bedroom means I'll be able to store my things somewhere, and it means I'll be able to wear a neat suit to job interviews. I won't be bound to curfews, either."

"You're right," I whisper. "I'm sorry, Silas. I just... I just really believe in you, you know? I just know you're meant for so much more."

He falls silent for a moment, and I wonder if I've misspoken. "I'll get there," he says eventually. "One step at a time. Per aspera ad astra."

"What does that mean?" I ask, the words sounding vaguely familiar.

"Through adversity to the stars," he says, his voice soft. "Those are the words I remind myself of when things get tough. The biggest accomplishments don't come without hardship, and this is the same. Things might feel tough right now, but that's because I'm reaching for the stars. The loftier the goal, the tougher the obstacles, but it's worth it."

I twist in bed as I think over his words. The two of us are quiet for a moment, but it's a comforting silence. "Hey, Si?"

"Yes, my love?"

"You owe me a question."

"Ask," he says, his tone lazy. I wonder if he's in bed, like I am. We've been on the phone for far longer than I thought we'd be, and I'm enjoying it more than I expected.

"Can I call you again?"

He chuckles, and I grin. "Yes," he says, his voice low. "You can call me whenever you want, Alanna."

"You don't mind? Please be honest with me, Si. I don't want to be a burden to you, and I don't want you to be nice to me because Ricardo made you."

Silas is quiet for a moment, and I worry I was right. "Alanna," he says eventually. "Despite the situation I'm in, I'm not easily coerced. No one has ever made me spend time with you, nor is anyone forcing me to speak to you. I'll probably regret this, because I know damn well I should keep my distance from you, but I'm going to say it anyway. You brighten up my days, and though I shouldn't, I enjoy being around you. Call me, Alanna. Call me every night if you want to."

I can't help the way my heart races, giddiness washing over me as a wide grin spreads across my face. "Okay," I whisper.

"Okay," he repeats.

I don't know how he's done it, but Silas managed to turn a lonely evening into one of the best nights I've had in a long time, and he isn't even with me. I'm already looking forward to the conversations we're going to have, and I suspect he might be too.

Chapter Ten

Alanna

"Dad?" I clench my phone tighter as I look in the mirror in the restaurant's bathroom. "Where are you? It's getting pretty late."

I've been trying to call him all night, and by the time he finally picked up, I'd already given up our table. I don't think he even realizes it's my birthday today.

"Sorry, darling," he says, sounding tired. "There's so much going wrong at work that I had to stay late. I won't even try to hide this from you anymore, Alanna, because I can't. The company is collapsing, and I'm trying to keep it together with my bare hands, but I can't. I can't do it."

I don't get why he even tried to keep this from me. Did he truly think that I didn't notice the things that went missing from our house? First it was his watch, then it was the paintings he loved so much. After that, Mom's diamonds disappeared. My credit card hasn't worked in months, and I never even told him, because he fought so hard to keep this from me.

"What can I do, Dad? How can I help you?"

"Nothing, sweetie. Just keep doing what you do, okay? Keep staying strong for me, keep smiling for me, and please, sweetie. Please be patient with me. I won't be able to get away from work for another few hours, so don't worry about me. You just have dinner, all right?"

I inhale shakily, part of me wanting to remind him that today is my seventeenth birthday, but I won't. "Of course, Dad. Don't worry about me. You just focus on work. I'll be fine."

Dad pauses for a moment, and then he sighs. "I love you, Alanna. I'll make this up to you. I promise."

I force a smile onto my face, though he can't see me. "I'm looking forward to it," I tell him. "See you later, Dad. Don't be home too late, okay?"

I end the call as I walk out of the restaurant I made a reservation at several months ago. I've been looking forward to tonight for so long, but I should've known something would go wrong. Every time I think I'll get to spend some time with Dad, something happens, and I end up being all alone.

I'm getting tired of it, but volunteering at the shelter makes me understand why he works the way he does. I can see his fears, and I don't dare act selfish. I don't dare tell him that I want his time, that I miss him. I'm shaking as I get into my car, unsure where to even go.

For a little while, I did what Silas told me to do, but even when I'm at his office, he doesn't really notice me. I was hoping to chat with him every once in a while, and I really wanted to better understand what Dad does, but my presence only seemed to stress him out more, so I stopped going.

I drive around aimlessly, only half surprised when I find myself pulling up at the shelter without even consciously realizing that I drove there. I park in front of the building and check the time. It's eight o'clock, so there are two hours left before *lights out*. I grab my phone, unsure of whether or not I should call Silas.

Over the last couple of weeks, we've definitely become friends, and we talk to each other almost every night, but somehow I feel conflicted about calling him tonight. I don't want to force him to spend time with me, and I know that if I call him, he'll come out to see me.

I bite down on my lip, but in the end, selfishness wins, and I press the dial button. He picks up almost immediately, and I can't help but smile.

"If it isn't the birthday girl. Happy birthday, sweet girl."

"Thank you," I murmur. I wonder if he realizes that he's the only one who's wished me a happy birthday today. I doubt it, and I want to keep it that way.

"How was dinner with your dad? I kinda thought it'd last much longer."

"Oh, it's great," I lie. "I just went to the bathroom to touch up my lipstick, and somehow I found myself thinking of you. I wasn't sure how long the evening would last, so I thought I'd call you. Don't want you to feel neglected, after all. What would you do with yourself if I don't call you before bed? I'm not sure you'd be able to sleep, you know? How could I do that to you?"

He bursts out laughing, and a soft giggle escapes my lips. I've barely spoken to him for a minute, and he's already turned my night around. I lean back in my seat and let my eyes fall closed as I focus on his voice.

"Yeah," he murmurs. "I've kinda grown accustomed to hearing your voice before bed. I wasn't sure I'd get to speak to you tonight, but I was hoping I would."

Our daily calls are the highlight of my day. Even now, he's rarely at the shelter when I go to volunteer, but I don't mind it as much. When I see him, things are somewhat odd between us. He's distant in person, but over the phone? Over the phone, it feels like he's *mine*.

I'm startled when I hear knocking on my window, and my eyes fly open. I sit up, surprised to find Silas standing next to my car, his phone still against his ear. "I had a feeling I'd find you here." He walks around the car and I unlock the door for him as he ends our call.

"What are you doing here?" I ask when he gets in beside me, shocked. "How did you know?"

He smiles and leans back in the passenger seat. "Your voice, Alanna. Over the last couple of months, I've learned to read every single one of your emotions through your voice. You've never sounded as upset as you did tonight. I knew you weren't at the restaurant, so I followed my instincts, and they led me right to you."

I let my eyes roam over him, taking in the slight stubble that only accentuates his strong jaw, the slightly long hair, and those lips I've been wanting to taste. "You can't read every one of my emotions, Si," I whisper.

"Yeah," he whispers back. "I can."

His eyes drop to my lips, and then he tears his gaze away. Silas has never crossed the line with me, and each time I try to, he reminds me that he's five years older than I am. He's been rejecting me subtly, but that doesn't make it hurt any less.

"That dress looks just as beautiful on you as I knew it would," he whispers, but he isn't looking at me. He's looking out the window. I stare at him, trying to figure out if he's just being nice, or if he means it.

"Thanks," I murmur, glancing down at my lap. I fell in love with this dress at first sight, and I told Silas it made me feel like a queen. It's a nude-colored midi dress with a corseted top, and it makes every single one of my curves stand out in the classiest way. It's the perfect birthday dress, and if nothing else, I guess I'm glad at least Silas got to see me in it.

"What happened tonight, Alanna?" he asks, turning back to me.

I shake my head. "Same old," I whisper. "Dad has been working, and I don't think he even realizes it's my birthday today. I didn't say anything, because I don't want him to feel guilty, you know? Even if he does come home now, my night is ruined, so there was no point."

He nods. "Come on, birthday girl. There's somewhere I've been meaning to take you. I didn't think I'd actually be able to do it on your birthday, but I guess it's my lucky day."

I frown, and Silas smirks at me as he puts a location into my navigation system. "Where are we going?"

He shakes his head. "You'll see. It's a surprise."

I smile as I follow the directions, curious. I drive down one windy road after another, until Silas tells me to park on the side of a dirt road. "Where are we?"

"Let me show you."

He gets out and walks around the car to open my door for me. Silas offers me his hand, and my heart races as I place mine in his. He entwines our fingers as he pulls me along, frowning when he realizes that my heels are sinking into the grassy grounds.

He bends down slightly, and before I realize what he's doing, I'm lifted off the ground and into his arms. He holds me close, his eyes briefly running over my body. I could've sworn I saw a flash of desire in them, but then it's gone, and he's striding forward with me in his arms. "What are you doing?" I whisper. "You don't need to carry me."

He shakes his head. "It's a bit of a walk."

I tighten my grip on him, reveling in his proximity. I allow myself to drink him in shamelessly, taking in his long lashes, the stubble on his skin, his strong jaw. His body feels strong against mine, his grip tight. I've never been this close to a guy before. "This is a first for me," I whisper.

Silas looks at me and blinks in confusion.

"It's the first time a boy has carried me in his arms like this."

Silas chuckles and tightens his grip on me, his eyes on mine. "I'm no boy, Alanna," he says, his voice soft and sexy.

"Oh no," I whisper. "Does this count as putting myself in a dangerous situation?"

Silas smirks, and my heart skips a beat. It's a lazy, intimate smirk, and it's all for me. "Damn right it does, baby. Don't you ever find yourself in another man's arms like this, late at night with no one else around. No one but *me*."

"Just you, Silas," I whisper.

He stops walking, his eyes on mine, and I wonder if he can see me blushing in the darkness. "We're here," he says, but he doesn't put me down.

I'm so mesmerized by his beautiful emerald eyes that I struggle to tear my gaze away. When I eventually manage it, I find us standing underneath a beautiful pink blossom tree. "Wow," I whisper. The air feels fresh, and the breeze carries a soft floral scent. This place feels magical. I glance around, my eyes settling on the stone cottage behind us.

"Silas," I whisper. "Are we trespassing?"

He smiles as he puts me down and places his hands on my shoulders. "Yes, I suppose we are." Silas has always kept his distance from me, but tonight feels different. "Happy birthday, Alanna," he murmurs.

He lets go of me and reaches into his back pocket, taking out a pink envelope. He holds it in both hands, his gaze downcast. Silas inhales deeply, and when he looks up at me, my heart starts to race. I've never seen him look at me like that before. His eyes are filled with every feeling I try so hard to hide.

"Alanna, there isn't much I can offer you other than my friendship... but I've learned the hard way that the most precious things in life truly are free. Maybe someday, I'll be able to give you diamonds and expensive flowers, but for now, please accept this."

He hands me the envelope, and I take it with trembling hands. My heart is racing as I open the envelope carefully, not wanting to tear it open. Silas shifts his weight from one leg to the other, seemingly just as nervous as I am.

I gasp when I slide a birthday card out of the envelope, a portrait of me on it... except the girl in the drawing looks nothing like me... she's far more beautiful than I ever hope to be. "Did you draw this?" I ask, shocked.

Silas nods and looks away. I've never seen him look so vulnerable before. "It's beautiful," I whisper. I open the card, taking in the simple birthday message in his handwriting. Instead of his name, it's signed with the ψ symbol. "I love it, Silas." My voice trembles, and I hug the card to my chest. "This... thank you. Thank you so much, Si. I don't need expensive flowers or diamonds, Si. Nothing could ever beat this."

He smiles at me and nods, but I see the insecurity in his eyes. Before I have a chance to even attempt to reassure him, he reaches back into his pocket and takes out a thin glass canister with paper inside it. "This," he tells me, "is for next year."

He tips his head toward the tree, and I follow his gaze. "My mother and I planted this tree over a decade ago," he says. "Every year, my father would take me here for my birthday, to my mother's favorite place. She and I had a tradition, you see... every year on my birthday, she'd draw me a picture, and I'd draw her one. We then put them in glass bottles and buried them. Throughout the year, we'd try to guess what the other had drawn, right down to the last detail. Whoever got closest would win a wish that the other had to fulfill. It was a silly competition, but it was ours."

I look around again, seeing this place through fresh eyes. We aren't trespassing at all, not really... this place should belong to Silas, and I have no doubt that one day it will again. "Si, that's your tradition with her," I whisper. "Something like that... you should share that with someone special."

He kneels down in front of me and looks up at me. "I *am*, Ray," he whispers.

"Ray?"

He nods. "I've been calling you by your name for far too long. You need a nickname. I thought of calling you sunshine, but I've spent too many days in the blistering sun, desperate for a glass of water. You're a *ray* of sunshine, a ray of light, a ray of hope in an otherwise dark, bleak world. You're enough to illuminate my path, yet I always want more."

My eyes widen, and Silas smiles at me, his expression tender.

When he looks at me like that, he gives me hope that someday, he and I could be more than friends.

Silas tears his gaze away and I watch as he digs through the dirt with his bare hands before burying the bottle, my heart racing wildly the entire time. He pushes the dirt flat onto the ground, securing the treasure he buried before brushing his hands against each other.

Si rises to his feet, towering above me, his eyes on mine. "Now you've got one of my firsts too, Alanna. You're the first woman I've ever drawn a portrait of, unless we're counting the childish doodles I shared with my mom. You're the first woman I've brought here, the first one to have received a birthday card from me."

I take a step closer to him and place my palms against his chest, my heart racing. "Next year," I whisper. "Next year, I'll bring a gift of my own too. I can't draw, Si... but I'll think of something."

He smirks and places his hands on my waist, his touch far more intimate than usual. "I'm looking forward to it," he whispers. Then he takes a step away from me, almost as though he physically wants to distance himself from me, and I sigh. Every once in a while, I catch a glimpse of what could be, if he'd let it... and tonight I want it more than ever before.

"Will you tell me about your favorite memories in this place?"

"Not counting the one we're creating right now?" he replies, and I blush.

Si drops back down to the ground with a smile on his face. I watch him as he takes off his hoodie, his t-shirt riding up with it and exposing his abs. He places it on the ground and tips his head toward it. My eyes widen, and I freeze. Why would he do that for me? I know how long he has to wait to wash his clothes at the shelter, yet he so carelessly threw his hoodie on the floor... for *me.*

My heart aches as I sit down next to him. Si smiles at me, and my heart starts to race. I'm falling for him, and I know I'll never have him. Silas has made that much clear. Even if there's a spark between us, he won't act on it.

"My darling Ray, let me tell you about the time I peed my pants because a squirrel attacked me," he says, and I grin. He's single-handedly turned the worst birthday I've ever had into the best one I could've wished for. I'm already looking forward to next year, and I have a feeling he is too.

Chapter Eleven

Silas

I stare at the notice on the door, informing us that today's seminar was canceled. Why didn't I receive an email about that? I'd have left straight after my last lecture if I'd known. I groan and turn back around in a rush to get back to the shelter. Maybe I'll get to see her today, if I'm fast enough.

"Hey, Silas?"

I pause, surprised at the sound of my name. A tall blonde smiles at me, her expression hopeful. I've seen her in my seminars before, but I don't think we've ever spoken a word to each other. To say I'm a loner at college would be putting it mildly. For one, I'm older than most of my classmates, because I started two years later than I was supposed to. Besides, it's unsettling to be around people who are so carefree, who take the educational opportunities they're given for granted. It's strange to be surrounded by people who are exactly what I'd be like if Mona hadn't kicked me out.

"Regina, right?"

Her eyes widen, as though she's surprised I know who she is, and then she smiles. How could I not know her? I hear guys talking about her at every turn. We might never have formally met before, but I know she's a cheerleader, and she seems to be every guy's biggest fantasy. Personally, I don't see it. I much prefer petite women with dark hair and sassy mouths that hide a heart of gold... perfect hazel eyes, and lips I'm dying to taste. Yeah, Regina is not my type.

"I'm throwing a party tonight. I'd love to see you there, if you're up for it?"

I'm not into the whole college party scene. I don't have time for it, and if I were to attend, I'd miss the shelter's curfew. My agreement with Ricardo meant I could never miss curfew, or I'd risk losing my bed. Now that I'm officially employed by the shelter, it's probably different, but I still won't risk it. Besides... it's Wednesday. Alanna volunteers on Wednesdays.

"I can't," I tell her. "But thank you for inviting me."

I haven't seen Alanna for nearly two months now, because of this damn seminar. It's ends so late that she's usually gone by the time I get back. Today is the first time it's ever been canceled. Speaking to her on the phone isn't enough, not anymore. There's no way I'll pass on a chance to see her, just to go to some party.

I smile at Regina and walk past her. "Wait!" she says, sounding mildly panicked. I turn back around to face her, and she smiles nervously. "Um, could I... could I maybe have your number?"

"Why?" I frown, confused.

She looks at me, her eyes wide and her cheeks rosy. What is wrong with her?

"Um, it's just, we've been in the same seminar all semester. I thought it would be good to exchange notes every once in a while."

"Right," I murmur, nodding. I take out my phone and unlock it before handing it to her. She takes it from me and dials her own phone number before saving it for me. For some reason, she hesitates before giving it back to me. Why is she being so awkward? As far as I'm aware, we've never spoken before today.

"Thanks," I tell her, taking my phone back from her. She nods and looks at me as though there's more she wants to say, but I don't have time to hang around. Not today. "See you at our next seminar."

She nods, and I walk away in a rush, worried I'll miss the next bus. I can barely remember the last time I saw Alanna, and I'm looking forward to spending some time with her again. Thanks to my new job and bedroom at the shelter, I get to talk to her until whatever time I want now. Our conversations usually last until either of us falls asleep, but it isn't the same as seeing her. It's strange, but Alanna and I can go weeks without seeing each other, and our friendship never changes.

"You're back earlier than usual today," Ricardo says when I walk into the shelter. I pause and nod, suddenly feeling awkward. "She's in the kitchen."

"Who?" I ask, playing dumb.

Ricardo shakes his head and glances back at his tablet, his gaze thoughtful. I was sure he'd have warned me away by now, and the fact that he hasn't means he trusts me with her. I know I can't take this any further. It isn't just the age difference, it's everything else too. There's no future for us. I can't have her, but I allow myself this much. I allow myself her company and her friendship, for as long as she's willing to give me that.

I pause in the kitchen doorway, the sound of her laughter stopping me in my tracks. I watch her as she smiles at one of the kitchen employees. She's no doubt being told some type of outrageous story. I wonder if she realizes that she brightens up all our days. I'm not the only one who looks forward to her visits.

I push away from the wall and walk up to her, wishing I could just take her into my arms. She's so ridiculously beautiful, yet I can never tell her that. Not without making things weird between us. "Ray," I murmur, fighting the possessiveness I feel.

She looks up from the soup she's cooking, and my heart starts to race when her eyes find mine. "Silas." The way she says my name has me taking another step toward her. Fuck. If I could kiss her right now, I would.

"Let me help you."

I feel her eyes on me as I wash my hands and grab an apron and gloves. Does she realize what she's doing to me? It's been a year and a half since she first started volunteering here, and in that time, she's managed to wear me down. I remember how badly I wanted to stay away from her when she first came here, yet now I can't even fall asleep if I don't hear her telling me goodnight first. Each time I saw her, she left me wanting just a little more of her. One more smile, one more conversation... and that just turned into a phone call, and another. My friendship with Alanna developed slowly, forged by my inability to resist her.

I take the spoon from her, and she grabs a bag of cornstarch to thicken the soup with. "I think we should add some more vegetables," she says, and I nod.

"You look tired," I murmur, my voice low enough for our conversation to be private in this busy kitchen. "Did I keep you up too late last night?"

I smirk when her cheeks turn rosy. So beautiful. It's insane how stunning she is, and somehow she just gets more beautiful each time I see her. "Silas," she admonishes. "If anyone heard you say that, they'd misunderstand."

I bite back a smile and shake my head. I'd tell her that there'd be no room for misunderstandings if I ever took her to bed, but I can't say that. I can't joke around with her like that, crossing the boundaries she's been pushing. "I'm serious," I tell her. "You look exhausted. Things not going well with your dad?"

She shakes her head. "No. He's sold most of his cars and pretty much every other valuable thing we own other than our home, but I don't think it's enough. We're receiving letters from debtors every week, sometimes multiple times a week. I don't know what's going on, Si, and he won't talk to me. If I try asking him anything at all, he just tells me not to worry. I don't know what to do."

"I wish I could tell you to take his advice, but I know it isn't that easy to simply not worry. Truthfully, there's nothing you can actually do, Alanna. All you can do is offer your dad the moral support he might need. I can imagine that what he's worried about more than anything else is letting you down. He won't want you to see him at his weakest, so for now just have faith in him, okay?"

She nods, but I can tell she isn't listening. She's anxious, and nothing I say will change that. I can't blame her, either. I'd be the same in her situation.

"Your phone," she says.

I blink in confusion, and Alanna points at my pocket.

"Your phone keeps dinging."

I take off my gloves and unlock my phone, surprised to find several messages from Regina with her address and information about the party, in case I change my mind. Why couldn't she just put all of that information in one single text? Why did she need to send me five?

"Who's Regina?" Alanna asks, her tone different, harsher.

"No one."

She looks at me then, a flash of hurt in her eyes. Fuck. When she looks at me like that she's got me ready to sink down to my knees and beg for forgiveness for whatever crime she thinks I committed.

"Regina is just some girl from school. She's in one of my seminars. I'd never even spoken to her before today."

"So today was the first time you spoke to her, yet somehow you have her phone number already? That was fast, Si. Good for you." She forces a smile, but she can't hide the pain in her eyes. Not from me.

"Ray, she asked for my number so we can exchange notes. That's all it is."

Alanna nods and looks back at the soup she's making. "Is she pretty?"

What? What am I supposed to say to that? "No? I'm not sure."

"You're not sure?" she repeats. "You've seen her before, right? Do you think she's pretty?"

Is she... *jealous*? I can't help but smile at the thought of it. She and I have been dancing around each other, both of us well aware that we can't cross the line, but every once in a while she slips up, and I love it when she does. I love it when she shows me how deeply she cares.

"No, Ray. I don't think she's pretty."

Her shoulders slump in relief, and she smiles. "Oh," she says, trying to act nonchalant when she can't keep her smile off her face.

I'm done for. I'm falling for her, and no matter how hard I resist, I can't stop. I can't stop wanting more of her. More of her smiles, more of her company, more of her touch.

I can't stay away... but I have to.

Chapter Twelve

Alanna

I sit up when I hear the front door open, my eyes wide. I don't remember the last time Dad made it home for dinner. It's been months since we even had a real conversation.

"Alanna, sweetheart."

Dad looks exhausted, but it's more than that. His work has always been his passion, and these days his eyes look vacant. The fire I'm so used to seeing in him is gone. He still hasn't told me what exactly is going on, but from what I understand, the company is struggling worse than it ever has before.

"You're home early! Come have dinner with me, Dad." I pat the seat next to mine as I get up to grab him a plate. I feel Dad's eyes on me and look back, a smile on my face. The way he's looking at me has me worried. I've never seen Dad looking so lost, so discouraged. The last time I saw him wearing that expression was at Mom's funeral.

"I made some spaghetti." It's simple, but it does the job. If I'd known that Dad was going to be home tonight, I definitely would've tried to make something nicer.

"Looks great, honey."

I sit down next to him and watch him for a moment. "It's so good to have you home for dinner," I murmur. "I can't remember the last time we had dinner together." It's been months, for sure.

Dad looks down at his plate and nods. "I've let you down, Alanna." His voice is soft, his regret palpable. "Work has overshadowed everything, and even so, it isn't enough."

I place my hand over his and shake my head. "No, Dad. You could never let me down," I tell him. "I know how hard you work, and you were right, you know? Volunteering at the shelter truly did make me appreciate everything we've got so much more. I get why you work so hard."

He smiles at me, and I breathe a sigh of relief. This is the first real smile I've seen on his face in months. "Your eighteenth birthday is coming up soon," he says, tightening his grip on my hand. "The months are flying by, each day filled with nothing but work. I haven't even had time to make up for missing your seventeenth birthday. How about I take you to that restaurant you wanted to go to back then? Or is there something else you'd rather do?"

I shake my head. "I'm not sure, Dad. It's so pricey, and it seems unnecessary. How about we just have dinner at home together? I just want to spend my birthday with you. It doesn't matter where."

Dad looks at me and shakes his head. "No, I'll take you there. I insist."

I grin at him and nod. I walked out of there that night without even sitting down, because I'd been waiting for Dad by the entrance. I've been wanting to go for so long now. "I can't wait!"

Dad smiles at me and shakes his head. "You're all grown up, and I've missed so much of it. I kept telling myself that there'd be time to make it up to you, that I just needed to save the company first, and everything else would come after... now I see how wrong I was. I'm sorry, Alanna."

"Dad," I murmur. "It's okay, honestly. I've been super busy with college applications, and school's just been a lot lately. I've kept myself busy, I promise."

It's true that I felt lonely at the start, but that was before Silas. Once he and I started to talk to each other every day, the loneliness faded.

"Hmm," Dad says, smiling. "There's a boy, huh?"

I freeze, my eyes widening. "What? No!"

Dad chuckles and takes a bite of his spaghetti, his eyes on me. I have no doubt that I'm blushing fiercely, but even if I wasn't, there's no way I could keep anything from Dad. We might not be as close as we used to be, but he's still my best friend. I've never kept anything from Dad, and I won't now either.

"Who's the lucky boy that gets to date my little girl?"

I shake my head. "I'm not dating anyone," I tell him honestly. "He doesn't even know I like him. We're just friends, and I know he wouldn't want that to change. He doesn't see me that way."

Dad smiles and takes another bite of his food, his gaze thoughtful. "He does. Of course he wants to date you, Alanna. The man would have to be blind not to. You're my daughter, after all! How could he not want to date someone with my genes?"

I burst out laughing and shake my head. "Right," I mutter. "So that's where I got my humbleness from."

Dad chuckles, and I smile back at him. It's been so long since we joked around together. Every conversation lately has felt strained, like I was bothering him, no matter how nice I tried to be.

"Sweetheart, that boy is the luckiest guy in the world because he gets to have your friendship. My marriage with Mom was built on friendship. She friendzoned me for years before we finally started dating. We met when we were both homeless, and though we clearly loved each other, we both knew that wasn't a good time to be together. We needed to work on ourselves before we could work on being a couple, because relationships really do take *work*. Don't worry about him not wanting to be anything more than friends for now, okay? You've got so much on your plate already, and what's meant to be truly will be."

I nod, my thoughts turning to Silas. "I didn't even know you knew the word *friendzoned*."

Dad nods. "Oh honey, I know all the lingo. I know *YOLO* and *LOL* too."

A giggle escapes my lips, and Dad laughs with me. The two of us sit at the table together, just enjoying each other's company. For once, Dad seems truly present in the moment, and I have every intention of enjoying every second of it. Who knows how long it'll be before I get to have a fun evening with him again? I have no doubt his focus will shift back to work the second he's done eating.

"I never knew that Mom and you met when you were both homeless," I murmur, unable to suppress my curiosity. "Ricardo has mentioned her before, but all of his stories were from after you left the shelter. He never told me she used to live there too."

Dad turns to me and nods. "We did. Your mother loved me at my lowest, and for as long as she lived, I've done my best to repay her for it. She was always the woman of my dreams. I knew she was the one the moment I first met her at the shelter. We quickly became friends, both of us eager to turn our lives back around. She helped me set up the company, and she helped me become the man I am today. Without your mother, I'd be nothing. Without her, I *am* nothing."

"Your love is out of this world," I murmur. "How could you two possibly have stayed away from each other for years?"

Dad looks away and sighs. "I felt like I had to prove myself before I could ever be with her. All I wanted for your mother was a life better than what I could offer her at the time. I wanted to give her the world, and I could never ask her to be with a man who couldn't even buy her dinner. I managed to achieve what I set out to do, and the moment I had a flat of my own and a steady job, I asked her to marry me. I didn't even ask her to be my girlfriend, because there was no point. I knew she was it for me, and she knew it too. I thought we'd made it, you know? I didn't realize it wasn't just the two of us in our marriage. It was us, and the demons that haunted your mother. No matter how much help I tried to get her, it was never enough. Homelessness leaves scars, Alanna. You can never truly escape it."

I don't understand how Mom could ever take her own life when she was this loved. I've tried so hard to make sense of it, and it wasn't until I started to volunteer at the shelter that I began to understand just a little. I have no doubt that Dad isn't telling me the full story, and I'll probably never know exactly what Mom has been through in life to lead her down the path she chose... but I can finally let go of the resentment.

I can't help but wonder what my story with Silas will be. When he achieves everything he's working toward... will he want me then?

Chapter Thirteen

Silas

I smile when Alanna pulls up at the shelter. She gets out of the car, and my heart starts to race. Fucking hell. She looks stunning tonight. I thought she looked irresistible on her birthday last year, but she looks even more beautiful tonight... and I'm pretty sure that tight black dress is all for me.

"Happy birthday, Ray," I murmur. "I didn't get to say it to you in person yesterday. The phone call doesn't count."

She walks up to me, and for a moment I think she'll hug me, but then she holds her car keys up for me. "Thank you, Si," she says, her cheeks rosy. Things have been different between us lately. It's almost like we're both at our breaking point, neither of us able to keep up this act much longer.

I don't think I can pretend not to want her tonight. Not when she looks like that. Not when I'm taking her back to the tree my mother and I planted. I wrap my hand around her car keys and open the passenger door for her.

"I wish I could've spent yesterday with you," she tells me as I get into the car, and I shake my head.

"No, beautiful. You've been looking forward to having dinner with your dad for so long now. I'm glad you finally got to go."

She looks at me, her gaze lingering. "I want to take you there someday, Si. Will you let me?"

I tighten my grip on the steering wheel, feeling conflicted. I want to be the person she goes out with, but I can't afford to take her on a date. I don't mind her picking up the bill every once in a while, but I can't in good conscience go when I know I'll never be able to do the same for her. I don't ever want her to feel like I'm using her, and this would quickly become a slippery slope.

"Someday," I promise her. Someday soon, I'll be able to take her wherever she wants to go. I'm only a year away from graduating, and if all goes well, I'll find a nice entry-level IT job. It might not pay much, but it should be enough to get a small place of my own. Now, more than ever, I'm desperate to get out of the shelter.

"How was it? Tell me all about it." Yesterday was the first day in weeks that we didn't talk to each other for very long. She came home late and fell asleep minutes into our phone call.

"Si, it was just the *best*. I don't think I've ever seen Dad so happy before, and the food was just amazing. It'd been so long since we spent some quality time together, and it felt just like old times. It was the first time in *forever* that he didn't seem stressed."

I love this about her. She went to one of the most expensive restaurants in town, and what she was most focused on was her father, and whether he had a good time. She's something special, and she doesn't even realize it.

Alanna turns to me, a wide grin on her face. "I almost forgot to tell you! I've got a bottle of my own this year. Do you want to guess what's in it?"

My heart fills with tenderness, and it takes all of me not to stop the car and pull her into my arms. I adore her. There's no other way to describe this feeling.

"Is it a birthday card?"

Alanna pouts, and I know I guessed correctly. "*Si*," she

complains. "I know you got me a card too, but the point is to guess correctly what kind of card it is."

"Who says I got you a card?"

"Wait, what? I thought you were going to draw me a card every year?"

I smile at her and shake my head. "The gift can be different every year. My mother always drew me something, yes, but that doesn't mean I'll do the same."

I feel her gaze on me as I park the car, and I can't help but smirk. Just being around her makes my heart race. I've been fighting this for so long, but I don't think I have it in me to resist any longer.

"It's a card, isn't it?" she asks.

I chuckle as I get out of the car and walk around it to open the door for her. "Only one way to find out, babe."

I grab her hand and pull her along, the two of us walking toward the tree hand in hand. I rarely touch Alanna. We don't usually even hug each other in greeting, but tonight is different.

"Si, I might actually die from anticipation. What if I *die*?"

I bite back my laughter and shake my head. I love that she only shows this dramatic crazy part of herself to me, and no one else. She acts spoiled around me, and poised around everyone else.

"I think you'll be okay, Ray. But just in case, I'd better dig up that bottle for you, huh?"

She reaches into her handbag and takes out a small gardening shovel, holding it up for me with a triumphant smile. "I came prepared. I've got this."

She drops to her knees in the same spot we were last year, and I shake my head as I take the shovel from her. "Let me," I murmur. I don't want her hands to get dirty, and I don't want her digging up dirt by herself.

She sits on her knees as I retrieve the bottle we buried last year, her eyes wide with excitement. There's something so beautiful about her, and it isn't just her looks. It's the fact that she's always treated me the same. She's always treated me as a regular human being, and despite the struggles I face, she's clearly falling for me as hard as I'm falling for her. I shouldn't even be on her radar, yet here she is, trespassing with me to dig up a bottle, and it looks like there's nowhere else she'd rather be.

Alanna gasps when I lift the bottle up, and she all but snatches it from me. "You have no idea how long I've waited for this," she whispers.

I smile, the feeling bittersweet. "Not as long as I've waited." My words are soft, barely above a whisper, but she hears them nonetheless. She has no idea how hard it's been to resist her. I kept telling myself that I wouldn't even consider being with her until she turned eighteen, but the truth is that I've been falling for her, little by little, day by day, for two years.

"Can I open it?"

I nod, and Alanna stares at the glass bottle for a moment before finally opening it. She takes out the card and unrolls it, her hands trembling. I watch her closely, my heart pounding. When she looks up at me, her eyes are filled with the same need I've been battling.

"It's us," she whispers. "Standing underneath this tree."

I nod.

"You're kissing me in this drawing."

I nod again.

"But... you drew this last year. I saw you bury this on my seventeenth birthday."

I smile and look away. "That's how long I've been wanting to kiss you, Alanna. At the time, you were obsessing over firsts, and you weren't happy that you didn't have any of mine, so I gave you *this*. You and me, this tradition... that was a first, but it wasn't the one I wanted."

"What *do* you want?" she asks, her eyes filled with hope and desire.

"You," I whisper.

I rise to my feet and pull her up with me. Her eyes widen, and

I smile when I pull her closer. "This is how we were standing in the drawing," I whisper.

She smiles at me, nerves and desire dancing across her eyes. "I was even wearing a similar dress in your drawing. Tell me, Si. Can you see the future?"

I smirk at her and lift my hand to her face, the back of my fingers trailing over her cheek. "I can, and both of ours are entwined, starting today."

"Is that so?" she whispers, her gaze dropping to my lips. "In that case, I can't wait for the rest of our lives."

I don't think I've ever been this nervous before, certainly not over something as simple as a kiss, but this is different. I want this to be perfect. I lean in, tilting my face toward hers, a small part of me still scared of crossing the line with her. There's no going back from this, but I don't want to. I don't want to be friends with her anymore.

My lips brush against her, and Alanna freezes, pulling away. I tense and take a step away from her, confused.

"Si, no," she murmurs. "It's my phone. It's buzzing. No one ever actually calls me but my dad, so I have to take it."

I breathe a sigh of relief as she answers the phone. This isn't exactly how I saw tonight going. I've replayed this evening in my mind countless times, but I never expected to be interrupted at such a critical moment. I'm nervous as hell, and her speaking to her dad isn't helping. It just reminds me that I shouldn't be doing this, that I'm not good enough for her.

"*What*? Which hospital?"

I straighten, instantly on high alert. Alanna's eyes fill with tears, and by the time she ends the call, I've got her keys in my hand. "What happened?"

"They said my dad was injured when someone tried to rob him, and he's in the hospital. What do I do, Si?"

I wrap my arm around her as I lead her to the car. "I'll drive you. Come on, let's go."

Alanna is barely holding back her panicked sobs as I drive her to the hospital, and I hold her tightly as we walk in, taking the lead. She's shaking, and she seems in no position to be asking for directions. It takes a moment, but eventually, we find her father's room.

The two police officers standing in front of it have me instantly worried. "Alanna Jones?" one of them asks. She nods, and the pity in his eyes has me tightening my grip on her. "They tried all they could, Ms. Jones. They couldn't save your father, but I promise you that my partner and I will do all we can to catch the man who shot him."

"What?" she asks, her voice breaking. "This... what... it can't—"

She pulls out of my embrace and rushes into her father's room. My heart breaks as I follow her in, knowing what I'll find. "Please," she begs, her voice breaking.

I watch as she shakes his arm, but it's too late. He's gone. I walk up to her and wrap my arm around her waist, offering her silent support as she continues to plead with her father, her tone getting more and more frantic as realization dawns.

"Silas, please," she pleads, her breathing weighed down by the sobs she's trying to restrain. She looks at me, and the desperation in her eyes destroys me. "Please wake him up. *Please.*"

I pull her into me, hugging her tightly, one hand in her hair, and the other around her waist. She struggles in my embrace for a moment, and then she collapses against me, loud sobs tearing through her throat as she falls apart in my arms.

The two of us stand there together, clinging to each other. I've never felt more powerless than I do tonight. Her heart is breaking, and there's nothing I can do.

Chapter Fourteen

ALANNA

I stare at my parents' tombstones as my phone rings non-stop. I know that it's probably Silas calling me, but I don't have it in me to pick up the phone. The more he speaks to me, the more concerned he gets, and I really don't want him to worry about me. I sink down to the floor opposite my father's grave and cross my ankles, unsure where else to go.

The last two weeks have been a blur, and I feel like I've just been going through the motions, following Dad's will. He had plans for every single thing that needed to happen in the event of his death, and all that was left for me to do was execute them. He'd even already contracted the same funeral home that handled Mom's funeral to ensure they had his wishes on record. There wasn't much for me to do at all. Part of me is grateful for it, but a small part of me also feels like it robbed me of doing one final thing for my father.

"I miss you," I whisper. "The police are still trying to find the man that shot you, but I haven't heard much at all. I feel like I won't be able to rest easy until that man is caught and brought to justice. Was the money he stole from you really worth a life? I know I shouldn't, but I hope he has a family that'll miss him when he's put in jail, so he'll feel at least a fraction of the pain I'm feeling."

I let my eyes fall closed, my face tipped up toward the sky. I watch the clouds move past me, a reminder that the world keeps turning despite the loss that upturned my entire life. "I lost the company," I whisper, as though I'm scared to even admit it. "The company was declared bankrupt when you died, and there's nothing I could do about it. Everything you've worked for… I wasn't able to hold on to it. The only thing I've been able to do that'd make you proud was paying all your employees their outstanding wages. That, and thanks to that life insurance policy you always insisted you should have, I've been able to pay back the loans you took out with the house as collateral, so I haven't lost our home… but that's all I've really got, Dad. I had no idea just how much debt you were in, but I've paid back everything that I became liable for. You'll be happy to know that the majority of your debt disappeared when you did. It was tied to you, and I didn't inherit it. I'm not sure if that's a good thing or not. To be honest, Dad… I don't know anything at all. I'm lost without you. I'm trying my hardest to figure out what I should be doing, but it's all so overwhelming. I'm not ready to be an adult. I'm not ready to live a life you aren't part of."

I draw my knees up to my chest and drop my head down, inhaling shakily. "Can't you please come back to me? Please, Dad. You promised me you'd make up for all the lost time, but you haven't. You *left* me. I'm glad you're with Mom now, but I *need* you."

I stare at the tombstones, both of my parents side by side. I wish I could hear my father's voice just one more time. I can barely remember Mom's voice, and I'm scared Dad is going to become a memory I struggle to recall.

A slight drizzle falls from the sky, and I look up at the clouds above me. Would it matter if I just stay here and let the skies drown me? Would it numb the pain?

I bite down on my lip harshly as I force myself to my feet. I know this isn't what Dad would have wanted for me, and I can't lose myself in my pain. I'm not sure how, but one way or another, I need to find a way to keep going.

I'm in a daze as I somehow manage to get myself home, surprised to find the police officer in charge of my father's case standing on my doorstep, a man dressed in a black suit next to her.

"Ms. Jones?" Officer Thomas says, her voice carrying a hint of compassion. "We found the perpetrator. Would it be okay if we spoke inside?"

I nod and lead them to the living room. "I'm Tom from Vita Insurance," the man tells me, but Officer Thomas shoots him a look, and he sits back in silence.

"Here's the thing, Alanna," she says carefully. "We found the assailant, and he confessed. The problem lies in the confession. Your father... he seems to have arranged his own assassination in order to give you his life insurance money. We've looked into it as best as we could, and your father was in tremendous debt. I can only imagine that he saw no way out, and this seemed like the best way to shield you from imminent poverty."

Tom sits up and starts to tap his foot. "Regardless of his motivations, it's insurance fraud. It's essentially assisted suicide, which is specifically excluded in our policies. Since you were the recipient, you'll have to pay back everything you were given."

"What?" I murmur, barely comprehending what they're telling me. Dad... he... he did this? He chose to die, even though he knew how hard it was for us to get past Mom's death? What did I do that made him think I'd rather live without him than live in poverty?

Officer Thomas holds her hand up and shakes her head. "He'll still be punished for your father's death, Alanna. But this complicates matters in terms of the insurance money."

"It can't be," I tell her. "Dad would never in a million years do that. He just wouldn't. Not after my mother took—" I can't even finish my sentence. It can't be.

She nods in understanding. "I promise you that I've gone over the evidence myself. The assailant had proof of conversations between your father and him, and there was a paper trail, too. Your father tried his best to hide his tracks, but the evidence is all there. We just didn't know where to look for it, initially."

He may not have pulled that trigger, but Dad took his own life, just like Mom did. Why would he do that to me? Why would he leave me here, all alone? He and I were left scarred by Mom's decision, so how could he, in good conscience, follow her lead?

"We understand that this is an unconventional situation, so the insurance company will work with you to figure out the repayments if you don't have the full sum anymore."

I nod, my thoughts still reeling. I thought the loss left me numb, that my heart couldn't possibly break more, yet it does. "I spent some of the money to pay back loans that Dad took out using the house as collateral, and then there's all of the funeral costs too. I also paid all of his employees their outstanding wages before the company was officially declared bankrupt."

"In that case, it'll become tricky. You'll owe more than you're able to pay back, and we'll have to look at your assets," the insurance guy says.

I nod, but I can barely focus on the conversation. All I can think about is the last few weeks of Dad's life. Were there any signs I missed? Is there anything I could've done to prevent this? I wish I'd tried harder to get through to him, to make sure he knew I loved him more than anything in the world, more than any of our belongings. I wish he'd known I'd happily live in poverty, so long as I get to have him by my side. I wish I hadn't tried to act strong and brave, so he wouldn't ever even have considered leaving me.

I wish I could go back in time, so I could convince him to stay.

Chapter Fifteen

ALANNA

I walk out of the home I grew up in for the very last time, my heart heavy with regret as I hand the keys to Tom. I spent more of the insurance money than the house is worth, so my home isn't the only thing I'm losing. Had I not paid my father's employees their outstanding wages, I might not have been in as much as trouble as I'm in now.

"I'm sorry it came to this, Alanna," Tom tells me. "I wish there was a different way, but I've done all I can for you."

I nod in understanding. Considering my case was ruled as insurance fraud, he really has done all he could. Tom worked with me to assess the value of all of my belongings, and the insurance company agreed to write off my debt, provided that I give them everything I have, on compassionate grounds. I lost my car, my mother's jewelry, and even all the paintings Dad and I collected throughout our travels. I've got nothing left to my name. Nothing but the contents of my backpack.

The only thing they let me keep was the truck I'm staring at. It's one of Dad's most precious belongings, and though I'll have to give them the cash I'll get for it, they allowed me to ensure it'd go to a good home.

When I was younger, I never understood why Dad loved it so much. I remember seeing scrap books with pictures in it, and I realize now that Mom and Dad created those when they were still homeless. This truck was part of the future they envisioned and worked towards, and it must have been one of the first things Dad bought for himself after escaping that life. To him, it wasn't just a truck; it was proof that he changed his circumstances. That's why he took such great care of it, and why he loved it above all of his far more expensive cars. It's probably why it's the only car he kept as he sold our belongings.

It kills me that I couldn't protect the truck he loved so much. It's strange to be so heartbroken over it, when losing the house should hit me much harder. I suppose selling his baby really makes me feel like I'm letting him down. I know that this is the one thing Dad never would've let go of. Selling this car would've felt like admitting defeat to him, and that's exactly what it feels like to me. I feel like I've failed him.

I brace myself as a kind-looking man steps out of a car parked across the street. After countless offers, it's his that I accepted. He walks toward me with his young son in his arms. The boy can't be older than five, and he's adorable.

"Is this our truck, Daddy? I love it so much!" he says, his voice soothing my aching heart.

"Alanna?" he asks.

I nod and shake his hand. "Mr. Brown, right?"

"Please call me Rob," he tells me, and I force a smile to my face as he takes a thick envelope out of his pocket. "Please go ahead and count it. It should be the exact amount of money we agreed on. I'm so glad you're selling this to me, Alanna. My son is obsessed with trucks, and this is the exact one we've both been wanting."

I nod and hand the cash to Tom. It isn't mine to keep, after all. "That's why I'm selling it to you," I admit. "This was my father's car, and I really wanted it to go to someone just like him, someone with a little kid who'll love sitting so high up, like I always did. This car holds so many happy memories for me, and I hope you'll create some of your own too."

Tom nods at me, and I take the car keys out of my pocket. My hands tremble as I give the keys to Rob, and he smiles at me in understanding.

"I'll take good care of her," he promises. "It's clear your dad loved his truck, and I promise I'll love her the same."

I nod, trying my hardest to blink away the tears gathering in my eyes as he puts his son down on the ground, the two of them inspecting the car together. Their excitement is reassuring and enviable all at once. I still remember all the times Dad let me help him wash his car, the two of us making a mess on Sunday mornings.

This is the car Dad drove me to school in for years, and on hot days, we'd drive far out, and Mom and I would have a picnic on the tailgate. Losing this car hurts more than I expected it to.

I watch as Rob drives away in my father's truck, and tears burn in my eyes as the last fragment of my life slips through my fingers, leaving me with nothing but the meagre contents that fill my backpack.

My attempts to blink away my tears only have them falling down my cheeks harder, until it becomes hard to see. My lungs burn as I inhale, trying my hardest to keep from sobbing and failing. I bite down on my lip as hard as I can, the pain distracting me from the blinding sorrow I can't push aside.

Within a matter of weeks, I've lost everything. I lost my father, our home, everything he worked for. If he's looking down at me from heaven, he must be filled with anguish, with regret. I'll never understand why he did what he did, and the anger I feel fights for dominance with my pain. He knew what impact losing Mom had on us both, yet he walked down the same path, knowingly.

"I'll leave the rest to you," I tell Tom, my voice breaking.

"I wish you well, kid. I'm sorry about everything you've gone through, and the role I was forced to play in it."

I smile at him as best as I can. "You're just doing your job," I remind him. "But it really is a shit job. You should really find something else."

Tom chuckles then, and for a single second, my own smile is a genuine one. Then my gaze drops to the home behind him, the one I'll never step foot inside of again, and a tear drops down my cheek.

I turn away and place one foot in front of the other, forcing myself forward, one step at a time. I've got nowhere to go, no one who will take me in. The only place I can think to go is the one place my father never would've wanted me to go to — not in these circumstances. This is exactly what he tried to prevent, yet it's his good intentions that are leading me there.

After what feels like hours, I find myself looking up at the shelter, my heart breaking in a different way as I push the door open.

Ricardo rises from his cubicle by the entrance, his eyes wide. "Alanna! We've all been so worried about you. What's going on? Where have you been?"

I look at him, a small part of me wanting to cling to the pride I no longer have a right to. "Ricardo," I whisper, my voice hoarse from the tears that haven't stopped falling since I lost my father. "I need a place to stay. Please, will you take me in?"

Chapter Sixteen

Silas

I stare at my phone, watching it ring, knowing she won't pick up the phone. Alanna has been declining my calls for weeks now, and I'm worried. I've walked all over town, going to every single place she could possibly be, yet I can't find her. I even went to her school, only to be told that they let her take a few weeks off on compassionate grounds.

I look up at the sound of knocking on my door and end the call with a sigh. "Come in," I shout, knowing it can only be Ricardo.

He opens the door, his expression grave as he leans in the doorway. "Silas. She's here."

I jump up from my bed, my eyes widening. "Alanna?"

He nods. "She asked me for a place to stay, so I pointed her toward the sleeping hall. She was distraught, to say the least, and the backpack she's carrying seems to be all she's got. I don't know what happened, but it doesn't look good."

I nod and run a hand through my hair. "She can't stay in the sleeping hall. It isn't safe for her. She isn't used to this, and she..." She's too beautiful. I'm worried about her safety.

Ricardo nods. "I know, but there's nowhere else for her to stay. I've already broken the rules by not making her fill out all the required paperwork tonight, and I didn't even check her bag. I can't break even more rules."

He looks down for a moment before looking back at me, his gaze meaningful as he glances past me, at my bed. My bedroom is mine, no strings attached. There is no rule against me bringing someone back here, so there should be no problem with me letting Alanna have my bed. The words he can't say are registering loud and clear.

I nod at him, and he breathes a sigh of relief as he nods back at me. Ricardo lets the door fall closed as he walks away, and I stare at it for a moment. Part of me is scared to go find her. For Alanna to have come here for shelter means she must have been through hell and back in the last couple of weeks. She knows how rough the living conditions are here. She wouldn't be here if she had any other choice, and I know how prideful she is. It's possible she won't want to see me tonight.

I inhale shakily and walk toward the door resolutely. I won't risk her getting hurt or being robbed in her sleep, simply to save her pride.

My heart races as I walk to the sleeping hall I spent every night in for two years. I've purposely never entered this room at night since I got a bedroom of my own. Escaping this place was one of the hardest things I've done, yet here I am, walking back in here willingly. For her.

I spot her almost immediately. Even in her darkest hour, she shines brightly. I watch her for a moment, taking in the despair in her eyes, the way she stares at the bunk bed in front of her in disbelief. She looks so broken, so unlike the girl I've fallen in love with, yet there is still so much strength in her posture. She's beautiful, perhaps even more so now than before.

I watch as one of the men hops off his bed and approaches

her, his expression spelling trouble. Alanna tenses, and a rush of pure venom rushes through me as I walk toward her. He leers at her, and I lock my jaw.

"Alanna," I snap, my tone harsher than I intended. She turns to face me, her eyes filled with regret, as though she wishes she could have avoided me tonight. She can barely meet my eyes, her lashes hiding those brilliant hazel irises of hers before I've truly had a chance to take them in.

I pause in front of her and lift my index finger to her chin, tipping her face up toward mine. Her lashes rise slowly, reluctantly, her gaze filled with defiance. Even with those dark circles underneath her eyes and the defeat she's coated in, she takes my breath away.

"Silas."

Fuck. It's been so long since I last heard her say my name, and never before has she said it with such need. I doubt she even realizes that her voice betrays her.

"Come with me."

She shakes her head and looks away, refusing to face me.

"That wasn't a request, Alanna."

She crosses her arms, and I pull my hand back.

"Last I checked, I was still the House Manager. You know the rules as well as I do. You *will* follow me."

She looks at me then, her eyes flashing. "Last I checked, you had no right to abuse your authority."

The edges of my lips turn up into a reluctant smile that I instantly suppress. "Alanna," I murmur, my tone softer. I reach for her hand, entwining it with mine before I pull her along. Thankfully, she doesn't resist.

I lead her to my room, my heart uneasy. I haven't heard from her in weeks, and it hurts that she never thought to rely on me, to at least inform me of what she was going through. Part of me is angry with her, but a larger part of me is just relieved to see her again.

I push my bedroom door open and lead her in. The moment

the door closes behind us, I pull on our entwined hands, pulling her closer until I've got her in my embrace. She looks up at me, her eyes filled with devastating pain that I wish I could take away.

"Where were you?"

She looks away and shakes her head.

"Why didn't you at least call me? Do you have any idea how worried I was?"

She pushes against my chest, and I take a step away, releasing her. I run a hand through my hair, unsure what to do or say. I've been in her situation before, and I get it. I get that she doesn't want to talk, that she closed herself off to the world as it came crashing down on her, but *fuck*. It fucking hurts. It hurts that I wasn't the person she reached out to, the one she let in, the one that held her together when her heart was breaking.

I turn away from her and stare up at the ceiling for a moment, taking a deep breath in an effort to calm my racing heart. "Sleep here tonight," I tell her, my voice betraying the defeat I feel. "You can have my bed. I'll take your spot in the sleeping hall."

"No, Silas. You said you'd never spend another night there. I won't be the reason you break that promise to yourself."

I turn back to face her and sigh. "Alanna," I whisper. "Take the bed. You aren't putting yourself in a dangerous situation on my watch, you hear me? You aren't walking back into that hall tonight."

She looks up at me, her expression disarmed. "Neither are you." Alanna looks past me, her gaze lingering on my bed. "There's enough room for us both."

My eyes widen, and my first instinct is to argue with her, but this is a battle I know I can't win. She won't stay here if I don't. Her pride won't allow her to. "Fine."

Her shoulders sag in relief, and her eyes fall closed for a moment. I watch her every movement, still in disbelief that she's standing here with me tonight.

"There's a small bathroom through that door. It isn't much, but it's private. I've got a spare towel for you."

She nods and smiles at me, her expression showcasing her exhaustion. "Thank you, Silas." Her voice trembles, a hint of shame in it that goes straight to my heart. Everything about tonight kills me. I get that I'm the last person she wants to show this side of her to, but I really wish she would. I wish she'd rely on me.

"Go on," I murmur, handing her a towel. I place my palm on her lower back and push her toward my tiny bathroom. She glances back at me once before disappearing through the door, and I sink down on my bed, my thoughts reeling.

This is the very last thing I expected. What is she doing here? What the fuck happened for her to end up here? Though I try my hardest, I can't escape the way my heart aches at the thought of her finding herself all alone, with nowhere to go but this shelter. I vividly remember the day I first walked into this building, and it isn't an experience I'd wish on anyone. I'd give the world to ensure it never happened to her.

I straighten when Alanna walks out wearing leggings and a loose t-shirt, her cheeks rosy. She pauses halfway and looks up at me, her insecurity shining through. "Let's go to bed," I murmur, knowing she won't want to talk. It must be awkward enough for her as it is. I won't make it worse, even though I desperately need answers.

I fold my bed covers over and tip my head toward the bed. My bed is pressed against the wall, and though it's a queen-size, I barely fit in it by myself. It'll be a squeeze with both of us in here.

Alanna hesitates for a moment before walking toward me, both of us tensing when she crawls into bed. I rise to my feet and turn the light off before joining her in bed, trying my hardest to keep some distance from her.

I listen to the sound of her breathing, my heart shattering as it becomes more ragged, a soft sniff disturbing the silence that surrounds us.

She turns toward me, and I open my arms for her. Alanna bursts into tears, and I hold her as tightly as I can, her face buried in my neck. "Silas," she cries, her entire body rocking from the force of her sobs.

I rub her back soothingly, my own heart breaking alongside hers. "Per aspera ad astra, remember?" I whisper. "*Through adversity to the stars.* I know everything feels hopeless, and I know you're hurting, my love. I know. Just remember that this type of hardship will pass. It might not feel that way, but it will. Your path still leads straight to the stars. You're just taking a detour, that's all. Everything is going to be okay."

She nods and tightens her grip on me, hugging me with all her strength. "It just hurts so much."

"I know," I whisper, wishing I could take her pain away and make it my own instead. "I know, baby."

I hold her until her sobs die down and her breathing steadies, my arms wrapped tightly around her as she cries herself to sleep. I wish I could take away her sorrow and give her back her smile. I don't know what the future holds, but I know it's filled with adversity before she and I reach the stars.

Chapter Seventeen

ALANNA

I blink slowly and snuggle closer before freezing suddenly, memories of last night coming to mind. I tense in Silas's embrace when I become aware of his naked chest underneath my cheek, his arms wrapped tightly around me. I push away from him, and he startles awake.

"Ray," he says, his voice low and sexy. This is how he always sounded on the phone, right before he fell asleep.

Silas sits up, facing me, a lazy smile on his face. I've missed him more than I dare to admit. It broke my heart each time I declined one of his calls, and I know I've hurt him too.

"I'm sorry," I whisper.

Silas reaches for me and cups my cheek, his touch gentle. "Don't be sorry, Ray. I'm just glad that you're okay, that you're safe."

He runs a hand through his hair and sighs, drawing my attention to his chest and abs. I remember he was wearing a t-shirt when we went to bed... did I do something to him in my sleep?

Silas catches me staring and grins. "Sorry, Ray. I'm not used to wearing clothes to bed, so I must have taken my t-shirt off in my sleep. The less I wear to bed, the less washing I need to do, you know?"

I nod. "Right." I suppose those are the kind of lessons I'll learn the hard way too. "I'm sorry, Si. I didn't mean to make you uncomfortable in your own bed. I—"

"You didn't," he interrupts. "I'd be far more uncomfortable lying here knowing you're out in the big hall all by yourself, vulnerable."

I nod and look down. "Thank you," I whisper. This is exactly what I wanted to prevent. Silas already has so much on his plate. The last thing I want to be to him is yet another burden. I knew he'd want to help, and he and I both know he's not in a position to do so.

"Ray, where have you been? Do you have any idea how worried I've been?"

I nod. "I'm sorry. I wanted to talk to you, but I... I just couldn't."

He looks hurt for a moment and clenches his jaw as he looks away. "I wish you'd leaned on me, Alanna. Don't you see that I want to be the person you turn to? I get that there isn't much I can do, but if nothing else, won't you let me be the person who gets to be by your side when life is tough?"

He bites down on his lips as though there's more he wants to say, but can't.

"Letting others be there for us is a way of offering consolation too," I murmur, my voice barely above a whisper. That is what he told me the day we met at the cemetery.

Silas looks up, his eyes flashing with surprise. "You remember?"

I nod and look away as I wrap my arms around myself. "I remember everything about you, Si."

"That feels like a lifetime ago. I was a different person then."

I shake my head. "You've always been that person to me. The one who cheered me up on one of the worst days of my life and gave me the strength to keep going. You still have that same effect on me... except now I no longer want to be a little girl who needs you."

He looks at me, his gaze intense. "You're far from a little girl now, aren't you, sweet girl?"

I nod, heat rushing to my cheeks. "Yeah," I whisper.

Silas reaches for my hand and entwines our fingers before raising our joined hands to his chest. "I never considered you needy, Alanna. You have *never* been a burden to me. You're my guiding light, my ray of sunshine on days where the darkness feels inescapable. I'm worried about you, baby."

The pain in his eyes hits me right in my beaten, battered heart. He isn't pitying me. He's asking me for consolation. "Si," I whisper. I need this as badly as he does, but I'm not sure I can say the words. I've been living in denial even as I deal with the consequences of my father's choices. I suppose that is part of the reason I avoided talking to Silas, because he'd ask me what happened, and I wouldn't be able to tell him anything but the full truth. "My father arranged his own assassination so he could commit insurance fraud for my benefit," I tell him, the words tumbling out of my mouth in one swift gush of courage. "He might not have fired that gun, but he took his own life, just like my mother did."

Hot tears fill my eyes, and though I try to blink them away angrily, they run down my cheeks nonetheless. I can't look at Silas, scared of the disgust or horror I might see in his eyes. What my father did was horrible, yet I can't be mad at him, not truly.

Silas pulls me closer, wrapping me in a tight embrace, and I fall apart in his strong arms. Loud, painful sobs tear through my throat as I burst into tears. "I... I don't k-know what to do," I sob, my entire body shaking with the force of my grief.

Silas tightens his grip on me and buries one hand in my hair, pressing my face deeper into his neck as he holds me tightly. "Ray," he whispers, his voice sounding as broken as mine. "We're going to figure this out, okay? You're going to be okay."

He strokes my back soothingly, keeping the broken pieces of

me together as I fall apart in his arms. "I won't," I whisper. "I won't ever be okay again."

He squeezes me tightly and shakes his head. "One step at a time, my love. We're going to move forward one step at a time, until someday, you look back in surprise at how far you've come. I'll be there with you every step of the way. You and I, Alanna. We're going to make it. We're going to defy the odds." He tightens his grip on my hair and pulls away a little to look at me. "You might feel like you're all alone, and like you've lost everything, but you haven't, Alanna. You've got me, and I'm not going anywhere."

I look into his eyes, taking in the fierce determination, the affection, and a tiny fraction of my broken heart starts to beat again.

"I promise, Alanna. We'll get through this together, okay?"

I nod. Silas is the last person I wanted to burden with my problems, but he's the one person I need most. I just hope I don't drag him down with me.

Chapter Eighteen

Silas

I lean against the doorway as I watch Alanna wash a huge stack of dishes. She's been trying to make herself useful all morning, a hint of discomfort and fear in her demeanor. I know exactly how she feels. I still remember how I felt when I lost the sense of safety and comfort a *home* gives you.

"Alanna."

She turns around and turns off the tap before pulling her gloves off. "Silas?"

"Follow me."

She freezes and nods slowly as she walks toward me. Ricardo tasked me with Alanna's intake process, and part of that includes discussing her future with her. We require all of our long-term residents to have a feasible plan to get back on their feet, so whether I like it or not, I'm going to have to ask Alanna what *exactly* happened, and how she's going to escape this place. I hate having to ask this of her, because it's clear she's not ready to talk, but I have no choice. Ricardo won't allow her to stay another night if she doesn't comply with our terms.

I close the door to our small office behind her and gesture toward the seat opposite the desk Ricardo and I share. She seems nervous, and I can't shake the dread I feel as I take my seat.

"Si," she murmurs. "I know what you need to ask me, and it's okay. I'll tell you everything."

I exhale in relief and sit back as she gathers her courage. Alanna knows our procedures as well as I do, and I'm grateful for it.

My heart breaks as she tells me about everything she tried to keep from me. The insurance company, the debt, the eviction notices, the repossession of her house and the sale of her father's beloved truck. She's been through so much in the last couple of weeks, and she did it all alone.

I clench my fist underneath the desk, my heart aching for her even as a strange sense of anger washes over me. Why didn't she rely on me? Does she truly see me as someone so useless that she didn't even consider asking me to stand by her as her entire life fell apart?

"I have to ask you how you're going to get out of this, Alanna. I can let you stay in my room for as long as you need to, but I can't share any of the shelter's resources with you long-term without proper registration."

She nods and looks away. "I came to an agreement with the insurance company, so I no longer owe them anything, but I also have nothing left to my name. I'll start looking for jobs today. I'm pretty sure I saw a job listing at the supermarket near here recently."

I shake my head. "That isn't a long-term plan, Alanna. You had an offer from Astor College, didn't you?"

She nods and looks down at her lap. "I did, but I can no longer afford to attend. I'm no longer eligible for any loans because of the debt I incurred, and I didn't have any scholarships."

"If nothing else, you should attend community college, Alanna. We'll start looking into scholarships and loans tonight, okay? You can get a part-time job if you want, but you can't just give up on college entirely."

She nods, even though she looks hesitant. "Come on," I tell her as I rise to my feet. "I'll lend you the laptop Ricardo got me for college. Start looking into the options, and we'll discuss them once I get off work. How about that?"

Alanna looks up at me, her expression forlorn. I can tell she's trying her hardest to keep it together, and I'm so proud of the strength she's portrayed so far.

Alanna is silent as I walk her back to my bedroom. "I'll get you a duplicate key."

"Silas," she says, turning toward me as the door closes behind us. "I can't stay here with you. If I become a resident, I should sleep in the big hall. I really don't want to inconvenience you, and I feel like I'm invading your privacy."

I take a step closer to her, and she takes a step back, until she's pressed up against the door. "Alanna," I murmur. Her eyes widen, and I smile as I rest my forearm against the door, right beside her face. "You sleeping in the big hall would be a huge inconvenience for me, because I'd hate having to worry about you. Besides, you sleeping with me means we can offer someone else a bed. There are no downsides to this for me, but if you're uncomfortable with us sharing a bed, just let me know. I can see if I can arrange a sleeping bag for myself. I'll just sleep on the floor. It isn't a problem at all."

"No! You can't do that, Silas. I'm okay with sharing a bed, but I just didn't want to bother you. Si... I just... I'm worried you'll start to dislike me if I depend on you too much. I don't want to be a burden to you. You're all I've got left."

My heart skips a beat at her words, and I sigh as I drop my forehead to hers. Now, more than ever, I wish I could properly take her into my arms and make her see that she'd never be a burden to me. Living the way I do means having to become selfish, but she's my only exception. I just wish she knew that.

Alanna's eyes fall closed, and I inhale shakily when she wraps her arms around my waist. I hesitate for a moment before pushing my body against hers, hugging her back. I thread my hand through her hair and hold her tightly, my need for her making every other thought fade away.

"You've got me, baby. You'll always have me. I get how hard it is to rely on someone when you've never had to do that before, but I swear to you, nothing would make me happier than you letting me be there for you, okay? It isn't charity, it isn't pity." *It's love.*

Alanna nods and turns her head, her lips brushing against my neck. A shiver runs down my spine, and I pull away from her before I start to want more than she's willing to give me.

"I need to get back to work," I murmur. "Start looking at scholarships, and we'll go through them together later, okay?"

Alanna nods, her eyes on mine. For the first time since I found her in the sleeping hall, those beautiful eyes of hers are filled with cautious hope. For now, that's enough.

Chapter Nineteen

ALANNA

I jump up from the bed when the door opens and Si walks in. He looks exhausted. I never quite realized just how hard he works every day. "Hey," he says, his voice soft. "Did you get some research done?"

I nod. "I made a spreadsheet with all available scholarships and their eligibility criteria, and I've already started drafting some essays, too."

He smiles, a hint of pride sparkling in his eyes. "Good girl," he murmurs, and my heart skips a beat. I know he means it as a compliment, so why do those words make me feel so flustered?

"Wait for me, okay? I just need to take a quick shower, and then I want to see this spreadsheet of yours."

I nod and watch him disappear through the bathroom door, my heart racing. Somehow, tonight feels different from last night. When I first walked into the shelter, I was so filled with worry and shame that I didn't have the emotional capacity to think of anything else. Tonight, all I can think of is the way I woke up in

Silas's arms, and the fact that we're about to share a bed again. There's so much left unsaid between us, and part of me wants to ask about the drawing he gave me on my eighteenth birthday, yet a larger part of me doesn't dare to. Not now. Not considering the situation we're in.

I'm startled out of my thoughts when Silas walks out of the bathroom in nothing but his towel, a few drops of water dripping down from his shoulder to his abs. I bite down on my lip, unable to tear my gaze away. I know Silas has always used exercise as an escape, but I never realized just how strong his body is. He's even sexier than he was in my fantasies.

"Alanna," he groans, his voice different to usual.

I drag my eyes up to his, only to find him looking at me in a way he never has before. My heart starts to race, and heat rushes to my cheeks. Silas runs a hand through his hair, and the movement just draws my eyes back to his abs. He clears his throat as he rushes toward his wardrobe, and I finally snap out of it when he walks back to the bathroom with a change of clothes in his arms.

My cheeks are still flaming when he emerges fully dressed, and I struggle to meet his eyes. He totally just caught me checking him out, in the worst way.

"Let's see it," he says, and my eyes snap up to his. Si smiles and shakes his head. "The spreadsheet, Ray."

"Oh!" I bite down on my lip, praying my cheeks aren't as flushed as I suspect they are. My heart is hammering in my chest as Si sits down next to me, the scent of his body wash invading my senses.

He leans into me and looks over my shoulder. Having him so close is wreaking havoc on my senses. It's insane just how soothing his presence is when it's simultaneously got my heart racing a thousand miles an hour.

"This looks really good, baby. It looks like there actually are quite a few you can apply to. I'm not sure it'll be enough to attend Astor College, but I think it'll be enough for community college.

Maybe, if you really want to, you could transfer to Astor College at a later time. I'm not sure if it's possible, but I wouldn't rule it out."

I turn my face toward his, my lips accidentally brushing over his jaw. Silas inhales sharply, his eyes finding mine. He's so close that I could just tilt my face and kiss him. How would he respond if I did that?

Just a few weeks ago, he told me he'd been wanting to kiss me for far longer than I could've imagined, and I wonder if that's still the case. Does he see me differently now, or does he still feel the same way about me?

"Alanna," he whispers. Silas clears his throat and pulls away a little, disappointment hitting me hard. "Let's see some of the essays you've drafted. Ideally, I really want you to apply for these tomorrow morning."

I nod, and together we rework some of my essays. Silas is so patient as he points out what I should or shouldn't include. He's clearly exhausted, yet he's taking his time with me.

I'm so worried that he's going to get tired of me. I used to be the girl who understood his world, but wasn't part of it. I allowed him to escape this shelter, and now I'm the person trapping him here.

"Promise me you'll submit as many as you can tomorrow? Don't even think of trying to find a part-time job before you do that, okay?"

I nod. "I promise."

"Good girl," he murmurs. "I'll take you out on a date tomorrow evening, provided you finish up all of your applications."

My head snaps up, and Silas chuckles as he gently brushes my hair out of my face, his hand lingering. The back of his fingers trail over my cheek, and my heart starts to race when he looks at me the way he did on my birthday. "Silly girl," he whispers. "Stop overthinking, okay? Nothing has changed between us. You're still my

Ray, and you always will be. I know that being here is tough for you, but it's a dream come true for me. Do you have any idea how much I've missed speaking to you before bed?"

Silas pushes against my shoulder, and I fall back on his bed. "I've imagined this, Alanna. Your long hair spread all over my pillows just like that. I still want everything I told you I wanted. The way I see you hasn't changed in the slightest. If anything, I just adore you even more. The strength and resilience you've shown me inspires and astounds me. I thought you were amazing before, but this? There aren't many people who would handle everything you've been through with as much grace as you have. How many people would pay outstanding wages of employees when they have absolutely no obligation to do so? Alanna, in my eyes, you've only become more beautiful."

"Then why... why..."

He smiles at me and turns to lean over me, his body hovering on top of mine. "Why what, baby? What is it you want?"

My cheeks flush, and I tear my gaze away from his.

"Look at me, Ray," he pleads, his voice soft.

I give in, my eyes finding his. "I once told you that it's when you're at your weakest that people are most likely to take advantage of you. Do you remember that?"

I nod, my heart thumping loudly. He's so close, and I'm so tempted to pull him fully on top of me. I get what he's saying, but it's different for us. "You wouldn't be taking advantage of me," I promise him. "You'd just be keeping a silent promise you made me on my birthday."

He smirks and drops his forehead to mine, his breathing uneven. "You make a compelling argument."

"Then don't keep me waiting," I whisper.

Silas pulls away a little before pressing a lingering kiss to my forehead. "Go to bed, baby girl. Let me take you on a date tomorrow. I know how important firsts are to you, so let me do this right, okay? I want you to remember our first kiss for the rest of our lives, so let me make it special."

Silas pulls away, and I watch him as he runs a hand through his hair, his expression tormented. I can't help but chuckle at the sight of him. He wants this as much as I do, yet he insists on doing it right. If I could fall any deeper in love with him, I would.

Chapter Twenty

Alanna

I grin as I send off my last scholarship application moments before Silas walks into the bedroom. "Perfect timing," I murmur, grinning at him.

He closes the door and leans back against it, his gaze filled with barely suppressed need. The last couple of days have been bittersweet. My thoughts keep drifting back to Dad, and each time, my heart stings with fresh pain. But then I think of Silas, and the way he's helping me, the way he holds me at night, and some of the bitterness fades away.

I should have relied on him from the very start. I never should have pushed him away. The couple of days have proven to me that the way he sees me truly hasn't changed at all. If anything, the divide between us seems much smaller. He seems more comfortable with me, more open.

"You sent all of them out?"

I nod. "Every single one of them."

"Well, well, well... who would've known you'd be that desperate for a date with me, Ray?"

I giggle and shake my head. "How is that a surprise to you? I've been dying to go on a date with you since I was *sixteen*. I've waited for two years, Si. I might actually die if you make me wait any longer."

He smiles at me with so much affection in his eyes that my heart starts to race. This is how I always imagined he'd look at me. I wonder when he started looking at me differently. I had the biggest crush on him when I was younger, but he never even remotely reciprocated my feelings. When did he stop seeing me as a child? When did he start taking me seriously?

"One day, Ray," he murmurs. "One day, I'm going to buy you a beautiful dress with some expensive ass shoes, and I'll ask you to change into that before taking you on a date. I'm going to make you feel like a princess every single day. You won't lack anything at all. I'm going to make sure that this period of our lives will be something we look back on fondly. It'll be a time when things were tough, but hope and love kept us going. If we ever find ourselves second-guessing our relationship or our commitment to each other, we'll remember this period of our lives. If we can make it through this, we can make it through anything. Per aspera ad astra."

I stare at him wide-eyed. "Our relationship, huh?"

He smirks and looks down for a moment. "I might be getting ahead of myself," he says, unable to suppress his smile. "But before the day is over, I'm making you mine. Officially. Irrevocably."

My heart pounds so wildly that I can hear my heartbeat thrumming in my ears. He has no idea how long I've waited to hear him say those words, how patient I've been, how long I've been burying my hopes and feelings.

"Let's go, Ray. Let's go on our very first date."

I nod with the biggest smile on my face and place my hand in his outstretched palm. Silas entwines our fingers and pulls me out of the room, his grip tight and his smile as big as mine. When I lost my father, it felt like I'd never smile again, but Silas lit a spark in my charred heart, reigniting it.

"Where are you taking me?"

"You'll see."

I smirk as the route the bus takes becomes more and more familiar. "The blossom tree," I whisper.

Silas nods. "It only seems right. It's there where I first buried my feelings for you, so it seems like the perfect place to give into them."

Silas and I walk hand in hand, and the closer we get, the more nervous he seems. For the longest time, he seemed so unapproachable, someone I admired from a distance but could never get too close to. Yet here we are, together at last. I'm at my lowest point, and it doesn't faze him.

I pause in surprise when the tree comes into sight. "Si... did you... you did this?" I stare in shock at the picnic spread laid out underneath the tree, countless wildflowers spread all over. It looks so romantic, and I can't believe he did this for me.

He smiles as he leads me to the blanket. "Ricardo helped with quite a bit. He let me use the shelter's ingredients to make us a spread. I offered to pay him for it, but he wouldn't let me."

I sit down next to him, and Silas turns toward me so he's facing me. "We were interrupted last time, and I didn't want this place to become a source of pain for you when we've created so many amazing memories here."

"Si," I whisper. "You didn't need to do this for me. I don't need dates and all of these things. You already work so incredibly hard. How did you even find the time to arrange all of this?"

He shakes his head and cups my face. "I will always make time for you, Alanna. I will never force you to fit in between the margins of my life. You will *always* be the center of everything I do, everything I am. Throughout the last two years, you've been a constant source of hope for me. You kept me going when life felt tough, when I thought I couldn't escape my circumstances. You gave me something worth fighting for, and if you let me, I want to offer you the same. I know things are about to get incredibly hard for you, for both of us, and I can't shield you from all of it. But if you let me, I'll be there every step of the way. Though I can't take away the pain, I'll share your burdens. Will you let me be to you what you've always been to me?"

He looks into my eyes with such hope, such unyielding love. "*Yes*. There's nothing I want more, Si."

He smiles, and I don't think I've ever seen him look happier than he does at this moment. Si bites down on his lower lip, his gaze dropping to my lips, and my heart starts to pound wildly. His eyes travel back up to mine, and he chuckles as he pushes against my shoulder.

I gasp as I fall backward onto the blanket, and Si smiles the sexiest smile I've ever seen as he moves on top of me, his lower body flush against mine and his forearms on either side of my head. "Do you remember when you and I were packaging food together two years ago? At the time you were upset you'd never have some of my firsts."

I purse my lips in annoyance and glare at him. How could he remind me of that right now? Silas merely chuckles and lowers his face to mine. He kisses my cheek gently. "Hear me out, baby." He presses another kiss to my face, inching a little closer to my lips with each touch. "I don't even know when it happened, Ray, but you took my most important first without me even realizing." He kisses the edge of my lips, and I tilt my face, wanting more. He's kept me waiting for this for so long now, and I don't think I can wait even a second longer. "You are my first love, Alanna... but more importantly, you'll be my last."

His lips brush over mine, his movements hesitant. I arch my back and tilt my head, giving him easier access, and Silas groans as he finally kisses me fully. One of his hands moves into my hair and he grips tightly as the tip of his tongue brushes over my lips, and I open up for him, my entire body feeling strange. I've never felt this kind of need before, and the way his tongue tangles with mine has me wanting more, though I'm not entirely sure what it is I want more of.

He moans against my lips as I kiss him back, my hands roaming over his back impatiently. I've never felt this restless before, this needy. Silas kisses me harder and grinds his hips against mine, igniting a new type of desire in me. He's hard, and knowing he wants me that badly has me feeling something I've never felt before. It makes my awkwardness melt away, and I slip my fingers underneath his t-shirt.

"Ray," he moans, pulling away a little to look at me. "You're going to drive me insane. Do you have any idea how difficult it is for me to take things slow with you?"

"Don't then," I plead.

He leans in and presses a lingering kiss to my lips. "I love you," he whispers. "I love you so fucking much. I'm done keeping the words buried within. I love you."

Silas wraps his arms around me and turns us over, so I'm lying on top of him, and I can't help but giggle as I push myself up against him. I look into his beautiful emerald eyes, my heart racing. "I love you so much more, Silas."

He smiles at me, and I lean in to kiss that smile right off his face. He's right. This is a moment I'll remember for the rest of our lives.

Chapter Twenty-One

Silas

The last couple of weeks have flown by in a daze of happiness overshadowing our sorrows. There are nights Alanna still cries herself to sleep, and more often than not, she dreams of her father, waking herself up with the force of her tears. Despite that, our days are filled with happiness and hope for the future we're working towards.

I was worried she'd lose her spirit, but she hasn't. Whenever she gets discouraged, she adds something to her digital scrap book depicting our life together. My crazy girlfriend has already picked out our home and our car, as well as the color scheme for all of it. I can't wait to someday sit in a living room of our own, her vision come to life.

I check my watch as I head to our room. Alanna should be back any time now. We've managed to coordinate her shifts at the supermarket with my work, and we've gotten into a good routine. During the day, she goes to school and I attend my lectures, and afterwards we both go to work. As much as we can, we leave our evenings open for each other. We're blessed that we have Ricardo's support. While our circumstances aren't ideal, it could've definitely been much worse. We've made sure to count our blessings as we work toward a better future.

"Si!"

She walks into our room and smiles at me, her eyes shimmering with love. This will never get old. I'll never tire of seeing her after a long day.

Alanna runs up to me, and I catch her as she jumps into my arms. Yeah, this will *never* ever get old. She wraps her legs around my waist, and I turn around with her in my arms, pushing her up against the bedroom door as my lips find hers. She moans against my lips, her body moving against mine as I kiss her, taking my time with her.

"Did you know? I *was* starting to feel a little tired," I murmur against her lips in between kisses.

Alanna giggles and captures my bottom lip between her teeth teasingly. "Then let me recharge you." She threads her hand through my hair and grips tightly, her touch possessive as she deepens our kiss. Alanna's hands move over my back, her fingers slipping underneath my t-shirt. Things have been moving fast between us lately, and I know she wants more, but I'm worried she's using lust as a distraction from her grief, and I don't want her to regret anything between us. I want her to take her time and be really sure. I have every intention of spending the rest of my life with her, so I can wait as long as she needs me to if it means we're building a solid foundation.

I tear my lips off hers reluctantly and drop my forehead to hers, my breathing ragged. "I desperately need a shower, baby." A cold one, preferably.

I put her down carefully, and she looks at me through narrowed eyes for a moment, but then she nods. I disappear into the bathroom instantly, my heart racing. This woman will be the death of me, without a doubt. How much longer can I resist her? I want to take my time with her and let her experience every step of a relationship slowly, one after another, but *fuck*. I want her so fucking badly. It was only last week when I made her come on my fingers for the very first time. I'll need to be much *much* more patient.

I let my eyes fall closed as I wrap my hand around my cock, images of Alanna flooding my mind. I don't think she realizes what it does to me to have her in my space like this. Seeing her wearing my t-shirts, falling asleep with her in my arms, kissing her whenever I please. Then there's the way she's touching me lately, her hands wandering every time I make out with her. I thought I'd die when her fingers wrapped around my cock last night. Just one touch, and I'm ready to burst.

I freeze when the bathroom door opens, my hand still wrapped around my cock. Alanna pushes the shower curtain aside, and my heart skips a fucking beat when I find her standing in front of me, naked.

"What are you doing?" she asks, her eyes on my hands. "Do you need some help with that?"

She steps into the shower wearing a nervous expression, her touch hesitant as she places her palms flat against my chest.

"Ray, what do you think you're doing?"

She smiles up at me, and my heart starts to race. "Forcing you to give in," she whispers. "I've been trying to seduce you for a while now, but every time I think I've convinced you, you pull away."

She inhales deeply, as though she's gathering her courage, and then she pushes her body flush against mine.

Fucking hell. She's really testing my patience today, huh? "What exactly is it you're asking for, baby?"

She glares at me. "You'll really make me say it?"

I smile at her and wrap my arms around her, pulling her against me, my cock pressing against her stomach.

Alanna looks up at me, her gaze pleading. "*Si*," she whispers.

I smirk and turn us around so I've got her pressed up against the wall. Alanna's eyes are filled with so much passion that I swear I could come just looking at her. The girl of my dreams, wet and naked, water droplets running down her breasts. She's so fucking beautiful, and she has no idea how much power she holds over me.

I grab her wrists and pin them above her head. "Keep them there," I order.

She nods and bites down on her lip as I grab some soap and lather it in my hands. Watching her chest rise and fall, her nipples rock hard for me. Yeah, she has no idea what she's doing to me.

I run my hands over her neck and down her collarbone, to the top of her breasts. She instinctively arches her back for me, and I smirk as my hands dip lower, cupping her tits. "Beautiful," I whisper as my thumbs brush over her nipples. Soft little moans escape her lips as she stands against the wall, her arms raised up and her eyes on me.

I take my time torturing my girlfriend, lathering up her body, slowly running my fingers down her stomach, pausing at her hip. Alanna looks at me, panicked, and I can't help but chuckle. She's so scared I'll stop here, but how could I?

"Silas, please," she moans, and I smile as my fingers trail lower, disappearing between her legs.

"Is this what you want, Ray?"

Alanna nods and I bite down on my lip as I push a finger into her, my thumb brushing over her clit. It's so fucking insane knowing I'm the only man that's ever touched her like this, the only one who's ever seen her expression as she tries not to come for me.

I watch her as I finger her, the water pouring down on us as I lean in and kiss her, swallowing down her moans. "I can't," she murmurs against my lips.

I smirk and push another finger into her, curling them in an attempt to hit her g-spot while my thumb brushes over her clit. Her eyes widen and she gasps, her lips falling open as a moan escapes her lips. "Silas," she groans, her pussy contracting all around my fingers.

I chuckle as I drop my forehead to hers. I fucking love this. I love that she's all mine. I love having my name on her lips as she comes. I love everything about her.

I pull my fingers away and grab the soap to clean her up, taking my time, enjoying that post-orgasm look in her eyes. She looks so satisfied, so happy, and knowing I made her look that way is a complete power trip.

Alanna smiles lazily as I turn the shower off and grab a towel to dry her off with. "I want more, Silas." She takes the towel from me the second I've got her dry and moves it over my body with as much care as I just showed her, drying me. "I want it all with you. I came in here to seduce you, and I won't stop until I've succeeded."

I grin and lift her into my arms, the towel falling away as I carry her out of the bathroom. "Is that so?"

I carefully place her on our bed, and Alanna nods as she lies back. I love that she isn't overly shy around me. She has no reason to be — I'm fucking obsessed with her.

I watch her for a moment before reaching over and grabbing a sharpie from my desk. I smirk as I climb onto bed with her, my cock still as hard as it was in the shower. "Consider me seduced, baby. I'm bewitched, enamored, head over fucking heels." I lean in and press a kiss to her rib, right below her breast.

I look into her eyes as I open up my sharpie and draw the Ψ symbol just below her breast, right between her ribs. "And now I've officially marked you, so you're mine. Forever."

"Then make me yours, *fully*," she pleads, her voice husky.

"You don't know what you're asking for, baby. It'll hurt."

"I don't care. I want it all with you, Si."

I join her on our bed and lie down next to her, my hand roaming over her body. I watch her carefully as the tips of my fingers brush over her pussy, my eyes widening when I realize she's wet.

Alanna blushes, and it's the most beautiful sight I've ever seen. How the fuck does she just keep getting more and more beautiful every goddamn day?

"I told you," she whispers. "I want you."

I smirk as I roll on top of her, my lips finding hers. I kiss her slowly, leisurely, enjoying the way she moves her body against mine, making my cock slip against her pussy with every move. I keep myself raised on top of her with one arm and bury the other in her hair, fisting a handful of it as I lower my lips to her neck, sucking and teasing, loving the way she moans for me.

"You really do want it, don't you?"

"Yes," she moans. "*Please*, Si. It's not just physical, I swear. I need you."

I pull away to look at her and align my cock with her pussy. "Baby," I whisper.

She nods at me. "*Silas*," she begs.

I push the tip into her, my eyes falling closed as I try my hardest to restrain myself. "You're so fucking tight," I groan. "I'm worried, Ray. You're wet as fuck, but this is still really going to hurt."

She wraps her arms around my neck, her eyes on mine as I push in another inch. Her lips fall open, and I pause as she takes a moment to adjust. With each movement, I feel her pussy clench around me. I won't last long when her pussy is this good.

"You okay, baby?"

She nods, but I see the pain she tries to hide.

I push in a little deeper, and she groans. "You're doing so good," I tell her. "You're taking it so well, baby."

She pulls on my neck, and I lean in closer to kiss her. Alanna lifts her hips, taking me a little deeper, and I lower my body on top of hers fully, thrusting all the way into her. She groans against my lips, and I hold as still as I can, trying my best to make this easiest for her.

"Finally," she whispers against my mouth. "I've wanted this for so long, Silas."

I pull away a little to look at her and pull out of her a little. "I love you," I whisper.

"I love you more, Si," she says, her hand finding its way into my hair.

I bite down on my lip as I push back into her, moving slowly, carefully. "Does it hurt?"

She shakes her head even though she has tears in her eyes, and I press a kiss to her forehead as I take her with strong, slow moves, trying my hardest not to hurt her. It's the toughest goddamn thing I've ever had to do. I so badly want to fuck her roughly, but I can't. Not today.

"I swear it usually lasts a lot longer, but I've wanted you for so fucking long, Alanna..."

She giggles and threads her fingers through my hair, her gaze filled with so much love that my own heart overflows. I can't get enough of her.

"I want to watch you lose control over me, Silas."

I smirk before showing her just that, taking her harder, faster, until I'm coming deep inside her. I collapse on top of her, and Alanna wraps her arms around me, hugging me tightly.

"That was even better than I imagined," I admit. "Your pussy is unreal."

She kisses my neck, my pulse racing against her lips. "Thank you," she whispers. "For not making me wait any longer, for not rejecting me."

I pull out of her, somewhat startled at the redness coating her thighs. Blood. I expected it, but it still surprises me. Alanna clenches her thighs together, her cheeks heating, and I smile to myself as I get out of bed to grab her a towel.

"Si!" she murmurs as I place a warm, wet towel between her legs, wiping her clean carefully.

Happiness... I didn't expect to find it in this place, but I did. I found it in her.

Chapter Twenty-Two

ALANNA

I flex my fingers a few times, trying to relieve the soreness from the hours and hours of folding I just did. It's not much, but the hundred paper cranes staring back at me make for the perfect birthday gift.

We usually exchange our real gifts for the year on my birthday underneath the tree, but every year so far, I've tried to give Silas something small and nice on his birthday. Last year, I got him a really nice pen to use during his finals. I never used to get him something so expensive that he'd feel burdened and always made sure it was something useful. This year I can't afford to buy him anything, but I'm hoping he'll still love the paper cranes.

I tense when the doorknob rattles, and seconds later, Silas walks in. I scramble off the bed, trying my hardest to hide my cranes, but that just sends them flying everywhere. "Si! Why are you home? You had a late seminar today, didn't you?"

He leans back against the door and grins as his eyes roam over my disheveled state. I spent all day in an old t-shirt of his, letting my hair air dry into the wavy mess it is now. I'd been planning to get all dolled up before he got back, but it's too late now.

"I love you, Ray," he says simply, his eyes sparkling.

I pause and grin up at him. "Happy birthday, Si. I know I said it this morning, but I was still half asleep, so it doesn't count." I walk up to him and throw my arms around his neck as I rise to my tiptoes. "Happy birthday," I whisper against his lips, right before kissing him.

Si groans and slips his hands underneath my t-shirt and around my waist. "Wanna tell me what happened to our bedroom?"

I turn in his embrace and lean back against him. "These," I tell him, "are paper cranes. I read somewhere that folding a thousand paper cranes will grant you a wish."

I turn back around to look at him, trying to keep the somberness off my face. "I made them out of twenty-five sheets of printer paper Ricardo was willing to give me, but he couldn't spare any more. So while this isn't the thousand cranes I wanted to make you, it's a beginning." I grab one off the floor and hold it up for him. "And! *And and and*, because I knew I wouldn't be able to give you a thousand cranes for your birthday this year, I made these cranes really special. Folding a thousand cranes might grant you one big wish, but each of these hundred cranes will grant you one small wish." I unfold one and show it to him. It's got the word *Kiss* written on it, and Silas takes it from me with a smile.

"They're coupons?"

"That sounds so lame. These are way cooler than that."

He chuckles and cups my cheek. "I love them. Thank you, Ray."

I look into his eyes, my smile fading away. "I know it's been tough, the two of us in this small room, so much of our future uncertain. You haven't been getting very far with your job applications and I haven't heard back about any of my scholarships. Your deal with Ricardo comes to an end once you graduate, and that will change everything for us. Right now, we don't know where we'll be or where we'll live. I know you're worried, Si. Despite that, you continue to put our happiness first. These," I gesture around at the cranes, "are my attempt to help. When you feel like our circumstances are impacting our relationship, open one of these cranes. When I upset you, or when you've had a hard day, or even when we just had a silly argument because we're both too stressed, open one up. One day, when we don't need to worry about the cost of origami paper, I'll make you a thousand, and I'll make one big wish. Hopefully, I can do that before you run out of your hundred cranes."

He buries his hands in my hair and smiles down at me. "What would your one big wish be?"

"For you to be happy," I say without a single doubt. "Not the kind of happiness that we have now, but the kind that we dream of. Us having a home of our own and not having to check the prices of anything in the grocery store. That kind of happiness."

Si nods, a sweet smile on his face. "We'll get there, Alanna. You and I. We'll have a home of our own sooner than you think. It's only a matter of time until I find a job, and when I do, I can find us a place to live. It might just be a tiny little studio, but it'll be ours. I'll go to work every day, and you'll go to college thanks to the scholarship I know you'll receive. Step by step, we'll build the life of our dreams, you and I. Per aspera ad astra."

I nod, my heart filled with cautious hope. "I can't wait," I whisper. "I'm already so happy with you, Si. When I lost Dad and everything that came with it, I didn't... I thought I'd never feel okay again. I was so scared to approach you, terrified I'd become just another burden to you, but instead, you've given me back my smile when I thought the tears would never stop falling. I don't know how I'll ever repay you for everything you've done for me."

He leans in and presses a kiss to my forehead. "Let's not keep score, baby. If we did, I'd come out at a loss. Before you, my life revolved around revenge and regaining everything I lost. It's all I could think about. I was so focused on it, that I forgot to live in the present. I kept thinking to myself I'd only be happy once I regained ownership of my home and the cottage by the blossom tree. Every single night, I went to bed dreaming of owning my father's company and leaving my stepmother penniless like she did me. It wasn't until you walked into my life that I realized I was poisoning myself, punishing myself far more than my stepmother ever could. If not for you, I'd let years pass me by without truly living, always waiting for a moment of revenge, after which I'd no doubt be left feeling as empty as I did before you. So, Ray, you don't owe me anything, except for this." He holds up the unfolded crane and smirks. "You owe me a kiss."

I smirk as I rise to my tiptoes and kiss my boyfriend with all I've got. Our future may be uncertain, but one thing I know for sure is that we'll be together.

Chapter Twenty-Three

Alanna

My heart sinks as I delete yet another rejection email. There's no way I'm going to attend Astor College, but at this rate, even community college won't be an option. I was so certain I'd get at least a partial scholarship somehow, but so far I've only received rejections.

I look up when Si walks into our bedroom, and he shoots me a sympathetic look. "Another one?"

I nod and hold my arms up in a plea for a hug. Si grins at me as he walks up to the bed and sits down next to me, leaning in to hug me tightly. My lips tip up into a smile as I rest my head against his chest and listen to his heartbeat.

Silas strokes my back tenderly, his lips pressed to the top of my head. "Give it time, baby. You've applied to everything that was available, and you've done your best. I have full faith that your hard work will pay off."

I wish I had as much faith as Silas does. With each passing day, my worries increase. Silas hasn't been able to find a job yet, and Ricardo made it clear he won't let us have this room once Si graduates. It's his way of forcing us to stand on our own feet, but I'm scared. Silas firmly believes that me getting into college will set me up for a good future, but I'm more worried about our *immediate* future. What are we going to do? I can't rely on Silas as much as I have been. I don't want to put even more pressure on him, and depending on him for a place to stay isn't right, and it isn't fair. He's come so far, and I'm just pulling him down with me. I know how hard he's worked throughout the last few years, and I don't want to shackle him.

"Hey," he whispers. "Your phone just buzzed. I've got a good feeling. Open it."

I turn in his embrace and rest my back against his chest so he can look over my shoulder as I unlock my phone. I click on the email, nerves settling in my stomach. This is one of the very last ones I've been waiting to hear back from.

"Congratulations," Silas reads, his voice brimming with excitement. He chuckles and tightens his grip on me as he drops his head to my neck, kissing me just below my ear. "I knew you'd do it, Ray. Read out the rest. What does it entail?"

My heart is hammering in my chest as I read the rest of the email in complete disbelief. "Tuition with a discounted student room," I whisper. "It's a smaller college, but they have a solid IT programme."

"How long do you have to reply to their offer?"

I scroll down the email and bite down on my lip. "Seven days."

"Accept it, Ray."

I turn to face him and frown. "What do you mean, accept it? Accept the tuition offer, you mean?"

He shakes his head. "Accept both. Tuition and the discounted accommodation. You should be able to pay for it with your current part-time job at the supermarket or something similar, maybe something closer to your college."

"Si, that makes no sense. If I accept the discounted room, we'd be paying for two places to stay. This is a shared room, so we wouldn't get away with both of us staying there. My roommate would definitely complain."

"I know."

I look into his eyes, for once finding him impossible to read. Something about his expression is making my heart ache, and I bite down on my lip when he looks down.

"Alanna," he says, his voice soft, pained. "You need to accept that offer. You and I... we don't have the luxury of being dreamers. When faced with a guaranteed place to stay for an entire year versus the uncertainty you'd have with me, the choice is obvious."

I pull away from him and clench my jaw. "Silas, I thought we were in this together. Weren't we going to find a small studio that we'd share? You'd go to work, and I'd go to college? Wasn't that part of our plan?"

Silas rises to his feet and starts to pace the room. "Alanna, my plans haven't changed. I still want to regain everything I lost, which means the next couple of years aren't going to be much easier than the past few have been. If nothing else, I want to be sure you have a safe place to stay."

"I know that," I tell him. "I know what your plans are, and I'll fully support you. I admit the last couple of weeks have been tough, but we've done our best, and we were happy, weren't we? I don't think we should spend money on two places to stay when we'll always be together, anyway."

He looks at me with a pained expression and shakes his head. "Alanna, you have your whole future ahead of you. You're meant for so much more than I can give you. I don't want you to struggle the way I always have. I want you to go to college and have fun. I want you to enjoy the experience and look back on it fondly. You can't do that when you're tied to a man like me."

I tense and look into his eyes. "What are you trying to say, Silas?"

He nods and runs a hand through his hair, his expression pained. "You're about to go to college, and I don't want you to be with me because you have no other choice, because our circumstances forced us together. If you accept that room, you'll always have the freedom to leave. You'll have a space of your own."

"That's not what I want, Silas. I want the future we envisioned, every single part of it, not just the good parts. I *know* it isn't going to be easy, yet I'm *choosing* to walk this path with you. I have no intention of leaving you, so stop this, *please*."

"I won't *let you* walk this path with me, Alanna. This isn't what *I* want. I want more than that for you."

I freeze, my eyes filling with tears I can't blink away. "W-what does that mean, Silas?"

He looks up at the ceiling and inhales shakily. "I don't know, Alanna."

I sniff as a tear rolls down my cheek and rush past him. Si reaches for me, but I shake my head. "Get away from me," I snap. "I can't... I can't deal with this right now, Si. I really can't. Just leave me alone."

I turn and rush out the door, my tears running down my cheeks uncontrollably. Just as I round the corner, thunder erupts in the sky, followed by a heavy downpour. It's as though the heavens are weeping with me, and I burst out crying in earnest. How could Si believe we won't last? How could he not believe in us?

I don't know how to reassure him, and I don't know what to do. The expression in Silas's eyes told me he wouldn't budge. He truly wants me to accept the discounted room I was offered, but what would that mean for us? He's in every single one of my plans for the future, but am I truly in his?

I'm so distraught that I don't hear the car approaching over the sound of the rain, not until it's too late. I look up into blinding headlights, seconds before I'm lifted off the ground by the impact of the collision, my body landing with a loud thud. The pain barely registers as my eyes fall closed, bathing the world in darkness. The last thing I think of before I lose consciousness is Silas, and how I wish I'd told him that I love him one last time.

PART TWO
The Present

Five Years Later

Chapter Twenty-Four

Silas

I open my desk drawer with trembling hands, taking out one of the hundred cranes that I keep hidden in there. I still remember the smile on Alanna's face as she gave them to me, each of them folded out of gifted printer paper because origami paper wasn't something we could afford.

I open it up, my finger tracing over her handwriting. *Hug*, it reads. There's nothing I wouldn't do to have Alanna in my arms today, a sweet smile on her face as she leans in to kiss me. She told me that she'd hoped these one hundred cranes would last me until she was able to fold me a thousand, and I'm starting to run low.

Each time missing her becomes too hard to bear, I unfold one of her little cranes, imagining her right by my side as I show her the writing on it and cash in my coupon. It's torture. It's a reminder of everything I should have had with her, but simultaneously, it's the one thing that makes me feel closer to her.

Today marks five years since Alanna went missing, and I only have three paper cranes left. Maybe I'm crazy, but a small part of me is still convinced I'll find her before I give into temptation and unfold the last one.

What would she think if I told her I founded my entire company in an effort to find her? She still is at the core of everything I do, everything I am. Sinclair Security is the result of my search for her. Starting off with only private investigation services, we've grown to encompass all kinds of security, yet we still haven't accomplished our main aim. Finding Alanna.

According to our case file, she was in a car accident five years ago. We traced back her movements until several months after her accident, after which the trail ran cold. Seven months after her accident, Alanna disappeared entirely, and I haven't been able to find her since.

I know every detail about her case by heart. She was flown to an out-of-state hospital due to the extent of her injuries, making it impossible for me to find her at any of the hospitals near us.

Legally not being family made it even harder to enquire about her whereabouts. I still distinctly remember walking into the police station to file a missing person report, and they wouldn't help me, purely because Alanna and I were both homeless. I can still hear their voices mocking me, telling me I was wasting taxpayer resources on someone who probably just left me. Over time, I've started to wonder if perhaps they were right.

After all, she was released a few weeks after her car accident, but she never came back to me. The accident report states that her phone was run over, but she memorized my phone number in case of emergency, so why did she never call me?

I look up at the sound of my office door opening and frown. Amy, my secretary, never walks in unannounced, especially not a day like today.

She looks at me with wide eyes, a hint of panic in them. "Boss, I have an update for you on Project Sunshine."

My heart sinks as a thousand fears fight for dominance over my thoughts. I've had recurring nightmares about Alanna, and the ones in which I *didn't* find her were better than the ones in which I did. In some of my dreams, she simply just walked away from me, from us, agreeing with the words I uttered that day, words I've regretted every second since. In other dreams, I don't find her alive at all.

Amy smiles, her eyes twinkling. "We *found* her."

I rise from my seat, my eyes widening. *Alanna.* "Where is she?" I grab my suit jacket and slip it on, intent on finding her this very second. It's been five years. *Five years* without Alanna. Alanna's disappearance was Sinclair's Security's first project, and it has to date been our only unresolved case. Until now.

"Where is she?" I repeat, my tone harsh.

"Astor College," Amy tells me.

Astor College? That's only a few minutes from my office. "How is that possible? We were monitoring student applications, weren't we?"

Amy nods. "We were, but she didn't show up in any of our systems. Boss... the only reason we found her is because she applied for a job at Sinclair Security. She specifically applied to join the Ψ division. We were able to use her job application details to figure out her location."

"What is her current exact location?" I ask. I just need to see her. The rest can wait.

Amy glances at her watch. "Her lecture is finishing in about ten minutes, after which she'll head to the coffee shop on campus where she's currently working part time. I will email you the exact location."

I nod and rush out of the office, impatience dictating my every move. I've waited five years to see her again. I can't wait a second longer. I don't care where she's been or why she's stayed away, so long as I get her back in my life. I need some answers, but more importantly, I need to see for myself that she's safe.

I walk into the small coffee shop on campus in a rush, nerves thrumming through my veins. Alanna is nowhere to be seen as I pick a seat in the back, and I glance at my watch impatiently.

Nostalgia washes over me as I listen to the chatter around me while I wait. How many times did I politely refuse to come here with my classmates because I couldn't afford the coffee here? I studied at Astor College for four years and today is the first day I'll be having a drink here. This is the college Alanna always wanted to attend, so I shouldn't be surprised she ended up here. What I don't understand is why she never even called. Why did she walk away from me without a word? What happened after that accident to make her stay away?

A shiver runs down my spine all of a sudden, and I *know*. I just know Alanna walked in. My lips tip up into a smile as I turn toward the entrance, my heart in full fucking disarray when I see her. Long dark hair, the same hazel eyes I've always loved. Five years, and there she is.

Alanna pauses halfway toward the barista counter, her eyes finding mine, and everything fades away. *Fuck*. It's been so long since I looked into those beautiful eyes of hers, and every feeling I thought had dimmed comes rushing back in full force. She still looks the same, except a little older, a little more mature, a little more *beautiful*.

She smiles tightly, not a single hint of recognition in her gaze as she walks past me. It isn't until she disappears into the staff room that I realize the only reason I caught her attention is because I stood up in the middle of a crowded room, staring at her. She didn't seem to recognize me at all. What the fuck?

My heart twists painfully as I sit back down, my thoughts reeling. How could this be? She looked at me as though I'm a complete stranger. Something isn't right. That wasn't just her ignoring an ex. She didn't *recognize* me.

I bite down on my lip harshly as I dial Amy's number. "Please double check Alanna's medical files," I tell her the moment she picks up. "Something isn't right. She doesn't seem to recognize me at all, Amy. Her reports mentioned a bad concussion but I never read anything about amnesia. Check if Alanna was ever referred to anyone else, other than her main doctor. If so, have him brought to our interrogation room. Something is wrong with her."

I end the call when Alanna walks up to the counter, switching places with her colleague. I'm nervous as hell as I approach her, unsure what I'm even hoping for. It's been five years, so it's not as though I expected to pick back up where we left off, but I'm feeling oddly unsettled.

"Hi," she says as I walk up to the counter, a friendly smile on her face. My lips drop to her mouth, a memory of her kissing my neck coming to mind. Does she truly not remember me? How could that be possible?

"Hey," I mutter awkwardly. "Can I have a long black, please?"

She looks into my eyes, and for a split second, I see something flicker in her eyes, but then she shakes it off and tears her gaze away. "Of course," she says, ringing me up.

My hopes are thoroughly dashed when she hands me the receipt and moves away to make my drink, not even remotely hesitating or lingering. I'm just another customer to her. I've been looking for her for years, not a day going by without me thinking of her, and here she is... staring at me as though I'm no one to her.

Alanna's colleague leans into her, a smile on her face. "Hey," she says. "Is your boyfriend picking you up again later? Your shift ends pretty late today."

Alanna nods, and my stomach lurches. The pain that sears through me has me placing a steadying hand on the counter. Boyfriend? What fucking boyfriend? What the fuck is going on?

Alanna's colleague takes my drink from her and walks over to the end of the counter I'm standing at, a flirtatious smile on her face. "I haven't seen you before," she murmurs. "Are you a new professor?"

I shake my head and take the cup from her with trembling hands. All I can think about as I walk back to my little table are the words I just overheard. Not only does the love of my fucking life not remember me... she's also dating someone else. Out of all the scenarios I imagined when I finally found her again, this never even occurred to me.

Chapter Twenty-Five

Silas

"What is the meaning of this?" the doctor asks, his eyes wide with panic that he's trying his hardest to contain. "Don't think I won't report you. This is *kidnapping*. It's, it's *illegal*!"

I sigh and push Alanna's file toward him. "Five years ago you treated Alanna Jones. She was referred to you because she was in a car accident. She seems to have suffered from long-term amnesia as a result. Alanna still hasn't regained her memory, it appears. What are her chances of recovery?"

The tension in his shoulders eases just a fraction, and he glances at the folder. "Who are you?"

"Someone who cares a great deal about her wellbeing."

He looks back up at me, his gaze accessing. "I cannot discuss my patients with you, whoever you may be."

I nod. "I understand, Dr. Jameson." I clasp my hands and lean forward. "Let's, for a moment, just assume that this is a hypothetical case. Let's say it's about your daughter, Cindy. She's fourteen, isn't she? Goes to Astor High School? Such a sweet little girl, isn't she? Let's just assume it's Cindy who got into that car accident and lost her memories. What would the chances be of her recovering her memory?"

Dr. Jameson starts to tremble, a bead of sweat dropping down his forehead. "Y-you leave my daughter out of this," he says, his voice shaky.

I nod. "This is all just hypothetical, of course. I just want answers. So long as you give me that, you'll walk out of here within a few minutes. This doesn't have to take long."

Dr. Jameson looks down, clearly distraught and uncertain about his next move, but I've got all the time in the world. He'll talk. My only question is whether he'll do it willingly.

"If a patient hasn't regained their memory after five years, they likely won't ever. Often, amnesia is a patient's way of protecting themselves. If there were any particular traumatic events they experienced, the brain may decide they're better off without those memories altogether. A fresh start, if you will."

I lean back in my seat and tap my finger on the table as I digest his words. Could it be that she didn't want to remember the loss of her father and the homelessness that followed? Or was it more than that? Did she want to forget *me*? We may have struggled at times, but I thought we were happy.

"What if I tell her about our past?"

The doctor shakes his head. "I don't recommend that. If she's told about her memories, it'll create false memories, and there's a chance these false memories will fully overwrite her true memories. Have you ever heard of witness testimonies being false, despite the witness being 100% certain of what they saw? Simple leading questions can distort a memory entirely, convincing someone of something when the truth was entirely different. Our memories aren't as reliable as we think they are, and they're easily distorted."

I continue to tap my finger on the table, unsure of what to do. I still remember her crying herself to sleep at night, the way she'd zone out with that vacant look in her eyes whenever she thought of her father. If I remind her of our past, she'll also remember everything she lost — and there's a chance that she won't truly remember our past. I don't want to instill memories in her that aren't hers. I don't ever want to manipulate her like that.

"Very well," I murmur. "You may leave. I'll find you if I have more questions."

The door opens, and two of my men walk in to escort the doctor out, Amy right behind them. I look up at her, feeling lost. I finally found Alanna, yet I... *didn't*. I always thought finding her would put me out of my misery, but I'm in just as much pain.

"Tell me where she went after her accident. Why did she just disappear?"

Amy nods and sits down opposite me as she pushes a file toward me. "We couldn't find her because Alanna left the country a few months after her accident."

I look up from the files in my hand. "She left the country? How? Where did she go?"

"She received a scholarship and attended a university in London, returning here only because of an exclusive exchange programme her university has with Astor College. Her name never flagged in the admissions system because she's an exchange student. She isn't officially enrolled at Astor College. She's finishing her last few months of college here, earning her remaining few college credits."

"That's impossible. How could she possibly have gotten a scholarship to a foreign university? Alanna and I went through her scholarship applications together. There's no way that's possible." I run a hand through my hair, frustration clawing at me. Finding her resulted in more questions than answers. "Why is it we couldn't find her until she came to us? We should've found her the second she returned to the country. What the fuck do I pay you guys for if you couldn't even do that?" I snap, on edge.

Amy shakes her head. "I'm still trying to figure out why she never showed up on any of our radars. We set extensive markers to identify her presence, but she eluded them all. I also can't find out who was behind the scholarship. It appears to be an individual, sir. It isn't an organisation."

I rise from my seat and start to pace, my head spinning. What the fuck is going on? Could it be Mona? I shake my head. What would she stand to gain by keeping Alanna away from me? That doesn't make any sense.

"What did you learn about the boyfriend?"

"Boss," she says, her tone worried. "You may want to sit back down for this one."

Chapter Twenty-Six

Alanna

"He's here again," Savannah murmurs, a dreamy expression in her eyes. She sighs happily as she leans over the counter, her head propped up on her elbow. I follow her gaze curiously, finding a handsome stranger seated in the corner of the coffee shop. He looks like he's far too big for the small wooden chair, yet it doesn't seem to bother him. He's got his laptop in front of him, his gaze intense. He's been coming here every day for two weeks now, and I find myself curious about him.

The man looks up, and my heart does this funny thing, almost as though it skips a beat. His eyes are the darkest green I've ever seen. They're the color of expensive emeralds.

Everything about him screams luxury. He's got cheekbones straight out of a magazine, and that hair... I bet it'd feel amazing to run your hand through that. He smiles at me, and I tense as I force a polite smile before dragging my eyes away.

"He's been watching you ever since you started your shift," Savannah says, a crestfallen expression on her face. "He's been sitting there for hours, pretending like he isn't watching you, when you're so obviously all he can see. I should know. I've tried catching his attention more times than I can count."

I glance back at him, surprised. He looks *unattainable.* It's not just the obviously expensive suit, or the way he sits at that tiny table with his laptop that probably costs more than I spend on rent every month. It isn't even his ridiculously good looks, that dark hair or those cheekbones. It's something else. Something I can't quite pin down.

Men like him don't pay attention to girls like me.

"I have a boyfriend, remember?" I murmur as I finish making a mocha for one of our regulars. Oat milk. Extra shot of caramel. She orders the exact same thing every single day, and there's a strange sense of comfort in that. "Here you go, Michelle," I tell her as I hand her the mug.

Savannah smiles and tilts her head as she stares at me, a curious look in her eyes. "I never understood why you would date Ryan. He's such an asshole, and while he seems to be faithful to you, he's known to be a fuckboy, so I'm not sure how long he'll remain loyal. Is it the money?"

I tense involuntarily and clench my jaw, swallowing down the insult. I can't blame her for thinking it. At least she isn't gossiping behind my back like everyone else is. Ryan is filthy rich, and I'm just a nobody. It's no surprise to me that everyone around us thinks I'm a gold digger, but it doesn't ever hurt any less.

"No, of course not. I know he's a bit... rough around the edges, but when he's with me, he's wonderful. He treats me well, and he's kind."

She stares at me as though she's trying to figure me out, and it immediately has me feeling defensive. "He's a good man," I tell her, keeping my voice cheerful.

Ryan is different. He keeps people at a distance and uses his wealth as a shield. But underneath that? Underneath the extravagance and the occasional obnoxiousness, he's a genuinely good person. He helps at the soup kitchen I volunteer at every once in a while, and just last week we spent a day collecting plastic on the beach. It was a perfect day — *he* was perfect that day. I just wish others could see it too. I wish they could see the version I see, and not the one he insists on showing the world.

My shoulders slump in relief when four girls walk in, chatting and laughing about their latest book boyfriend. I smile as I grab cups for them, writing their names before they even reach the counter. Nicole, Sara, Gladys and Megan always order the exact same thing. They sit and chat for hours, each of them trying to lay claim on the main character of whatever book they just read. Just seeing them brings a smile to my face. The friendship they share warms my heart, but it's their kindness that always brings a smile to my face.

"You have to read this, Alanna," Nicole says, holding up a paperback that looks pristine. I've never dared accept one of her books because it's obvious she handles them reverently. I wouldn't even be surprised if they're all signed.

I'm too clumsy. I'd spill coffee on her book and she'd hate me forever. I smile at her as I decline her offer. Nicole's smile drops just a fraction, but it's back in place as soon as I hand her her coffee. I have no doubt these girls have made it their personal mission to get me to read one of their books, and by the determined look in their eyes, I know I'm destined to cave someday.

The green-eyed stranger rises from his seat, and my heart involuntarily skips a beat. I can feel his eyes on me, and a shiver runs down my spine. He makes me nervous, and it's rare for anyone to have that effect on me.

His eyes never leave me as he walks up to me. By the time he reaches the counter, my heart is racing, and it unsettles me. Something about him leaves me feeling thrown.

"Alanna," he says, his voice deep as he draws out my name, his eyes on my name tag. He smiles at me, and I tense. Most people are so absorbed in their thoughts and their own day as they order a coffee that they don't even look me in the eye. His intensity is unsettling.

"Could I ask you to make me a long black, please? To go, please."

I smile involuntarily. There's something so sexy about politeness, especially coming from a man like that — someone whose cufflinks could likely pay for a month's worth of groceries.

"Of course." I grin at him as I grab a cup, and for a second, our eyes lock. "What's your name?" I ask, my voice soft. He usually has his coffee here and prefers ceramic cups, so I've never had a chance to ask his name before.

He hesitates for a split second before speaking. "Simon."

I drag my gaze away, moving to hide behind the massive coffee machine as I write his name on the paper cup.

I'm flustered. I rarely get flustered. Even Ryan complains that he never succeeds in making me blush, yet here I am... feeling out of it because of a stranger. This is weird, and I feel guilty instantly.

I take a deep breath as I pour his coffee into his cup, my eyes drifting up to the large clock opposite me. Thank God, this shift is done now. I've got so many class notes to get through, and then there's tonight's dinner. It's the first time I'm formally meeting Ryan's family, and truthfully, he seems more nervous about it than I am. I can't help but wonder if Ryan's family thinks I'm a gold-digger too.

It's all I can think about as I hand Simon his cup. He takes it from me, his gaze inquisitive, but my thoughts are elsewhere. I hope I'll make a good impression tonight, but there's this niggling sense of unease I can't push aside. I've always trusted my intuition, and I can't help but feel like tonight is going to be a disaster.

I bite down on my lip as I take off my apron and walk into the staff room to grab my bag. By the time I walk out of the coffee shop, I'm overthinking everything. It took me an entire week and close to two weeks' worth of my salary to select an outfit, yet now all of a sudden I wonder if I might end up looking like I'm trying too hard. I'm worried they might not like me, and that they won't be able to see past my messed up past. They won't want their son to date someone who doesn't even know who she truly is, will they?

I'm so lost in thought that it takes me a moment to heed the warnings my intuition is sending me. I blink as I realize that I'm not alone in the narrow alley that leads to the bus stop, and a chill runs down my spine.

I pause and inhale shakily as I turn decisively. In my experience, most weirdos will let you be if they think you'll put up a fight or confront them. My eyes find the man behind me, his dark green eyes squarely on mine.

"Simon," I murmur, before straightening my shoulders. Savannah's words ring through my mind again. *You're so obviously all he can see.* A chill runs down my spine as I stare him down. He pauses and raises his brow.

"Are you *following* me?"

Chapter Twenty-Seven

SILAS

Alanna glares at me, and the dim lights in the alleyway just make her look even more beautiful.

I take a moment to drink her in and smile, enjoying the way her bravado wavers as her eyes widen ever so slightly.

"*Me*? Following *you*?" I ask, feigning ignorance.

I wonder what she sees when she looks at me. Does she see beyond the expensive clothes? Does she see *me*, or does she see the persona of Silas Sinclair, CEO of Sinclair Security? I've spent two weeks coming here every single day, waiting for a sign to prove that a small part of her remembers me, but she's given me nothing. I'm just a stranger to her, and it kills me.

Just looking at her has my heart clenching tightly, every fiber of my being begging me to take her into my arms. I so desperately want to tell her about us, but I can't.

I can't risk distorting her memories. If the doctor is right, and her amnesia is truly caused by her subconscious desire to forget her painful past, then I cannot force her to remember. I can't make her go through the pain of losing her father, of homelessness. Not again. Not because of my own selfish desires.

Besides, there's no guarantee that would accomplish anything. Even if I do tell her, there's no way to know how her mind will respond, *what* she'll remember.

Alanna narrows her eyes and crosses her arms over her chest, drawing my attention to her breasts. She's still so fucking beautiful. I take my time trailing my eyes back up to hers, a smirk finding its way onto my lips when I find her staring me down.

"Yes. *You*. My colleague tells me you only ever hang around the coffee shop when *I'm* there."

Alanna looks at me like I'm some random stranger, and it hurts. I'd hoped that seeing me would spark a memory, but no such luck. I'm truly no one to her.

"Is that so?" I ask, my voice soft. I grin at her and take a step toward her. She tenses, and then she takes a step back, retreating until her back is against the wall. She looks up at me with wide eyes, a hint of panic simmering below the surface.

I lean my forearms against the wall, caging her in. There are only a few inches between us, and part of me wants to push further. I want her against me, but only if she comes willingly.

"You should've run," I warn her. "When you find yourself alone in an alley with alarm bells ringing in your head, you *run*, Alanna. You don't pick a fight you can't win."

She places her hands against my chest, as though she's about to push me away, but then she pauses. She looks me in the eye, and at last I see a hint of recognition. It fades so quickly that I'm left wondering if I imagined it.

"I have a boyfriend," she whispers. Her hands are palms flat on my chest, the heat of her skin sinking through my shirt. This is the closest I've had her in years.

"And where is he now?" I whisper back, pushing down the pain her words caused.

Alanna swallows hard, and I watch her gather her courage. Good girl. "He isn't someone you can mess with. If you so much as touch me, he'll make you disappear," she warns me, and I smile. No one in this city is untouchable, certainly not her *boyfriend.* Not to me. Besides, he won't be her boyfriend for much longer. Out of everyone in this world, he's the only person she can never be with. Not him. I can't figure out how they ended up together, but I'm putting an end to it.

I lean in and brush the back of my hand over her cheek, my touch soft. "Is that so? I'd love to see him try."

She blinks in disbelief, as though that isn't the response she expected, and disappointment washes over me. The Alanna I used to know never would've hidden behind a man. She'd have tried to knee me in the balls the second I cornered her.

I pull away with a sigh. "You should've run," I repeat. "You shouldn't be alone in these dark alleys at all, Alanna. When you do inevitably find yourself here, be quick. Don't zone out. Don't linger. When someone approaches you and your intuition tells you that something is off, you run, you hear me? Don't put yourself in dangerous situations."

She nods and wraps her arms around herself protectively, her eyes on mine. There's so much I want to say, yet now that I finally have her alone, nothing feels right. I take a step away and run a hand through my hair.

"Did you... did you follow me to make sure I was safe?"

I look away and shake my head, lying to her. "No," I say, tipping my head toward the end of the alley. "My car is parked there."

Her cheeks darken as my words sink in, and I smile. Embarrassment looks cute on her. "I... I'm sorry. I misread the situation. I didn't mean to..."

I smirk. "You didn't mean to *what*? Didn't mean to assume I was interested in you?"

She bites down on her lip and I follow her every movement, all the while wondering what those lips will taste like. Does she still taste like cherry chapstick? I'll find out soon enough.

"I... yes. I'm sorry. That was... God, I'm so embarrassed. I'm sorry."

I smile at her, enjoying that sheepish expression on her face. She's still so cute, and I still love teasing her.

"I am," I tell her. "I *am* interested in you, but I'll never hurt you, Alanna. Not unless you ask me to." I smirk at her, enjoying the way her cheeks turn redder still. "And when I take you, it won't be without your consent — you'll be begging me for it."

I turn and walk away, leaving her staring after me. This isn't how I expected that conversation to go, but hell... when do things ever go to plan with Alanna?

Chapter Twenty-Eight

Alanna

"You look beautiful tonight," Ryan says, his eyes lingering on my chest. "Don't be nervous, okay? You'll do great."

I look up at him and smile tightly. I should be nervous about meeting Ryan's family, but I'm still thinking about Simon. That look in his eyes... what was that?

I bite down on my lip, my stomach twisting with anxiety. The things he said... I should be scared, but I'm not. There's something about him I can't quite place, something familiar and *safe*.

"Hey," Ryan says, his arm wrapping around me. "You aren't still worried about that weirdo from the coffee shop, are you? I'll take care of him, I promise."

I shake my head, my anxiety turning to dread. I never should've told Ryan what happened, but I just couldn't help myself. That entire exchange with Simon just felt so... sinful. I know I did nothing wrong, but somehow I felt like I did, like hiding what happened would be wrong.

"No, that's not it," I lie. "I'm just nervous about meeting your family." It's not a total lie. I truly am nervous about meeting them.

I know next to nothing about the Sinclairs. I know they come from old money, but googling them mostly resulted in investment reports and financial news. There was no tabloid news. Nothing to tell me who they are. I briefly met his mother when I was volunteering at the beach, on the day Ryan and I met, but we haven't been formally introduced before, and I'm not sure she even remembers me.

"It's just my brother and my mother tonight, sweetheart. You'll do great."

I nod and stare at myself in the mirror. I'm wearing a dress I can barely afford, and I'm worried I look as uncomfortable in it as I feel.

"You look like you might actually be even more nervous than I am," I murmur.

Ryan looks away and sighs. "I am. My brother and I... we aren't that close. We haven't really spoken in years, and we're only just getting to know each other again. He reappeared in our lives under somewhat strained circumstances, and we're kind of trying to find a way to be a family again, he and I."

I frown, confused. "You never told me that. In fact, you never really talk about your family at all." I haven't dared to ask, because I don't want to seem like I'm prying. I'm scared asking too many questions will make him think I'm after him for who his family is, but I'm also scared of saying the wrong thing tonight simply because I don't know enough about the Sinclairs.

Ryan stares at me and runs his hands down my shoulders, nodding. "Well... it's complicated. My brother, Silas... he's my half-brother. Our father passed away when I was young, and Silas left home shortly after. He kind of fell off the grid until recently. I want us to be close again, like we were when I was younger, but it isn't that simple." He sighs and runs a hand through his hair. "Tonight means everything to me. We only really have dinner together every few months."

I bite down on my lip, worried. "Are you sure I should be there tonight? It sounds like it's a family occasion."

Ryan lifts his hand to my face and brushes the back of his hand across my cheek. The move has a tremor running down my spine. Simon touched me in the exact same way, but his hands were bigger, rougher... and when he looked at me, it truly was like I was all he could see. Ryan isn't even looking at me. He's lost in thought — he always is.

"Of course you should be there. You're bound to become part of our family, and my brother is going to love you."

My eyes widen and Ryan smiles. We've only been together for a few months, and marriage hasn't even been on my mind yet. To have him mention it so casually... that's pretty special.

"He's a lot like you," Ryan says, a sad smile on his face. "He cares about giving back to the community, and he does a lot of volunteer work like you do. You two will get along great. Having you around will break the tension."

I smile nervously, the pressure weighing down on me. I can't shake that nervousness as Ryan leads me to his car, and my anxiety only increases as I get in. Ryan loves this car, and every single time he picks me up, I'm scared I'll damage it somehow. There's no way I could afford repairs on a car like this.

"Hey," he says as he places his hand on my thigh. "Relax, okay? It'll be fun tonight. The food will be good, and my family will love you."

I nod, trying my best to control my breathing. I feel so out of place. I feel like a fraud, and at any second Ryan is going to realize that I don't belong in his world, that he can't introduce me to his family after all.

My heart starts to race when a large iron gate swings open to reveal an actual mansion. The house makes me feel the same way this car does. Inadequate. Out of place.

I'm only barely keeping myself from shaking by the time we reach the front door and I glance at Ryan for support, but his attention isn't on me. He's staring up at the house with an expression I've never seen before... almost like a mixture of longing and contempt.

I follow him through the house, my heels clicking loudly on the marble floors. Somehow that just adds to my embarrassment, even though I can't help it.

"Mother," Ryan says as he walks into what appears to be the dining room. "I didn't realize you were here already."

I take in the long table and the woman sitting at the head of it. She stands to kiss Ryan on the cheek before turning to me.

"Alanna, right?"

I nod as I walk up to her, hesitating. I'm not sure how to greet her, but thankfully she takes the decision out of my hands by wrapping me in a brief, firm hug.

"I'm Mona," she tells me. "It's great to finally formally meet the woman that has my little boy so smitten. Ryan hasn't shut up about you since that day at the beach."

I smile and breathe a sigh of relief. "It's lovely to officially meet you too." She's nice. It seems like I was worried about nothing. Maybe tonight won't be so bad after all.

Mona's eyes widen, an excited glint in her gaze. "Oh, Silas! There you are, darling."

I tense. Silas Sinclair. Ryan's older brother and the CEO of the country's largest security firm. The same firm I just applied for a job at. He's a man shrouded in secrecy, allegedly one of the most dangerous people in the city. I'm nervous as I turn around to greet him.

My heart skips a beat when I look into his emerald green eyes, the same eyes I haven't stopped thinking about since earlier today.

"Simon?" I whisper.

Chapter Twenty-Nine

Alanna

He smiles at me and offers me his hand. I'm trembling as I place my hand in his, our earlier encounter still fresh in my mind.

"*Silas*," he says, correcting me. "You must be Alanna. I've heard so much about you."

I stare at him in disbelief. Just today, he told me his name was Simon. Did he do that on purpose? Was he watching me because I'm dating his brother?

My cheeks fill with shame once more. To think I actually believed he was hitting on me, when all he was doing was looking out for his brother. Was he provoking me to see if I'd betray Ryan?

He shakes my hand, a polite smile on his face. I can't tell what's going on. Why is he pretending not to know me? I'm not sure if I'm supposed to play along or not. Is this a test?

Before I can make up my mind, he lets go of my hand and walks toward the dining table, a frown on his face.

"That's not my seat," he tells one of the uniformed maids in the corner. She looks up at him with wide eyes and nods before rushing forward to rearrange the table setting, placing him at the head of the table instead of Mona.

Mona and Ryan both tense, and I can't quite figure out what's going on. I expected to feel out of place, but this... this is different.

We're all quiet as we take our seats, Silas at the head of the table with Ryan and me closest to him. The setup leaves Mona sitting a little isolated with no one opposite her. I guess Silas is more traditional than I expected.

I can't help but think back to our conversation. The more I think about it, the more embarrassed I am. To think I threatened him... he's *Silas Sinclair.* I can only hope he found it amusing and won't hold it against me. Especially considering that I applied for a job at his company.

"So, Alanna," he says. My eyes snap up to his, and I pray my nerves aren't as obvious as I think they are. "How did you and my brother meet?"

"I... I..." I stammer, my mind suddenly blank. I'm beyond nervous and a little scared that he'll bring up our conversation today. I'm mortified and *terrified* I'll just make things worse.

Ryan wraps his arm around my shoulder and pulls me closer. Silas's eyes drop to Ryan's hand, his gaze chilling. "We met at the beach," Ryan says. "Mom and I volunteered to gather plastic, and there she was. I'm not sure what I did to deserve Alanna, but I'm grateful she gave me a chance that day."

Silas looks up at Mona, who is smiling back at him. "I see," he says, his gaze unreadable. "So tell me about you," he says, turning back to me. "I'm curious about the girl that tamed my wild little brother. What do you study? What are your plans for the future? I assume you have plans... or were you planning on letting my brother provide for you?"

I freeze, deeply insulted... but there's pain there too. His words hurt, and I can't even pinpoint why. I should be used to this by now, after all.

"I study Computer Science," I say, my voice wavering. "I'm nearly done and I'm interviewing for graduate jobs right now."

The way he looks at me makes me uncomfortable. He looks mad, but I've barely said anything. He can't still be mad about what I said earlier, can he?

I breathe a sigh of relief when he nods and shifts his gaze to Ryan. My thoughts are all over the place, and I wish I could just sink through the floor and disappear. I expected dinner to be awkward, but this is on another level.

"I meant to ask you a favor," Ryan says. "Some guy harassed Alanna today. She was so rattled. She was barely coherent when she called me."

The blood drains from my face as I stare down at my plate. This can't be happening.

"Is that so, Alanna?" Silas says, his voice tinged with amusement. "What did that guy say to you?"

His words reverberate through my mind, heightening my embarrassment. *When I take you, it won't be without your consent. You'll be begging me for it.*

My cheeks are burning as I look up at him. "It was nothing, really," I murmur, my voice barely above a whisper. That look in his eyes... he's enjoying my torment, isn't he?

Silas grins at me. "That bad, huh? What should I do to the poor sucker? Should I make him disappear?"

I bite down on my lip and tear my eyes away. He's definitely mocking me. What would Ryan think if he found out that the person I'd been complaining about was Silas?

"I... um, excuse me." I rise from my seat in a rush, needing a moment to compose myself.

I freeze when Silas rises too. "I'll show you the way." He gestures toward the large doors and walks away before I can decline. I follow him reluctantly, my heart hammering loudly in my chest.

By the time the dining room doors close behind us, I'm

certain I can hear my heartbeat thrumming in my ears. I don't remember the last time I was this nervous.

I almost run into him when he pauses abruptly in the middle of the hallway. He turns around to face me, and I take a step back.

"Break up with him," he orders, his eyes flashing with an intensity that takes my breath away.

"*What*?"

Silas takes a step closer to me and places his index finger underneath my chin, tilting my face up toward his. "You heard me, Alanna. Break up with him."

Pure devastation rushes through me, rendering me silent. I expected Ryan's family to find me lacking, but this? I didn't expect this.

I start to tremble and try my hardest to keep my tears from forming. I'm so tired of always feeling like I'm not good enough. All my life I've felt like a stranger looking in from the outside, until Ryan. To know that those closest to him don't want me with him... it hurts. It kills me, because I know Ryan will always choose his brother over me. I see the admiration in his eyes, the regret in his voice when he talks about Silas.

Silas takes a step closer to me and tightens his grip on my chin, our bodies brushing against each other. "Break up with him while I'm still giving you a choice."

Silas walks away, leaving me staring after him once again. What just happened? How do I even tell Ryan what his brother just said to me? He'll never believe me... and something tells me that Silas meant what he said.

He doesn't want me with Ryan, and I have a feeling that Silas always gets what he wants.

Chapter Thirty

Silas

"Where are we with the lawyer?" I ask, frustrated. I've been on edge ever since Alanna came over for dinner. I've always wanted to see her in the home I grew up in — I just never expected she'd be sitting there as my brother's girlfriend. It fucks me up endlessly.

I'm at a loss. She doesn't remember me, and even worse, she seems *happy* with Ryan. I suspect that Mona orchestrated them meeting each other, but his feelings seem sincere. From what I can tell, he's innocent in this situation, a mere pawn in his mother's schemes.

What the fuck do I do? What am I supposed to do when she seems to be in love with my *brother*. I don't want to hurt either of them, but I can't just sit back and watch them together. My heart can't take it. I can't fucking stand watching him drape his arm around her, I can't stand to see her look at him the way she once looked at me. Fuck that. I can't do it.

I spent years searching for her, only to find her in my little brother's arms. Had it been anyone else, I may have been able to walk away and wish her well, but Ryan? He's the one person she can't be with. Especially because I'm certain Mona orchestrated this somehow. Ever since I took back what she owed me, she's been trying to find a way to gain the upper hand, and I'm scared she's succeeded. She found a way to manipulate me, and neither Alanna nor Ryan appear to be aware of the role they're playing in her plans.

Amy straightens and shakes her head apologetically. "One of the two witnesses that oversaw the signing of your father's will passed away recently, and the other still hasn't been found. As far as we can tell, he left the country shortly after your father died and hasn't returned since. The moment he steps foot into the country, we'll know."

I nod, my thoughts reeling. In the last few years, I've managed to gain back most of what I lost, fighting dirty to get it. For years, I anonymously purchased my father's stocks until I had enough to make an impact. Then I sold it all off, sinking the share price until it was nearly nothing, allowing me to buy back a larger share at a lower price. I brought Mona to the brink of bankruptcy and then pretended to save her from it. I never should've had to play such dumb games at all. It all should've been mine from the start.

"What about Alanna? Have you figured out how she ended up with Ryan? Is he even remotely aware of our past?" Part of me wishes that my brother is in on this. If he is, I can tear Alanna and him apart without a single ounce of remorse. If he isn't... then that complicates matters. I've already taken so much from him as it is. I took his home away from him the way Mona once took it from me, evicting them both. I couldn't risk letting him stay, because she'd just use him to regain access to the house. I want to keep Ryan out of my revenge on Mona as best as I can, but I can't shield him entirely. Now that Mona has involved Alanna through him, I'm not sure what to do. My hands are tied. I don't want to hurt either of them.

Amy shakes her head. "Alanna doesn't have social media accounts, which is part of the reason we could never trace her. Ryan, on the other hand, has never posted anything about her.

We're still checking both of their location data history, but it'll be a bit longer before we'll have any meaningful conclusions. I thought checking whether their location data intersected at specific places would give us a clue, but nothing so far. The best I can come up with is that they met at the beach like they told you and started dating shortly after, but there must be more to it than that. I can't prove that their initial meeting was orchestrated by Mona, but I suspect it was. From what I've observed, there has been no indication that Ryan is aware of your past with Alanna."

I nod and run a hand through my hair. Five years, and all I've found is a fucking mess. My girl doesn't remember me, and everything I've regained feels empty without her.

"Silas," Amy says, her voice soft. "I know that the current circumstances aren't ideal, but I firmly believe that the two of you are meant to be. If you give it some time, she'll find her way back to you. I just know it."

I smile at her, a spark of hope lighting in my cold heart. "I suppose in many ways, this is a new start. It's like we're meeting all over again, but this time I have a lot more to offer her. I guess it's a chance to win her back and treat her the way I've always wanted to, right from the start."

Amy grins at me. "Exactly. Besides, you know what your brother is like. Alanna can't truly be happy with him. I suspect she's only with him because somehow, he reminded her of you."

I lean back in my seat, taking in the disgust in her eyes. "Why do you hate my brother so much? You've always been my most professional employee, yet you've always failed to hide your hatred for him."

Amy looks away. "I don't hate him, per se." She hesitates before she looks back at me. "I just see what you refuse to see. When you look at Ryan, you see a chance to make up for lost time. You see him as the kid he used to be, and even though I think it's too late, you see a chance to save him from his mother's influence. I get it, boss. I do. I'm just worried about you. He's using you, and you're letting him. Him dating Alanna? There's no way there's no foul play there, Silas. It's true that so far, he seems innocent, but I just don't believe that he is. I can't prove how or why yet, but I can't be wrong about this. You're blinded by him, blinded by your guilt and your shared past, so you don't see it, but *I do.*"

She starts to pace in my office, looking back at me with anguish burning in her eyes. "You once saved me, Silas. You took a chance on a young widow with two kids I could barely keep fed, and you saved us all. Throughout the last couple of years, you've become family to me. To me, you're the brother I never had, so keep that in mind when I tell you that your real sibling is using you as a walking, talking ATM. He isn't interested in a relationship with you — he's only interested in not losing the lifestyle he used to have. When you bought out Mona, she wasn't left with enough money to maintain their previous living standard, so they came after *you*. I know you don't want to believe me, but you need to be careful. It doesn't sit well with me that he went after Alanna. This *cannot* be coincidence."

I rub my face and nod. "I hear you, Amy," I murmur. She's been worried about me from the moment Ryan became part of my life again, disliking the fact that I've given him access to whatever he wanted. I know what she's saying, but I don't think Ryan is beyond salvation, and while it would be convenient for me to believe he went after Alanna with an agenda, there's no proof of that. He truly seems to love her, and though it fucking kills me, she seems to feel the same way about him. My brother isn't that good of a liar, and there wasn't a single hint of deception in his expression over dinner. If he was faking it, I'd know. He loves her.

I sigh as I run a hand through my hair and stare up at the ceiling, unsure what to do. I still remember how hard it was for me when Mona threw me out, and I'm trying my best to shield Ryan from my actions as best as I can. Suddenly losing everything pushed me into a downward spiral, and though I wasn't willing to give up on my revenge, I'm trying my hardest to shield Ryan from the consequences of it. I want Mona to suffer, but I don't want

Ryan to be caught up in it. I know he's spoiled, but deep down, he isn't a bad kid. He was just raised by a terrible person.

Had I been around, he wouldn't have been the way he is now. When Dad died, I promised him that I'd protect Ryan, and that's exactly what I'm trying to do. Maybe it's too little too late, but I have to try. I owe it to our dad.

If I can, I'll give Ryan everything he would've had if I hadn't stepped back into his life and forcibly taken it from him — except for Alanna. It's going to kill him to lose her, but one way or another, I'm making her mine... even if it comes at the cost of my relationship with my brother.

My only worry is that it's no longer me she wants. If Alanna really is happy with Ryan, can I truly take away that happiness? Can I knowingly break her heart because of my own selfish desires?

Chapter Thirty-One

ALANNA

I stare up at the entwined double S on the building in front of me, wondering whether I should just walk away. I was so excited about this interview just a few weeks ago. The idea of working with Ryan at the company that bears his surname was amazing.

Now? Now I'm second-guessing myself. I've embarrassed myself in front of Silas enough now. The last thing I want to do is run into him again.

Not that I would. The building has twenty-seven floors. Surely the CEO doesn't sit in on graduate interviews?

I take a deep breath and force myself to walk into the building. I'd be crazy not to attend this interview just on the off chance I might run into Silas. Sinclair Security is my dream company. I've wanted to work for them long before I even met Ryan.

"Good morning, Ms. Jones," the lady behind the receptionist counter says before I can even tell her what I'm here for. My eyes widen, a thrill running down my spine. I've heard rumors about the staff here. They're what I always imagined the FBI would be like — except privatized.

I look around for a name card, but there isn't one. I nod politely, wondering whether this is a test. Should I have known her name too?

She smiles as though she can read my mind. "I'm Amy, and I'd honestly be quite upset if you knew that, because it'd mean I wasn't doing my job." She winks at me as she rises from her seat and guides me toward the elevators.

Her kind smile puts me at ease and I listen attentively as she tells me about the security measures in place at the elevator. "Fingerprint scans are sufficient for the lower floors, but any floor above fourteen requires a retinal scan," she says as she leans into the scanner.

I only barely manage to contain my excitement. I knew Sinclair Security was high tech, but this is better than I even imagined. Amy presses the button for the top floor, and I blink in surprise as unease washes over me.

The top floor for graduate interviews… surely not. My suspicions are confirmed when she leads me through the quiet floor, until we're standing in front of a corner office — one fit for a CEO.

"You'll do great," she tells me as she knocks on the door. "I have no doubt that we'll be working together soon."

She opens the door and takes a step back to let me pass. I hesitate, taking a moment to gather my courage and push down the dread that threatens to overwhelm me.

My stride is confident as I walk into the office, finding Silas sitting behind a large black desk. He looks up and smiles politely, his expression completely professional. I'm nervous as I sit down opposite him, but I'd like to think I managed to keep my cool.

Silas glances at a document in front of him, and I quickly realize that it's my resume. "Tell me, why do you think you'd be a good fit for Sinclair Security?"

I stare at him in surprise. Is he serious? He can't seriously be conducting my interview himself, can he? I force myself to get it together and answer the question the way I practiced.

"I... I've followed the growth of Sinclair Security for years now. I'm aware you started with private investigations and ended up growing this business to encompass security of all types, including cybersecurity. The research you do and the company's trajectory are astonishing. I think Sinclair Security will become even more of a powerhouse than it currently is, and I'd love to be part of it."

It's true. I truly admire this company and all he's done with it. It might be near impossible to find information on him online, but I hear the rumors from the industry experts I know. This company is astonishing and barely anyone even knows it even exists.

"You specifically applied to be part of the Ψ division, even though it's the toughest division to get into. If you did your research at all, you'll know that we mostly hire internally for this division. Why did you apply here instead of the other departments that are much easier to access?"

I look down at my hands for a moment, startled by the question. "I'm intrigued by the secrecy surrounding this department, and I love a good challenge. The opportunity to work with some of the brightest minds in the country isn't one I could let slip by, even if my chances of joining are slim."

He stares at me as though he knows I'm lying and shakes his head. "Tell me the full truth, Alanna."

I look into his eyes, finding encouragement in them. "I don't know," I whisper truthfully. "I don't know, Silas. All I know is that I belong here. When I first heard of the Ψ division, I just knew. That makes no sense, and I know that it doesn't, but it is the truth. I feel like I'll find the answers I'm seeking here."

"What answers are you seeking?" he asks, his voice soft.

"I'm looking for someone," I admit. "Someone I keep dreaming of. I can't keep this from you because I know you'll do a full background check before you'll even consider hiring me, but I suffer from amnesia. Despite that, there's someone I keep dreaming of. I don't know who it is, but I feel like someone out there is waiting for me. I have no intention of using corporate resources to find this person. Please don't misunderstand. I just... I just feel like being here gets me a step closer."

He stares at me, and for a moment, I'm certain he'll ask me to leave his office and never return, shredding my resume in the process. Instead, he nods and proceeds to ask me basic interview questions. Much to my relief, the interview proceeds that way, with Silas asking questions I've prepared for.

Just when I think I'm in the clear, Silas drops his pen on top of my resume and stares me down. "Have you wanted to work here since before you met Ryan?"

The personal question throws me off. He's been so professional since I walked in here that he made it easy to forget what he told me. If he doesn't think I'm good enough to be with his brother, why would he think I'm good enough for his company?

"That's right," I tell him, unsure what else to say.

Silas nods. "So you don't solely want to work here to be with Ryan?"

I grit my teeth in annoyance. I hate this. I hate that so many people assume I'd be nothing without him, that I'll follow wherever he goes. Ryan is a great guy and I do see a future with him, but that doesn't mean I'll forget about my own plans and goals.

"No," I say, my voice deceptively sweet. *Silas Sinclair.* I wish I could throw something at him and walk out of his stupid office, but I want this job too badly.

He stares at me, an irritating smile on his face, and it becomes harder to resist temptation. I want to walk away and slam his door as loudly as I can, preferably in his stupid, annoyingly handsome face. Instead, I smile back at him.

He turns his laptop to me, his gaze unreadable once again. "Crack this, and you're hired. I want the password to this email address within ten minutes. You can use any of the software already installed on my laptop, including the software you'll need if you know what you're doing."

I glance at the piece of paper he hands me and frown. Silas@

sinclair.com? He's asking me to give him the password to his own email address? I bite down on my lip, unsure if he's giving me a near impossible task just to keep me from joining his firm. The man is an enigma.

"Have you asked this of all applicants?"

Silas smiles. "Yes."

"Has anyone managed it yet?"

He nods. "One person."

I breathe a sigh of relief. If it's possible, then I can do it too.

"Do you interview all applicants yourself?"

He smirks. "Why? Did you think you were special?"

This man. How does he always get under my skin? Why can't he just be sweet and kind like Ryan is? The two of them couldn't be more different.

I grit my teeth and start to type, channeling all my annoyance into my work. This is the one thing I'm good at. I might fail at most things in life, but when it comes to security testing, I never fail.

My heart races as I type, and I barely keep from smiling. This doesn't even feel like work. I could do this all day, just for the hell of it. I love the thrill.

Ten minutes. That's all the time it takes me, considering everything he's got installed. I smirk when Silas's password is revealed, only for that smile to melt off my face when I realize what it is. *Perasperaadastra. Per aspera ad astra.* Through adversity to the stars. It's the exact same phrase I have tattooed on my rib. How could it be?

I swallow hard as I look up at him, slowly turning his laptop back to him. Silas... there's no way he could've known. Is he mocking me somehow? Did Ryan tell him about my tattoo?

He stares at me, and I wish I could read him. I want to know what he's thinking. I want to know the story behind his password. Is it all just to throw me off, or is there more to it?

"You're hired," he says, his voice soft.

I nod, my thoughts whirling. "I... thank you, Silas." I hesitate before asking a question I know I shouldn't ask. "You aren't going to make me breaking up with Ryan a requirement for hiring me?"

He looks at me, his expression entirely blank. "No," he says, sounding... *tired*. "I keep my personal life and my business strictly separate. I expect you to do the same if you wish to succeed here. This isn't an easy firm to be at."

My cheeks heat of embarrassment. I shouldn't have asked. All I accomplished was making myself look unprofessional. Why is it that I constantly feel unlike myself when I'm around Silas?

"Of course," I nod, rising from my seat. I need to get out of here before I make an even bigger fool of myself.

"I'll see you on Monday. Congratulations."

I turn back to him when I reach his door. "See you on Monday," I say, praying to God that I won't. With a bit of luck, I'll be able to avoid him at work just fine.

Luck... yeah right. When has Lady Luck ever smiled down on *me*?

Chapter Thirty-Two

ALANNA

I'm giddy with excitement as I walk up to Ryan's apartment, my set of keys in hand. He gave them to me last week, and today seems like a great first time to use them. I can't wait to tell him the good news. The two of us working together is a dream come true.

I'm surprised when I walk in to find the lights dimmed and loud R&B music playing. Ryan never listens to this kind of music. It's far more my taste than it is his. He's the one that taught me all about classical music, and though I still don't enjoy it, I hate it a little less.

My gaze trails over the packed living room, and I pause in confusion. What the hell? Ryan hates partying. He's a loner, like I am. Why would he be throwing a party without even inviting me?

I walk through the crowd of dancing people, not a single person I know in sight. Who *are* these people? I breathe a sigh of relief when I spot Ryan standing on the balcony with some guys I vaguely recognize. I've only ever met them briefly, but I believe the one standing next to him is his childhood friend.

I'm about to walk out there when I hear my name being

mentioned. Something about the way Ryan's friend said my name has me pausing, my instincts alerting me that something is... *off.* I lean back out of view and listen, curiosity getting the better of me.

"How much longer are you going to date Alanna? She's fucking beneath you. I get secondhand embarrassment just watching you with her."

I expected Ryan to snap at his friend, but he just laughs. "I have to keep playing this game a bit longer. My brother would never believe I changed otherwise. He'll believe she caused the change. He told me he wouldn't give me shit until I cleaned up my act and stopped drinking and partying, withholding what should've been *mine*. She's everything that asshole loves. The fucking charity bullshit, the vanilla *everything*. I swear, the way she fucking kisses is boring as fuck. The sex is even worse. I've got her believing I want her so much that I can't last more than a minute with her, but honestly, I just can't stand fucking her for longer than that. She's so goddamn boring. The only reason I can get it up at all is because she's hiding a hot little body underneath all those goddamn oversized layers she wears."

His friends all laugh, the sound in sharp contrast with the pain in my chest. He's dating me as a front? To make Silas believe he isn't the playboy everyone has been warning me he is? I swallow down the sob that threatens to rise up my throat and squeeze my eyes closed. It can't be. I must have misheard it. Ryan... he loved going to game night at our local senior complex last week. He's the one that's constantly suggesting ways for us to give back to the community.

I think back to our relationship, wondering what was real and what wasn't. Even the music in this place isn't something I thought he enjoyed. If something as simple as his music taste was fake, then what else was?

"If she's everything your brother wants, why not just give her to him? That's bound to get you in his good graces."

I jump when I hear glass shattering. I turn to peek outside, finding large shards right next to Ryan's shoes. He's staring his friend down, his expression terrifying. I've never seen him like this. He's nothing like the sweet man I know.

"Fuck no. That bastard took everything from us. He gained control over all the Sinclair assets to the point that I have to beg him for a fucking job. I'm not giving him anything else. He can't have her. Never her. I'm never letting anything that's mine fall into his hands again. Nah. I'm going to use Alanna to gain his trust. Behind that rough exterior, he's still the same guy I grew up with. He puts family above all else. Once I'm in, I'm taking back everything we lost, starting with our fucking house. I can't wait to throw him out the way he did with my mother and me. That asshole is going to pay."

I'm shaking so hard I'm certain someone is about to notice me and ask if I'm okay, betraying my presence. My thoughts are whirling, and I'm barely able to comprehend what I'm hearing. He's using me? I'm just a way to improve his damn *image*?

I should've known. I should've believed everyone that warned me, everyone that told me that guys like Ryan don't date girls like me. I wanted to feel loved so badly that I ignored the warning bells.

I can't tell if I'm more angry or hurt. I'm mad at myself for being so blind, for truly believing someone could want me the way Ryan pretended to. By the time I walk out the door, my pain has given way to blinding fury.

That fucking asshole.

I gave him everything. All those evenings we stayed up together, the long talks, the dates. Was all of it fake? How much of the man I thought I knew was even real? To think he couldn't even bear touching me... I can't believe he faked it. At least I now no longer have to feel bad for never enjoying the sex.

I pause in the middle of the street, my eyes dropping to Ryan's beloved car. Out of everything he showed me, his love for this stupid car was definitely real.

I glance at the keys in my hand and back at his car. Before I realize what I'm doing, I'm digging his house keys into the side of car, ruining what I'm sure is an expensive paint job. I take my time spelling out A S S H O L E, but it does nothing to ease my anger.

He used me. He took my love for my community and used it as a fucking PR stunt. He led me on, talking about how I belong in his family, making me think he was serious about me, when all along it was all a game to him.

I turn around, in search of something to throw at his car. I narrow my eyes when I find a couple of decently large rocks near the trees. I grab them and walk back, hesitating for a split second before throwing one of the rocks straight through his window. The glass shatters beautifully, damaging his leather seats, and I smile. It doesn't make up for the pain he put me through, but it's a start.

I lean into the car, digging my keys into the leather headrest, keying M I C R O D I C K and M I N U T E M A N into it. I can't believe I suffered through shit sex over that asshole. I can't believe I spent so much of my time with him. I ignored well-meant warnings because of him, alienating some of my closest friends. He played his part so well that I was none the wiser. If I hadn't overheard him tonight, then what? Would he have wasted more of my time? How much of my life did he intend to sacrifice for his selfish, petty goals? For the first time in years, I felt like I belonged with someone, and it was all fake.

I wipe away the tears I hadn't even realized had fallen and kick his door as hard as I can, denting it. I want him to find his car tomorrow and feel at least a bit of the pain he's put me through. He clearly doesn't care about me, but this? This will hurt him.

"Microdick? Nice."

I whirl around in shock. "*Silas.*"

I didn't hear him approach. The streets have been eerily silent. The only thing disturbing the peace was the sound of me damaging Ryan's car.

I drop the keys in my hand, my face draining of color. Fuck. What have I done? I can't afford repairs on this car. What was I thinking? A fresh wave of panic overwhelms me, and I try my hardest to keep from shaking.

Silas stares at me, his expression calm. His attention isn't on the car. It's on me. "What happened?" he asks.

I open my mouth to answer, but the words won't come. How do I tell him that Ryan was using me? It's hard enough for me to come to terms with myself. Admitting it to someone, to *Silas*? That's beyond me right now.

He sighs and walks up to me, pausing right in front of me. Silas places his hands on my cheeks and swipes at my tears with his thumbs. "He hurt you."

I nod, my eyes falling closed as another fresh wave of tears fall from my eyes. Silas catches them all, his touch gentle.

"I'm sorry," I whisper. "I... I wasn't thinking. I'll get the car repaired, I promise. Please don't report me to the police," I beg.

Silas chuckles and brushes my hair out of my face, tucking it behind my ear instead. "This isn't what I expected to find when the car's silent alarm went off," he says. "I'm impressed. You did quite a bit of damage in the few minutes it took me to get here. What is it with you and damaging cars, huh?"

Silent alarm. Of course. Why didn't I think of that? I must've truly lost my mind. I'm done for. I'm going to be in debt for the rest of my life, and it wouldn't surprise me if Silas decides not to hire me anymore.

I bite down on my lip harshly. What did I do? I let Ryan use me for months, and right till the end I'm the one that suffers most. I put my own future at stake and he isn't even worth it. I swallow down a sob and squeeze my eyes closed. Years of hard work, all gone because I couldn't control my pain.

Silas sighs and takes a step closer to me. Before I realize what's happening, he's got his arms wrapped around me. He hugs me tightly, and I burst into tears while he just stands there, stroking my hair with one hand and keeping the other wrapped tightly around me.

"What happened, my love? What did he do?"

I shake my head and hug him back, squeezing him tightly, as though holding onto him will keep me from falling apart.

"I'll get the car fixed," I murmur. "Don't fire me, *please.* I swear I'm not usually like this."

Silas chuckles and holds me tighter. "Fuck the car," he says. "It's mine anyway. It's not his. Don't worry about it. I'll have it towed in a minute."

I pull back to look at him in surprise, and he smiles. "Oh God," I whisper. "It's not Ryan's?"

Silas smirks and shakes his head. "I loaned it to him because he loved it so much."

His words bring fresh tears to my eyes. I damaged a car that isn't even Ryan's. The small amount of vindication it gave me drains away, leaving me feeling empty, deprived of my revenge and heartbroken in more ways than one.

Ryan's words run through my mind, filling me with fresh contempt. *He can't have her. Never her.* I swallow hard, my eyes running over Silas. "I'll repay you," I tell him.

Silas frowns, and I smile bitterly.

"Right now."

"How are you going to pay me back, Alanna?"

My heart starts to race as I look into his eyes. "Silas, I'm ready to beg for it."

Chapter Thirty-Three

SILAS

"Silas, I'm ready to beg for it," she says, a vindictive glint in her eyes. Her eyes are roaming over my body, but it's not me she's seeing. What she sees is an opportunity for revenge. What the fuck did Ryan do to her?

"Did you break up with him?"

She looks up at me, surprised. "We're done," she says, her voice soft. I'm relieved at the lack of heartbreak in her eyes. She seems angry and hurt, but not heartbroken. Maybe there's still a chance for us, after all.

"Does he know that?"

She shakes her head and grabs her phone. "No, but he's about to find out."

I watch her as she texts him, breaking up with him over a text message. Damn. He really fucked up, huh? I should feel sorry for my brother, but all I feel is relief. For weeks, I've been trying to figure out what to do. I've been wanting to break them up, but I couldn't stand the thought of forcibly breaking her heart, depriving her of the happiness she sought out. I will always place Alanna's happiness above all else — including my own.

She smiles as she puts her phone away and takes a step closer to me. I won't even pretend to lie to myself. I want her. I always want her.

All I could think about when she interviewed with me was what it'd be like to work with her, to steal a kiss from her here and there. I imagined her in a sexy skirt, her legs spread on my desk. I've wanted her in my bed from the moment I found her. Her dating my brother didn't change a thing for me. I still love her the same. I still want her as much as I always have — but not like this.

"Come on," I tell her. "Let me take you home."

She blinks in confusion, and I watch her emotions and thoughts dance in those beautiful eyes of hers. "I... how about we go to your place instead?" she asks. Her sweet smile is in contrast with the calculative look in her eyes, and something about it breaks my heart. When I eventually fuck her, I don't want her to be thinking about Ryan, and tonight he's all that's on her mind.

"No," I tell her, and the devastation in her eyes nearly wrecks me. She wraps her arms around herself, and it's not hard to guess what she's thinking. The sting of rejection is clear in her demeanor.

"I see," she says, her voice shaky. She looks down at the floor and takes a step back. It only takes her a second to paste a smile on her face, and then she nods at me politely. "You don't need to take me home, but thank you for offering. I think I'll head back inside."

I cross my arms and stare her down. "And do what, exactly?"

She grins. "Find one of Ryan's childhood friends to spend the night with," she says, shrugging. "Before the night is over, I'll have hurt him in the best way I can, with or without you."

This woman... she makes my fucking blood boil. "Like hell you are." I grab her wrist and pull her along. She resists, but there's no fucking way she's going back in there. "You want to fuck the pain away tonight, baby? Fine — but you won't be doing it with anyone but me."

She's still the same fucking psycho with a heart of gold that I used to know. Once she's set her mind to something, there's no talking her out of it. This isn't how I imagined being with her, but fuck it. If it's Alanna, I'll take what I can get.

She's quiet as I drive us to my home, parking into the elevator that takes us straight up to my penthouse. I glance at her, wondering if she's changed her mind, but the glint in her eyes tells me she hasn't.

I step out of the car and walk around it to open the door for her. She takes my hand, and when her eyes meet mine, I smile. I've missed her, and having her here in my home is a bit of a dream come true. She has no idea that I modeled it after the plans we made together.

"This... this is your house?" she asks, her voice filled with disbelief. I smile at her and nod. "This is my home. The house you came to for dinner is my family home. It's where I grew up and where I might eventually live when I settle down, but this is where I live on a day-to-day basis."

She nods and looks around, taking in all the glass and the beautiful skyline. The view is the main reason I bought this place, and I have a feeling she appreciates it as much as I do. When we were cooped up in that tiny room without a window, we both dreamed of large windows and a beautiful skyline. Now we've got it.

"Wow," she whispers, and I grin. I walk over to the kitchen and grab a bottle from the wine fridge.

I hand her a glass and she takes it with shaking hands. "Changed your mind?" I ask, wanting to tease her.

She looks at me, her eyes slowly roaming over my body before moving back up. "No," she says, placing her glass on the counter. She takes a step forward, pausing in front of me. I tense when she places her hand on my chest and slides it up, until she's got it wrapped around the back of my neck. "Did you?"

I smile and tilt my face toward hers. "What will you do if I say that I changed my mind?"

She grins and rises to her tiptoes. "I'll just have to seduce you," she whispers, her lips brushing over mine.

Her eyes flutter closed as she kisses me, her touch cautious, hesitant. I smile against her lips and thread my hand through her hair, pulling her closer roughly. For a while, I wondered if I'd ever hold her like this again. I thought I'd lost her to Ryan, and I was too scared to make a move, too scared to hurt her. I thought I'd have to live off the memories we created for the rest of my life, the ones only I remember, but here she is, back in my arms.

She moans as she kisses me properly, her body moving against mine, betraying her desire. I've waited years to feel her against me like this, and it's even better than in my memories. I push against her, making her take a step back.

I walk her toward the mirror in the hallway that way, step by step, her lips never leaving mine. Alanna moans against my mouth, her tongue tangling with mine in a way that has me wondering what her hot little mouth will feel like around my cock. I have a feeling it'll be a thousand times better than my memories. I turn her around in front of the mirror and place my lips right below her ear, pressing a featherlight kiss to her skin.

"If you're going to do this, Alanna... if you're going to use me to take revenge on Ryan, then you're going to watch yourself in this mirror. You're going to watch me fuck you."

Chapter Thirty-Four

Alanna

Silas stands behind me and looks at me through the mirror. The way he looks at me… I've never had a man look at me that way. His desire is on display, and he doesn't try to hide it. His eyes trail over my body hungrily, and I bite down on my lip in an effort to control my emotions.

"Look at yourself, Alanna," he whispers, his hands trailing up from my waist to my breasts. His thumbs graze over my nipples, and he grins. "Already turned on, and I've barely even touched you. Fucking look at you."

He places his hand at the top of my dress, taking his time, teasing me. Silas smiles when he pulls the zipper on the back down, exposing my skin inch by inch. My heart is racing by the time his hand reaches my lower back. He grins at me in the mirror before leaning in and presses a kiss to the back of my neck, sending a shiver down my spine.

He pulls away to look at me, his eyes on the mirror as he pushes the straps of my dress off my shoulder. It pools at my feet, the air cold on my bare skin. I shiver, and Silas presses a kiss to my shoulder. "Beautiful," he whispers. "You're even more beautiful than you were in my fantasies."

I stare at him with wide eyes, and he grins. "I've been wondering what your lips would taste like," he says, his hand wrapping around my throat. He tilts my head to the side and kisses me, his movements slow, sexy. His every move is powerful, filled with the promise of *more.*

I'm breathless by the time he pulls his lips away to move them to my neck instead. His teeth graze over my skin, and then he sucks down on my neck, leaving a mark. "I need a taste of your pussy," he tells me.

I gasp, and Silas chuckles as he turns me around to face him. "Yeah, baby," he whispers. "I wanted you from the moment I walked into the coffee shop. You dating my brother didn't change that. I knew I'd have you in the end. What I didn't expect was you coming to me so willingly."

He drops to his knees and places his lips against my breast, kissing me softly before twirling his tongue over my nipple. It hardens instantly, and he smirks as he pulls away a little to admire his work. Silas blows against my skin, and the air feels different against it.

He freezes all of a sudden, his gaze on the tattoo hidden just below my breast. It's the phrase he's using as his password, followed by a tiny Ψ symbol. I had it tattooed on myself in London, though I could never pinpoint why both mattered to me so much. I may not remember anything from my past, but these two things I found myself scribbling on my notepad whenever my thoughts drifted.

"This," he groans, his finger tracing over my tattoos. "What is this?"

I shake my head. "It's nothing. I don't actually know. It's complicated, so please don't ask."

He looks into my eyes, his expression surprisingly tender. "Okay, my love," he whispers. "I won't ask. Not now."

Silas moves his attention to my other breast, trapping my

nipple between his teeth as a reprimand. This time, a moan escapes my lips, and he rewards me by teasing me with his tongue. "Silas, please," I whisper, unsure of what I'm even asking for. I have no idea what I'm even doing here. I was mad and impulsive, but I can't get myself to regret it. Not when his touch makes me feel this good.

"Please what, baby?" he asks. "Tell me what you want. Do you want me to lick this delicious pussy of yours?" he adds, his fingers trailing over my navy silk underwear. He grins when he realizes how wet the fabric is and my cheeks slowly turn crimson.

He looks me in the eye as he places his hands on either side of my hips, dragging down my thong until he's got it around my ankles. "Bare," he murmurs. "I knew it."

I smile at him and raise my brow. "You've been fantasizing about your brother's girlfriend's pussy?"

He leans in and presses a kiss to it. "Damn right I have. Turn around."

He doesn't wait for me to turn. Instead, he wraps his hands around my waist and makes my body obey.

"On your knees," he orders, and this time I don't hesitate. I want more of whatever he's doing to me. I want it all.

"Good girl," he whispers as he makes me face the mirror. I barely recognize myself. My lips are swollen, and my eyes are filled with an expression I've never seen in the mirror before. My breasts are on display, my nipples rock hard. The image I'm presenting Silas with is a version of me I never knew existed.

"I'm going to make you come on my face," Silas says, and the mere thought of it has me clenching my thighs. "And you're going to look yourself in the eye as you come harder for me than you ever did for Ryan. When your pussy tightens and wave after wave of pleasure rocks your body, it's my name I want on your lips."

He leans in behind me and does exactly what he told me he would. He licks my pussy like it's his favorite flavor of ice cream, lapping me up and teasing me as he circles his tongue around my clit, withholding his touch where I want it most.

I look in the mirror, startled by the lust I see reflected back at me. I'm being eaten out by my ex's older brother, and I look like I've never been happier. A moan escapes my lips, and Silas finally gives me what I want. His tongue expertly strokes my clit, and within minutes I'm closer to an orgasm than Ryan has ever gotten me.

"Silas, please," I beg. "*Please.*"

He gives into my pleas, and my eyes fall closed as my muscles tighten, my orgasm washing over me in waves. It's unlike anything I've ever felt before, going on and on. Silas doesn't let up. He continues to lick circles around my clit, not quite touching it, yet within a minute I'm coming all over again.

I moan his name as he pushes me over the edge, coming so hard that I feel dizzy for a couple of seconds. Silas pulls away and straightens, a smug smile on his face as our eyes meet in the mirror.

I turn to face him and place my hands on his shirt. I'm naked, but he's still fully dressed, and I want more of him. I want his skin against mine. I want all of him with a possessiveness I've never felt before.

He stares at me as I undo the buttons of his shirt, and the intensity of his gaze just turns me on further. I don't think anyone has ever wanted me the way he wants me. He's rock hard through his trousers, and I swallow hard as I pull his boxers down.

My expression must betray my thoughts, because Silas laughs. "I take it my little brother isn't quite the same size, huh?"

I shake my head. "You're huge," I whisper, a little intimidated. I'm worried he'll hurt me.

Silas cups my cheek, his touch so gentle that it makes my heart skip a beat. The feeling startles me. I'm not here to catch feelings. I'm here for revenge.

I bend down and wrap my hands around his cock, placing the tip against my lips. "It's your turn to look in the mirror, Silas. Look at you letting your brother's girlfriend suck your cock. How would he feel when he finds out you've fucked my face?"

I smile, imagining the pain in his eyes. I wish he could see us right now. I wish he could watch me suck his brother's cock. I want him to see Silas take the one thing Ryan said would never be his — *me*.

I take his cock into my mouth, taking my time with him, teasing him the way he teased me.

"So fucking good." He threads his hand through my hair and pulls tightly, moving my head up and down, fucking my face the way I wanted him to.

"Look at you taking my cock. You're loving every second of it, aren't you? You pretended to be such a devoted, loving girlfriend, but look at you now. I always knew you'd be mine, eventually. Ryan could never handle you."

I suck him harder, twirling my tongue around the tip of his cock every time he pulls back. It doesn't take long for his movements to become more erratic. Just knowing that I got him close within seconds sends another wave of desire through me. I never realized how sexy it is to be truly wanted.

Silas pulls away and I groan in dissatisfaction, wanting more. He shakes his head and twirls me back around to face the mirror. He pushes me onto my knees, his left hand on my lower back. "I can't take it," he says. "I need your pussy. Right fucking now."

I moan when he pushes the tip of his cock into me. Silas moves his hand to my hair and pulls on it, making me look up into the mirror. He holds me like that as he pushes all the way into me, his eyes never leaving mine.

"Fuck," he groans when he's finally all the way inside me. I've never felt this full before, this stretched. "Your pussy is out of this world, baby."

He pulls almost all the way out before pushing back into me, and then he does it all over again, his movements slow and strong. Silas looks at me, and then he raises his hand. "This is for being with my brother when you always should've been mine," he warns, before bringing his hand down on my ass.

I gasp, the sting painful for a few seconds, before morphing into a delicious type of heat. My pussy clenches when he raises his other hand. I never thought I'd enjoy this, but it turns me on far more than I ever could've imagined.

"And this is for taking so long to come back to me." He brings his hand down, slapping my ass hard. I gasp as I breathe through the sting, and Silas grabs my ass, massaging my skin as he continues to fuck me slowly.

"Look," he orders. "Look at who's fucking you, Alanna. When you're taking my cock, I want your thoughts on me."

I grin at him through the mirror. "Silas, you've ruined me for anyone else."

He looks pleased and fucks me harder. I watch him just like he ordered me to, enjoying the connection. His eyes never leave mine, and I love seeing him slowly lose control.

Silas reaches around, his fingers finding their way between my legs. He starts to finger me while he fucks me, and I gasp. It's too much. "I can't take it, Silas."

He shakes his head. "You can, and you will."

He's right, because within seconds, I come for him all over again. Silas isn't far behind. He moans my name as he comes deep inside me. "Alanna," he whispers as his eyes fall closed.

He drops his head to my back and presses soft kisses to my skin as both of us try to catch our breath. Silas pulls out of me, and the moment breaks.

I look in the mirror, realizing what I've done. I slept with my ex-boyfriend's older brother. I stare at myself, but I don't recognize the woman looking back at me. What have I done? I pull away and grab my clothes, wanting to run and hide.

He watches me as I walk away, his expression unreadable once more. "Alanna," he says as I reach the door. I pause and turn back to find him leaning back on the floor, his irresistible body on display. "Don't be late for work on Monday."

I blink, realization dawning. I slept with Silas Sinclair. He's not just Ryan's older brother... he's also my future *boss*. I'm done for.

Chapter Thirty-Five

ALANNA

I'm trembling as I walk into Sinclair Security, my cheeks blazing as memories of Silas and me run through my mind. What was I thinking? How could I have slept with him knowing who he was?

"Good morning," Amy says, a smile on her face. She glances down at her tablet for a moment before tipping her head toward the elevator. "We're going to get your biometrics put into the system, and then you'll receive your company phone and laptop. I've got your training schedule and department details here, too."

I open my mouth to ask for more information, but she smirks and holds up her finger, silencing me before I have a chance to say anything at all. "You'll have to wait. Sinclair Security is big on proper procedure, so I'm not allowed to tell you anything until all the final paperwork has been taken care of."

I nod and follow her, my nerves somewhat settled as she shows me around and finishes up my intake procedures. This company is so huge that there's little to no chance of me running into Silas on a regular basis, right? I don't think I can face him after last weekend. Just as I've begun to relax, Amy leads me back into the elevator and presses the button for the top floor.

"Why are we going there?" I ask hesitantly, fear evident in my voice.

She smirks. "The Ψ division is located on the top floor. It's our most prestigious department, and the only one that gets to work directly with the boss."

I let my eyes fall closed for a moment and draw a shaky breath. *No*. This cannot be happening. Of course I applied for the one division that works directly with Silas.

"You don't look excited," Amy says, a hint of confusion in her tone.

"I... um, is it possible for me to switch divisions?"

Amy chuckles and shakes her head. "You're a perfect fit for the Ψ division, you'll see."

I bite down on my lip nervously. It isn't the division I'm worried about. It's Silas. The last thing he and I need is to be around each other. I don't even know how to face him now. He's my ex's older brother and my boss. I shouldn't know what he looks like naked... I shouldn't know what it feels like when he's deep inside me.

By the time the elevator doors open, I'm shaking. I'm bound to do or say something stupid, or I'll make things awkward between us. I can't afford to lose this job, and being around Silas pretty much guarantees that I will.

"Here we are," Amy says, placing her tablet down on an empty table. "Meet Jessica and Josh, your team members." They wave at me briefly before turning back to their work, both of them looking overwhelmed and overworked. The atmosphere is definitely very tense. "The Ψ department is incredibly small because each person here is hand selected by the boss. There are a few team members who are currently working at a client site, so you probably won't meet them for another few months, and then there's me. I'm not officially part of this team, but I assist where I can."

I nod, taking note of everything she's telling me.

"This entire floor has flexible seating, so you can pick whichever desk is free. We do that because you won't always be working with the same team members, and you might not be able to disclose what you're working on even within your team. The Ψ division is somewhat different. It's the department that's closest to all the rumors you hear about Sinclair Security. They truly handle Black Ops. Not even I know exactly what everyone works on. This is the department with the highest clearance, salary and perks, but it's also the department with the longest working hours and the highest level of confidentially, hence the various non-disclosure agreements you've been asked to sign."

I nod nervously and tuck a strand of hair behind my ear.

Amy smiles at me, a look of understanding in her eyes. "You'll be fine, Alanna. Every person on this team was handpicked by the boss."

That's exactly what I'm afraid of. What motive does Silas have for accepting me onto this team? Was it truly because I passed his test? Could it be that simple?

"Follow me," Amy says. "Mr. Sinclair told me to bring you to his office once we finished up with all the admin and onboarding."

Oh no. *No, no no.* Before I can even think of an excuse, she's knocking on Silas's door. Amy grins as she opens the door, not realizing that I'm mentally losing it. I don't think I've ever wanted to sink through the floor more than I do in this moment, yet I try my hardest to paste on a poker face as I follow her in.

Silas looks up from the papers on his desk, and I pause in the middle of his office. Damn it. Why does he have to look so good in that suit? This man is the devil. That look in his eyes instantly transports me back to the night we shared, and a shiver runs down my spine.

"Alanna." The way he says my name has my heart skipping a beat. He's a danger to my sanity.

"Mr. Sinclair."

He smirks and glances at Amy. "I need that report I requested a bit sooner than expected. Do you think you could start working on it right now?"

She glances at me briefly before nodding. "Of course, boss."

No, don't leave, I silently beg, but she merely smiles and walks away.

I'm unsure how to behave, unsure what to say. When I headed to work this morning, I was so sure I'd be able to keep it together, but now that I'm standing in front of him, I'm nervous and scared. I have no doubt my cheeks are bright red, too.

"Alanna."

I look up at him and swallow hard as I square my shoulders. I still remember the way he looked at me in the mirror as he pushed into me. I remember the way his lips felt against mine, and even worse… I want another taste of him.

"Mr. Sinclair," I mutter, my voice lacking the confidence I tried to inject in it.

He chuckles and shakes his head. "Call me Silas, like you did last weekend."

My eyes widen, and I shake my head. "I can't. We never should've… can we please just forget that even happened? *Please.*"

"You regret sleeping with me?" His tone is harsh, and when my eyes meet his, all I see is anger in his gaze.

"Don't you? I'm your brother's ex. It never should've happened."

"Alanna, even if I wanted to, I'm not going to forget about the way your lips felt around my cock or the way you moaned my name. You were hungry for my cock, baby, and you know it. That pussy of yours is the best I've ever had, and I won't pretend otherwise."

I stare at him in shock, my cheeks blazing. "It was barely memorable," I lie. "I've had better."

Silas sits up, his eyes flashing with anger. He looks away, but not before I catch a hint of agony in his gaze. It hits me straight in the chest and makes me wish I could take my words back.

"I see," he says simply. "It looks like I'm the only one who was affected then, huh? Very well. I read too much into it, clearly. As you wish, I'll pretend nothing happened. You'll be working directly with me, after all."

I nod, but I feel oddly defeated, even though I got exactly what I wanted. I watch Silas as he runs a hand through his hair and sighs. He looks... *hurt*, and my own heart aches in response.

"Has Amy informed you about our mentorship programme?"

I nod, unable to face him.

"Congratulations," he says drily. "You'll be my mentee from today onwards, meaning you'll be shadowing me closely. I'll be overseeing your training myself, and I'm far stricter than most of our other mentors. I expect you to be at your best, every single day. Fail to meet my standards, and you can kiss your job goodbye."

I tense and narrow my eyes at him, my earlier remorse fading away. "Did you become my mentor so you could find a way to get rid of me? I promise you that I won't let my personal life interfere with work, so there's no need for you to worry. I'm not going to give you a chance to fire me. This job is everything I've ever wanted, and I won't let you down, no matter what you throw at me."

He stares at me for a moment, his eyes moving over my face. "You think you have what it takes to be part of the Ψ division?"

My confident smile wavers for a moment. I don't think I'm worthy of being here, but now that I *am* here, I'm going to fight to maintain my place. This is my dream job, and I won't let him sabotage it for me. "I do, and I'll prove it to you."

He looks away and nods. "We'll see. This department is only for the best of the best. It only takes a small mistake to lose your job... and I'll be watching you closely."

I cross my arms, mimicking him. "Watch me all you want. You won't catch me slipping."

His eyes roam over my body, and then he chuckles. "Well... I do love watching you."

I stare at him in shock for a moment, heat rushing to my cheeks as I remember the way he looked at me in the mirror. "You... I..."

"Yeah?" His voice is husky, his eyes filled with that same look he wore when he took me home.

I shake my head, praying I'm not blushing. "I look forward to learning from you," I tell him, a wide smile on my face.

He chuckles and nods. "And I look forward to teaching you a lesson or two."

My eyes widen a fraction, and then I shake my head. He's trying to get a rise out of me, and I won't give him the satisfaction. Instead, I merely nod at him before turning and walking away.

There's nothing he can throw at me that I can't handle. He thinks he can get rid of me easily, but he's wrong. Silas Sinclair doesn't know it yet, but he's met his match. I won't go down easily.

Chapter Thirty-Six

Alanna

Yesterday was my first official day of work, but since it mostly consisted of setting up my laptop and learning about the numerous company rules and security measures, I didn't do any actual work. I'm nervous and worried about far too many things that shouldn't even be a factor. I keep thinking of Silas and the way he touched me last weekend, the way he provoked me in his office. Then my thoughts inadvertently turn to Ryan, and shame hits me hard.

I run a hand through my hair as I walk toward where Jessica and Josh are seated. From what I understand, I'll be receiving my first assignment today, and I'm equal parts excited and scared. I'm worried that I truly don't belong in this department, and that it'll show. My team members all seem so extraordinary, and I don't fit in. Josh graduated at the top of his class at Astor College and then worked for Grayson Callahan's IT firm for years, and Jessica worked for the government before joining Sinclair Security. Though she'll neither confirm nor deny what she did exactly, I know it's something impressive. From what I can tell, our other team members are equally impressive.

"Alanna?" I freeze a few steps away from my desk, my stomach churning at the sound of his voice. *Ryan.* My heart starts to race, a familiar ache making me take a step back. The last time I saw him was when I overheard him talking shit about me... the night I slept with his brother.

"Alanna, what's going on? You broke up with me over text and I haven't been able to reach you since then. What happened? Did someone do something to you? Honey, there's nothing we can't resolve together. There must be a misunderstanding of some sort."

He looks at me with the same gaze that won me over in the first place. When he looks at me like that, it feels like he's laying his soul bare to me, showing me vulnerability that no one else gets to see. He looks so distraught that I find myself second-guessing what I heard that night.

"It's nothing," I murmur, aware of the curious looks we're getting from my team. "This isn't the right time or place to talk about this." Silas must really have had his car towed, or Ryan would've been far more angry with me. Too bad he never saw the damage I did.

Ryan stares at me for a moment and grits his teeth before nodding reluctantly. "Fine, but I won't let you avoid me any longer. We need to talk. *Today.*" He walks past me and straight into Silas's office, and my stomach drops. Surely Silas wouldn't say anything, right? I shouldn't care, but the thought of Ryan finding out what I did fills me with shame.

"So you're the boss's brother's girl, huh?" Josh says. "I was wondering how you got into the Ψ division. We've never had a rookie join."

I stare at him, unsure what to say. "I'm *not* his girl. I get how this looks," I tell him. "But I can assure you that I applied to join Sinclair Security long before I started dating Ryan. Give me a chance, and I'll prove to you that I belong here as much as you do."

I sound much more confident than I feel, and I wonder if Josh realizes it. He looks into my eyes as though he's assessing me, and then he nods before sitting down, dismissing me.

"Don't mind him," Jessica says. "He's just mad he's no longer the youngest on the team. Silas mentored him because he was our newbie, but you've stolen that role and his mentor. He'll get over it at some point."

"Silas used to mentor Josh?"

She nods. "He always mentors our newest team member himself. We've all had the privilege of learning from Silas, but Josh definitely had him as his mentor the longest."

I bite down on my lip, embarrassment washing over me. I accused Silas of mentoring me so he could get rid of me, but that isn't what he's doing at all. He's granting me a privilege, yet I treated it as punishment.

I look up when Ryan storms out of Silas's office. "Alanna!" Silas shouts immediately after, his tone filled with barely restrained anger.

I jump up, and Josh smirks at me. "You're crazy if you think you're going to be treated differently just because you're the boss's sister-in-law. He's going to be just as tough on you as he is on us, so good luck with that. You've just made a terrible impression by letting your boyfriend come here during working hours. You're doomed."

"Shut up, Josh," Jessica says. "The only reason the boss hired you is because he's friends with Grayson Callahan, and you had a personal recommendation from him. So sit your ass down and mind your business."

Josh glares at her, but she merely smirks at me, making me smile in return. "Go," she says. "Best not to keep the boss waiting. He doesn't get mad often, but he has a zero tolerance policy for unprofessionalism. This really wasn't your fault, but you'll be implicated nonetheless. Just beg for mercy. He's not as bad as he seems."

I nod at her gratefully and rush toward Silas's office. Whatever Ryan just said to him can't have been good. Is Ryan going to cost me my job?

"Close the door," Silas snaps.

He grits his teeth and runs a hand through his hair as he walks around the desk. The anger in his eyes has me taking a step back, until I'm backed against the door.

"Explain to me why the fuck Ryan just asked to be transferred to the Ψ division."

He walks right up to me and rests his forearm against the door, caging me in. Silas leans into me and looks into my eyes, a mere inch separating his body from mine. The scent of his cologne washes over me, the familiar smell sending a rush of desire through me. My heart starts to race, memories of the two of us dancing through my mind.

"I don't know," I tell him honestly.

Silas smiles humorlessly and lifts his free hand to my face, cupping my cheek tenderly despite the fury in his eyes.

"You don't know, huh?" He murmurs. His thumb brushes over my lip, and my breathing accelerates. I can't think straight when he's this close. "He told me you two had an argument, and he wants a chance to make it up to you. Ryan all but begged me to let him join the Ψ division. He doesn't seem to be under the impression that you two are over."

Silas's fingers slowly trail from my cheek to my ear before he tangles them through my hair. He tightens his grip and tilts my face toward his, making my body arch toward him until my breasts brush against his chest. "You saw the text I sent him," I remind him. "I broke up with him before you took me home. I swear." There isn't just anger in his eyes, there's pain, too. I can deal with his anger, but I can't stand the thought of hurting him. It's irrational, and it's crazy, but my heart aches when he looks at me that way.

Silas takes a step toward me, pressing his body against mine so I'm fully trapped between him and the door behind me. "I did see that text, but I have no idea what you've said to him since."

I look into his eyes, trying to decipher his expression. "Why do you care?" I ask, my voice soft. "Even if I get back together with Ryan, why do you care?"

"You won't."

I narrow my eyes at him. "What makes you so sure? He and I have history together."

"*History*," he repeats mockingly, his tone low and angry. "You want to know why I'm so sure, baby?"

I nod against better judgement, and Silas smiles. He untangles his hand from my hair and smirks as his fingers trail over my neck, down to my collarbone, until he's brushing over my nipples. I bite down on my lip, resisting the urge to arch my back in a silent plea for more. "It's because he can't fuck you like I can. After being with me, you won't go back to him." I feel him harden against me, and my pussy clenches at the memory of him inside me. "Your body won't let you. You're standing here in my office, your pussy soaking wet for me when I've barely even touched you. You pretend you want to forget about that night, but you can't. It replays in your mind, over and over again, just like it does in mine. That's why you won't go back to him. The question is... have you made that clear to him?"

I laugh nervously and try my hardest to control my breathing. He's right. I haven't been able to look at him without wanting him, and I'm not even remotely thinking of getting back with Ryan. Even worse, I'm not even heartbroken when I should be. Silas consumes all of my thoughts, making the pain fade away. "You're so full of yourself. I haven't thought about you once since that night, and no, Silas, I'm *not* wet for you. If anything, I'm just embarrassed on your behalf."

He chuckles, some of his earlier anger replaced by lust. He leans into me, his lips brushing over my ear. "Your nipples are so hard, I can feel them straight through your bra," he whispers.

"The next time you want to pretend you don't want me, make sure your body isn't betraying you."

He pulls away, looking far too pleased with himself, and I cross my arms, hiding my goddamned traitorous nipples from him. Silas smiles at me, and there's something about that smile that hits me right in the chest. His earlier worries seem gone, and I shouldn't care about that, but I do. Something about our interaction just now set him at ease, and I really shouldn't encourage this, but I'm just relieved he's no longer angry.

"Come on," he says. "You're attending a meeting with me. After that, I'll brief you on your first project."

He smirks as he walks back to his desk to grab his briefcase, and I stare at his back. Silas Sinclair... he'll be the death of me, and I'm scared I'll go willingly.

Chapter Thirty-Seven

ALANNA

I frown when I notice the pile of clothes at the entrance of my building. This... this is all *mine*. Why the hell are my clothes on the street? I bend down to pick up as much as I can, only to freeze in shock when my landlord walks out of the building carrying a box filled with my belongings. "Mr. Smith?" I ask, confused. "What is going on?"

He smiles at me, but it doesn't reach his eyes. "Sorry, kiddo. I'm going to have to evict you."

"*What*?" I stare at him, struggling to comprehend what he's telling me. "Why? I've never missed a rent payment. You haven't even given me any notice or warnings."

He shrugs and drops the box he's holding to the floor, sending some of my books flying out of it. "You're subletting, kid. I don't have to give you shit. I want you and your things out of here. *Now*."

I start to tremble and tears gather in my eyes. It took me weeks to find this place, and it'll be impossible to find something this cheap quickly. Even if I do, it might not be safe, and I can't afford anything more expensive until I get my first paycheck. "Where am I supposed to go?"

I see a hint of sympathy in his eyes, but it's gone before I can utter another word. "Not my problem," he says, shrugging. "I've already had the locks changed, so don't bother trying to get into the studio." I watch as he walks back into the building, the door slamming closed behind him.

I sink down to the floor, surrounded by every single thing I've ever owned, all of it scattered over the floor. A hint of something I can't quite place flickers through my mind, filling me with pure agony. Memories of a hall filled with bunk beds and dim lights, a man's voice calling my name… just as I think the memory will solidify, it's gone, leaving me feeling empty.

I have nowhere to go, no one to turn to. There are a few people I know from college, but I'm not close enough to anyone to ask for help. The only person I've ever dared to rely on was Ryan, but I can't call him. I won't.

I gather my things together as I try to think of a solution. There's one place I can go to right now. If nothing else, that'll give me a few hours to figure out what my options are. I bite down on my lip as I open up the ridesharing app on my phone and order a taxi to Sinclair Security.

If I get caught sneaking into the office after hours with all of my belongings in tow, it isn't just my pride that'll be at risk. It's my job too. Sinclair Security doesn't condone a lack of professionalism, and I've already angered Silas once. But what else can I do?

I'm terrified as I walk into the building, my arms trembling under the weight of the boxes I'm carrying. Just a few more steps until the elevator. *Please*, I silently beg. *Please don't let anyone see me.*

For once, my luck holds up, and I make it to my floor undetected. I place my boxes underneath the desk I used today and sink into my chair, trying my best to keep from crying.

At times like these, I find myself wondering if there's anyone out there who misses me, who'd want to be there for me... but then I remember that in all these years, no one has ever come looking for me.

I grab my phone, wondering if there's anyone I could call, only to find twenty-two missed calls from Ryan. I unlock my phone and frown at the countless messages he's sent me.

Ryan: *Where are you?*

Ryan: *Why aren't you picking up?*

Ryan: *I'm in front of your house*

Ryan: *Please, can we talk?*

Ryan: *Seriously, Alanna. Where are you?*

Ryan: *Call me as soon as you see this*

Ryan: *I'm worried, honey*

I hesitate for a moment. If I asked, he'd help me. He might have been talking shit about me, but he's never actually treated me badly otherwise, and even though I've been going out of my way to avoid him lately, he hasn't stopped trying to contact me. I don't have anyone else I can turn to. He's all I've got.

"*Alanna*?"

I tense, a surge of panic rushing through me. My heart starts to race and my stomach drops, fear rendering me speechless.

"What are you doing here at this hour?"

I turn to face Silas, trying my best to keep from trembling. Tears start to gather in my eyes, and though I try my best to keep them in, I can't keep them from spilling. He told me I'd lose my job if I messed up in the slightest, and I barely lasted a week. Showing up even remotely hungover can cost you a job, let alone this. Using company assets for personal purposes is strictly prohibited, and I've definitely crossed the line. "Please," I beg. "Let me explain. Please don't fire me, Silas. *Please*. I swear I can explain."

He walks up to me and places his hands on my shoulders, his gaze reassuring. "Okay," he says. "I won't fire you."

I blink in surprise, and he nods at me. "I won't fire you, Alanna. Just tell me what's going on, okay?"

"I... I was evicted without notice. I had nowhere to go, and I know this is unprofessional, but I just came here because I needed somewhere to think. I won't stay here, I swear. It had started to rain, and I just didn't know where to go. I'm so sorry. I know you want to get rid of me and you have a zero tolerance policy for unprofessionalism. I know that... but please, *please*... I-I'll call a friend now to come get me."

He looks into my eyes and takes a step closer to me. I tense when he cups my cheeks and sighs, his thumbs swiping at my tears. "Get rid of you, huh? Your mind really is quite peculiar. I wonder how you came to that conclusion, little overthinker." He runs a hand through his hair and sighs. "Come with me," Silas says, his voice soft yet firm. He grabs my hand and pulls me along before I can protest.

"Where are we going?" I ask when he leads me to the elevator. I'm scared he's personally escorting me out of the building, and I don't know how to convince him to let me stay.

He tightens his grip on my hand and pulls me into the parking garage. Before I realize what's going on, he's holding the door to his bright red Ferrari open for me. I stare at him in confusion, and he tilts his head toward the door. "Get in," he orders.

I don't dare object and cautiously get into the car, scared of dirtying his seats somehow. I've already destroyed one of his cars. He won't let me off if I damage another.

Silas gets in beside me and leans over me as he reaches for my seatbelt, his face inches from mine. I inhale sharply when my eyes meet his. He smiles, and I look away as he fastens my seatbelt for me. He doesn't seem angry, and the tenderness in his gaze takes the edge off my anxiety.

"Where are you taking me?" I whisper, my heart uneasy. Something about today's situation makes me feel restless. It's almost like being thrown out of my studio flat rubbed salt into wounds I didn't know existed. I feel heartbroken, and it's about more than just being evicted. It's got something to do with my lost memories, but I can't figure out how or why. Have I been in this situation before?

"I'm taking you home, baby," Silas says as he starts the car.

Chapter Thirty-Eight

Silas

My heart races as I hold the passenger door open for Alanna. What would have happened if I hadn't been at the office tonight? Where would she have gone? Thoughts of her with Ryan assault me, and my stomach churns. Would she have gone back to him?

"Silas," she whispers, a hint of fear in her voice. It kills me to see so much insecurity in her eyes and no acknowledgement of everything we used to be. She has no idea what she means to me.

"I have a spare bedroom," I murmur, my heart heavy. "Since you're shadowing me at me work, I prefer for you to be on call 24/7. Josh stayed in that room more nights than I can count, and so will you."

She stares at me as though she doesn't believe me, and I can hardly blame her. Josh was my mentee for nearly two years, but in that time, he only stayed here a handful of times. It was only ever when we were swamped with highly confidential work that he'd stay the night.

"Josh stayed here too?"

I nod and walk away before she can question me further.

Alanna has always had an uncanny ability to see straight through my lies. She might not remember me, but I have no doubt that deep down, her heart still beats with mine.

I lead her through the house and pause in front of the guest room, holding the door open for her. It's a nice room, done up in neutral colors, yet filled with the same luxury that surrounds the rest of this place. This home is my sanctuary, and that extends to this guest room. It's another room that's a fulfilled fantasy she can't even remember. She doesn't know it, but she designed this room, back when all we had was a handful of dreams.

Her gaze wanders over the interior, her discomfort apparent in the way she wraps her arms around herself. I'd give the world to take her in my arms right now and hold her until she's feeling better.

"Alanna, you haven't even received your first paycheck yet, so you won't be able to put a deposit down, even if you find a place. I doubt you can afford a hotel, and I'm not so heartless that I'll have you stay somewhere unsafe. If you're worried about what people might say, then I'm happy to keep you staying here a secret. Will that make you feel better? It's not like Josh and I informed anyone whenever he'd stay over."

She stares at me, her expression unreadable. "I want to say no, Silas... but I have nowhere else to go. Would you let me stay here until I find somewhere to live? In the meantime, I can pay you rent, and I can help with chores, too."

I smile at her even though my heart is aching. What would she say if I told her I designed this place with her in mind? This penthouse is everything we've ever wanted, our every dream and fantasy come true. This is exactly where she's supposed to be.

"Just do some of the chores," I murmur. "If you do that, I'll consider that payment for the spare bedroom. Stay as long as you want." *Ideally, forever.*

She starts to object, and I shake my head. "Do you have any idea how expensive a housekeeper is? It's a good deal for me."

Alanna hesitates, clearly unwilling to commit to living here, but eventually she nods. "Okay," she whispers. "It'll only be a few weeks. I won't bother you for long at all, I promise."

I'm so tempted to take a step closer to her. I want to bury my hand in her hair the way I used to and tip her face up toward mine. I want her body against mine and tell her that I'm never letting her go now that she's finally found her way back to me. But I can't.

"You're not bothering me at all, Alanna. Do I seem like the kind of man that goes around doing his employees favors? The only reason you're here is because it's more convenient for me, and I happen to need a housekeeper. You don't need to feel obliged, since this is a mutually beneficial deal."

She looks at me and tilts her head, as though she's assessing me. "You say that, but your words are never in line with your actions."

I frown. "What do you mean?"

She smiles tightly and shakes her head. "It's nothing. Would it be okay if I looked around?"

I smirk, unable to help myself. "Didn't you see most of it last time? Or were you too focused on getting my clothes off?"

Her eyes widen, and a blush stains her cheeks pink. "Silas," she says, her voice soft. "You can't... we... we work together, and we'll be living together for a little while too. We can't... please don't bring up that night. I really don't want things to be awkward between us. Please, can we forget about it?"

I take a step back as her words pierce straight through my heart. That night was the first night I truly felt whole again, yet to her it's a shameful memory. How did Alanna and I end up this way?

"I understand," I tell her, and I do. I get it, but there's no way I'm forgetting about that night. She wanted me then, more so than she ever has before, and that couldn't have been fake. She might not remember me, but her body does. "Go ahead and take a look around. Nothing is off-limits to you, so just treat this place as yours."

I force a smile before walking away, needing a moment to myself. What would she do if she knew how much she's hurting me? If she hadn't lost her memories, would things be different now?

I walk into my bedroom and look around, seeing it through fresh eyes. Would I be sharing this bedroom with Alanna, instead of having her sleep a few doors down? I inhale slowly as I sit down on my bed. I won her over once, and I'll do it again.

Her being evicted is one of the best things that could've happened to me, but there's no way this is a coincidence.

I grab my phone and call Amy. "Hey, I need you to find out why Alanna was suddenly evicted from the place she was renting. Something isn't right, and I want to know what it is. Please also send someone over to pick up some boxes from the office and have them delivered to my house."

Chapter Thirty-Nine

Silas

I look up when Alanna walks into the kitchen at seven in the morning, biting back a smile when she freezes, her eyes running over my bare chest. I turn toward her, giving her a better view, and her gaze drops to my low-hanging shorts. If she keeps looking at me like that, I'm going to embarrass myself. She tells me she wants to forget about our night together, but she's clearly lying. I've always been able to see through her lies, and I'm glad that hasn't changed.

Too bad she's already dressed for work. I want to see her in one of my old t-shirts, the ones she used to love. She has no idea how many times I imagined us having a lazy morning together. I'd make her coffee, and she'd sit on the kitchen counter wearing one of my shirts. This isn't the exact future I imagined, but it's close enough to make me smile like a fool.

My eyes roam over her body, taking in the pencil skirt she's wearing and the pink blouse that's just about low enough for me to catch a hint of her breasts, but not low enough to be indecent. She looks sexy as hell, and I almost wish I could just keep her home so her colleagues won't get to see her looking like that.

"Morning," I tell her.

Alanna snaps out of it, her cheeks turning rosy as she bites down on her lip, her gaze wandering all over the kitchen nervously. She clearly still wants me, and that's enough for me. Even though she can't remember me, it's still me she wants. It's still me she instinctively trusts, or she wouldn't be here with me. After years of searching for her, here she is, exactly where I want her to be.

"Morning," she says, her voice so soft I barely hear her.

"Coffee?" I hold up a coffee I'd just made her, and she takes it from me hesitantly. I watch as she musters up the courage to ask me something before shaking her head and raising the cup to her lips. Silly girl. Of course her coffee is oat milk with two shots of espresso and more sugar than she should have. It's exactly the kind of coffee we couldn't afford but that she loved before she lost it all. I wonder what she'd have done if I handed her a black coffee. Why won't she just ask me for what she wants? Do I intimidate her?

Her eyes widen as she takes a sip, and I bite back a smile. "It's perfect," she says, giving me the biggest smile. Fucking hell. She's still so fucking beautiful, and that smile of hers still disarms me. Alanna's smile drops all of a sudden, her delight replaced by confusion. "How did you—"

"I made it for myself," I lie. *Shit.* I need to be careful with my knowledge of her. "I wanted to try out something sweeter, but decided it isn't for me, so you can have it."

She nods as she takes another sip and I lean against the counter, enjoying the way she's sneaking glances at me. It's surreal to me that we're standing here together. She has no idea how happy I am just having her around. I need to find a way to make her stay, because I don't think I can ever let her go again. I don't ever want to spend another morning by myself, not when I can have *this*.

"Wait for me," I tell her. "Let's go to work together."

"Oh no," she begins to say, but I hold my hand up and shake my head.

"Wait for me," I repeat, my tone firm.

Alanna freezes, and I walk away before she's able to throw any excuses my way. I get that she wants to keep our living arrangements a secret, especially because her team is already wary of her. In that regard, she's still the same. She still wants to earn people's respect and loyalty the honest way. Even at the shelter, she always worked harder than anyone else, wanting to earn her right to be there. A lot may have changed in the last five years, but deep down, she's still my Ray.

My thoughts are so filled with her as I get ready that I almost miss the sound of my ringing phone. "Amy?"

"Boss," she says. "I found out that Alanna's landlord was paid ten grand to evict her. The payment was made in cash, but I accessed your brother's bank records, and a few days ago, he took ten grand out of the account you let him use. From what I understand, Alanna has been avoiding him ever since he came to find her at the office, and since I took away his access to the top floor, he was probably getting desperate."

That fucker. He's trying to force her back to him. Thank fuck I was at the office last night, or she really might have gone back to him out of sheer desperation.

"Got it. Good work, Amy. Limit his transactions to $100. Anything above that will require my approval."

I end the call with fury coursing through my veins. This motherfucker put my girl on the streets, nearly putting her through the same hell she barely survived the first time. Maybe Amy is right about him after all. This isn't the first time he's done something that made me question whether I'm just wasting my time trying to salvage our relationship, constantly choosing to see the best in him, even when he proves me wrong. The guilt I feel toward him is the only thing that's holding me back. I haven't just taken his home from him now... I'm taking Alanna back from him too.

I want to confront him, but if I do so, I'll have to admit that I know Alanna was evicted. With her being as wary as she is, I don't want to do anything that'll give him a chance to swoop in and accomplish what he set out to do, forcing her back to him. For the time being, no one can find out that she's living with me. Not until I've convinced her to stay.

Alanna looks up when I walk into the living room, her gaze searching. "What's wrong?"

She still reads me the way she used to. I could never tell how she did it. Even when I try my hardest to keep my emotions from showing, she sees through the facade. What do I tell her? Would she believe me if I tell her about her landlord? I have no concrete evidence, because the money came out of *my* account.

"Nothing. Let's go."

She nods and follows me to the car. I hold the door open for her, enjoying the way her body brushes against mine as she gets into the car.

"I've never seen anything like this, you know? A car lift that goes all the way to your house and parks your car in the middle of the living room. It's very... manly?"

I get into the car and bite back a smirk as I lean over her under the guise of buckling her in. I love how nervous she gets around me, how her breath hitches and her eyes widen. She thinks she's acting reserved, but her body is betraying her in the very best way.

"You don't like it? The floor of the lift is just marble tile, so if there's no car in there, the living room floor is seamless. I can just park the car in the regular garage, where I park the others. It's just that this specific car is quite expensive, so it's an insurance thing."

The seatbelt clicks into place, and she exhales slowly. I just love stealing these little moments with her. I can't push her too far, or she'll just move out and I'll be back at square one, but this much I can do. At some point, she's going to have to admit to herself that she wants me. Even if all she feels for me is lust, I'll take that. The line between love and lust is a blurry one, after all.

"Oh, no. That's not what I meant. I shouldn't have said anything at all. I'm sorry. I just meant that it's pretty cool."

I nod and smirk at her. I'm going to have to find a separate garage for my Ferrari. She definitely doesn't like having it in the living room.

"Your tie is the same color as my blouse," she remarks as I start the car.

I glance over at her, pretending to only just notice her blouse. "Hmm, you're right. We look good together."

Alanna's outraged expression makes me laugh, earning me a look of wonder and astonishment. "I've never seen you laugh before."

She raises her hand to her chest, making me wonder if her heart skips a beat around me, the way mine does when she smiles.

"You'd better enjoy it," I tell her. "It's a rare sight."

She turns to me and rests her cheek against the car's headrest. "How so?"

"For the longest time, there wasn't much in my life to smile about, let alone laugh. For years, I've felt like the most important part of me was missing." *Until now.*

Alanna nods. "Yeah," she whispers. "I know how that feels."

I glance at her and smile. I'm going to have to make it my mission to make her laugh now. One way or another, I want her to feel the happiness she brought back into my life.

"Oh, please stop here, Silas."

I frown. Why would I stop a block away from the office?

"Please, Silas."

I sigh and pull up to the curb. "Why am I stopping here?"

She undoes her seatbelt and smiles nervously. "If we're seen arriving together, everyone will be asking me questions about it and I won't know what to say. When Ryan came to our department, I was teased about it for days on end, including by people I don't even know. I just want to focus on work and not invite more rumors."

I run a hand through my hair in annoyance. If it were up to

me, I'd be shouting from the fucking rooftops that she's living with me, but I don't seem to have a say in this matter. "Fine."

Alanna smiles at me before rushing out of the car, and I shake my head as I watch her for a moment. How long is it going to take to truly make her mine once more? I'm already running out of patience.

Chapter Forty

Silas

Amy's tense expression instantly puts me on edge, and I straighten in my seat. She grimaces as she closes the door behind her, taking a moment before turning toward me, almost as though she's bracing herself.

"What is it?" I ask, my voice soft. "Just tell me."

She nods and clutches her tablet tightly. "I found out where Alanna's scholarship money came from." She walks up to me and puts her tablet down before turning it my way and sliding it over. "You won't believe this, but I triple checked my sources and even asked Aria Callahan to assist me with this, and it's correct. The money came from the man who was convicted for Alanna's father's death."

I pick the tablet up and go through the files, struggling to believe what I'm reading. It looks like he was paid a hundred grand to assist Alanna's father with his insurance fraud.

"He never expected to be caught. They'd planned the hit in detail, but they were caught by an eyewitness. He may not have realized that him confessing in return for a more lenient sentence also meant Alanna didn't get any of the insurance money she would have gotten, and I suppose he felt some remorse. He knew what her father was doing it for, after all. When she lost her memory, he thought a fresh start would be good for her, so he had his family make the arrangements and used some of her father's money on her."

The road to hell truly is paved with good intentions. I understand the sentiment behind the decision that was made, but I'm not sure it was what was best for Alanna. I suppose she got a better education than she would have been able to afford here, but I also lost her in the process.

"Thank you," I tell her.

Amy smiles at me and shakes her head. "Once we learned she'd been in London, it became a lot easier to track down more details. I'm sorry it took so long to find her, but the way she came back definitely seems like fate to me. Her applying to join Sinclair Security when we'd so desperately been trying to find her? I know you don't like to hear these types of things, but maybe it's a matter of it finally being the right place and the right time."

I chuckle and lean back into my seat. "You really are a hopeless romantic, aren't you?"

Amy shrugs. "Your story is the stuff of legends. Do you have any idea how exciting it is for me to watch it unfold in real life? Someday, someone is going to write a book about you two."

I shake my head at her, but before I can even retort, my door opens and Ryan storms in. Amy and I both tense, and she crosses her arms in annoyance.

"Silas," he says, his tone aggrieved. "Why are you doing this to me?"

I frown in confusion and sit up. "What, exactly?"

"I told you that Alanna and I had an argument, and not only did you refuse to let me join her department, you also revoked my access to this floor, so I can't even come see her. I had to wait for someone to take the elevator up to this floor just so I could ride up with them."

I hate having her name in his fucking mouth. I hate that he knows anything about her at all. I glance at my watch, thankful that Alanna is in a meeting right now. I don't even want him seeing her. "My office is not some goddamn playground," I snap. "You can't just go wherever the fuck you please. Besides, you two broke up, didn't you? Am I just supposed to let you harass my employees?"

"It's just a misunderstanding," Ryan says. "It's just temporarily. I hurt her, but I'll make it up to her."

Like hell he will. I won't give him the chance. "Why did you break up? What did you do to her?"

Ryan tenses and shakes his head. "I said some things I didn't mean, but I'll make it up to her, and she'll forgive me. Just please, Silas. Reinstate my access to this floor and please stop limiting my credit card transactions. I tried to send her a large bouquet of flowers today and couldn't even do that."

I frown at him, my finger tapping on my desk. Alanna never told me what he did to her and I didn't want to upset her by questioning her. If it truly is a misunderstanding, is there a chance she might forgive him?

"So this is all about the money?" I ask. Does he think I'll lift the restrictions on his card if he leads me to believe he wants to spend money on Alanna? What game is my little brother playing? Was I truly wrong about him?

Ryan grits his teeth and shakes his head. "No, Silas. It isn't. Not entirely, but yes, that's one of the reasons I'm here. When you bought Mom out and took back the house and all our assets, you told me I wouldn't be impacted by it at all, and that I wouldn't lose the lifestyle I'd gotten accustomed to. You swore to me I'd always have a place to live and that I'd never have to worry about money, so long as I got my act together and stopped partying and drinking. You told me to be a person you could be proud of, and I tried. I've done all I could. I barely drink, I only go out every few weeks, I work for you at Sinclair Security, and I even volunteer once a month. Yet you randomly restricted my credit card. I don't understand what I've done."

I stare at him, wondering if he truly is innocent or if he approached Alanna knowing what she means to me. Was it his mother's orchestrations, or was he in on it? If he's innocent, then I can't hurt him more than I already have. I can't break the promise I made my father.

I run a hand through my hair, torn. I don't want Alanna to remember her past when her brain decided that she's best off without those memories. I don't want to put her through pain or risk distorting her memories, so I can't let him know about my past with her if he truly is unaware. So far, he hasn't given me any indication that he knows about us, but can I trust him? I'm starting to worry that Amy is right about him. I've been so focused on the fact that he's my only remaining family member that I've turned a blind eye to too many things.

"Your credit card is for dinner, groceries, that kind of thing. It isn't for large purchases, that's what I gave you a job for. So why is it you took out 10k in cash?"

Ryan shifts his weight from one foot to the other nervously. "I... um," he stammers, clearly flustered. Maybe I wasn't wrong about him at all. He isn't that good of a liar. If he knew about Alanna and me, he'd have let it slip already.

"I'm not lifting the restrictions until you can tell me what you used the money for. Until then, I need you to get back to work. Do not fuck around at work, Ryan. Do not come here during working hours if you don't have a legitimate reason to be here. You're not exempt from maintaining professional standards just because you're my brother. I *will* fire you."

He looks at me contritely and nods before turning away, his shoulders slumped. The more I observe him, the more certain I am that he's just a puppet in his mother's schemes. He's just an angry kid, like I once was. Mona must have pushed him toward Alanna, but to what end?

Chapter Forty-One

Alanna

I step into the hallway and pause in front of the mirror, my heart racing as memories of Silas and me dance through my mind. I can't look into this mirror without thinking of the way he bent me over in front of it, his eyes on mine as he pushed inside me.

The dress I'm wearing tonight hangs around my frame loosely, and I bite down on my lip harshly as I reach for the zipper on the back. I sigh softly as I stare at my reflection, admitting defeat to the little zipper that refuses to budge.

"Need help?"

I freeze when Silas walks up to me, pausing once he's stood behind me. His eyes find mine through the mirror, our position similar to that night.

"You're home." We've been living together for a few weeks now, and in that time, he's been home at night no more than a handful of times. I see him every morning, but never in the evenings. I'm unsure if he just works late every day, or if he's spending his nights elsewhere.

My gaze roams over his body through the mirror, a dull ache

spreading through my chest at the thought of him spending his nights in someone else's bed. It's irrational, and it's crazy, but I can't help the tinge of jealousy I feel. I keep trying to remind myself that sleeping with him is something I should be ashamed of, something I should regret, but being here in his home just makes me want it more.

Silas takes a step closer to me, his fingers trailing over my bare back as he takes his time to do my zipper up. "Where are you going, dressed like this?" His tone is commanding, a hint of possessiveness laced through it.

"The bar around the corner from the office."

"With who?"

Silas places his hands on my shoulders and looks at me, our reflection staring back at us. Does he feel what I feel?

"Why do you ask?"

He smirks and turns me around, making me face him. Can he tell that I'm nervous? My chest rises and falls rapidly, my body tense. Being this close to him in this private space unnerves me. It makes it so much harder to pretend I don't want him.

"Why can't I ask?"

I smile at him nervously. "Jessica asked me to come. She told me the company does a mixer every month, so I thought it'd be good to go." I haven't really been able to get on well with my colleagues. Since I'm part of the ψ division, I'm not allowed to talk about any of the work I do, which makes it so much harder to have a conversation with any of my colleagues. It doesn't help that rumors spread about Ryan and me dating, so now everyone thinks I'm only here because of him. I'm hoping tonight will give me a chance to set the record straight, if nothing else.

Silas nods. "I'll drive you."

"I... um, I can make my way there myself."

He shakes his head. "I'm heading out, anyway."

I hesitate for a moment before heading to my room to grab my clutch and slip on my heels. I've grown accustomed to seeing him every morning, and it's rarely awkward. We usually just have a coffee together and make some small talk, both of us preoccupied with the day ahead, but tonight feels different.

Silas smiles at me when I walk back into the hallway, his eyes roaming over my body. The flash of lust in his eyes has me clenching my thighs, heat rushing to my cheeks. When he looks at me that way, it gets hard to remember that he's my boss, my ex's older *brother*.

"Let's go," he says, leading me down to the carpark.

"You're taking a different car tonight?"

He nods as he walks toward a blue sports car, holding the passenger door open for me. I'm oddly nervous as I get in. We drive to work together most days, but something about tonight just feels different.

I sneak a glance at his forearms as he starts the car. The sleeves of his shirt are rolled up and the top button of his shirt is undone. Silas always looks neat and professional, but tonight he looks laid back. "Where are you going tonight?" I ask, before I even realize what I'm saying.

I clamp my lips shut immediately, but it's too late. He glances at me, a lazy smirk spreading across his face.

"Why do you ask?" he murmurs, throwing my earlier question back at me.

I smile at him provocatively. "Why can't I ask?"

Silas chuckles and shakes his head. "I'm having dinner with some of our senior staff tonight. I learned early on in my career that the best collaborative ideas come from less rigid settings, so tonight we're doing a strategy session over dinner."

I breathe a sigh of relief and nod. So not a date then. I shouldn't even care, but I can't help the possessiveness I feel. I hate the idea of Silas going on a date with someone. Ever since we slept together, I haven't been able to stop thinking about him. It's like I'm enchanted, wanting more of his touch.

Silas parks the car and steps out, surprising me. I thought he'd just be dropping me off. "I'll go in and say hi," he tells me, following me in.

"Alanna!" Jessica shouts from a small table next to the bar. I grin and wave at her, making my way through the crowd toward her, Silas on my heels. I expected him to leave me the moment we stepped foot inside, but he hasn't.

"Boss?" Jessica shouts, holding a shot glass up in the air. "Wow, you never usually attend these events! So I guess the secret is inviting your sister-in-law, huh?"

I feel Silas tense beside me and glance up at him. His expression looks calm, but I can feel the anger radiating off him. He wraps his arm around my waist and looks into my eyes. "*Sister-in-law?*" he asks, his eyes dropping to my lips. "You were never going to become my sister-in-law," he says, his tone harsh. "Besides, didn't Ryan and you break up before you even started at Sinclair Security? What is this bullshit?"

Jessica giggles, clearly intoxicated. "It's just a *joke*, boss."

He locks his jaw and stares her down. "It's slander."

"Silas," I whisper, placing my hand on his chest. He looks so distressed by her words, and all I want to do is take away his anger. "Just leave it. She's drunk."

He looks into my eyes, his gaze searching, though what for, I'm not sure. He nods but doesn't let go of me, his thumb drawing circles on my waist. I should pull away, but I find myself not wanting to.

"Look who it is!" Josh shouts, walking up to us with even more shots in his hands. Just how long have they been drinking? They're both wasted. Josh holds a shot glass up to Silas, the drink spilling over the edges and onto his shirt. I'm relatively certain that Silas really regrets walking me in now.

He sighs and pulls his arm away to dab at his shirt, and I root through my clutch to find my handkerchief. I raise it to his chest and carefully wipe off the stain, though the damage is already done.

Silas wraps his hand over mine, but his gaze is on the handkerchief. He pulls it out of my hand and stares at the embroidered ψ logo on it.

"Oh! That's not... it's got nothing to do with the ψ division," I tell him. "I'm not some kind of crazy person. This is mine. It's something I've always had."

He looks at me, his gaze intense. "Is that so? You carry this with you everywhere?"

I nod hesitantly. "Is there something wrong?"

Silas shakes his head and hands it back to me with an intimate smile on his face, his eyes filled with affection. "No. Nothing at all."

His fingers brush against mine as I take the handkerchief from him, unable to look away. Silas Sinclair... he's addictive, and I'm not even sure he realizes it.

"I wish I could stay and endure this with you," he tells me, glancing back at my drunk colleagues, "but I need to head out or I'll be late for dinner. Don't be late, okay? And please, don't end up like these two. Let me know when you're done and I'll come pick you up."

I nod at him, unable to deny him even though I know I'll take a taxi home, and then he walks away, leaving me staring after him, my heart racing.

"Damn it! I wanted to ask him about the rumors!" Jessica complains.

I turn back to her and frown. "What rumors?"

"I want to know if it's true that Sinclair Security was founded because of a woman."

Josh nods and holds up his finger. "It was. Everyone knows this," he says, slurring his words.

I frown as I grab one of the shots he's holding. The company was founded because of a woman? Who is she?

White hot jealousy sears through me as I listen to Jessica and Josh's theories, my thoughts drifting. Could any of this be true? What kind of woman could possibly have Silas Sinclair so obsessed?

Chapter Forty-Two

Alanna

I sigh as I flex my fingers, tired from the hours of typing I've done. Sinclair Security was hired to investigate foreign influences on our elections, and our division has been put in charge of social media monitoring. We're supposed to create an algorithm that'll flag fake news, and I've been tasked with the initial design of it. I'm worried I can't pull it off. While I understand how to get this done in theory, I've never had to do something like this in practise.

"Hot damn," Josh mutters, and I glance over to find a beautiful dark-haired woman walking our way. She walks straight to Silas's office, and much to my surprise, no one stops her. "Looks like our boss is taking his *lunch break* early today. What a snack."

"Who is she?" I ask against better judgement.

Josh looks at me in surprise. "Are you serious? She's a supermodel, and our boss's girlfriend. Her name is Raven."

Girlfriend? Silas has a girlfriend? My heart twists painfully as pure venom settles in my stomach. Did he touch me when he belongs to someone else? Is she the reason he's rarely ever home at night? I see him every morning, but that doesn't mean he's sleeping in his own bed. He might just be coming in to change. Once, when I asked why he's rarely home, he told me he's just been busy with work. Was that all a lie?

I tense when the sound of Raven's laughter fills the office, followed by Silas's office door slamming closed. Josh laughs and shakes his head. "Lucky bastard," he mutters.

I try my hardest to focus on my work, but all I can think about is Silas. In my mind, I see the two of them together, his hands on her body, the way they were on mine. This isn't just simple jealousy. It hurts to see him with someone else, and I can't figure out why.

I gather the files on my desk and shuffle them, barely able to think straight. Before I know what I'm doing, I'm out of my seat and halfway to Silas's office. Amy looks up at me, and much to my surprise, she grins at me instead of stopping me from storming into Silas's office.

I open his door with more force than I intended, freezing in the doorway when I see him leaning against his desk, Raven standing in between his legs, her hands on his chest. I grit my teeth as I resist the urge to tear her away from him.

"Alanna," he says, frowning. Silas straightens and gently pushes Raven aside, but it isn't enough for me. I want her out of his sight altogether.

I walk right up to him and put my folder down on his desk with barely restrained anger. "I have some questions about the work you assigned me."

He looks at me, an intimate smile on his face. I'm standing closer to him than is appropriate, but I can't get myself to care. "Is that so?"

"Yes."

"And it couldn't wait?"

I glance at Raven then. She's watching the exchange between us with a curious expression. Just looking at her hurts. She's so beautiful and elegant that it's easy to see why Silas would have fallen for her. The thought of him comparing me to her kills me. When he's been with a woman that beautiful, everyone else must fall short. What am I even doing?

I turn back toward him, my heart aching and my stomach clenching. Why did he sleep with me when he's got a girlfriend? I feel terrible in more ways than one. Never once did it occur to me that I was *the other woman* that night.

I can't stand here and pretend I did nothing wrong. I can't take more from her than I already have. I rarely act impulsively, but today I couldn't stop myself. It's almost like I truly couldn't think straight when I thought of the two of them together, but what right do I have to behave this way?

"You're right," I tell him, my tone defeated. "It can wait."

I turn to walk away, my throat closing up. I never felt this upset about Ryan, so why am I reacting this way now?

Silas grabs my wrist, stopping me in place before I have a chance to escape. "Alanna," he says, his voice soft and intimate. This is how he said my name that night. I turn back toward him but can't get myself to raise my head and look at him.

"Raven, it was lovely seeing you, but I need to get back to work. Let's catch up some other time, shall we?"

She nods and walks away with a smirk on her face, seemingly not at all offended. It's clear she doesn't remotely consider me competition, and for some reason, that just fuels my turmoil.

"Alanna," Silas repeats the moment the door closes behind Raven. He pulls me toward him roughly, and I stumble, ending up in his arms. Before I have a chance to step back, he wraps his arms around me, caging me in.

"Look at me." His tone is harsh, yet there's a hint of the same need I feel. I reluctantly obey, my eyes finding his. "I broke up with her weeks ago. It was never serious in the first place. It was just convenient. That's all it is. She has no feelings for me, and I definitely don't feel a thing for her."

I grit my teeth, unable to restrain my anger. "You asked me if I'd broken up with Ryan and watched me text him. I-I..." I hesitate, unsure what I'm even trying to say. In the end, the right words elude me, and I push against his chest.

Silas lets go of me, but his gaze follows my every move. "Forget it," I tell him. "It's none of my business what you do or who you do it with. I just hate the thought of playing a role in your adultery. If you two were truly over, she wouldn't have been here today."

Silas leans back against his desk, his hands on either side of him. "None of your business, huh? Yeah, I guess it isn't. So you won't mind if I take Raven home and fuck her the way I fucked you? You won't mind hearing her moans in your bedroom?"

His words are like daggers that assault my already battered heart, and I take a step back. I inhale shakily and force a smile onto my face. "Of course I won't mind, Silas. It would be somewhat awkward, though, so please let me know when you have a woman over, and I'll be sure to leave the apartment. As it is, I don't expect to be there for much longer. I'd hate to invade your privacy that way."

He looks at me and shakes his head. "Little liar," he whispers. "The only one you're fooling is yourself."

I bite down on my lip and turn away, rushing toward the door. I need to get away from him. What was I even thinking, storming in here the way I did? Why is it I never act rationally around him? I'm disappointed by my own behavior, yet I can't control the way he makes me act.

"Alanna," he says, and I pause with my hand on the door handle. "You're the only woman I've ever taken to bed in my home. I've never taken a woman I was seeing to the home you and I live in."

I glance back at him, surprised. If that's true, why did he take *me* home? With each interaction, Silas leaves me more and more confused.

Chapter Forty-Three

Silas

I stare at Alanna's bedroom door and sigh. She's been avoiding me since Raven visited my office a few days ago, and I'm not sure what to do. It's clear that she's confused by her feelings for me, and I don't want to push her too hard, because I'm scared she'll run.

Just as I'm about to walk away, a soft sound stops me in my tracks. Is she crying? I hesitate for a split second before pushing her door open. Her room is pitch dark, and I can just about make out the shape of her in bed. She's twisting and turning, her breathing labored. "Si," she groans.

I freeze and stare at her in shock. I never thought I'd hear her call me Si again. I approach her cautiously, my heart pounding loudly. She's fast asleep, but she seems to be dreaming... of *me*.

"Please, Si," she begs, her tone desperate. "*Please*." A tear rolls down her cheek as she whispers my name again.

I lift the covers and slide into bed with her, turning onto my side so I'm facing her. "I'm right here, baby," I whisper. "I'm with you."

Her body relaxes, but her expression remains tense. I lean in and brush the tip of my finger over her scrunched up brows, and slowly but surely, the tension in her body drains away. Alanna sighs and turns toward me, draping her leg over me. "Si," she whispers, a hint of relief in her voice. Is she dreaming of me? She's given me no indication that she remembers me at all, but she's clearly calling for me.

I wrap my arms around her as she snuggles closer, until she's got her head on my chest, the two of us lying together the way we used to. She still fits against me perfectly.

"I've missed you," I whisper, needing to say the words. "I still love you as much as I did then. It's always been you, Alanna."

She snuggles closer, her nose brushing over my neck. I bite down on my lip as she moves against me, wishing I could just turn us over and kiss her the way I've been wanting to. Now that I've finally got her back in my life, it's hard to take it slow. I want everything we've missed out on. I hold her just a little tighter, needing her with a desperation I haven't felt in years. She's the only one who's ever made me feel this way.

Alanna tenses in my arms and I freeze. She pulls away from me, her eyes widening when she sees me. "Silas?"

I look into her eyes, noting the redness in them. "Do you often cry in your sleep?"

Her lips fall open and she looks away, clearly not wanting to answer me. I sigh as I pull her back into my arms. "You don't have to tell me if you don't want to." I rub her back soothingly, and she relaxes in my arms.

"At least once a week," she admits. "Sometimes more often. I can never remember why, but every time this happens, I wake up feeling heartbroken. It feels like my dreams are showing me someone important, but the moment my eyes open, the images fade away. I just know it's someone I love."

"Someone you love?" I ask, my heart aching painfully. I wish I could tell her all about us and the history we share. Would she be mine once more if I tell her the truth?

I bite down on my lip as memories of her crying herself to sleep come to mind, her small frame shaking from the force of her sobs. If Alanna regains her memories, she'll also be reminded of the pain she went through when she lost her father. I can't put her through that. Besides, perhaps this is a blessing. It's a chance to make her fall for me all over again, without the burdens of the past.

"I told you that I lost my memories when I was eighteen, right? I have no memory of anything before that point. I woke up in the hospital with no idea who I was or where I came from. I had a driver's license on me that told me my name, but I could never recover my memory. In all these years, no one has come looking for me, yet I can't help but feel like there's someone out there." She sighs and buries her face in my neck. "But maybe that's just wishful thinking."

"Maybe, but maybe it isn't." I hesitate for a moment and inhale deeply. "What would you do if you met someone who knew all about your past? If you were told about it, there's a high chance you'd never recover your full memory, because there'd be a risk that your real memories would be overwritten by whatever you're told, until you can no longer tell what's real. Would you still want to know?"

Alanna hesitates, her finger drawing circles on my chest the way she used to when she was thinking. She might not remember anything, but she still behaves the way she used to. She's still my Ray in every way that matters.

"No," she says. "I have a feeling that the memories I lost are important and precious ones, and I wouldn't want them to be corrupted. I've spent years by myself and I've done just fine without those memories. Even if I were given the chance, I'd rather wait for them to return to me naturally, without anyone manipulating them."

I nod, unsure how to feel about her answer. "This person you dream about..." I don't even know what I'm asking her. "Who do you think it is?"

She sighs and tilts her head. "I think it's a man. I can only assume it's an ex-boyfriend, but this would've been years ago. He never came looking for me in all this time, and he's probably moved on."

"Impossible," I murmur. "I'm certain he never stopped looking for you, Alanna. There's no way he would've moved on."

She tenses in my arms, and I tighten my grip on her. "That's sweet of you," she whispers. "But we both know it isn't true."

She pushes away from me and sits up. "I'm sorry if I woke you up, Silas. Thank you for consoling me. I... I didn't mean to — I wasn't trying to..."

"I know."

"You should probably go back to your room."

I put my hands behind my head and glance at her. "I'm perfectly comfortable right here."

She looks at me and shakes her head. "You have a girlfriend."

"Do I? When did we agree to start dating, Alanna? I'm all for it. I just wasn't aware. This is definitely a pleasant development."

She looks at me like I've lost my mind, and I can't help but laugh at her expression. I thought I'd set her worries at ease when I told her I wasn't dating Raven, but her insecurities must have gotten the better of her. She's always been one to overthink things, and I should've anticipated that. I love how jealous she gets, because it gives me hope... but I'm going to have to tell her the truth about Raven soon.

Her gaze turns dreamy all of a sudden, reminding me of the way she used to look at me when she thought I wasn't looking. "You laughed again."

"It's an unfortunate side effect of being around you. You're ruining my broody imago."

Alanna stares at me, and I lift my hand to her face, stroking her cheek with the back of my fingers. "I swear to you, Alanna. I don't have a girlfriend. I'm not seeing anyone. Not now, and not when I took you to bed, either." From the moment I found her, she's been all I can see. Even when she brought my brother to my home for dinner, being with someone else never even occurred to me.

"You never took me to *bed*," she whispers accusatorially.

I smirk. "I'm happy to remedy that."

She looks like she's about to snap at me, so I pull her back to me and hug her tightly. "I'm tired," I say, my voice soft. "Let's go to bed."

I expect her to fight me on this and kick me out, but instead she settles against me and nods. Part of her still wants me, and not just physically. It might take time, but I have no doubt she and I can get back to where we used to be. Day by day, I'm going to steal tiny pieces of her heart, until one day, she's mine again.

Chapter Forty-Four

Silas

I grin at the text messages Alanna sent me, rereading them for the thousandth time today. We woke up together this morning, and she's barely looked me in the eye all day. She's been awkward and tense at the office, yet her texts tell a different story.

Alanna: *I was just wondering if there's any chance you'd make it home for dinner tonight?*

Silas: *If you want me home, I'll be home.*

Alanna: *It's okay if you're busy. I just wanted to repay you for consoling me last night. Usually that kind of dream leaves me feeling hurt and upset the entire next day, but thanks to you, I'm feeling fine today.*

Silas: *I'm never too busy for you, Alanna.*

Alanna: *Then... would you have dinner with me tonight? I can cook for you, if you'd like?*

I chuckle to myself, my heart skipping a beat every time I read this text. It's been hard, taking things slow with her, but moments like these make it all worth it.

Silas: *I'll see you at home tonight then.*

I wonder if she has any idea how many of my mundane fantasies she's realizing. Simple things like having dinner together in a home of our own... that's what I've always wanted.

I'm smiling as I finally walk through the front door, barely managing to contain my excitement. Amy had to make a lot of changes to my schedule in order to free up tonight, but it's worth it. I don't care how long ago some of my meetings were arranged. They aren't as important as this.

I follow the smell of something delicious to the kitchen and find Alanna standing behind the stove, wearing a loose t-shirt and some cotton shorts. She looks cute as hell.

"Smells good," I murmur.

She whirls around, her eyes wide. "Silas! You're home earlier than expected." She looks down at her clothes and grimaces, making my heart skip yet another beat.

"You look beautiful just the way you are," I tell her, and she bites down on her lip in an attempt to hide her smile. Fuck. I've waited so long for this. She's kept me at a distance for so long, and for a while I worried I wouldn't be able to win her over. Watching her cheeks redden over such a simple compliment has me all kinds of excited.

I lean back against the counter and pull my tie loose. "Besides, weren't you the one who asked me if I'd like to have dinner with you?"

She nods, her cheeks tinged pink. "I lost track of time, and I didn't actually think you'd say yes. I've been here for a few weeks now and I can count the times you had dinner at home on one hand."

"I've spent every evening in the last couple of weeks socializing with clients, but today my schedule was free for once, so this worked out perfectly. What are you cooking?"

She smiles at me awkwardly. "It's spaghetti bolognese, and I know that sounds a little boring, but I made the sauce myself and it's going to be amazing."

I nod, my heart racing as I try my hardest not to stare at her. I wish I could spend more evenings at home with her, but my schedule is jam-packed. I didn't use to mind it, because I never used to have anyone to come home too, but it's different now. Somehow, I'm going to have to find a way to work a little less. I want more of this.

I take a seat by the kitchen island and watch her as she cooks, humming a tune I don't recognize. This was part of our fantasies. We'd work, and then we'd come home and cook dinner together. It's the simple things in life we wanted most. Does a small part of her remember?

"So, what is this all about?" I ask, curious. "Not that there needs to be a reason for us to have dinner together. I was just curious."

Alanna puts the knife down and looks up at me, her expression sincere. "I genuinely just wanted to thank you. It's hard for me to explain, but a dream like the one I had last night can truly ruin my entire week. Often I'll find myself trying so hard to remember what I dreamed of that I get the worst headaches, and it makes me unable to focus on anything else in life. But somehow, it was different today. Instead of feeling heartbroken and empty, I felt oddly... complete. Usually, it's almost like there's a huge chunk of *me* missing, and it's not just about my memories. But I didn't feel that way this morning."

I smile at her, wishing I could just come clean and tell her everything. "Hey, maybe it's because I'm the man of your dreams? Are you having wet dreams about me, Alanna?"

She grins at me and picks her knife back up. "To be fair," she says. "The only wetness you can draw out of me *is* tears. I guess that explains why I woke up crying, huh?"

My lips fall open, and I point a finger at her. "Alanna, I feel like I need to defend my honor here. If you weren't holding a knife, I'd walk over there, spread your legs right on top of this kitchen counter, and show you just how wet you can get for me."

Her eyes darken, but then confusion flickers through them.

She puts the knife down and rubs her temples, her eyes falling closed. "Defend your honor?" she whispers.

I freeze. That's an inside joke of ours and I said it without thinking. I didn't think it'd trigger a memory. I walk around the kitchen island and wrap my arm around her waist. "Hey," I whisper. "What's wrong?"

She drops her head to my chest and inhales deeply. "It's nothing," she whispers. "It's just... sometimes random words make my head hurt. Almost like a part of me wants to remember, but a larger part of me refuses to." She pulls away and looks at me. "Sorry, Silas. It really is nothing." She takes a step away from me, and I reluctantly let her go. "Come on, the food is pretty much done, anyway. I've already set the dining table."

She's quiet as she plates our food, and I help her carry it all to the dining room, both of us silent. She's lost in thought now, and I can't help but wonder if she remembered something. I never even realized that it physically hurts her to recall anything about us at all, and it fills me with guilt.

Alanna is absentminded as she takes a bite, and I'm worried. "Are you sure you're okay?" I ask.

She nods and smiles at me sweetly. "Yeah. This happens every once in a while, but it's all fruitless. I never remember anything, no matter how hard I try. For a really long time, I was so obsessed with my past that I forgot to live in the present, and I no longer want to do that. It isn't easy, having so very few memories, but it is what it is. I guess that's why it was so hard for me to find out that Ryan had been using me. I know you don't like hearing about him, but he's the only one I really have memories with, so finding out he used me just hit me so hard. I spent so long chasing my memories, and the moment I decided to stop doing that, I placed my trust in the wrong person. It left me feeling scared to trust anyone, to trust myself. After all, I trusted the wrong person once and I never even realized it, so what if it happens again?"

I look into her eyes, unsure how to reassure her. Without her memories, she doesn't have her previous life experience to fall back on, and that's what shapes our decision making. I know she's instinctively still making the right choices, but it must be hard not being able to logically think through why she does things or why she feels a certain way, especially for an over thinker like Alanna.

"That night... you never told me how he hurt you, and I haven't brought it up because I didn't want to upset you. Will you tell me what he did?"

She nods. "He didn't cheat on me, if that's what you thought. He used me to create a better image of himself for you. I overheard him saying that he was only dating me because I'm exactly the kind of girl you'd like, and that you wouldn't believe he'd changed overnight, but you'd believe it if it was because of a girl. Maybe I shouldn't have reacted the way I did, but it just really hurt, because it made me wonder if anything we had was real."

So he was knowingly using her against me, but why her? It looks like my little brother isn't as innocent as I'd hoped, and I'm not sure what to do with that information. "How did you two meet?" I ask, not wanting to hear about the two of them, but needing to know so I can set my worries at ease.

"Ryan told you we met at the beach one day, right? I volunteer to gather plastic once a month, and one day he showed up with his mother. She and I made small talk, and she kept telling him to be more like me, and that he should learn from me if he wants to clean up his act. I just thought it was funny, the way she somewhat jokingly berated him. At the end of the day, he asked if we could hang out, and we just chatted for a bit. That was it, really."

That can't have been a coincidence. Mona must have gone there knowing Alanna was there, but how did she find her before I did? How did she know about Alanna at all?

"Did you see Mona often?"

Alanna shakes her head. "Not at all. Just that first time at the beach, and then at your house for dinner. Why do you ask?"

I shake my head. "It's nothing. I was just curious."

She smiles and takes a bite of her pasta, the two of us eating in silence, both of us lost in our own thoughts.

"Oh! I forgot to tell you," she says, dropping her fork. "I found a few places I think could work, so I won't be bothering you much longer."

The mere thought of her leaving has my heart aching. "Don't leave," I murmur, my tone pleading. "There's plenty of space here, and as you've noticed, I'm rarely home. There's no need for you to leave."

She looks up at me, wide-eyed. "I, um, I can't stay here."

"Why?"

She blinks, as though she isn't quite sure herself. "It isn't appropriate, and I don't want to invade your privacy." Her expression turns anguished, and I know exactly what she's thinking of.

"You were jealous last week, weren't you?" I murmur. "You brought Raven up last night too. Did her coming to the office really bother you that much?"

I wonder if she has any idea how hard it was for me to see her with Ryan, the two of them sitting opposite each other in my own goddamn home. I don't want her to hurt the way I did, but part of me is glad that she's jealous too. It gives me hope.

Her head snaps up, her eyes wide. "*No,*" she denies. "I wasn't jealous."

I nod and bite back a smile when she shoves her plate away, her expression serene but her demeanor betraying her. "I thought the way you stormed into my office was pretty cute. The way your eyes flashed with possessiveness was hot. Honestly, I really wanted to kiss your anger away."

Alanna looks away, her expression flustered, and I can't help but smirk. She's so fucking cute. Every time I worry about our future together, she gives me a little sign that proves she still cares. She might not understand why, but she does.

"Alanna, Raven and I never truly dated," I tell her. I was going to keep this from her because the jealousy she shows me is evidence of the feelings she has for me, but I can't hurt her like this. "I admit that I slept with her a handful of times throughout the years, but only ever when she and I were both drunk enough to—" *to pretend the person in our arms was someone else.* "She and I… we're just friends. We realized that people left us alone whenever we were seen together, so we pretended to date simply to make both our lives easier. Inevitably, Raven would decide that she wanted to date someone for real in an effort to get over the person she's in love with, and we'd part ways. The rumor mill is one we fueled ourselves, on purpose. Raven and I don't have feelings for each other. Our relationship isn't what the world thinks it is. It isn't what *you* think it is."

Alanna looks at me, her eyes widening as relief sets in. How do I explain to her that the only person I've ever loved is her? How do I convey that the only times I gave in were when I was convinced she'd simply left me to pursue a better life?

"I want you, Alanna," I admit. "I've wanted you for far longer than you can imagine, and your past with my brother doesn't change that."

She looks down at her plate and shakes her head. "And this is why I need to leave," she whispers. "Because a part of me wants you too, and we can't go there. The entire company knows me as Ryan's ex-girlfriend, and you're my *boss*. If things go wrong, they'd go *really* wrong, and we can't afford for that to happen. This job means everything to me, Silas. Besides, do you really want to hurt your brother like that? Us being around each other outside of work is a terrible idea."

I shake my head and inhale deeply. "Or it's a great idea, baby. No one needs to know. This is our own space, separate from work. Ryan has no access to my home, so it's not like he can show up here."

She looks into my eyes, clearly tempted, yet she shakes her head. "I can't. It was wrong of me to sleep with you that night, and with us living together the lines are blurring even more. I don't know what it is about you, Silas… I know I should walk away, yet I keep finding myself gravitating toward you. It's wrong, and I hate myself for it, but I can't stop myself either. I know I should leave, but I desperately want to stay."

"Then stay," I whisper. "Just stay with me, Alanna. Stop looking for a place to live, and just let me take care of you. I won't lie and pretend I don't want you, but I won't actively pursue you if that's not what you want. So just stay with me."

"Aren't you worried about hurting your brother? You and I… we barely know each other. What is it about me that makes it worth the risk? Ryan will never forgive you if he finds out. You're his *brother*, Silas. That's not a relationship you can just walk away from."

I look into her eyes, trying to figure out the best way to answer her. "Alanna, all I know is that I feel like myself around you. You say that you aren't sure why you gravitate toward me, and it's the same for me. I don't know why I want you so badly, why you make me smile like no one else ever has before, and I'm not sure why I want you in my space when I've always loved being alone, but I do."

"I don't get it," she whispers. "Why me?"

I lean back in my seat, my eyes roaming over her face. I've missed her so fucking much. As the years passed, I wondered if I'd even want her as badly when I finally found her, if perhaps we'd find we've outgrown each other, but no. I still need her as much as I need the air that fills my lungs.

"Because you're the only woman who's ever made me smile when it feels like breathing is near impossible. You breathe live into my broken heart, mending my soul when I thought it was forsaken. You do something to me that no one else can, and I don't know how or why, but I know I can't get enough of it."

Alanna bites down on her lip, her cheeks flaming. Sitting opposite me at the table, she's never looked more beautiful.

"So stay," I whisper. "Stay here with me."

Chapter Forty-Five

Alanna

I look up from my desk when Silas walks in. He smiles at me, and my heart skips a beat. All I've been able to think about all day is the way he looked when he asked me to stay. I've analyzed our situation countless times in my head, but he doesn't stand to gain anything by being with me. He doesn't seem to be lying about wanting me either, but I find it hard to believe he'd be willing to hurt Ryan over me. Unless he's just after a secret fling? But if that's the case, why would he want me to live with him?

I think back to the way he held me after I woke up from my dream. Every time I'm around him, I find myself doing things that are out of character for me. I've never sought out company after a dream like that, yet being in his arms made me happy. It set my restless heart at ease.

I can't figure out what's so different about Silas. Is it because I slept with him? Or is it the kindness he always shows me, despite his rough manner? I'm not sure what it is, but I feel safe and comfortable around him. It's a feeling that's eluded me ever since I woke up in the hospital five years ago. He makes me want to stay with him, even though I know better.

"Alanna?"

I'm snapped out of my thoughts by the last voice I wanted to hear. "Ryan?"

"Can I speak to you, please?"

My colleagues are all staring at us, and I instantly feel awkward. "Sure," I say, even though I don't want to.

Ryan smiles, his expression portraying relief as he leads me down the hallway toward an empty meeting room. "You've been ignoring my calls ever since you sent me that breakup text, and you haven't replied to any of my messages, either. I've been trying to get hold of you for weeks now. How long are you going to keep avoiding me? I even went to your house yesterday and was told you'd moved out. Where are you living now? I'm really worried about you."

The concern in his voice sounds so real that I find myself second-guessing everything I heard that night. The way he looks at me can't be fake, can it?

"You don't need to worry about me."

He reaches for my hand, and I pull away, crossing my arms defensively. "Alanna, what is going on? Can't you see that you're killing me by treating me this way? You broke up with me over text and never even told me why. What have I done to deserve this? Did the time we spent together mean nothing at all?"

I stare at him, startled by the sincerity in his voice. "I heard you talking about me at the party you threw that night. I came over to tell you about the job offer I'd received, and there you were, telling all your friends that you only dated me because it'd improve your image in front of your brother. *You* tell *me*, Ryan. Did the time we spent together mean nothing at all?"

His eyes widen, and he looks away as he runs a hand through his hair. "Alanna," he says, his tone regretful. "I was drunk, and I didn't mean a word. They'd been teasing me about being with you, because they think you're a goody two-shoes, and instead of defending you like I should have, I came up with some garbage because I wanted to look cool and act aloof. I fucked up. I swear that I didn't mean a word. I love you, Alanna. Why would I spend so many months with you if any of what I said was true? What about all our dates, our endless phone conversations? Do you really think I'd have put so much time and effort into a relationship that didn't matter to me?"

I can't tell if he's lying to me or not. He looks and sounds so sincere that I feel stupid for breaking up with him and doing what I did, when I should have just confronted him. Instead of that, I seduced his older brother. There's no going back from that. I can't undo that night. I'm not even sure I want to.

"It doesn't matter anymore. It was just the push I needed to end a relationship that wasn't working for either of us."

"You can't mean that."

I look into his stunning green eyes. It's his eyes that captivated me when we first met. One look, and I was a goner. Yet somehow, when I look into those very same eyes now, they just look like a diluted version of Silas's eyes.

"I mean it. I feel like I don't even know you, Ryan. Everything you said that night made me wonder how much of our relationship was even real."

"Everything about it was real, Alanna. Just give me a chance to prove it. You can't just expect me to accept this. We can't break up and throw away months worth of memories over words spoken in a drunken stupor. Please, Alanna. You know me. You know the real me better than anyone else does. I know I'm a dick sometimes and I fuck up occasionally, but my heart is in the right place, and it only beats for you. It always has."

I bite down on my lip, memories of the two of us flooding my mind. Most of the memories I've got are with him, and he's right, it's hard to walk away from that. But how could I possibly be with him when I slept with his brother behind his back? He'd never forgive me. If we were to get back together, we'd be on borrowed time. At some point, he'd find out, and that'd be the end of us. Besides... it isn't him I see when I close my eyes now. It's Silas.

"I can't be with you," I whisper.

"Why?" His voice breaks, true pain reflected in his eyes. "I love you, Alanna. There's nothing you and I can't get through together. Please, sweetheart. Give me a chance to prove to you that I'm better than the version of me you saw that night."

I look away, suddenly uncertain. Even though I want to, I struggle to deny his request. "I don't think you and I can be anything more than friends," I murmur. "I just... I don't see us getting back together. Our relationship wasn't as happy as either of us pretended it was. We weren't a good fit, and this incident was just what we needed to show us that."

He shakes his head and takes a step closer. Ryan cups my cheek tenderly and sighs. "Give me a chance to prove you wrong, Alanna. After the months we spent together, don't you owe me that much at least? At least give me a chance to mend our friendship. We were such good friends before. Even if you never want to get back together, surely our friendship is still salvageable?"

I bite down on my lip and nod against better judgement. "Maybe," I whisper.

He leans in and presses a kiss against my cheek, startling me. "Thank you, sweetheart. You won't regret this."

I pull away from him and put some distance between us, his proximity making me uncomfortable. I thought I loved him, yet within the span of a few weeks, I can barely stand the sight of him. "Don't misunderstand," I warn him. "I think we can be friends, and I'm willing to work on that, but that's all I'm willing to give you."

He smiles and nods. "We started off as friends, Alanna. Remember? A chance is all I need."

Ryan smirks and walks away, leaving me standing here wondering what just happened.

I walk out in a daze, annoyed with myself for agreeing to his request when I didn't truly want to. Before I even reach my desk, Silas calls for me, his tone angry. "In my office. *Now*," he barks.

I follow him in, jumping when he slams the door closed behind us. "What did Ryan want?" he asks, pacing in his office.

I can barely look him in the eye. I'm so overwhelmed with guilt that I shouldn't even be feeling. I don't owe Silas anything, yet I'm nervous standing here, my heart beating a strange rhythm of fear and guilt.

"He wanted to make up. He asked me for another chance."

Silas pauses and turns toward me. He walks up to me, and I resist the urge to take a step back. "Will you?" he asks. "Will you give him that chance?" Only a few inches separate us, and unlike with Ryan, I find myself wanting him closer. Silas reaches for me the same way Ryan did, his hand wrapping over my cheek tenderly. His touch feels different, more intimate somehow.

"You can't," he adds, his voice pained. "You can't go back to him, Alanna. Not after what we did."

I look into his eyes, reveling in the possessiveness he's showing me. "I won't. He just wants a chance to be friends again."

"You know he wants more than that."

I pull away from Silas and look away. "He's in all of my favorite memories, Silas. I can't walk away from him when he's such a huge part of who I am. It's just friendship he's asking for."

Silas grits his teeth and reaches for a strand of my hair. "What about the memories we created? What about that night when you fell asleep in my arms? What about the way you moaned my name as my cock sank deep inside you? Don't those memories count?"

I blush and look down at my shoes, flustered. "Silas, that night we fell asleep together was... I'm not sure what that was, but both instances were mistakes."

"Were they?"

I nod.

He grabs my hand and pulls me toward him, and I stumble into him. Silas buries a hand into my hair and tips my head up as he lowers his lips to mine. "If it was a mistake, then why did it feel so right?" he whispers, his lips hovering over mine. All I need to do is rise to my tiptoes, and I'd get a taste of him. I've been craving him ever since the night I try so hard not to remember, when it's all I can think about.

I inhale shakily and pull away from him. He's my ex's older brother and my boss. I can't go there. Not again. "You just want what you can't have," I murmur.

His expression hardens. "Alanna, make no mistake. I will never let you be with my brother. If that means that he learns all about the way I made you come on my floor, then so be it. I have no problem telling him all about how his girlfriend came onto me and begged me to fuck her."

My eyes widen, a chill running down my spine. "You never wanted me with him in the first place. In your eyes, I was never good enough for your little brother. Is that why you slept with me? To ensure he and I would be over? To prove to yourself how unworthy I am?"

"No," he tells me. "I fucked you because you asked me to, and because you always should've been mine. You made your choice when you came home with me, Alanna. There's no going back now."

Chapter Forty-Six

Alanna

I tense when I hear Silas walk into the house and escape into my bedroom before he sees me. I don't know how to face him after what he said to me in his office.

I fucked you because you asked me to, and because you always should've been mine. You made your choice when you came home with me, Alanna. There's no going back now.

Silas is confusing me, and everything he's making me feel is terrifying me. He and I… we can't happen. I can't be with my boss and my ex's older brother. The world would mock us. They'd judge me so much harder than they'd ever judge him. I know all of that. I know it, and I still can't seem to stay away.

I jump at the sound of knocking on my door and look up at my closed bedroom door, imagining Silas standing on the other end of it.

"Alanna?"

I bite down on my lip, wondering whether I'll get away with pretending I'm not here at all. Seeing Ryan again filled me with a fresh sense of guilt, and I can't escape it. I'd started to believe that

Silas and I really could exist in our own little bubble, but seeing Ryan again forced me to face reality.

"Alanna," he repeats. "I need you to accompany me to a business event tonight. Open the door. I know you're in there."

I inhale deeply as I walk toward the door cautiously, annoyed with myself for being unable to calm my nerves. I pull the door open and find Silas standing right in front of me, looking every bit as angry as he did earlier today. He holds up a bag for me and grits his teeth. Is he still mad because I gave Ryan a chance to be friends again?

"Change into this. You've got ten minutes to get ready."

I take the bag from him and force a smile to my face, but Silas storms off before I can even thank him. I'm the one who should be angry after the conversation we had and the way he threatened me, so why is it that *he's* angry?

A soft gasp escapes my lips when I pull out the nude colored floor-length designer dress with matching heels and a clutch, all in my size. I've never worn something so beautiful before, and I have no doubt I could never afford to replace this if I damaged it. Just the beading on this dress would've taken hours to do. Normally, I would've argued with Silas about wearing this, but not tonight. Though I shouldn't indulge him, I find myself wanting to placate him. I want to tell him not to worry about Ryan, and that I haven't even thought of Ryan since that night, but I can't. I shouldn't.

Silas is leaning against the wall opposite my bedroom when I walk out exactly ten minutes later, his eyes on his watch. He's wearing a black tux that makes him look every inch the powerful CEO he is, and I hate the way my heart skips a beat.

Silas's gaze moves to my feet, pausing at the slit in my dress before slowly moving up toward the sweetheart neckline of my dress. "Damn," he whispers, his eyes finding mine. "You look gorgeous."

I don't think any man has ever looked at me the way Silas

does. It's as though I'm all he can see, as though he's been waiting for me all his life.

"Let's go," I whisper.

He nods and offers me his arm, and I take it hesitantly. I can't help but wonder what Silas truly thinks of me. He hired me when he could've easily rejected my application, and he offered me a place to stay when he should've fired me for being unprofessional when I showed up at the office with my belongings. He isn't the tyrant everyone thinks he is. Everything he's done so far showed me that he's a good person, so it makes no sense that he doesn't think I'm good enough for his brother. I'd think that it's just because I slept with him that night, but he wanted me to break up with Ryan long before that.

"We're attending a charity auction," he tells me as we get in the car.

I frown and turn to face him. "I thought you said this was a business event?"

He nods. "It is. It's hosted by one of our biggest clients, and I'll have to go. Usually, Amy attends with me."

"So why did you ask me?"

He glances at me, his gaze lingering for a moment before he turns back toward the road. "Her time is more valuable than yours. She has two kids who need her at home. You, on the other hand, have no plans other than sulking all night."

Asshole. I cross my arms and look out the window, annoyed. He isn't wrong, but it's still a shitty thing to say.

"I'm expected to buy something tonight," he murmurs, his tone relaxed. "I'll leave that to you. You can buy one thing that you'd like to have. No budget."

I smirk at him. "So if they auction a diamond necklace worth millions, I can buy it?"

"You can buy whatever you want. There really isn't a budget, but you can only bid on one thing."

I nod. "Must be nice, having so much money."

He looks at me then, his expression complicated. "Yeah," he whispers. "It is."

I can't help but chuckle as I shake my head. "At least you're honest about it."

Silas steps out of the car and walks around it to open the door for me before handing the keys to the valet.

My heart starts to race as we walk into a large ballroom filled with the city's rich and famous. I unknowingly tighten my grip on Silas's arm, and he places his hand over mine reassuringly.

"Silas!"

I tense when I see Raven walking toward us, looking beautiful in a tight red dress that matches the shade of her lipstick. I should let go of Silas and let him greet her, but I can't.

"Raven," he says, nodding politely.

Her eyes drop to my hand on his arm, and instead of pulling away the hand Silas covered mine with, he starts to draw circles on the back of my hand.

"We meet again," she says, a sweet smile on her face. "You're Silas's assistant, right?"

I shake my head. "His mentee. I'm part of the Ψ division."

She nods knowingly. "So you're one of his most elite team members, huh? I'm surprised you made it to that division at your age. Well done."

I force a smile to my face as I resist the urge to drag Silas away from her. Seeing her just reminds me of the history he has with her, the years they've spent together. I know he says they *pretended* to date, but it can't all have been fake. Not with a woman who looks like her.

I shouldn't, but when I see her, I can't help but compare myself to her, and it becomes painfully clear why Silas thought I wasn't good enough for his brother... or for him.

"Silas," she says, drawing out his name. "I heard you're taking part in the eligible bachelor auction? I'm definitely winning a date with you. I can't wait." She winks at him before walking away, her expression provocative. It's clear she isn't in the least intimidated by my presence, as though she knows other women come and go in his life, but she's his constant. Is that because she knows they'll always be friends, or is it more?

I looked her up after Josh mentioned her, and Silas always seems to end up back with her, no matter how long they break up for. His name is never mentioned in the articles, but I've seen photos of them together. Those photos didn't look like it was all pretend. He seems to genuinely care about her.

"What is she talking about?"

He lets go of me and turns to face me, a mere inch between our bodies. "I'm up for auction tonight," he says, grinning. "Several other bachelors and I will be auctioning off dates. I was a little worried that I'd stand there without anyone wanting to bid on me, but I worried needlessly."

Thoughts of the two of them going on a date together plague me, and my mood plummets even further than it already had.

"I'd better get ready for the auction," he tells me. "Don't forget. You need to buy one thing tonight on behalf of Sinclair Security. I won't be able to do it."

I nod and watch him walk away, interrupted every few steps by women who seem far too eager to speak to him. The second he goes up on that stage, all hell is going to break loose. It's obvious that most of the women that surround him have every intention of winning a date with him, and it doesn't sit well with me.

I stand in the corner as several items go up for auction, including a gorgeous diamond necklace that I would've bought just out of sheer spite, yet I find myself holding back.

"At last, the highlight of our event." I look up at the woman on stage, who seems to be a celebrity of some sort. "I hope you've got your chequebooks on you, because we're about to auction off dates with the city's most eligible bachelors."

Five men walk onto the stage, but the only one I've got eyes for is Silas. He smiles at the crowd, yet somehow, his eyes find mine within seconds. I swallow hard as he holds me captive with his gaze, unable to look away.

With each man that gets auctioned off and exits the stage, I get more nervous. I noticed Raven standing at the front, clearly expecting to win, and I know I should let it be, but I can't.

He said I could bid on one thing that I wanted tonight. What if it's him? What if what I want... is *him*?

"I don't need to introduce Silas Sinclair to you, do I?" the hostess says, and the women in the crowd go wild. "Let's start the bidding at a thousand dollars. One thousand dollars, anyone?"

"Five thousand!" Raven shouts, holding up her number.

"Eight thousand," another woman shouts instantly.

"Ten thousand," yet another woman adds.

I look around the room, a sense of dread overcoming me as I take in the countless women that want nothing more than a date with Silas. The bidding quickly gets out of hand, the amount of money they're willing to spend on a single date making me uncomfortable.

"Sixty thousand," one woman says.

Many of them are celebrities, heiresses, and prominent business women. They're all more qualified to be with him than I'll ever be, but I don't care. I raise my hand and gather my courage. "One hundred thousand," I say, and heads turn as the room quietens. I feel countless gazes on me, everyone assessing who I am and what I'm worth.

"Going once," the hostess says.

Silas smirks at me, his eyes betraying how pleased he is.

"Going twice."

Raven twists her hands, and for a moment I fear she'll outbid me.

"Sold to the lady in the back!"

My shoulder slump in relief, and Silas chuckles as he exits the stage. My cheeks are blazing and my heart is thumping so loudly that every other sound fades away. What have I done?

"Good girl," Silas murmurs, his hand wrapping around my waist.

He pulls me flush against him, and I look up into his eyes,

unsure what to say. The truth is that I didn't want him to go on a date with any of these women.

"There's no avoiding me now," he tells me as he pulls me onto the dance floor. "I meant what I said earlier, Alanna. You made your choice when you came home with me. I won't do anything that you don't want me to, but there's no way in hell I'm letting you get back together with my brother. Not ever."

I look into his eyes, startled by the passion blazing within them. "I know," I whisper. "I won't."

He nods, looking pleased as he twirls me around, the two of us swaying together, our bodies far closer than appropriate. "Tell me, baby. Why did you bid on me?" he whispers eventually.

"You told me to bid on something on your behalf. I figured I might as well do you a favor. Those ladies seemed really viscous."

He pulls me closer, the two of us falling into a steady rhythm. "I told you to bid on something you *want*, my love." His hand roams over my back, his touch possessive.

"I don't want you."

He smiles. "You will by the time the date you just bought wraps up."

Chapter Forty-Seven

Silas

I smile to myself as I knock on Alanna's bedroom door early in the morning. She won a date with me, so that's exactly what I'm going to give her. The only reason she's even considering forgiving Ryan is the memories she shares with him. She has no idea of our shared past, of our history. If I want to compete with Ryan and make her fall for me the way she once did, I'll have to give her new memories to replace the ones she lost.

"Silas?" she says, surprised. I smirk as I take in her workout gear. As expected, she was going for a morning run, as she always did when I managed to fluster her.

"Oh, good, you're already dressed. I was about to ask you if you wanted to join me for a morning run."

She looks at me wide-eyed and starts to shake her head, but I grab her hand and pull her along before she has a chance to decline. "Let's go. I've got the perfect trail in mind."

"Silas, running is more of a solitary activity for me."

I know, but not with me. You've always loved running with me. "That's fine. We don't need to talk."

I start jogging toward the trail the moment we reach the street, and much to my surprise, Alanna maintains my pace, running alongside me instead of behind me. We remain silent for most of the run, and I don't try to engage her. Alanna has always hated talking while running, but she's always loved having me by her side. It's been years, and in many ways she's no longer the woman I used to know, yet the essence of her stayed the same. It's strange feeling like I know her better than she knows herself, yet not knowing her at all.

"Let's go left here."

She follows me, and nerves assault me as we get closer to the place I've been leading her to. I pause in front of the elaborate picnic setup, complete with a tent behind it for privacy and protection from the rain we're expecting today.

I turn toward her and smile. "You paid good money for a date with me, so I'd better deliver. Hundred grand, was it?"

Her eyes move from the picnic spread back to me, widening as realization sinks in. "This... you did this?"

I nod and grab her hand as I pull her toward the blanket that's been spread out on the grass. She can't remember, but our first real date was a picnic too. She's the reason I am who I am today. I always intended to regain what I lost, but because of Alanna, I didn't lose my soul in the process. I always knew that someday, we'd find our way back to each other, and when we did, I wanted to be the person she thought I was. Her *Si*. Alanna is such an integral part of my life, even in the years we spent apart. Every one of my favorite memories revolves around her, and I know it used to be the same for her.

"Here," I murmur as I hand her the energy drink she always loved.

She stares at it for a moment and smiles. "Wow, this is my favorite flavor."

I grin and try my best to act surprised. "Is it?"

I watch her as she empties half the bottle. I've always loved the way she looks after a run. It's not much different from what she looks like after sex. Alanna out of breath is a sight to behold.

She breathes a sigh of relief when I hand her a disinfectant wet wipe for her hands. "Thank you," she says, taking it from me. She hates touching anything after a run. The first thing she usually does when she gets home is wash her hands. Usually she won't even grab a drink before that. While I couldn't provide her with a sink here, this thankfully seems to be good enough for her.

I feel her gaze on me as I spread out the food I had prepared for her. The first time I took her on a date we barely had anything to eat, and I remember thinking then that I'd someday redo this date the way I'd wanted to.

"Strawberries and champagne?" she asks.

I smirk. "You did pay a shit ton of money, after all."

"Technically, *you* did."

"It was a gift. So does that mean I gifted you *me*?"

"I suppose... does that make you mine for the rest of the day?"

I smile at her, my heart thumping loudly in my chest. "Considering the amount of money involved, I'm willing to extend that deal for the rest of our lives."

Alanna giggles and tilts her head up toward the sun. She looks so sweet lying back on her elbows. It's almost as though the years we spent apart never happened. "So if I want to make you my boy toy, I can?"

My cock starts to harden at the mere thought of it. "Are you threatening me with a good time?"

Alanna laughs, and I raise my glass to hers. "Here's to the rest of our lives."

She looks into my eyes as her glass clinks against mine. "To the rest our lives," she repeats.

She takes a sip of champagne as I lay out the assortment of pastries, fruits and salads. "You have good taste," she mutters. "These are all my favorite things."

I smile as innocently as I can. "Are they? I suppose we're more alike than I realized."

I hold up an apple beignet, and she takes it from me with a smile. "The only thing that's missing—"

"Is coffee?" I finish her sentence for her as I hold up a canister of the sickly sweet coffee she loves.

Her lips fall open, and she shakes her head. "There's nothing you haven't thought of, huh?"

I smile as I fill up a mug for her. I've also got freshly pressed orange juice and countless other things that she might want, but this will do for now.

Alanna looks at me, her gaze lingering. "I'm surprised you didn't take me to a fancy restaurant."

"Is that what you want?"

She hesitates. "Isn't that what you would've done if any of those other women had won?"

I look away, wondering how to answer her. "I suppose so, but that's mostly because I don't care whether that date is special to them or not. I'd just be fulfilling an obligation. It's different with you. I wanted to spend some quality time with you and I wanted to do something memorable. Since you're my mentee, you'll be accompanying me to countless formal business dinners, and I didn't want our first date to be another one of those."

"First date?"

I nod. It's our *second* first date, and though I often hate the fact that she lost her memory, it's also a chance for me to do things the way I've always wanted to with her. The memories she and I shared were filled with poverty and despair. Now, I can give her anything she wants. Money doesn't just buy *things*. It also buys experiences, and those in turn become treasured memories.

"What would you have done if Raven had won the auction?" she asks.

There's jealousy in her eyes, and I can't help but smile. She clearly misinterprets my smirk, because she grits her teeth and looks away. "Never mind," she snaps. "I don't need to know."

I lie down beside her and look up at her. "I'd have taken her for dinner."

"Dinner," she scoffs, as though she doesn't believe me. "Is that what we're calling it these days?"

"You're jealous." She doesn't seem to believe me when it comes to Raven. There truly isn't anything between us, but I'm enjoying every second of the jealousy Alanna shows me because of her.

She looks outraged at my words and crosses her arms, not realizing that she's betraying herself. "*Jealous*? Why would I be jealous?"

I'm tempted to tease her, but I know we're not quite there yet. I'm scared to do anything that'll push her away. Or worse... into Ryan's arms.

I stare up at the clouds, watching the world move slowly. She has no idea how long I've waited for her, how long I've been searching for her. If she hadn't lost her memories, would we have reunited sooner?

"You told me that you lost your memories when you were younger," I say cautiously. "What were the last few years like for you if you didn't have your memories?"

Alanna sighs as she lies down next to me, our heads close together. "It was strange. I woke up in the hospital with no idea who I was or where I came from. If not for the driver's license in my pocket, I wouldn't even have known my name."

I bite down on my lip to keep from telling her everything. If I hadn't argued with her the way I did, would I have been able to prevent that accident?

"The police came in, but I didn't match any of their missing person reports, and I didn't seem to have any next of kin. I was in that hospital all by myself, and no one was looking for me, no one cared."

She wraps her arms around herself, and though I want to pull her closer, I don't dare to.

"Social Services came in and found me a place to stay. After a couple of weeks, I received a scholarship offer, and I moved to London. I had a really great professor there, and she's a big part of the reason I came back. It's thanks to her that I dared to reach for a little bit more. She taught me that it's okay to dream, and that trying to make my biggest dreams come true is a worthwhile purpose. I came back to figure out what I lost. The last couple of years were fine, but I felt incomplete."

I turn my head to look at her. She's staring up at the sky, her expression dreamy and content. "You mentioned that you often feel like there's a man you've forgotten. There's someone you dream about, right? How come you dated Ryan when there's someone you loved so much that even the loss of your memories couldn't fully erase him from your subconscience?"

She looks at me then, her smile bittersweet. "That is precisely why I started dating Ryan," she says, her expression crestfallen. "There was someone I loved so much that I couldn't fully forget him, even when I forgot my own name. Despite that, no one has come looking for me. Whoever he is, he didn't care enough to be a part of my life."

"Maybe he did look for you and just couldn't find you."

She looks away. "I used to think that. I used to hope that I'd one day run into him, and I'd just know that it was him. That's kind of what it felt like with Ryan. There was something about his eyes that stirred something deep within, almost like I recognized that shade of green, even though he insisted that we'd never met before. It's what made me interested in him."

I stare at her, my heart breaking. "Alanna," I whisper, unsure of what to say. Ryan and I both have our father's eyes. Emerald green with specks of brown. It's *my* eyes she saw in his. "What would you do if that guy walked back into your life now?"

She looks back at me, the hope in her eyes remedying fragments of my broken heart. "I don't know. I'd like to think that I'd recognize him the moment I see him, but I'm not sure anymore. Even if I did meet him again, how could he possibly live up to what I've imagined him to be? It's been years, and he's probably moved on. I need to do the same."

He hasn't moved on, is what I want to say, but I can't. Even now that I've finally found her, it feels like she can slip away at any moment. I'm tempted to tie her to me, but Alanna was never meant to be tied down. I need her to stay with me willingly, so I'll have to give her a reason to. This date is only just the beginning.

Chapter Forty-Eight

Alanna

I smile to myself as I think back to the way Silas and I spent hours chatting in the sun, never running out of things to talk about. It was the perfect date, and I don't think I've ever been happier. I keep trying to remind myself that I shouldn't fall for Silas, that he's my boss and my ex's older brother... but it's a losing battle.

"Monitoring these computers is tedious as hell," Josh complains, and I snap out of my daydreams as I look back at my screen.

When we were first assigned this project, I thought it'd be far more exciting than it is. I feel like a cop on a stakeout, just waiting for something interesting to happen. We're assessing our algorithm to see what it's flagging, and more importantly, what it's missing, but it's a really boring and lengthy process.

"Alanna?"

I freeze at the sound of Ryan's voice. He's been calling and texting me non-stop, and even though I said I'd give him a chance to be friends again, I've been avoiding him. Every time I want to reply to one of his messages, I'm reminded of the way Silas looked at me when he told me to stay away from Ryan. His words were harsh, but there was something in his eyes that had my heart aching.

"Ryan," I mutter, forcing a smile to my face.

"Are you free for lunch?" he asks hesitantly.

I glance at Josh nervously, scared he's going to accuse me of nepotism again, but much to my surprise, he simply nods. "You might as well go. I haven't seen you take a lunch break in weeks. You can't always eat at your desk. Bring me back something, though."

I nod, unsure if I'm grateful or not. I don't really want to go with Ryan, and part of me was hoping that Josh would provide me with an excuse.

I sigh as I grab my handbag and follow Ryan out. "Where are we going?" I ask, oddly nervous. I only told him that we could try to be friends again to alleviate the guilt I feel, but I'm worried about Silas. I'm worried he'll be hurt or angry if he hears about this. I shouldn't care at all, but I can't help myself.

Ryan reaches for my hand, and I pull away, moving my free hand to the straps of my handbag instead. His smile drops for a second, but he shakes it off quickly. "There's a nice little sandwich shop one block away. I think you'll really like it. They do some cool latte art."

Damn it. I'm a sucker for latte art, and he knows it. "Sounds good," I mutter.

He glances at me as though he's trying to find the right words to say to me, the tension between us awkward for both of us. I shouldn't have agreed to come with him at all, but I wasn't sure how to decline without making a scene. My colleagues already gossip enough about me as it is.

By the time we sit down, I'm anxious. Ryan might have fucked up, but I slept with his brother in retaliation. I'm terrified of him finding out, and shame uncurls in my stomach, making me feel sick. I feel guilty toward Ryan, and I'm worried about hurting Silas. No matter what I do, I'll be in the wrong.

"I'm sorry, Alanna," he says the moment our order is placed. "You said we could try to be friends again, but we can't do that with so much left unsaid between us. I can't undo the pain my words caused, but I can tell you I didn't mean what I said. I was drunk, and I was trying to look cool in front of my friends. It's fucking lame, and I know it. It's no excuse."

I look into his eyes, trying to determine whether the anguish in them is genuine or not. "Did you approach me because you thought I'd help you improve your image in your family's eyes?"

He closes his eyes and nods. "I did, but if that's the only reason I dated you, why would I have stuck around for so long? I only did that because I fell in love with you. By the time I said those stupid words, my brother had already given me everything I'd asked him for. He'd given me the cars I wanted and access to pretty much unlimited funds. There was no reason for me to keep you around, but I did. I admit that I'm a complete asshole who set out to use you, but I never even considered treating you badly, and every moment I've shared with you is precious to me. I know that it's hard to believe, but surely you felt it too? When we were together, there was nothing fake about it. What we had was real, and now that I've lost you, I feel it all the more. I'm not myself without you, Alanna. Being with you changed me for the better, and I can't see a life without you anymore."

My heart aches over everything we've lost, everything I thought we had. "I don't believe you," I whisper. "And I don't trust you."

"I know," he murmurs. "I'm not asking you to forgive me, because it's clear that I've really hurt you. I always knew I couldn't outrun the truth, and I'm willing to accept the consequences. If I have to start back at square one, I will. Just please don't ask me to give up on you entirely, because I can't do that."

The waitress smiles at me as she places our order on the table, and I welcome the interruption. I don't know what to say to him. I didn't expect him to be so honest and apologetic. I thought he'd make excuses and weave more elaborate lies. Instead, he's owning up to everything he's done.

I place my fork down halfway through our meal and shake my head. "You set out to use me, Ryan. You aren't the person I thought you were. It's terrifying to me that we spent so much time together, yet I don't even really know you. I only know the person you pretended to be. Can't you see how crazy that is?"

He nods. "That's exactly why I'm asking you to give me a chance. I'm in love with you, Alanna. It's the kind of love I can't forget about and it isn't something I can walk away from. Let's get to know each other all over again. Please?"

I shake my head, confused by my own feelings. Ryan is the only person I've ever opened up to. He's the only one I've ever loved as far as I remember, the only one I share memories with. He's my first kiss, my first date, my first love. Part of me wants to be friends with him purely so I can prove to myself that I wasn't a complete idiot for putting my trust in him, that at least some of what we shared was real.

"I'm not sure," I whisper.

"I just want to be your friend, Alanna. Let me buy you a coffee every once in a while. For now, that's all I'll ask of you. I know I don't deserve it, but please don't cut me out of your life. I've been miserable without you."

"Just a coffee every once in a while?"

He nods, his expression earnest.

"Fine," I say against better judgement, in part because of the guilt I feel. He might have used me, but if he were to find out what I did to him in return… I'm not sure which of us is worse.

Ryan places his hand over mine and squeezes, a grateful smile on his face. "Thank you," he murmurs.

I pull away and grab my bag. "I need to get back to work."

Ryan jumps up and nods. "Let me walk you back. I'd better

get back to work too, or Silas might actually kill me. You probably know how awful of a boss he is."

Just hearing him say Silas's name has a fresh wave of shame washing over me. "Yeah," I murmur awkwardly.

Ryan tries to make small talk as we head back to the office, but all he manages to do is make me incredibly nervous. I'm terrified of saying something that'll make him suspicious of Silas and me. I don't owe him anything, yet I still feel guilty.

He smiles sheepishly as we get into the elevator and looks down at his shoes. "I'd press the button for you, but Silas took away my access to the top floor after I came to find you at work on your first day."

My eyes widen in surprise as I lean into the scanner, the button for the 27th floor automatically lighting up. "How did you get up there today, then?"

He smirks at me. "Every day at lunchtime, I've been roaming around the elevator, waiting for someone to go to the top floor. I was starting to give up hope, you know? You said we could be friends, but you've been ignoring all of my calls and texts, so I was getting desperate."

I shake my head at him, oddly touched by his perseverance. "Aren't you going to press the button for your floor?"

He shakes his head. "I want to walk you back to your desk."

I stare at him for a moment. It's easy to see why I fell for him, but is any of it true? He seems kind and thoughtful, but is it genuine? He's right to say that he no longer needs me, but I'm still unsure.

"Here we are," I murmur as I drop my handbag on top of my desk.

Ryan nods, his expression crestfallen. "Would you have a coffee with me next week?"

I nod, despite not wanting to. I've never been good at saying no, and today I really wish that were different. Ryan leans in and pushes a strand of my hair behind my ear, his touch tender. "I'll see you soon then."

He turns and walks away, leaving me feeling confused. When I broke up with him, I thought that'd be it. I villainized him in my mind, convincing myself that nothing we had was real, but maybe not everything was fake.

"*Alanna*!"

I whirl around, surprised by the anger in Silas's voice.

"Follow me to my office."

I tense as I do as he says, a different type of guilt washing over me. With Ryan, my guilt stemmed from being judged for what I did, but with Silas it's different... I'm scared of *hurting* him.

I close the door behind me and stare at his broad back. He's turned away from me, a hand in his hair. I'm rooted in place when he turns around, his eyes filled with anguish.

"Why were you with him?"

"He just wanted to explain. I told you he asked me if we could be friends, and though I agreed, I'd been ignoring him, so he came to find me."

Silas scoffs. "I already told you he definitely doesn't just want to be friends with you, and you know it."

He walks toward me, and I know I should take a step back to keep some distance between us, but I don't want to. I want to be near him, and though I shouldn't, I want to reassure him.

He lifts his hand to my face, the tips of his fingers brushing over my lips. "Why is your lipstick smeared?" he asks, his tone low and dangerous.

"I just had lunch," I whisper.

"With him?"

I nod.

"Don't do that again. Don't meet up with him, just the two of you."

I look into his eyes, trying to figure out what he's thinking. "*Why*?" I whisper. "Why do you care so much?"

He cups my cheek, his gaze intense. "Because you're *mine*, whether you realize it or not."

My heart skips a beat as heat rushes to my cheeks, and I look away, flustered. Surely he can't mean that?

"I'm not a toy for you two to fight over."

"No," he agrees. "You're not a toy, Alanna, but you damn sure are worth fighting for."

Chapter Forty-Nine

Silas

I look up when Alanna walks into the house, my heart skipping a beat at the sight of her. She has no idea how many times I've fantasized about her coming home to me like this. It'll never get old. In ten years, I'll still feel the same level of excitement. I just know it.

Alanna pauses halfway into the living room, her eyes roaming over the countless candles I lit all over the living room. "What is this?" she asks, her tone carrying a hint of uncertainty. "Are you expecting someone?"

I finish setting the table and nod. "Yes," I tell her as I pull out a chair for her. "*You*."

Her eyes widen, and for once, she looks entirely disarmed. "This is… for *me*?"

I smile at her and hold my hand out. "Come here."

She takes a cautious step forward, and I wait patiently as she walks toward me, each of her steps measured and insecure. She looks into my eyes as she takes a seat, her gaze filled with questions.

"Why are you doing this? What is this, even? Is this supposed to be a date? You're never home early, and today..."

I lean in and push a strand of her hair behind her ear. "I told you that you were worth fighting for. This is me fighting."

"Why?"

"Because you're the woman I'm going to marry, and you might not quite realize it yet, but I'm the man of your dreams."

"Is this all because I went for lunch with Ryan? Is this all some type of weird sibling rivalry?"

The way she looks at me breaks my fucking heart. There's so much distrust in her eyes, and I have no doubt Ryan is the cause of it. She and I made so much progress when he wasn't in the picture. One lunch date with him, and she's doubting my intentions. I can't tell if it's because of something he said, or because he reminded her that she once blindly put her trust in the wrong person, and she's scared she's making the same mistake.

I reach for her hand and entwine our fingers. "No. I don't give a fuck about your past with my brother, and quite frankly, I don't want to hear about it. I want you for *you*. I've wanted you for far longer than you realize, and nothing will ever change that, not even you dating my brother. I'm tired of dancing around this thing between us when I know you feel it, too. "

"I want to believe you, Silas," she admits. "But you're surrounded by women that'd pay good money for a single date with you, and I... I'm no one. I don't know why you're doing this, but you must think I'm stupid if you truly expect me to believe you really want me. I'm not saying that to act coy either — it isn't a plea for compliments or reassurance. I'm just done with all of this. I'm tired of being led on, and I'm tired of deceiving myself. If you want me in your bed, just say so. Don't lead me to believe you have feelings for me."

I tighten my grip on her hand, the pain in her eyes going straight to my heart. Seeing Ryan clearly reminded her of the way he used her, and now she's convinced herself I'm doing the same thing to her. Weeks of progress, all destroyed within the hour she spent with him. Just how badly did he hurt her? No matter what I do or say, she won't believe I truly want to be with her.

"I understand," I say, my voice soft. "I'm not asking anything of you, Alanna. I just want to spend time with you, can I?"

She hesitates and I sigh as I look away, my thumb drawing circles across the back of her hand. Just having her so close to me is setting my worst worries at ease.

"You talk of ulterior motives," I murmur. "I'll admit that that's part of the reason I want to be with you. You don't have ulterior motives. You're not after my money or status. You're one of very few people who look at me and see the man beneath the persona I've crafted. I feel like I can be myself around you."

She looks up, her gaze searching, and I lay my soul bare, my expression disarmed and earnest. "Why me?" she asks, her voice catching on the last word.

"Because I love your smile and your tenacity. I love the way you and I are always in sync, the way we work together, and the way you seem to understand me like no one else can." My eyes roam over her lips and down her chest before I tear my gaze away. "And because I want you every waking second. I can't look at you without wanting to pull you closer and kiss you. I think of the way your pussy felt around my cock every time I close my eyes, and when I go to bed, I imagine you lying next to me, your long hair spread over my pillows, your lips on mine."

Her expression darkens and her breath hitches. Her cheeks turn a beautiful rosy color, and I squeeze her hand in an effort to keep myself seated when all I want to do is walk over to her and yank her out of her chair so I can kiss her the way I've been wanting to.

"Are those reasons good enough for you?"

She nods. "They sound good," she whispers. "But there's no way of knowing whether it's true or not."

"Tell me what it is you're worried about. You think I only want your body? That I'll tire of you eventually and leave you heartbroken?"

Her eyes widen, and I smile at her. I know her well enough to realize what she's thinking, but I'm not sure how to set her worries at ease.

"Marry me," I tell her. "Marry me, and if I ever leave you, you'll be able to take half of my assets. Would that set you at ease? Would that prove to you that I'll never let you go?"

"Bold move," she says, smiling. "What if I actually say yes? What will you do then? What if I'm really just after your money?"

I chuckle and lift our joined hands to my lips before pressing a soft kiss to the back of her hand. "If you say yes, you'll make me the happiest man in the world. And you know... if you're after my money, tell me. I'll just give it to you."

Her lips fall open, and she shakes her head as she pulls her hand back. "You really are crazy."

"Maybe," I whisper. "Or maybe I really am serious about you, and you're worth more than money."

She stares at me as though she's trying to figure me out and shakes her head. "Definitely crazy."

I watch her as she sits down at the table. "I'm not giving up," I promise her. "Truthfully, only time can prove whether or not I'm lying to you, but that's okay with me. I'd rather spend a year with you doubting my intentions toward you and having a chance to prove myself, than a year without you. Take all the time you need, Alanna. I know he hurt you, but I never will."

She nods, her gaze solemn. She may not have said it explicitly, but she's giving me a chance.

Chapter Fifty

Alanna

I walk out of the office and inhale deeply, my face tipped up toward the cloudy sky. My mind has been a mess lately. Now, more than ever, I wish I knew more about who I am, and what I left behind. I feel incomplete, and the few memories I did create all turned out to be fake, orchestrated by someone wanting to improve his image.

I so badly want to believe that Silas means what he says, and that he truly wants to be with me, but how can I? How do I believe him when the only other person that supposedly loved me used and deceived me? It's one thing for Silas to flirt with me and to want my body. That's something I understand and it's something I can believe. Him genuinely having feelings for me? That I cannot believe. I don't want to make the same mistake I made with Ryan. It'd be so much worse with Silas, and not just because of who he is. I don't think I could survive Silas breaking my heart.

"Alanna!"

I tense and inhale deeply as I turn to face Ryan. He's the last person I want to see right now. "What are you doing here?"

He grins as he holds up an umbrella. "I saw you leaving and wanted to give you an umbrella in case it rains. Or better yet, will you let me drive you home?"

I freeze instinctively. Ryan has no idea that I live with Silas, and he can't find out. It isn't just because I'm worried about hurting him, or because I can't face the shame my actions have filled me with. It's also because I don't trust him to keep it to himself. Ryan has always been competitive. If he finds out that I live with Silas, he'll only pursue me harder, purely because he won't want Silas to have me. He said it himself, after all.

"You can walk me to the bus stop," I tell him, knowing he won't give up unless I give in. I used to find it charming, but everything I used to love about him is now tainted with suspicion and disgust. It isn't because he's trying to be chivalrous, it's because he wants to get his way.

"You said we could be friends, but you keep avoiding me," he says as he falls into step with me.

"Yes, Ryan. I am. We both know you're capitalizing on my preference for avoiding conflict instead of giving me the space I need."

He nods, looking contrite, but that's probably all an act, too. If he truly felt any remorse for his actions, he'd just leave me alone.

"I'm worried that giving you too much space will result in me losing you forever. Besides, I'm not asking you out on a date. I'm just accompanying you to the bus stop. I just want a few moments of your time. You told me you feel like you don't even know me, and all I want is to show you who I really am. I want to show you that the time we shared was real. I might have approached you for the wrong reasons, but I stayed because I fell for you. Maybe I'm being insensitive by ignoring your need for space, but I can't take the risk of losing you completely."

I pause and turn to face him, a slight drizzle coating my skin as Ryan opens the umbrella and holds it over us. Does he stand to gain anything by doing this?

"Alanna, if all I'll ever have for the rest of our lives is your friendship, then I'll take that. I need you in my life in some shape or form. I just want to show you that I'm sorry for the way I hurt you and if you'll let me, I want to be part of your life."

I nod, more confused than ever. I don't think he's lying, and when he's standing here in front of me, all I'm reminded of are the good memories, the times we laughed together, the way he treated me.

Ryan leans in and cups my cheek, hurt and longing filling his eyes. "Do you remember our first date? We went back to the beach we met at. It was only meant to be a stroll, but we ended up watching the sunset together with a cheap bottle of wine from the supermarket. We spent hours chatting about our goals in life. The sun set, and the air cooled, so I wrapped my arm around you to keep you warm, and you smiled at me. That's when I fell in love with you. I didn't even realize it at the time, but I did. I've been yours from that moment onwards. I told myself that it was all a game, but you and I both know that it wasn't. Those feelings couldn't have been faked."

My eyes fill with tears and I look away, blinking rapidly as I continue to walk to the bus stop. That time at the beach was the first time I felt a real connection like that. Until that point, I'd been living my life trying to learn about my past, and in that moment, I decided to focus on the future instead.

"We're here."

He nods and takes my hand, wrapping it around the umbrella's handle, his hand on top of mine. "Take this."

I nod, my heart aching from the wounds he reopened.

"Does it upset you to see me? Do you truly want me to stay away, Alanna? Does our past really mean nothing to you anymore?"

I glance back at him as the bus stops in front of me and I collapse the umbrella. "I don't know, Ryan. I really don't know."

He nods and takes a step back. "So long as it isn't a no, there's hope."

I turn away from him and step into the bus. It's true that I'm not sure about my feelings, because it really is hard to walk away from what we had, but I'm not sure I should be giving him any hope at all when there's no way we could ever get back together. Not only did I sleep with his older brother, I'm living with him too. There's too much standing between us now, and it isn't just his lies and deception. It's my treacherous heart, too. When my thoughts drift, it isn't Ryan they turn to.

I'm absentminded the entire way home and barely even notice Silas standing in the hallway. "Where did you get that umbrella?" he asks, his voice strained.

I look up in surprise and glance back at the umbrella, guilt washing over me. "I... um."

"Ryan gave it to you?"

I nod and take a second look at the umbrella. I didn't realize it initially, but the Sinclair crest is on the handle.

"You were just with him."

I nod again, struggling to face Silas. "He walked me to the bus stop."

Silas leans back against the wall, his eyes roaming over my face. He's so close, yet he feels so far away. There's something in his eyes that makes my heart ache. It's a sense of loss, a hopeless desperation.

"Come with me." He grabs my hand and walks me back to the passenger elevator in the hallway. He entwines our fingers as we go down to the car park, his grip tight.

"Where are you taking me?"

He pulls me out of the elevator and points to a row of cars. "Pick any of these cars," he tells me. "Drive any of them. I don't give a shit if you completely damage every single one of them, but I don't want you taking the bus anymore."

"Silas, I... I can't do that. Are you crazy?"

"Yes," he deadpans. "I am crazy, and you're going to do as you're told."

He walks me to a locker on the wall and holds my finger up against it, unlocking it. "It's got the same biometrics programmed to it as the elevator. It holds all of our car keys, so just pick one and drive it. When you're done with it, you put it back here. From now on, I want you to drive to work, park in my designated parking area, and then use my private elevator to go straight up."

"Is this... this isn't about Ryan, is it?"

He nods. "Partially. For one, I don't want you taking the bus late at night, and I don't like the idea of you walking from the bus stop, but yeah. I'll admit, I also want to cut off Ryan's access to you. It's my fault for not giving you access to my cars sooner. I've been so caught up in work that I forgot to ensure you knew you can use anything I own, but you can, baby. Everything that's mine is yours."

I stare at him, trying to figure him out. "What's that covered car in the back?" I ask, curious. All of his cars are low sports cars, but there's something hidden in the back that looks like a truck.

"That..." he murmurs. "It's just an old car. Don't worry about that one and use any of the others."

I nod, knowing he won't let this go until I agree. Silas Sinclair... I can't figure him out. Is he leading me on like his brother did, or is this something else? I'm starting to want things that scare me, things I've never wanted with anyone else, not even Ryan. I know being with him would result in certain doom, but I don't think I can resist much longer.

Chapter Fifty-One

Silas

My eyes roam over the carnage in the living room, sofa pillows strewn everywhere. What the fuck happened? Why the fuck is everything such a mess?

I freeze when I hear the sound of sniffling and follow it to find Alanna on her knees, rooting through what appears to be her upturned bag.

I kneel down beside her and grab her shoulders. Her eyes are red from the endless tears she's cried, and her pain hits me straight in the chest. "What happened, my love?"

Her breathing is choppy, and she keeps choking on her sobs. "I-I… I lost it," she cries. "I lost my… my h-handkerchief."

The handkerchief my mother gave me? "The one with the Ψ symbol on it?"

She nods and bursts into tears all over again, loud heart-breaking sobs tearing through her throat. I pull her against me and wrap my arms around her, hugging her tightly. "Baby, it's just a handkerchief. It isn't worth your tears. I'll buy you a hundred of them. I'll get it replicated for you."

She pushes me away, pain and anger flashing through her eyes. "This isn't something you can throw money at, Silas. There's only *one* of it." Alanna sniffs, her anger overtaking her pain. "Someone like you would never understand how much it means to me."

I bite back a smile, which only infuriates her further. She has no idea that the handkerchief she's crying such bitter tears over is one of the last things my mother left me.

I cup her cheeks tenderly and wipe her tears away with my thumbs. "I'm sorry, baby. Let me help you look for it, okay? Where did you last see it?"

"I w-was playing with it in the living room last night, and now it's gone."

I nod as my eyes roam over the pillows and the deconstructed sofa. How did she even take that apart? "That explains the state of our living room."

She pauses for a moment, her eyes widening a fraction before she shakes her head and continues to look around. I join her in her search, my emotions in turmoil all over again. Each time I wonder if I'm wasting my time trying to win her over, she proves to me that a part of her still loves me too. Her only connection to that handkerchief is *me*.

I pat down the sofa cushions and smirk when I see her handkerchief poking through the zipper of one of them. "Baby," I murmur, leaning back against sofa's base. "Look at this."

She crawls toward me and leans over my lap as she grabs the handkerchief. "You found it! I've been looking for it for over an hour, how did you find it so easily!"

Alanna presses it to her chest and smiles so widely that my heart skips a beat or two. I'm pretty sure I straight up forget how to breathe for a moment.

She turns toward me and throws herself at me, her arms wrapping around me, the two of us entwined on the floor. I hug her tightly as she squeezes me, a relieved exhale escaping her lips. "Thank you, Silas! Thank you, thank you, thank you!"

Her lips brush over my neck, sending a shiver down my spine, and I hold her closer, my hand wrapping into her hair. "Why does that little thing matter to you so much?"

She pulls back to look at me, but I don't let go of her. It's been so long since I've had her so close.

"I don't know," she whispers, her face a mere few inches from mine. "I just know that it's important to me. Every time I see that embroidered Ψ symbol, my heart feels at ease. This handkerchief is the reason I wanted to join the Ψ division at Sinclair Security. I've always felt that Ψ means something to me, that it's an important clue about my past, but I just can't figure it out."

I look into her eyes, wanting to tell her everything. If I do, would she be mine the way she once was? Or would I be tying her to me with the knowledge I have about her? Would I do more harm than good?

"Every time I see the Ψ symbol, everything in my crazy mind feels calm for a moment. I might not know who I am or what happened to me, but when I see that symbol, I feel a sense of belonging. It's crazy, and I can't explain it, but it's just really precious to me."

I cup her cheek and brush my thumb over her lips. "Is that why you had it tattooed on your rib?" She had the Ψ symbol tattooed onto her rib in the exact same spot I once drew it with a sharpie. Some part of her clearly still remembers me, so what is blocking her memories of me?

She nods, her cheeks turning rosy. "One night, when I felt particularly lonely, I decided to get it done. I may not know why or how, but I know Ψ belongs to me somehow. It's something I care about. Maybe it's a project, or the name of a pet. I'm not sure. I just know I feel a deep sense of love and longing whenever I see it."

I move my face closer to hers, tempted to kiss her. I've been struggling with the crazy situation we found ourselves in, wondering what's best for her, and whether I'm being selfish by forcing her to stay with me, by keeping her from my brother. Just as I'd started to regret my actions, she's proven to me that it's all worth it.

"So now I don't just have to compete with the man you dream of, but also with this little Ɏ symbol?"

She smiles and looks away. "You don't consider Ryan competition?"

"Should I?"

Her smile melts away, and she looks back at me with uncertainty shimmering in her eyes. "You really aren't joking, are you?"

I shake my head. "I've never wanted anything more than I want you."

"But I'm your brother's ex-girlfriend."

"No," I whisper, leaning in a little further, until my lips are brushing over hers. "You're so much more than that."

I smile, relieved that she hasn't pulled away from me, and then I kiss her. Alanna tenses for a moment, but then she kisses me back, her body moving against mine as I deepen our kiss. I pull her fully onto my lap, wanting more of her, and the way she moves against me tells me she feels the same insatiable need.

My hands roam over her body, and I grab a handful of her ass, a moan escaping my lips as she grinds against me. Just as I'm about to turn us over so I've got her pinned down underneath me, Alanna pushes away from me, her cheeks flushed and her eyes wide.

"Oh God," she whispers, scrambling to her feet as realization sinks in. I lean back against the sofa and wrap one ankle over the other as I watch her disappear in the direction of her bedroom, a satisfied smile on my face.

I never should've worried about Ryan. She might not understand why, but it's me she wants. I just need to make her accept that.

Chapter Fifty-Two

ALANNA

I hide behind my screen as Silas walks past my desk and disappears into his office. "What's wrong with you?" Josh asks. "Did you do something?"

I glance at him and shake my head. "No, it's nothing. I'm behind on something the boss asked me to do, so I'm hoping he'll forget."

Josh rolls his eyes and looks away. "Idiot. Silas never forgets anything. You won't get away with that for long. You'd better go fess up and ask for more time."

I nod as I get back to work, wishing it were as simple as that. I can't believe he kissed me, and I let him. I don't know how to face him, or what this means for us. I'm more confused than ever. I've barely healed from what Ryan put me through, and Silas is the last person I should be getting with, but I also can't stay away.

I haven't stopped thinking about the way he felt against me, and the way he touched me, his hands rough and urgent. If I hadn't run away, we definitely would've slept with each other again, and that would've just complicated matters so much more.

I'm startled out of my thoughts by the sound of heels clicking on our quiet floor, and I tense when Raven walks in, heading straight for Silas's office. It annoys me that she can come here so freely when this is supposed to be a highly guarded floor.

She closes the door to Silas's office, and I grit my teeth as I grab a random folder from my desk and follow her. I walk in to find her standing next to Silas's office chair, leaning over him with her cleavage on display and a seductive smile on her face.

Silas looks up, his gaze following me intently. "Alanna?"

I place the folder on his desk with more force than intended and smile at him through gritted teeth. "I have some questions about the project I'm working on."

Raven straightens and smiles at me. "It's you again."

I smile back at her sweetly and cross my arms. "Are you authorized to be here?"

Raven opens her mouth and then snaps it shut again before pushing an envelope toward Silas. "Make sure you attend the show's afterparty," she reminds him. "Mr. Therza will be there. I'll be sure to introduce you."

The door closes behind her, and I stare at Silas, my anger overflowing. He kissed me last night, and today his ex shows up at his office? When he told me everything between them was fake, was that a lie?

He reaches for the folder, but I place my hand down on it and yank it back. I have no idea what documents are even in there. I just grabbed the first thing I saw. "Are you going to this party tonight?" I ask, the words leaving my lips involuntarily.

"Yes."

Disappointment hits me right in the chest and my shoulders slump. Of course he's going. "You can't," I tell him. "I noticed some suspicious behavior on one of the computers I'm monitoring, and I think we'll see some action tonight. I think it'll be a large-scale attack."

"If it happens, notify me, and I'll head straight to the office."

"I also need help with some of the coding that has to be done for the Astra project."

"Josh can help you."

I stare at him, wondering if I was mistaken about him. Why did he kiss me if he's still going out with his ex like this? Why did he lead me on? I take a step back and nod slowly, realization dawning. Maybe he really is just like Ryan, and I fell for it all over again.

"Alanna," he says the moment I turn away. "If you're free, I'd like you to join me tonight. Mr. Therza is a potential client I've had my eyes on for a while, and tonight's introduction could be a game changer for Sinclair Security. I have to go."

I turn back around to find him smiling at me knowingly, a teasing look on his face. "Oh," I murmur. "I mean... I suppose I can make time, if it's that important."

He nods. "That would be great."

I walk out of his office with a smile on my face and sit down at my desk, filled with cautious hope and butterflies that have no business fluttering the way they do. "I guess the boss gave you an extension?" Josh says, and I nod absentmindedly.

I try my hardest to focus on work, but for the rest of the day, all I can think about is attending this event with Silas, and the way he quietly put my worries to rest.

Chapter Fifty-Three

ALANNA

"Alanna?" Silas holds up a dress bag and grins at me. I didn't even notice him leaning against the wall next to my bedroom door — I've been too busy berating myself for my irrational behavior. I acted like a crazy jealous girlfriend when I stormed into his office today, and I expected him to be annoyed with me, but instead he's waiting for me with a smile on his face.

"Change into this. Can you be ready in thirty minutes?"

I nod and take the bag from him with shaking hands. Thirty minutes is plenty of time to turn my daytime makeup into a nighttime look. By the time I walk out of my bedroom wearing the stunning red dress Silas gave me, he's already waiting by my door, a black tux making him look irresistible.

"I wish I could just keep you home," he whispers. "No one should be seeing you in that dress but me."

My eyes widen at his comment and heat rushes to my cheeks. Sometimes he just says the sweetest things, and he does it with such a deadpan expression. Silas offers me his arm, and I take it nervously.

"Mr. Tharza is an oil giant, and I know he's been looking for a new firm to handle the encryption of his transactions. That's something we can do."

I nod and read through the documentation Silas compiled as we drive to the venue. Knowing that we'll be working makes me feel far less guilty about the way I'm crashing this event.

"Ready?"

I nod, and Silas steps out of the car. Cameras flash, and I gasp in surprise, freezing for a moment when Silas opens the door and offers me his hand. "Smile," he tells me. "Or the headlines will all be accusations of me mistreating my girlfriend."

He wraps his arm around me as I smile up at him. "What headlines? What girlfriend?"

Silas chuckles as he leads me into the hotel the fashion show's afterparty is being held at. "The ones about you and me. You're the first woman I've publicly been seen with in a while, so we'll end up all over the tabloids."

"Why do you seem so pleased with that?"

He looks at me, his gaze making my heart skip a beat. "There's nothing I like more than seeing your name next to mine." He pauses and shakes his head. "Wait, that's not quite true. What I'd like even better is your first name paired with my last. Alanna Sinclair. Sounds quite good, doesn't it?"

"You're crazy."

He shrugs. "Maybe, but you love it."

"Is that what you tell yourself?"

"You're not denying it."

I try to resist smiling but can't, and Silas chuckles as he hands me a glass of champagne. "I love being around you," he whispers, his voice so soft I nearly missed it.

His gaze turns intimate, and I'm instantly reminded of the way he kissed me last night. I was out the door before he was this morning and managed to avoid him for most of the day, so we haven't spoken about it at all, but the sexual tension between us is inescapable.

His eyes drop to my lips, and I inhale sharply. "Excuse me for a moment," I murmur, pressing my glass against his chest. He takes it from me, and I rush off to the bathroom, needing a breather.

There are cameras everywhere, and Silas is right. There'll no doubt be photos of us circulating tomorrow morning. Sinclair Security will have them removed before the day is over, but they'll never be gone completely.

I close the lid and sit down on top of the toilet, needing a moment to myself. Silas Sinclair is rapidly becoming my weakness. He's the one man I can't have, yet I can't resist him. I know I'll be judged harshly if I were to date him, yet I still want to. I'd have to endure rumors and suspicions of nepotism at work, and I'd be judged harshly for my previous relationship with Ryan... but I'm starting to wonder if being with Silas would be worth the stigma.

"Did you see?" I hear a woman say. "Silas showed up with another woman. If he isn't here with Raven, that means he's single again. He's only ever off-limits when he's with Raven. He doesn't date anyone else exclusively. I'm going to make a move."

I hear another woman huff. "Good luck," she says. "You know it's only a matter of time before he's back with Raven. He always goes back to her."

"Doesn't mean I can't enjoy him in the meantime."

I grit my teeth and push the bathroom stall open, a sugary sweet smile on my face as I walk toward the sink to wash my hands. Their eyes widen when they see me, no doubt recognizing me as Silas's date. "I just heard you talking about Silas," I murmur. "You should probably know that he told me he's got crabs. It's such a shame, but that's too vicious of an STD for me to overlook."

Both women gasp, and I smile sadly as I dry my hands and walk away, my fake smile turning into a real one as I walk back into the ballroom. That should keep them away from him for at least a little while, if not forever.

Silas is shaking Mr. Tharza's hand as I approach them, Raven by his side. I hate how good they look together, and for a moment I wonder if I should just stay away, but then Silas's eyes find mine from across the room. I walk toward him, and he pulls me against him the moment I'm within reach, his hand wrapping around my waist. "This is my date," he says. "Alanna, meet Mr. Tharza."

He looks at us and grins as he shakes my hand. "I had my reservations about you, Mr. Sinclair, but I feel much better now. You look at her the way I look at my wife. A man who knows the value of things beyond money is a man I can work with. I'll give you a call."

He walks away, and I gasp as I turn toward Silas. "Oh my gosh! You did it!"

He grins and wraps his arms around me, holding me in his embrace. "That went better than expected." He looks back at Raven, who's staring at us with a sweet smile. I expected to see jealousy in her eyes, but there is none. Maybe, just maybe, I've been judging her too harshly. Maybe Silas wasn't lying to me after all. Maybe they really are just friends. "I'll have to thank you properly, Raven," he says.

She nods politely, her attention stolen away by a woman who approached her. I feel her glancing at us curiously every few seconds, but Silas doesn't seem to care. Instead, he pulls me onto the dance floor.

"Aren't you worried about upsetting her?" I ask, unable to hide the insecurity I feel. "I hear she's the woman you always go back to, the only one you ever date exclusively."

"You're jealous again."

"You're evading my question."

Silas chuckles and pulls me flush against him, the two of us swaying to a slow romantic song. "No, Alanna," he answers. "I'm not worried about upsetting her. You're all I can see tonight, and every night to come. I've said it before and I'll remind you as many times as I need to. There's nothing between Raven and me. The rumors are just that — *rumors*."

The tension in my shoulders fades away, and I smile up at

him. Even if this is all a lie, and he's leading me on the way Ryan did, I don't think I'll ever regret this. Being in his arms, having him look at me the way he does... I want this, even if it isn't real, even if it's only temporarily.

"Now that we've accomplished what we came here to do, we might as well enjoy our night. I heard the food is pretty good," he says. "I was told that the crab cakes are nice."

I cough, my eyes widening as nerves run down my spine, straightening my back. Oh shit.

"They've got crab legs too, though that sounds a bit messy. Lots of crabs tonight, huh?"

"I... um," I stammer.

Silas chuckles and moves one of his hands to my hair, his fingers threading through my long hair until he's cupping the back of my head, his touch possessive. "You call me crazy, but it looks like I've met my match."

"I... I can explain."

"You don't need to," he murmurs, leaning in. His lips brush over my ear, sending a shiver down my spine. "I love your crazy side, baby. Spread all the rumors you want, because there's only one woman present tonight that I'll ever be interested in. Only you, Alanna. Always you."

He kisses my neck, and a soft moan escapes my lips. "Silas," I whisper. "Remember where we are."

He pulls back and grins at me. "You staked your claim, baby... now you'd better take responsibility."

He leans in again, his lips brushing over mine once, twice, before he gives in and kisses me in the middle of the dance floor, everything fading away until he's all I can focus on.

I can't resist him. Even if I could, I no longer want to. I want everything he's making me feel. Every warped emotion, every bit of heartbreak that I know will come from this. We're a disaster in the making, but what a beautiful sight it'll be.

Chapter Fifty-Four

Alanna

I stare at the text Silas sent me in dismay. He's working late *again*. Even though we live together, I rarely see him outside of the office. It's only really our mornings that we spend together. We don't even drive to work together anymore, because he doesn't want me to be without a car after work. It's strange, because I see him every day, but I miss him.

I miss the version of him that he only shows me. The intimate smiles, the flirting. He's entirely different at work, and I find myself wanting to spend more alone-time with him. He's turning me into a crazy, greedy person. I want his attention, and I want more of his kisses. I want him with a desperation that scares me, and it isn't just physically.

I stare at the display in the elevator as it moves down to the parking lot, surprised by my own melancholy. I've always loved being alone, so when did I start feeling lonely without Silas?

The elevator stops on the 12th floor, and Ryan walks in, his eyes widening when he sees me. Damn it. This is exactly why Silas told me to use the private elevator that's reserved for our VIP clients, but I was just too worried it'd draw my colleagues' attention.

"Alanna," Ryan says, his tone carrying a hint of relief. "Just the person I was thinking of. Mitchel just called me asking if we'd be up for volunteering today. He said the recent rain pushed a lot of plastic to the shore, and he needs our help. I didn't dare commit on your behalf, but are you free tonight?"

"Oh," I murmur in surprise. That's not exactly what I expected him to say. Ever since I ended things with Ryan, I stopped volunteering too. I didn't want to do anything that reminded me of him, and since I'd been avoiding him, I didn't want to go anywhere I'd run into him. I've really missed it. There's nothing better for my soul than spending a few hours making an actual difference.

"He asked about you, actually. He was worried since he hasn't seen you in a while. If you're not busy, why don't we go and help him out tonight? I was gonna go by myself, but since you're off work now anyway... the more helping hands, the better."

I study him for a moment, trying to assess if there's more to his request, but he seems genuine. I have a hard time saying no to things in general, but saying no to charity work is near impossible. "Sure," I end up saying. "I'm free tonight."

He smiles at me and walks out of the elevator when we reach the garage. "I'll see you there then. I just need to run home to get changed."

I nod, and he rushes off, leaving me staring after him in confusion. He truly doesn't seem to have any ulterior motives today. Have I been judging him too harshly?

I head straight to the beach, and just like Ryan said, it's littered with plastics of all kind. Mitchel waves at me when he sees me.

"Alanna! It's so good to see you, kid. I had to save a turtle from some plastic earlier today, and it's got me even more eager to get this trash cleared out as soon as possible. How have you been? I was worried about you, but you seem good. You look healthy and happy."

I smile at him as I take the tools he's handing me. "I am. It's good to see you too, Mitchel. I'm sorry I haven't been in a while."

He smiles at me and claps me on the back, but before he can say another word, someone shouts his name. "I hope that's not another turtle," he mutters. "I'll catch up with you later, okay?"

I nod and wave him off, working in solitude for a while. I love volunteering at soup kitchens and doing charity walks, but there's something about being on the beach, sand between my toes and a breeze dancing on my skin.

"You've got that same expression on your face," Ryan says, and I look up to find him standing a few steps away. He walks toward me, his expression complicated. "You looked just like this when we first met. I don't think I'll ever get that image out of my mind."

I grimace and look away, suddenly uncomfortable. This is exactly what I wanted to avoid. I don't want to reminisce with him.

"How is it that we work in the same office and still don't get to see each other?"

I purse my lips, unsure how to handle him. "It's a big company," I end up saying.

He nods and works quietly alongside me, the way we used to. Ryan and I were pretty good friends before we started dating, but I wonder if any of that was real. Would he truly have come here today if I hadn't agreed to join?

"Are you okay, Alanna? You're not usually this quiet. Is Silas overworking you?"

I look up, startled out of my thoughts. "No, not at all."

Just hearing Silas's name fills me with equal parts longing and guilt. What would happen to Ryan and Silas's bond if he ever found out what I did? From what I understand, things are already strained between them, and this could be the final straw.

Ryan sighs and looks away. "Just tell me if he is. I know there's nothing you can't handle, but when it comes to my brother, I can definitely help. I'm worried he's targeting you because of me."

I instantly want to defend Silas, but I know no good will come of it. "He's good to me, Ryan. He's a fair boss, and he treats all of his employees well."

Ryan stares at me, his expression pained. "Just be careful, okay? I know how charming my brother can be, and you're spending so much time with him now. I saw a photo of you two in The Herald last week, and the way he looked at you didn't sit well with me. I know employees of the ψ division often attend corporate events with him, but I don't know... I don't think you'd ever betray the love we shared in that way, but still. Silas can be hard to turn down. Just remember that he's always got an ulterior motive, and there's only one girl he's ever truly loved. *Ray.*"

I look up in surprise, the name sounding oddly familiar. "Who is Ray?" I ask, my heart squeezing painfully.

Ryan hesitates. "She's the one he calls for when he's drunk, the one he can't ever forget. He won't tell me anything about her, but it's her he calls for every single time he drinks too much. There are plenty of girls he has fun with, but she's the only one he'll ever love. Don't be just another girl, okay? If you never trust me again and there's no future for us, I'll find a way to live with that, but please, please... please don't ever get with Silas. If he goes after you it's really only to hurt me. Please don't let him use you like that. Don't let him do to you what I did."

I nod, my heart uneasy. The name Ray sounds familiar, and it's almost like I can hear Silas whisper it in a memory I can't quite grasp.

Realistically, there's no future for Silas and me. If people were to find out about us, we'd be judged harshly, and I have no doubt it'd harm Silas's reputation.

"You don't need to worry about that. He's just my boss."

Ryan looks into my eyes and forces a smile onto his face. "I believe you, but the photos posted by The Herald definitely made it look like there was something going on between you. They were also left up for much longer than Sinclair Security usually allows, almost as if Silas wanted everyone to see those photos. The way you two danced together, and the way he looked at you... it made me feel sick, Alanna."

I grimace and nod. That's probably how most people would respond if they found out about us. They'd call Silas sick or cruel for going after his brother's girl, and I don't even want to imagine what they'd say about me.

"Like I said," I murmur. "You don't need to worry about it. Besides, you two seem to be doing okay now, aren't you? You work for Sinclair Security and you guys have dinner together every once in a while. I'm not dismissing what you told me, but Silas seems like a good person. He works hard, and he clearly cares about you."

Ryan looks away and sighs. "I think he just feels guilty for taking everything from me and leaving Mom and me penniless. There isn't much left for him to take, so I guess he's feeling charitable now."

I shake my head. "Just talk to him. I don't think he's pitying you. To me, it looks like he cares about you and wants to salvage whatever relationship you can still have, but relationships are two-way streets, you know?"

Ryan nods and grabs my hand, squeezing tightly. "Yeah, I know." He hesitates and looks away for a moment. "Alanna, you and I... we're okay, right? We're still friends, right? I thought we were okay, but it feels like I'm losing you, and I don't know what to do."

My thoughts turn to Silas, and how upset he was when I had lunch with Ryan. I don't want to see him hurting like that again, but it's near impossible to cut ties with Ryan completely. My thoughts turn to the future I can't help but imagine, and for a moment, I wonder what it'd be like if I formally dated Silas. I wouldn't be able to avoid Ryan, and each family dinner would turn into hell.

"Yeah," I whisper. "We're fine."

We aren't fine at all, but I'm not sure what else to say. It doesn't matter what road I choose to walk — they're all dead ends.

Chapter Fifty-Five

ALANNA

I walk into the house after a fulfilling evening volunteering with Ryan, my heart filled to the brim with something that feels a lot like *closure*. The way our relationship ended left me questioning everything about who I am and who we were as a couple. Ryan might have been the one who broke my trust, but it resulted in me questioning everyone and everything around me.

It might have been different for someone who's lived a full life with enough memories to help them withstand the hits that life brings them, but it isn't the same for me. I was betrayed by the only person I ever remember trusting, the only person I've ever let in, the only one I've ever loved. It left me feeling stupid and inadequate, as though somehow, I deserved what happened, because I failed to see through Ryan, because I *chose* to trust him.

I walk into the living room to find Silas standing by the window, a whiskey glass in his hand. He turns to face me, his expression unreadable. "Where were you?" he asks, his voice soft.

I tense, unsure what to tell him. If I tell him the truth, would that hurt him? Would it anger him?

Silas put his glass down and walks toward me, his steps slow and measured, his gaze trained on me. My heart starts to race and I bite down on my lip in an attempt to keep my nerves under control. He pauses in front of me and raises his hand to my face, placing a finger underneath my chin to tip my face up toward his. "There's sand in your hair," he whispers. "Who were you with?"

I look into his eyes, my heart heavy with regret. I don't need to tell him who I was with. He knows. He just wants me to say it.

"Silas," I whisper, his name a plea on my lips. What I'm asking him for, I'm not sure. *Don't do this. Don't ask questions you don't want answers to. Don't look at me that way.*

He drops his forehead to mine and inhales shakily. "Alanna," he murmurs, his voice barely above a whisper. "Tell me you weren't with him."

He pulls away a little to look into my eyes and cups my cheek tenderly, his gaze pleading. "Silas," my voice falters. "It isn't like that. When I broke up with him, that truly was the end of our relationship. We were just volunteering together. All we did was gather plastic on the beach."

He takes a step closer, our bodies brushing against each other. "Was that really all it was?"

I nod, my heart breaking over the pain I see in his eyes. I put that pain there, and I don't know how to take it away.

"Did you go because he asked you to?"

I look into his eyes, unsure what to say. I can't lie to him. Not to him.

His thumb brushes over my lip, and I inhale shakily. "Why do you keep hurting me?" His voice breaks, vulnerability shining through his eyes. "I've done all I can to show you that I'm not playing games with you. I've put my heart on a silver platter for you, Alanna... but I never even stood a chance, did I? I can't compete with the history you share with my brother, can I?"

"Silas, I swear, there's nothing left between Ryan and me. It was just... we're just trying to be friends, that's all."

"Friends?" he huffs. "You know he doesn't just want to be

your friend, yet you're giving him chance after chance to be with you, to earn your forgiveness. What have you given me? Have you ever seriously considered giving me a chance?"

My eyes widen, and Silas chuckles humorlessly. "You haven't, have you?" His hand threads through my hair, and he holds the back of my head like that, his touch possessive even now. "Do you have any idea how much I want you? Do you know how patient I've been? I've given you space, never asking for more than you're willing to give me, quietly watching over you, always putting you first… but it'll never be enough, will it? I'll never be enough for you. You'll never see me as more than you ex's older brother."

He untangles his fingers from my hair and lets his hand fall to his side, a soft defeated sigh escaping his lips. He takes a step away and turns away from me, leaving me staring up at his broad back. Silas looks up at the ceiling, and for once, I allow myself to follow my heart, no matter how wrong it might be, no matter how harshly the people around us will judge us.

I take a step closer to him and wrap my arms around his waist as I press my cheek to his back, hugging him tightly. I can't stand to see him hurting this way, and watching him turn his back to me tears me to shreds. Why does it feel like I'm losing him when he was never mine in the first place?

"I don't feel anything for him, Silas. I really don't."

He places his hands over mine, but the tension in his body doesn't ease. "I can't do this anymore, Alanna." He pushes my hands away, forcing me to let go of him. Silas walks toward his bedroom, and every instinct is telling me to stop him, that letting him walk away now isn't something I'll survive.

I walk up to him and grab his arm, pulling him back to me. Silas turns back to look at me, his gaze cold, but I don't let that deter me. I rise to my tiptoes and wrap my arms around his neck before pulling him toward me, my lips finding his. I kiss him with every repressed and hidden feeling, every desire I pretend not to have.

Silas freezes against me instead of kissing me back, and my

heart sinks as I pull away, humiliation and defeat spreading throughout my body. I let my hands slide down his chest and pull them toward me, unable to look him in the eye, the rejection stinging.

"Silas," I whisper, my voice breaking.

Just as I think he's going to walk past me, he grabs my hair and tips my head up before leaning in and kissing me, his touch rough and impatient. I moan as I rise back to my tiptoes, my hands roaming over his chest.

Silas grabs my hips and lifts me into his arms, and I instinctively wrap my legs around his waist as he pushes me against the wall, grinding against me as he deepens our kiss, moaning into my lips. He pushes against me, pressing his hard cock against me, and a delicious shiver runs down my spine. I move my fingers to his chest, sending the buttons on his shirt flying in my impatience.

Silas chuckles and moves his lips to my neck as I push his shirt as far over his arms as I can, wanting it off entirely. "So impatient," he admonishes before sucking down on my neck.

"Oh God," I moan, rolling my hips against him. I need more of him. I need to feel him closer. I want him deep inside me, his thoughts filled with nothing but me. I want my body to tell him everything my lips can't.

Silas carries me to his bedroom, his lips never leaving mine as he blindly finds his way to his room, the two of us knocking over several things in the hallway in our impatience. He throws me onto his bed and shrugs off his shirt, letting it drop to the floor as he watches me.

He places his knee on the bed and leans over me with a scowl on his face. "Tell me, baby. Did you let my brother touch you today?"

I shake my head, and Silas grits his teeth as he stares at me for a moment, trying to ascertain my truthfulness. He pushes my dress up and looks into my eyes as he wraps his fingers around my thong, slowly dragging the fabric down my thighs.

"You're lying to me, aren't you?"

I shake my head again, and Silas leans over me. One of his hands moves between us, and he smiles when he realizes how wet I am. His touch is rough as he pushes two fingers in, his thumb brushing over my clit. I wrap a hand over my lips, trying my hardest to control the intense desire he makes me feel.

"No," he warns. "None of that." He yanks my hand away and pins it above my head as he looks into my eyes, his fingers slowly driving me crazy. "Say my name, Alanna. Beg for it, and I'll make you come."

"Si," I beg, "*please.*"

Silas freezes, his eyes widening. "What did you just call me?"

"Si?"

He groans and dives in, his lips taking mine roughly as his hands tear at my clothes, his touch tinged with a new kind of desperation. He takes off my dress, and I tug at his suit trousers, the two of us relentless. Silas moans when I wrap my hand around his cock and pump up and down, enjoying the feel of him.

"*Alanna,*" he warns. He sits down on the bed with his back against the headboard and pulls me on top of him, so I'm straddling him, his cock sliding against my soaking wet pussy. I rise up a little, and Silas grabs his cock, aligning himself with me as I sink down on top of him, taking all of him, inch by delicious inch.

"Oh God," I moan as Silas drops his forehead against mine. Our position feels so intimate, so close. I feel like I'm in his embrace, yet he's filling me up in the best way possible. He cups the back of my head and kisses me as I rock my hips, riding him slowly, leisurely, the two of us lost in each other.

"He can't fuck you like this," Silas whispers against my lips as his hands move to cup my breasts, his thumbs teasing my nipples. "He doesn't know your body like I do. No one ever will."

I nod. "No one has ever made me feel this way, Si. I swear it. No one but you."

He captures my lips as his hands move to my waist, and Silas starts to move me up and down his cock, keeping me at an angle that has me gasping. He nibbles on my lower lip as he teases me. "He doesn't know you can come just like this, with my cock sliding in and out of you slowly, the tip brushing past your clit over and over again." Silas pulls back to look at me and smirks. "You want to come for me, don't you?"

I nod, my gaze pleading. He's torturing me, keeping me right at the edge. I might be on top of him, but I'm not in control at all.

"Yeah... you've always been a little slut for me, haven't you? Couldn't resist me even when you were dating my brother. You've always been mine."

"Please," I beg.

"Please *what*, baby?"

"Please make me come, Si. I'm begging you. I can't take another second of this."

"Tell me you're mine, and I'll consider it."

I look into his eyes, half crazed with a deep need for this man that goes beyond the orgasm I'm craving. "I've been yours from the moment I looked into your eyes that day in the coffee shop. I haven't stopped thinking about you since."

"Good girl," Silas says. "You've been mine for far longer than that, but this'll do for now." He moves his hand between us and brushes his thumb over my clit as he finally lets me have all of his cock, and just like that, I shatter for him, wave after wave of pleasure making my pussy clench all around his cock.

Silas watches me with a satisfied expression and lifts his thumb to his lips, sucking it clean with a smirk on his face. The moment my breathing steadies, he turns us over, his hands pinning my wrists above my head.

"My turn," he groans as he places his lips against my neck, sucking down and marking me as his as he fucks me, the speed and strength of his thrusts getting me close all over again. Silas pulls back a little to look at me as he gets close, holding himself up on his forearms as he whispers my name.

"*Alanna*," he groans, right before coming deep inside me, his eyes falling closed as pure bliss takes over his expression. He drops his forehead to mine, his breathing irregular. This is everything I've been denying myself, everything I've ever wanted. This feeling... I've never felt quite this *complete* with anyone else. I wrap my arms around him and hug him tightly, my heart at ease. Something that feels this right can't be wrong, can it?

Chapter Fifty-Six

ALANNA

My heart is pounding as I walk into the office. I woke up in Silas's bed, all alone. He never leaves the house before me, and it doesn't sit well with me that he did today. Mornings are always *ours*. It's the only part of our day that's uninterrupted, and it's quickly become my favorite moment with him.

I can't help but feel uneasy. Last night felt perfect, but it also felt final, as though I was losing him even as he sank deep inside me. He seemed hurt and angry, and even as he kissed me, I felt him pulling away.

I glance at his closed office door as I sit down at my desk. "Is the boss in?" I ask. Jessica looks up and nods. "Yeah, he came in super early."

"Why? Is there an emergency of some sort?"

She shakes her head. "Not sure. He does this occasionally, but he doesn't seem to be in a bad mood, so I wouldn't worry about it."

I nod as I try to think of an excuse to walk into his office. I need to see him. I've felt unsettled from the moment I woke up, and I won't feel even remotely okay until I'm sure things are fine between us.

I sigh as I grab my tablet and walk toward his office, knocking briefly before stepping in. Amy and Silas both look up, and I freeze as I take in their intimate positions. She's leaning over him, looking at something on his laptop, their heads mere inches away from each other.

She straightens when she sees me and pastes a polite smile on her face, and I try to do the same, despite the white hot jealousy that uncurls in my stomach.

"Can I help you?" Silas asks, his tone overly formal.

I tense and hug my tablet to my chest as I approach his desk, unsure what to say. "Can I speak to you for a moment?"

"Go ahead."

I glance at Amy nervously. "In private."

Silas sighs, a hint of impatience in his expression. He's never looked at me that way before. He's never looked so cold and impersonal, not even when he interviewed me for this job. "Amy is my executive assistant. There isn't anything you can tell me that she can't hear."

I stare at him pointedly. "It's private."

"Then it can wait until work is over."

"It *can't* wait."

"Then you'd better speak up, Alanna. Stop wasting my time."

I glance back at Amy, who is watching the exchange between us curiously, and I cross my arms.

"*Fine,*" I snap. "You weren't in bed with me when I woke up this morning. Why?"

Amy coughs awkwardly and Silas stares at me with wide eyes, as though he genuinely didn't expect me to mention it. Amy takes a step away from Silas and grabs her phone from his desk before walking away briskly, a smile on her face. "I... um, I'll take another look at those files," she stammers as she walks out, shutting the door behind her.

Silas runs a hand through his hair as he looks at me. "I

thought you wouldn't want anyone knowing what happened last night."

"You left me no choice." Truthfully, I'm happy that he forced my hand. Something about the way Amy was leaning into him didn't sit well with me, and by behaving the way he did, he allowed me to stake my claim. Maybe I'm crazy, but I don't care.

"I had to work, Alanna."

"What was so urgent that you couldn't wait for us to go to work together?"

He grits his teeth and tears his gaze away. "Since when do I answer to you, Alanna? I'm *your* boss, not the other way around."

Why is he being this way? Why is he being so cold and distant after the way he touched me last night? I stare at him, speechless. Did I misunderstand?

"Silas, what's wrong?"

He shakes his head. "Nothing is wrong. What do you want, Alanna?"

You. "I... um, okay, well, let's talk about it over dinner, alright?"

Silas looks away. "I won't be home for dinner."

"Why?"

He sighs and stares out the window. "I'm going out for dinner."

My heart sinks. "Who are you having dinner with?"

He looks into my eyes, and it's almost like I can barely recognize him. "Why is it that you seem to think you have any right to question me? Who do you think you are? It seems I've been too kind to you, because you've forgotten your place."

I take a step away, my heart twisting painfully. He's pushing me away, and I don't know how to hang onto him when he's determined to let me go.

"Look me in the eye and tell me you're going on a date with someone else, Silas."

He smiles humorlessly. "You never did me the courtesy of telling me any of the times you went to see my brother. Why is it you expect something from me that you've never given me in return?"

"Who is it?" I ask, my voice breaking. "Raven?"

He looks into my eyes for a moment before nodding briefly. My heart shatters, and I take another step away as I lift my hand to my chest.

"Don't," I plead. "Don't go, Silas. I know you're mad at me, and I know that I've hurt you, but don't do this. *Please* don't do this."

He runs a hand through his hair and looks away. "Get back to work, Alanna. I don't pay you to waste working hours on personal issues."

I swallow hard and nod. I don't have the right to ask more of him than I already have, and if I keep pushing, he might try to get rid of me entirely. Losing this job is about more than my career prospects now. It's also the one thing that keeps us connected, even when he wants to cut our ties.

"I'm going to cook you dinner tonight," I murmur. "So please come home to me."

I turn and walk away, pausing at the sound of his voice. "I won't," he says, his voice decisive.

I lift a trembling hand to the door handle and nod. "I'll wait for you anyway," I murmur before I walk away on shaking legs, my thoughts reeling as I head back to my desk.

I'm on autopilot for the rest of the day, completing one task after another just to keep my mind off Silas. Silas walks past us at six, his stride impatient, as though he can't wait to get to his date. He doesn't even pause to look at me, not even for a moment.

Jessica chuckles. "Looks like the boss has a date."

"Why do you say that?" I ask, hanging onto the broken pieces of my heart as best as I can.

"The cologne," Jessica and Josh say in unison.

I nod as I sit back in my chair. He's really doing this. He's going on a date with Raven less than a day after sleeping with me. She really is the one he always goes back to, after all.

Chapter Fifty-Seven

Silas

"I didn't think I'd ever get to have dinner with you again," Raven says as she sits down opposite me.

"What makes you say that?" I push a glass of her favorite wine toward her, and she takes it from me with a smile.

"Because you found her, didn't you? You found your Ray. It's that girl, isn't it? Alanna. Your employee."

I look down at the whiskey in front of me and nod. "How did you know?"

Raven chuckles and reaches for me, placing her hand on top of mine. "I know you only agreed to our arrangement because I resemble the woman you love. I had my suspicions from the moment I met Alanna, but when I saw the way you look at her, I knew. I've never seen you look at anyone that way before — certainly never *me*."

I nod slowly and take a leisurely sip of my drink. Raven and I have known each other for years, and though we've never really been more than friends, we do care about each other. It's no wonder she knew about Alanna without me saying anything.

"So that begs the question, my dear Silas... what are you doing here tonight? I saw how you two interacted at the auction, and then again at the runway afterparty. Everything seemed to be going quite well, so why are you here with me tonight?"

I sigh and push the menu toward her. "Why are you so full of questions tonight? Can't I just catch up with an old friend?"

She raises her brow and shakes her head. "Not when that old friend is also your alleged ex. I remember how possessive your girl is. There's no way she's okay with this, and I'm not okay with you using me to hurt someone you clearly love."

I breathe a sigh of relief when the waiter walks over, saving me from this conversation. She's supposed to be on my side, isn't she? Why is she defending Alanna?

"Does she know you're with me?" Raven asks the moment the waiter walks away, and I grimace.

"Can you please drop this?"

She crosses her arms and stares me down. "I won't. I have no doubt you're being an ass, and I want to know why. If you're going to use me to make her jealous, you at least owe me an explanation."

I look her in the eye and inhale deeply. "She used to date my younger brother, and she isn't over him. I'm done competing with carefully orchestrated memories. I'm done wondering if it's him she sees when she looks at me. I'm just done with all of it."

"What do you mean, carefully orchestrated?"

I shake my head and take another sip of my drink. Everything about the person Ryan is around Alanna is fake, a persona created especially for her, the perfect man in her eyes. How am I supposed to compete with that?

I glance at my phone, a small part of me wondering if she truly is cooking me dinner tonight. Surely not, right?

I sigh as I log into our home security system and check the cameras, only to find Alanna standing in the kitchen. I switch cameras and zoom in on the dining table. She's set it for two, and she seems to have gone all out in an effort to make it look romantic. *Fuck*.

I lock my phone and put it away. Even if I go home, where will that take us? Alanna has always been possessive, so there's every chance she just wants me home tonight because she doesn't want me to be with Raven. It doesn't mean she truly wants *me*.

"Fine," Raven says. "Let's eat then. Just don't say I didn't warn you. If I were you, and the man of my dreams actually wanted me too? I'd never let go. I'd play dirty if I needed to. I'd give it my all."

I look at her as I take a bite of my steak. "You still haven't told me who he is. Who is crazy enough to walk away from you?"

"Other than you?"

I chuckle. "Touché, but you always knew my heart belonged to someone else. I never led you on."

She looks away, loneliness taking root in her dark eyes. "My soon to be brother-in-law," she says, her voice so soft I nearly missed it.

I clear my throat, my sip of whiskey having gone down wrong, and I narrow my gaze. "*What*?"

She shakes her head and smiles at me with a sad expression. "You don't get to judge me, Silas. You're in love with your brother's ex-girlfriend, and it's the same for me. I've been in love with my sister's fiancé for as long as I can remember, but he's never even looked at me twice. I loved him before she even met him."

"You loved him first," I murmur, the story sounding all too familiar.

"Yes, and if I thought for even one single moment that he could love me back, I'd risk it all. But he won't. He can't. Theirs is the kind of love most people don't even dare dream of, and I... I just want them both to be happy. But Silas, it's different for you. Your happiness is within reach."

I glance back at my phone and grab it hesitantly. The camera feed loads slowly, and my heart starts to ache as I watch Alanna sitting at the table by herself, staring at the candle burning in front of her, two filled plates on the table. I didn't believe she'd truly wait for me, but there she is.

I watch as she suddenly rises from her seat and stalks over to the living room, returning to the table with her laptop in hand. Just a few minutes later, my phone rings.

"Amy?"

"Boss... someone hacked your private phone and accessed your GPS data. The weird thing is that it seems to have come from your own address."

I chuckle and look up at the ceiling with the biggest smile on my face. She's such a psycho, but I love her so fucking much. I had my doubts about her feelings for me, but she wouldn't go this far if she didn't truly care about me. "Thanks," I say, ending the call.

"Raven," I murmur. "I need to go, before my girl comes to get me. I'm pretty sure I'm already in enough trouble as it is. I'd better not get you involved too."

Raven nods as she lifts her fork to her lips. "Go get your girl, Silas. And this time, *don't* let her go."

"I won't," I promise as I rise to my feet. My driver is already waiting for me as I walk out of the restaurant, and I can't help but chuckle. She never would've shown her crazy side to Ryan. That's always been only for me. This is the Alanna I know and love. The one who spray painted a car in high school because a guy wouldn't stop pursuing her, the girl who smashed *my* car because my brother hurt her, the crazy psycho who tracked me down because I didn't make it home for dinner when she told me to. She's insane, and I love every little thing about her.

Raven is right. My happiness is within reach, even if it doesn't always seem that way. She might not be fully over my brother, but her relationship with him is nothing in the grand scheme of things. When she and I are old and gray, she won't even remember him.

I walk into the house to find her by the door, putting on her shoes. She looks up at me, her eyes wide.

"Silas," she says, her voice breathy. "You're home."

I lean back against the closed door and nod. "Going somewhere?"

"I… um, no. I was just going for a walk."

I chuckle as I take in her outfit. She's wearing a black dress that looks way too hot on her with matching black heels that I bought her. I have no doubt my little psycho was on her way to bring me home, and she's dressed for battle.

I walk up to her, and she tenses. I can't help but smirk as I cup her cheek. "You wanted me home, Alanna… here I am."

She looks into my eyes and tips her face up toward mine. Her gaze roams over my face, and she tenses all of a sudden, her hand lifting to the edge of my collar. She looks into my eyes as she unbuttons the top button of my shirt. "There's a lipstick stain on your collar," she tells me, her tone deceptively calm. "How did that get there?"

I bite back a smile and thread my hand through her hair. "It's not quite what you're imagining, baby. It was just a simple greeting, that's all." She nods and continues to unbutton my shirt, her jaw locked. "What are you doing?" I ask, unnerved by her silence.

Alanna smiles up at me. "I'm going to burn this shirt."

I burst out laughing and pull her closer to me. "Okay, my little psycho… but can it wait?"

I lean in and kiss her, my heart finally at ease when she kisses me back, nothing standing between us. Any doubts I had are gone. Even if she doesn't love me as much as I love her, there's something between us that I'm certain she's never felt for my brother.

For now, that's enough for me.

Chapter Fifty-Eight

Alanna

"Why are you smiling like that?" I ask as Silas and I step into the elevator. The doors close, and he turns toward me with a wicked grin on his face. Silas leans in and twists his hand through my hair, tipping my face up as he kisses me, his touch possessive. I melt against him and lift my hand to his face, deepening our kiss, desire rushing through me.

The lift pings, and he steps away just as the doors reopen, straightening his tie as though nothing happened while I'm left feeling flustered and wanting more.

Si leans into me, his lip brushing over my ear as the elevator fills with more of his employees. "I was smiling because I've been wanting to do that for so fucking long now. One day, I'm going to fuck you in this elevator, with all of these mirrors around."

I bite back a smile as I elbow him, trying my best to send him a chastising look and failing. He hasn't stopped touching me since he came home to me, and I kind of wish we could've stayed in bed instead of having to go to work. For the first time in forever, everything feels right. I have no lingering doubts, and I'm done giving into my guilt and shame. Silas makes me happy, and that's all I'm going to focus on.

The lift stops on the 12th floor, and Silas and I both tense when Ryan walks in. He looks at me, a grin on his face, and I instinctively take a step closer to Silas. The guilt and shame I feel toward Ryan is nothing compared to my fear of hurting Silas.

"Alanna," he says, his tone relieved. "I was just hoping to come up because I need to speak to you."

Silas leans back against the wall and stares at Ryan through lowered eyes. "What the fuck is your deal, Ry? You know people think you're haunting the elevator, right?"

He glares at Silas. "Isn't that your fault? You took away my access."

"A normal person would've taken the hint."

Ryan ignores Silas and turns to me. "I know I don't have the right to ask something like this of you, but I just... I never told my mother that we broke up, and she insisted that I bring you over for family dinner tonight. I didn't know what to say, so when she initially brought it up, I just agreed. I'm really worried that she'll be upset if she finds out that we broke up. Please, can you do me the biggest favor and attend with me tonight?"

I shake my head. "No," I tell him resolutely. It isn't just because Silas is standing next to me. I'm just done with everything related to Ryan. I'm tired of carrying so much shame, of feeling obligated when I wasn't the one who sabotaged our relationship. "I can't attend your family dinner with you. I'm sorry."

Silas smirks and places his hand on the small of my back. "You should come," he tells me. "It was nice to have you over last time."

I look up at him, puzzled. He *wants* me to attend? I'd have thought he'd want to keep me away from Ryan.

"Yes," Ryan agrees. "Please, come tonight."

"I'll think about it," I murmur as we reach our floor.

Ryan sends me a pleading look as he steps back into the elevator, presumably to go back to his own floor now that he's accomplished what he set out to do, and I follow Silas to his office.

He looks relaxed, not even remotely annoyed, and that just confuses me even more. "Why did you tell me to attend dinner tonight?" I ask the second his office door closes behind us.

"I rarely get to have dinner with you as it is, and tonight will be much more bearable if you're there. I don't mind you attending family dinner, so long as you aren't his date."

I shake my head nervously. "I'd much rather stay home and catch up on work."

Silas shakes his head. "Come with me," he tells me again. "I want you to set the record straight tonight. Make it clear to both of them you and Ryan are over, or I'll do it for you."

I look into his eyes, finding a hint of insecurity in them. "Okay," I promise him. If this puts him at ease, I'll do it, no matter how uncomfortable it might be for me.

Silas smiles at me, a tinge of incredulity in his eyes, almost as though he expected me to deny him. I rise to my tiptoes and wrap my arms around his neck, my lips finding his. I'm falling for Silas Sinclair, and there's nothing I can do about it.

He groans in dismay when I pull away, and a giggle escapes my lips. "I have to get to work," I tell him. "My boss is a total meanie." Silas narrows his eyes at me as I walk away from him, my heart racing.

For the rest of the day, all I can think about is tonight's dinner. Just a few months ago, I attended this very same dinner as Ryan's girlfriend. Today I'll be going there knowing I'm sleeping with his brother, and I no longer even feel bad about it.

Chapter Fifty-Nine

ALANNA

"You've been quiet," Silas says as he parks in front of his family home. "Maybe I'm asking too much of you after all. Do you want me to take you home?"

Home. When did I start thinking of Silas's penthouse as *home*? I'm not sure, but it undoubtedly is. "No," I tell him. "I want to be wherever you are, Si."

He turns toward me and smiles, something indescribable in his gaze. "I won't ask you to tell him about us, Alanna. I know as well as you do that it'll strain my relationship with him. If we give it a bit of time, he'll be forced to move on, and eventually, everyone will forget you two ever even dated. I don't want our relationship to be stained by your past with him."

I grab his hand and nod. "Me neither," I whisper. I don't want to be the subject of countless rumors. I don't want Silas to endure it, either. I look down and smile, my heart skipping a beat when his words finally sink in. "Wait," I murmur. "What relationship?"

Silas chuckles and grabs my chin, pressing a swift, chaste kiss to my lips. "I fucking dare you to deny that you're mine, baby. Go on. Try it."

I bite down on my lip, tempted to tease him. "What will you do if I won't admit that I'm yours?"

Silas chuckles and shakes his head. "Alanna, my love... don't you provoke me. You won't like the consequences."

I smirk at him and step out of the car, my heart racing. The sound of Silas's laughter follows me as I rush up to the front door. I'll never tire of hearing him laugh. There's just something about it that makes my heart do funny things.

"Alanna!" a woman calls.

My smile melts away when I see Mona and Ryan standing by the front door, and I can't help but wonder if they just saw Silas kiss me in the car. Ryan smiles at me, and my worries melt away. He wouldn't be smiling like that if he'd seen us together. "Hey," he murmurs. "You made it."

Mona walks up to me and wraps her arm around me. "It's so good to see you. Ryan kept telling me you were busy with work and might not be able to make it, but I knew you'd be here. How have you been, sweetie?"

Silas walks up to us, and Mona tenses. She takes a step away from me, her eyes traveling up and down his body. "Silas," she says curtly.

He barely glances at her as he unlocks the door with the same biometrical security measures that we've got at our house. The door swings open, and he walks in, leaving us to follow.

Ryan falls into step with me as we walk toward the dining room, his arm brushing against mine. "I'm really glad you made it," he whispers. "Thank you. Honestly, thank you."

I nod at him and force a smile onto my face. I'm not here for him. I'm here for Silas. I'm here to overwrite the memory of me attending dinner as his brother's date. I'm here to make amends.

Much to my surprise, Silas sits down opposite Mona today, instead of at the head of the table, which earns him some curious glances that he ignores.

The same serving staff from last time step forward, placing large dinner trays on the table for us. "Wow," I whisper, taking in the variety of the food on the table. "This looks really amazing."

Mona forces a smile to her face. "Yes, Silas spoils us every time we come here. It's too bad it's only four times a year at most. It'd be so nice to have dinner more often."

Silas grunts and looks away. "If not for Ryan's incessant requests, I wouldn't be having dinner with you at all. The only reason I'm here is because he earnestly asked me to have dinner with his only two family members every once in a while."

She blanches and purses her lips in annoyance. Even after all this time, I don't fully understand their family dynamics. Ryan and Silas don't seem to have the best relationship, yet Si keeps trying his best to salvage it, going as far as having dinner with Mona for him. Despite that, Ryan still seems to resent Silas. I don't understand why.

Mona turns to me and forces a smile to her face. "It's been so long since I last saw you," she says. "How have you been? I understand Ryan and you work together now? That must be exciting?"

I feel a hand slip onto my thigh, down to the hem of my skirt and underneath it. I glance at Silas, but he's leaning back, seemingly relaxed, his expression blank. What is he doing? Is he insane?

"Yes," I murmur. "It's been great working at Sinclair Security. I work directly with Silas, and it's been an honor learning from him."

His fingers trail up my thigh until they brush against my underwear. Silas pries my legs apart, and I obey his silent command, shifting in my seat even as I grab my phone to text him.

Alanna: *what do you think you're doing?*

Silas glances at the notification on his phone and smirks, his finger slipping underneath my underwear.

"So you don't work with Ryan?"

I shake my head. "No. We don't even work on the same floor."

She looks at her son, confusion marring her beautiful face. "I thought you said you two worked together."

Ryan grimaces and picks up his spoon to take a sip of his soup, but I can't focus on him, not when Silas's fingers are drawing circles around my clit. I bite down on my lip as I smile at my ex while his brother finger fucks me. My phone buzzes, and I pick it up nervously.

Silas: *I told you that you wouldn't like the consequences, baby.*

I bite back a smile as I text him back.

Alanna: *what makes you think I don't like this?*

Silas chuckles and slips a finger inside me.

Silas: *you're such a good fucking slut for me, baby. Tell her Ryan and you are over, and I'll give you what you want. I'll make you come right here, right now, with him sitting opposite you.*

He's crazy, but so am I. I lock my phone and put it away as I lean back in my seat, spreading my legs wider for him, my dress bunched around my waist.

Silas takes a leisurely sip of his soup with his right hand while his left hand has me suppressing my moans as I pretend to focus on my food. I shift in my seat, wanting to ride his hand, and he smiles. This is what he's done to me. He's turned me into someone I barely even recognize. This version of me exists only for him.

"At least you two still get to see each other at work," Mona says eventually, her tone sour. She clearly dislikes that we don't work together, or maybe it's me working with Silas that she dislikes. I'm not sure, but I see her through different eyes today. Previously, I only ever saw her clear love for Ryan, but today I see her dislike for Silas. I'm surprised he tolerates her at all, but I shouldn't be. Despite his rough manner, Silas truly has a heart of gold.

He pushes another finger into me while using his knuckle to stroke my clit, and I bury my face in my hand. I can't take this. I really am going to come right here, with Ryan and his mother sitting opposite me.

"Are you okay, Alanna?" Ryan asks, concerned. "Your face is flushed."

I swallow hard and look at him, teetering on the edge of an orgasm that his brother has brought me to.

"Actually," I murmur, turning to face Mona. "Ryan and I broke up weeks ago."

I see Silas smile in my peripheral vision right before he gives me what I want, slipping a third finger in just as he teases my clit harder. I suck down on my spoon as I come for him, my hips moving against my will.

"You *what*?"

"Alanna," Ryan says, his tone pleading.

Silas leans into me, his lips brushing past my ear. "Good girl," he whispers. "I'll reward you later."

Then he pulls his fingers away and brings them to his lips, sucking them clean. Ryan doesn't seem to realize what just went down, and thankfully, neither does Mona.

I look down at my plate, surprised at the lack of guilt I feel. For so long, guilt is what held me back. It's what kept me away from Silas, and it's what kept me from reaching for the happiness he brings me.

I look up at Mona and smile. "Ryan and I broke up. We won't be getting back together. I'm here today as a friend, if that."

Ryan looks at me accusatorially, but I merely smile back at him. I don't owe him anything. Not anymore, and certainly not at Silas's expense.

Chapter Sixty

Silas

I lean back against the living room doorway, my eyes on Mona. She seems distraught, her gaze traveling over the family photos on the wall.

"Did you think you'd get away with it?"

She whirls around, her eyes widening. "Silas." Mona runs a hand through her hair, her movements coquettish and extremely irritating. "I have no idea what you're talking about."

I nod. "Yeah, when you've done so much fucked up shit, it could be anything."

She locks her jaw, and I smile at her sweetly. I still remember the way she threw me out of the house a mere few days after we lost my father. For years, everything went her way, but she should've known better.

"Alanna," I clarify.

She takes a seat on the sofa and crosses her ankles. "It doesn't matter that they broke up," she tells me. "They'll get back together."

I cross my arms and stare at her, confused. "Why are you

doing this? What did you think you'd accomplish through Alanna? What made you think I still cared about her after all these years?"

Mona leans back and smirks. "You carry a photo of her everywhere you go. I saw it in your wallet once, about a year ago, *My Ray of Sunshine* written on the back of it. I'd heard Ryan mention that there's a girl named Ray that you call for when you're drunk, and I've been curious about her ever since. A few months later, I saw her walking down the street. Now tell me, Silas. Don't you think that was a blessing from above? I found her through sheer coincidence. Your one and only weakness... and she doesn't even know who you are. It's priceless. I mentioned you a few times just to be sure, but she didn't recognize your name."

Fucking bitch. "Does Ryan know? About her and me?"

Her smile wavers. "No. Of course not. Despite my best efforts, he still thinks the world of you, even when he tries to convince himself that he doesn't. My little boy despises that you took everything from us, but he still loves you. I suppose that was a good thing, in the end. What would you have done to me if not for him?"

I nod, my shoulder slumping in relief. At least I wasn't entirely wrong about Ryan. Mona has him in her clutches, but he's not a lost cause. Not just yet.

"That must have been annoying, huh? You spent years talking shit about me, getting him to hate me, only for you to have to switch gears so you could use your own son to get to me. It's strange to me that women like you are allowed to be mothers at all."

She grits her teeth, and the way she's holding herself back is bringing me a strange sense of satisfaction. For years, she squandered away my father's fortune, only to find herself standing in the same house she once threw me out of, at my mercy.

"What were you trying to accomplish with Alanna? Was it just to hurt me?"

"Partially," she admits. "But let's be real, Silas. Would you deny her anything? I know you whisper her name in your sleep. I know you beg her not to leave you when you're drunk. Ryan told me all about your obsession with *Ray*. Even if she's with Ryan, you'll want her to have the best of everything, won't you?"

"You need help," I tell her. "I mean it. You really do. Ryan deserves better than this, but I'm done fighting his battles for him. You did this to yourself, Mona. You never should've touched Alanna, but you did, and you'll pay the price for it."

She smiles at me provocatively. "There's nothing you can do to me, Silas. Not without hurting Ryan, and by extent, Alanna. I know what you're like, and you won't let either of them suffer."

I grin at her and tilt my head. "Yeah, I definitely won't let my girlfriend suffer, not outside of bed anyway. My brother, though? I'm pretty damn pissed off he touched my girl. Now that she's finally back in my arms, I'm pretty inclined to retaliate for what he did, for taking what belongs to me."

She frowns, and I chuckle. "Why did you think she came here with me tonight, Mona? Why would she be so quick to clarify that she and Ryan broke up? I told her to."

I see the confusion and panic in her eyes, but it does nothing to ease my anger.

"Dating her comes at the cost of your relationship with Ryan. After everything you've done to salvage your bond with him, are you really going to do that to him?"

"Yes," I answer simply. "Without a second thought. I'll pick Alanna over anything and anyone, anytime. You should've thought of that before you set out to use Ryan against me. I've given him the benefit of the doubt because I'm well aware he's not the mastermind behind this little ploy, but I'm done. I'm out of patience. I have nothing left to fear now that she's chosen me all over again. You, on the other hand... I'd watch my back if I were you."

I walk back toward the dining room, where Alanna and Ryan are helping the staff clear the table. He looks somber, but my

Ray... she looks impatient. I have a pretty good idea what she's after.

"Your mother is ready to leave," I tell Ryan. He nods and glances at Alanna, but I shake my head. "I'll drive her home. You go with your mother."

He seems reluctant, but she pays him no mind and continues to stack plates, silently dismissing him. She's being such a good girl tonight. If I'd known going on a date with Raven would make her come to her senses, I'd have done it much sooner.

Ryan walks away, the dining room door falling closed behind him, and Alanna looks up, a sexy smile on her lips.

"I want my reward," she murmurs, her voice husky.

My heart skips a beat at the sight of her, and a soft chuckle escapes my lips. She's fucking perfection. I thought I loved her when I was younger, but it's nothing compared to what I feel for her now.

"You've been so good today, baby. Tell me what you want. Do you want me to fuck you?"

She nods. "You know I do."

I smirk at her and hold my hand out for her. She takes it, and I pull her into me. "I'm still upset, you know," I admit. "I hate that he once got to call you his. I'm not okay with it at all, Alanna, and I'm tired of pretending I am."

She wraps her arms around my neck and rises to her tiptoes, her lips brushing against mine. "How do I make you feel better? How do I make you forget?"

I bend down and lift her into my arms, carrying her toward the stairs. I intended to carry her to my childhood bedroom, but I pause in front of Ryan's instead.

"I'm going to fuck you in his room," I tell her. "I'm going to make you come all over his bed, my name on your lips and my cock buried deep inside your hungry pussy. I'm going to fuck you until you're begging me for mercy, and then I'm going to do it all over again in my own bed."

Alanna smiles at me, not a single hint of guilt or anguish in her eyes. "Is that a promise?"

I chuckle, the worst of my worries put to rest. "Yes, my little psycho. It is."

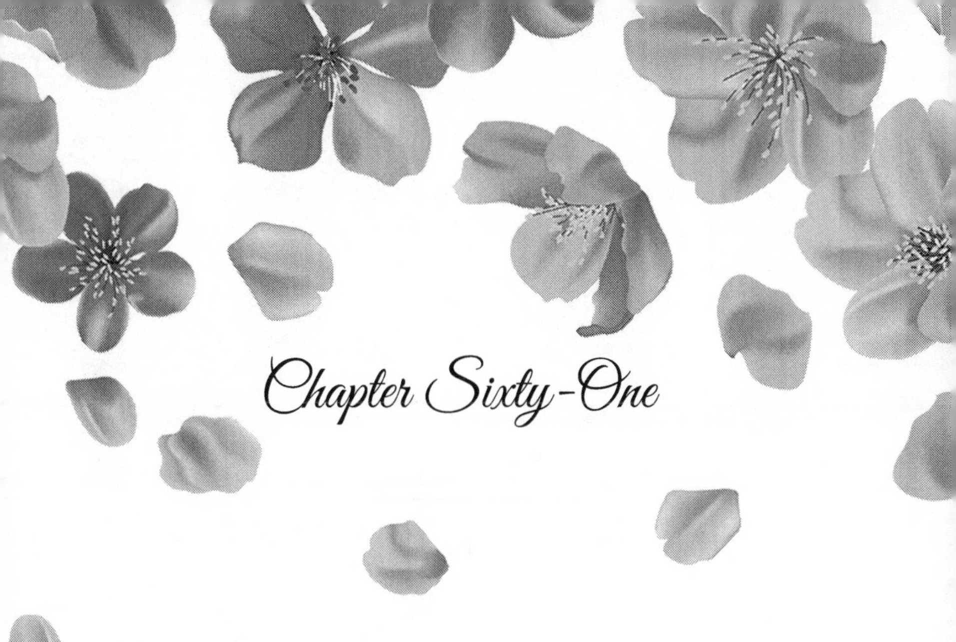

Chapter Sixty-One

SILAS

I lean back against the wall, trying my hardest to ignore the puppy eyes Alanna has been walking around with all morning. My Ray thinks I forgot her birthday. Little does she know, I've celebrated her birthday every year, even when she wasn't with me.

It's so surreal to me that we found our way back to each other. The last couple of weeks have been pure perfection. The only thing that could top my happiness is telling the world she's mine. I hate having to hide our relationship, and I don't think I can do it much longer.

"Alanna, can you please get me a report on our latest successful interventions? I need it before you go home today."

She looks up at me, a hint of disappointment in her eyes, and I bite back a smile. She never even hinted about her upcoming birthday, yet she's sad I supposedly didn't remember. I love watching her fall for me all over again. It's almost like our roles are reversed now, and she's the jaded one while I've got so much love to give that I can barely contain it.

I still remember how scared I was to expect anything from her when I was homeless, and she was my ray of sunshine. She didn't care about my circumstance, she only cared about me. From the very start, she was honest about her crush on me and the feelings that followed, and I was the one who was scared and insecure, worried I wasn't good enough for her. It took a few years, but I'm finally in a position to treat her the way I wanted to back then.

She's scared to expect anything from me, yet her heart clearly does. If only she realized that I'd never let her down. So long as it's within my power, I'll give her anything her heart desires. If I play my cards right, what she'll want above all is *me*.

Amy walks up to me, an agitated expression on her face. She smiles politely and averts her gaze as she leans in to speak to me. "Your brother has requested access to the top floor fourteen times since this morning. I've circumvented four attempts to send gifts up to Alanna, including flowers and balloons. I suspect he'll be waiting for her downstairs."

I sigh, irritated at his sheer grit. I can't even blame the guy. Alanna isn't the kind of girl you'd ever let go, but she was never his to take. I know she's been courteous with him in recent weeks, the two of them barely even friends, but he still won't give up. He may have approached her because his mother told him to, but it's clear the lines blurred at some point. He loves her.

I hoped he'd have given up on her by now, so being with Alanna won't cost me the relationship Ryan and I have only just rebuilt, but he's leaving me no choice. I refuse to keep dating Alanna in secret. She deserves better than that, and so do I.

I watch as Alanna rises from her seat, her tablet with the report on it in hand. She looks up at me and forces a smile to her face as she approaches me. "The data you asked for," she says, her voice soft.

I grin at her as I take it and hand it to Amy. "Thank you, baby," I murmur. Her eyes widen in alarm, and she glances at Amy, who dutifully ignores her worried expression. "Let's go. We've got somewhere to be."

Alanna frowns, and I grab her hand as I pull her into my

office. She freezes in shock when she sees the floor-length golden designer dress I bought her. "Change into that."

She turns toward me, her gaze filled with wonder and happiness, and I can't help but chuckle. "Did you really think I'd forget my girlfriend's birthday?"

"Girlfriend?" She repeats, her voice soft. I suppose I haven't really called her that before today, but that's exactly what she is.

I smirk and grab her chin, lifting her face to mine. "It doesn't sound right, does it? Don't you think *wife* would sound so much nicer?"

She shakes her head admonishingly. Alanna thinks I'm joking, and until she's ready, I'll let her believe that. I've got all the time in the world, after all. I've already spent five years searching for her. I'll spend another five making her mine all over again if I need to. Someday, I'm changing her last name.

I lean back and watch her as she changes out of her office clothes and into the dress I've been imagining on her. I thought it'd look sexy on her, but nothing could've prepared me for reality. I'm glad I'm not taking her to a crowded place tonight. The vision in front of me isn't one I want to share.

I kneel in front of her and grab the matching golden shoes I bought her. For what they cost me, the sparkles on them better be real diamonds and gold. I grab her ankle, and Alanna's breath hitches as I slip her shoes on for her.

I look up, our eyes meeting, and for a moment I consider throwing her onto my desk and fucking her raw, but there's time for that after dinner.

"Let's take the private elevator down," I murmur, wanting to avoid Ryan. There's no way he's seeing her today, and he certainly isn't seeing her in this dress.

I'm insanely nervous as I drive her to the one place I've gone to every single year on both her birthday and mine. Part of me wants her to regain her memory so she'll stop feeling so guilty about being with me, but a larger part of me knows that she'll have to go through the loss of both of her parents all over again, in addition to the memories of being homeless. There's a reason she's suppressing the most painful parts of her life, and I'm not selfish enough to force her to remember something that'll be bittersweet.

"We're here."

"Silas, are we trespassing?"

I turn toward her and smile, my heart aching at the familiar words. She has no idea that she said the same thing to me when I brought her here the first time.

"No," I tell her, my answer different to before. "I own the lands around us and everything on it."

This is one of the very first things I took back from Mona. It never should've fallen into her hands in the first place.

I offer Alanna my arm and walk her toward the blossom tree that I've visited every year on her birthday, except this time, there's a waiter standing by a table with dozens of candles around it.

Alanna gasps, and I smile to myself. I've always wanted to do this for her and never had the chance to. Even if she doesn't remember, I'm going to keep every promise I made her.

"Silas, this is... it's beautiful. Is this all for me?"

I cup her cheek gently and lean in, my heart overflowing with happiness. This might be for her, but it's also for me. It's for the young me who wanted to give Alanna the world and couldn't. It's for the girl who loved me when I had nothing and never treated me differently. "Happy birthday," I whisper, my lips brushing against hers. I kiss her tenderly before pulling away. She's far too beautiful tonight, and touching her is dangerous. I'll be tempted to lay her down underneath the tree, the breeze caressing her skin as I sink deep inside her.

Alanna chuckles as though she knows what I'm thinking, and I can't help but smirk as I pull out her chair for her before sitting down opposite her.

Her gaze drops to the jewelry box on the table, and I nod. "Open it."

She does as I ask, but instead of gushing over the diamond

necklace I bought her, she snaps the box closed in shock. "Are you insane? Those aren't real, are they?"

A surprised laugh escapes my lips, and I nod. "Of course they're real, my love."

"You're crazy, aren't you?"

I nod. "A little."

"What makes you think I won't just sell this?"

I shrug. "I'll just buy you a new one, baby."

She looks into my eyes with so much love in her gaze that my heart skips a beat. I know she isn't ready to say the words, but I hear them loud and clear nonetheless.

"There's more."

She raises her brows, and I push an envelope toward her. Alanna takes it with trembling fingers and opens the birthday card I made for her. Yet another tradition she's forgotten.

"Wow," she whispers. "Did you... did you commission this?"

I smile at her and shake my head. "I drew it."

She looks at me with such disbelief that I burst out laughing. "You don't believe me?"

"I didn't know you could draw. This... is this what I look like in your eyes?"

I drew a portrait of her standing in the sun, her face tipped up toward the light, a serene smile on her face. It's what she looks like on Sunday mornings, and it's an image so seared in my mind that I drew it from memory.

"Yes," I tell her, "and no. You're far more beautiful than that, Alanna. My drawing skills don't do you justice."

"Silas, I... I..." I lean in and watch her struggle to find the right words, even though I can see her feelings reflected in her eyes.

"Happy birthday, my love."

She nods, her eyes filling with tears. "Thank you," she says eventually, her voice breaking. "Thank you for letting me experience true happiness. Before you, I didn't know what it really felt like. I thought I did, but I was wrong."

I smile at her and nod. "This is nothing yet, baby. Every day we're together, I'm going to do my best to make you happier than the day before." *Even if you can't remember me, I'm going to make sure your heart always will.*

I glance at the waiter, and he approaches us with our starters. This is the birthday I once promised her, and I'm so glad I got to keep my promise.

Chapter Sixty-Two

Alanna

"I'm exhausted," I complain as Silas parks in the car lift. He rarely uses it anymore, and I think it's because I once vaguely indicated I didn't exactly love it. He's thoughtful like that, picking up on little cues that not even I am fully aware of.

He tips his head back against the headrest and smiles at me as the lift moves up. "I know, baby. Not much longer left now. I used to hate being so busy at work, but having you around makes it so much bearable. I love being able to see you all day, but I still want more."

Since the elections are coming up, the ψ division has been working non-stop, trying to prevent foreign interference, and every time we circumvent one attempt, three more are launched. It never ends. Silas, my team, and I have practically been living at the office. It feels like Si and I haven't been able to spend a moment alone in nearly two weeks.

"More?" I suppose we haven't been as intimate as we usually would've been. By the time we get home, we're both exhausted, and I often just go to bed after dinner.

"*More.*"

Silas steps out of the car and walks around it to open the door for me, offering me his hand as I get out. He entwines our fingers and pulls me along, leading me to my room silently.

"I've had enough of this," he tells me as he opens my wardrobe. I watch in confusion as he grabs as many of my clothes as he can before marching out of my room and straight into his. He walks into his walk-in wardrobe and puts my clothes down on one of the counters.

"I... what are you doing?"

He smirks at me. "What do you think I'm doing?"

Heat rushes to my cheeks and my heart begins to pound wildly as he starts to hang my clothes next to his. "Si..."

He chuckles, and the sound sets my heart ablaze. There's something about hearing Silas laugh that brings me a strange kind of joy and satisfaction.

"I've had enough, Alanna. I know you're exhausted, and I am, too. The next couple of weeks will not get any easier, so let me fall asleep next to you every night, okay? I barely get to spend any alone time with you, and it's killing me. I want to fall asleep with you in my arms, and I want you to be the first thing I see when I wake up. I may have to share you with my staff for most of the day, but your mornings and evenings are mine."

I stare at him, my heart wavering. I tried to resist as best as I could, but he's so easy to fall for. I know the happiness we share is limited, overshadowed by the inevitable pain we'll go through when people find out about us, but it's worth it.

"What's wrong? Any objections?"

I grin at him and shake my head. "No objections."

Silas smiles as he puts my clothes next to his, and I lean back to watch him. How is any of this real? When he and I got together, I thought it was just passing lust, but with each passing day, a life without him becomes harder to imagine.

"What's wrong?"

I shake my head. "Nothing, it's just... I thought you'd get tired of me eventually. I keep trying to remind myself not to fall for you so I won't get hurt, but you make it impossible to hold back. I want to be selfish with you, Si. I want all of you. I don't ever want to let you go."

"Then don't." He looks into my eyes, his expression serious. "Don't ever let me go, Alanna. No matter what happens, no matter what people might say."

I nod, my heart cautiously hopeful. Would it be okay to want it all with Silas? Can I really place my heart in his hands?

"Alanna?"

I look up, and Silas smiles.

"There's only one woman I've ever loved, you know? There's only one woman I've ever wanted to share my home with."

My heart skips a beat, and I clear my throat. He can't be saying what I think he's saying. I didn't bring this up so he could reassure me with lies. "I, um, I need to take a shower."

Silas looks disappointed for a moment, and then he nods. "Use this bathroom, then. From now on, it's *ours*, just like this bedroom is."

I blush and nod as I brush past him, flustered. The joy that surrounds us scares me. I can see us spending the rest of our lives together, just like this. Our happiness feels so fragile, and I'm terrified of everything falling apart around us. I don't think I could survive losing Silas. We were never supposed to fall for each other, but he and I... We were inevitable.

It's strange to be using his space tonight. Most nights, Silas joins me in my bed, and the few times I found myself in his, I'd slip out the moment he fell asleep, scared to overstep any boundaries between us.

Si uses the bathroom after me, and I climb into bed, listening to the sound of the shower. It's strange to have this last barrier between us fall away. It gives me hope I don't dare cling to. Silas is nothing like his brother, but a small part of me still wonders whether this is all a game, whether he approached me with an ulterior motive, and whether he'll tire of me, eventually. I struggle to see what a man like Silas sees in someone like me. Whatever it is, someday he'll wake up and realize that I don't measure up to the image he has of me. Where would that leave me?

The bathroom door opens, and Silas walks in wearing nothing but boxers. I take my time appreciating his body. He pauses halfway through the room and stares at me, a tinge of disbelief in his eyes. "You have no idea how many times I've imagined you lying in my bed with me, Alanna. You might think you know how much I want you, but I promise you, it's a thousand times more. I'll never tire of this sight."

I smile at him nervously as he gets into bed next to me, turning onto his side to look at me. His gaze carries an emotion I don't dare name, for fear I'm misreading him. I hope he'll always look at me this way, as though he can't believe I'm here with him, as though I'm the most precious person to him.

Silas leans in and kisses me tenderly before pulling away. "Goodnight, baby."

"Night," I murmur.

Silas chuckles and pulls me closer, until he's got his arms wrapped around me and my head on his chest. I smile as I listen to the rhythmic beating of his heart, feeling a sense of belonging I've never felt before. This, right here... this is where I belong, right in his arms.

Silas's breathing deepens as he falls asleep, and I hold on to him tightly, enjoying every second of this experience. It's a first for us, and I have a feeling I'll always remember it.

Silas sighs, mumbling something, and I lean in closer, curious. "I love you," he whispers. "*Ray*."

I tense in his embrace, my heart clenching painfully. *Ray*? I pull away from him and sit up, my stomach dropping. It's me he's got in his bed, but subconsciously, it's someone else he wants. Ray... that's the same person Ryan was talking about.

I stare at Silas, my heart breaking. I'm falling so hard and fast, but he won't be there to break my fall. If I keep going this way, I'll find my broken remains lying at his feet, and I have no doubt I'll have a smile on my face as I destroy myself over him.

Chapter Sixty-Three

Alanna

"Alanna!" Silas shouts, and I jump up from my seat as I rush toward his office, worried I messed something up. Now, even more so than usual, I really don't want to let him down. I'm worried he'll think us being together is impacting my work, and I can't let that happen.

"Silas?" I close the door behind me and walk up to his desk, mentally running through everything I'm working on.

"Come, take a look at this."

I nod and walk around his desk to look at his screen, frowning when I see the post-mortem of a cyber attack we circumvented. "That was close," I recall.

Silas sighs and leans back in his chair. "I want to see how you'd go about it if you were to replicate this. I'm having a hard time finding the remaining vulnerabilities in the system."

I nod and lean over him to reach for his keyboard, feeling oddly nervous around him in a way I never did before.

"Hey," Silas murmurs, the tips of his fingers running down my spine soothingly. "What's wrong?"

I look at him, caught off guard. How did he know? I shake my head and look back at the screen. "It's nothing." How am I supposed to tell him that I want to know about *Ray*? Would he think I'm crazy if I tell him I'm worried? That I'm feeling insecure?

"Tell me the truth," Silas orders, his tone rough.

I glance back at him and bite down on my lip. "You and I..." I shake my head, unsure how to even ask this without seeming childish.

"You and I," he repeats, "were inevitable."

Inevitable. That's exactly how I felt too. I look at him with wide eyes, and he smirks as he pulls me closer. I tumble onto his lap, and Silas grins as he cups my neck, his lips finding mine. He kisses me slowly, leisurely, without any regard for time or place. The way he groans as his lips move against mine, as though he's been dying for a taste, and I just gave him an excuse to cave... I can't get enough of it.

A soft pleading moan escapes my lips when he pulls away, and Silas drops his forehead to mine with a smile on his face, his eyes still closed. "Does that answer the question you can't voice, baby?"

I nod, relief rushing through me as the edges of my lips tip up into a smile.

"You're mine, Alanna. You've always been mine, and you always will be. Nothing and no one will ever change that. It doesn't matter what the world might say about us. All that matters is that we're happy together, okay?"

I look into his eyes, wondering if he truly means that. If he's truly happy with me, why is he proclaiming his love for Ray in his sleep while he's holding *me* in his arms? Who is she? Why does she have such a hold over him? Even Ryan seems to know about this mystery girl.

I place my knee between his legs and lean onto his chair as I wrap my arms around him, my lips brushing over his. It doesn't matter. I don't care who she is. She isn't here, but I am. It might take some time, but I'll make him forget all about her.

I kiss Silas with all I've got, letting his touch eradicate my every insecurity, until my mind is filled with just him. He pulls me onto his lap and deepens our kiss, his hands threading through my hair as his tongue brushes past mine. He kisses my lips the same way he kisses my pussy, every stroke turning me on just a little more, until I find myself squirming in his lap.

I tear my lips off his and move them to his neck, sucking down right below his collar. I'm feeling so restless, so needy. I can't push down my need to mark him as mine.

Silas groans and tightens his grip on my hair, his hard cock digging into me. "Baby," he moans.

I pull away and shake my head. "Say my name," I plead. I need to know he's here in this moment with me. I need to know it's me filling his thoughts.

"Alanna," he whispers. He strokes my cheek with the back of his fingers, his eyes on mine. "My love, is everything okay?"

Before I can answer, we're interrupted by a knock on the door. I jump off Silas's lap mere seconds before Amy walks in, her eyes moving between the two of us. She smiles with barely suppressed excitement and Silas sends her a warning look.

"This needs your signature," she says, handing him a document. "No rush! I'll come get it later."

She smirks as she walks back out, and I glance at Silas. "What was that all about?"

Si shakes his head, a reluctant smile on his face. "She loves our love story. Thinks someone should write a book about it someday. She acts like we're her personal Telenovela or some shit. Honestly, I ought to fire her, but I'm pretty sure the firm would collapse if I did that."

"A book, huh?"

Si smiles at me and brushes a strand of my hair behind my ear. "Now where were we? I think you were about to replicate the recent attack we only barely managed to stop."

Disappointment washes over me as I force a smile onto my face. "Right," I murmur. "Of course."

I bend over Silas's desk to reach his keyboard and start typing, forcing myself to focus on our work. I've been absentminded all day because of the words Silas whispered last night, and I should know better. We're at the office, after all.

Silas rolls his chair back and I glance at him over my shoulder, only to find him smirking at me. He grabs the hem of my skirt and pushes it up until he's got it bunched around my hips. "Keep typing," he orders.

Heat rushes to my cheeks and I blush fiercely as I obey his order, trying my hardest to keep typing when all I want to do is turn around and kiss him. Silas's hands roam over my ass, kneading and teasing, his thumbs brushing over my pussy.

I gasp when he grabs my tights and rips them right at the crotch, the sound loud in his quiet office. "Si!" I whisper.

"Keep working, baby," he tells me. "You've got ten minutes to replicate the attack so we can build a proper defense."

He pushes my underwear aside and chuckles as he drags his thumb over my pussy. "Wet," he whispers. "I love this about you. I love that a single kiss turns you on just as much as it does me."

He leans in and presses a soft kiss right between my legs, making me swallow down a moan. "Silas," I warn.

He merely chuckles in response. "Eight minutes."

I bite down on my lip as I continue to type, praying I'm doing a half decent job when all of my attention is on what he's doing to me.

Si leans in, his tongue lapping around my clit, evading the spot I want him at most, over and over again. He's torturing me.

"Six minutes."

Silas spreads my ass cheeks and leans in further, his tongue moving down from my clit, until he's sliding it into me, fucking me with his tongue in an effort to drive me insane.

"I'm not above begging," I moan.

He chuckles and finally drags his tongue to my clit, flicking over it, falling into a steady rhythm that has my orgasm building rapidly.

"Si," I plead. "I'm going to come. I can't hold it."

He takes me right to the edge, and then he pulls away. I gasp and try to straighten, but he keeps me pinned down with a hand on my lower back. "I'm not done with you."

My pussy clenches when I hear the sound of his belt unbuckling, and moments later, he slides his cock against me, teasing my clit and pushing just the tip in, repeating the motion a few times, refusing to let me come.

"Silas," I warn. "I'm going to kill you. I'm seriously going to kill you."

He chuckles and slams into me, finally giving me what I want. A loud moan escapes my lips, and Si wraps one hand around my lips, keeping the other on my hip. He fucks me like that, and everything fades away as I chase a high.

"Four minutes," he reminds me, and I try my hardest to refocus on the code I'm trying to write, when all I want to do is come for him.

The way he's got his hand wrapped over my lips has him pulling my head back, my back arched. I can't imagine what we look like right now. I'm bent over his desk, his thick cock thrusting into me and his fingers silencing me.

I grit my teeth and continue to type, praying to God any of what I'm typing is what I'm hoping it is. I can't think straight when he's touching me like that, and he knows it.

Si moves his hand away from my hip to my pussy, his thumb brushing over my clit as he fucks me from behind. He flicks my clit along with every stroke, and within seconds, I'm coming for him, his hand silencing my moans.

Wave after wave of pleasure rocks my body as Silas increases the pace, fucking me harder, his strokes stronger, deeper. Moments after my orgasm subsides, he comes deep inside me, my name on his lips. "Oh God, Alanna," he moans.

He leans over me and hugs me from behind, the two of us

leaning against his desk, still intimately connected. I smile as he presses a kiss to the back of my neck, setting my restless heart at ease. "I don't know what's got you so worried today, my love. Just know that you're the only one I want. You always will be. You're it for me, Alanna. Forever."

Silas slips out of me and grabs a paper napkin from his desk drawer, cleaning me up before pulling me upright. He turns me around and wraps his arms around me, his eyes on me. "You're all I've ever wanted," he promises. "You always will be."

The sincerity in his gaze startles me, and I rise to my tiptoes to kiss him, unsure what to say. How did he know I was feeling insecure?

Silas kisses me tenderly, taking his time with me. His touch takes away all of my worries and cements my decision. I don't care who Ray is. I'm taking every part of Si that used to belong to her, and I'm never letting go.

Si pulls away and presses his lips to my forehead, his touch lingering as he moves to my neck next. "You're out of time," he whispers.

I chuckle as I pull away from him and straighten my clothes before walking toward his door. I pause halfway through and turn back to face him. "Check the code," I tell him.

His eyes widen, and I smirk at him. Who does he think I am? This girl he can't seem to forget... there's no way she's as compatible with him as I am. No way in hell.

Chapter Sixty-Four

Alanna

I smile to myself as I fold the last paper crane. It took me a few weeks of waking up early and carefully sneaking around the house, but I've managed to fold a thousand little origami cranes for Silas. It still doesn't measure up to everything he's done for me, and the way he celebrated my birthday with me, but I hope it at least shows him my sincerity.

I just hope he won't find it silly. It's hard to find a present for someone who can afford nearly anything, but I hope that if nothing else, this will at least make him smile.

I'm nervous when I hear the sound of the car lift and glance at the cranes I've strung on thread and hung all over the living room. Now that I hear him coming up, I'm suddenly second-guessing myself. He might hate the mess I've made, and he might find me childish. Was this a bad idea, after all?

Silas steps out of the car and smiles when he sees me, but then he looks up at the origami birds and freezes. "Paper cranes?" he asks, his voice carrying a hint of uncertainty.

"One thousand of them." My voice falters, and I clear my

throat. "Ever since my birthday, I've been wanting to thank you, but words didn't seem enough. I can't remember where, but I once heard that folding a thousand origami cranes will grant you a wish. You already have everything you could possibly want, so I thought..."

He walks up to me, his gaze filled with tenderness. The way he's looking at me has my heart overflowing with love. He does this sometimes... he looks at me like I'm his every dream come true. Silas swallows hard as he cups my cheek, his thumb brushing over my lip. "So what is your wish for me?"

"I wish for you to be happy, Silas. Every second of every day, I want you to be happy."

He drops his forehead to mine and inhales shakily. "So long as you're with me, I'm happy. If I get one wish, I wish for you to be with me for the rest of our lives. Will you grant that wish?"

I smile to myself, never tiring of his allusions to marriage. It's something Ryan did too, but it feels different when Silas does it. It feels sincere, and it gives me a sense of security I've never felt before. "Yes," I tell him, though what it is I'm agreeing to exactly, I'm not sure. No one knows about us, and there's so much standing between us. There's everyone at work, Ryan, and the girl he calls for in his sleep... *Ray*. I let her upset me for so long, but I realize now that it doesn't matter. She isn't here, but I am, and I'm not going anywhere. I'm going to erase every memory of her until I'm all Silas can think of.

He leans in, his lips brushing against mine once, twice, before he dips in and deepens our kiss, a soft groan escaping his lips. He pulls me closer, his hands roaming over my body impatiently, and I smile to myself. Yeah, Ray isn't the one he wants. She isn't the one he's thinking of right now. All he wants is *me*.

I rise to my tiptoes and pull away a little, my lips brushing over his ear. "The cranes? They each have something written on them. Kind of like an IOU. They're all different, but some of the things on there include kisses, massages, dinners... and a few *other* things."

Silas pulls away and looks at me wide-eyed. "They're coupons?"

I blink, a foreign memory flashing through my mind. "They're coupons," I repeat. "One for each time I upset you. Hopefully there's enough of them so you'll never run out."

I take a step back and raise my hand to my lips, surprised at the words that just tumbled out of them. Have I ever said something similar before?

"Are you okay, Alanna?"

I look into Silas's eyes and my head starts to throb, a wave of déjà vu washing over me. I clutch my temples and blink rapidly, a vision of me folding paper cranes flashing through my mind. Have I done this before, for someone else?

"Alanna!"

Silas lifts me into his arms and carries me to the sofa, sitting down with me in his lap. I rest my head against his shoulder and inhale shakily, my head pounding. It's rare for me to recall any of my lost memories, but this one feels important. My heart aches with a sense of loss, and I can't help but wonder who I was folding those little birds for.

Silas rubs my back soothingly, and I drag my nose along his throat, inhaling his cologne and letting it put me at ease like it always has. "I'm sorry," I whisper.

"It's okay, my love. How do you feel? Is it your head?"

I nod, my stomach churning. "Don't be mad, okay?"

He kisses my temple and tightens his grip on me. "I promise I won't be."

"I think I've done this before... the paper cranes, I remember folding them. I only saw a flash of a memory, but I remember the feeling vividly. I was filled with love, hope, and nerves. I wanted to give them to someone I loved so much that it hurt. I've tried so hard, but no matter what I did, I could never remember anything, so why now? What is it about these paper cranes?"

Silas buries his hand in my hair and holds me tightly. "It must be because you loved that person so much that fractions of your memories with them shone through the locks on your mind."

I pull away to look at him, but there's no jealousy in his expression. If anything, there's just intrigue and a hint of a smile. "You're not upset."

Silas looks away and shakes his head. "I've got you in my arms, right now and every single night to come. There's nothing for me to be upset about. You're entitled to a past, Alanna."

"What if someday I remember that I had a boyfriend I loved more than anything, and I leave you for him?"

Silas chuckles and runs his hand through my hair. "Then you'll still find yourself back in my arms, Alanna. There's no escaping us."

I narrow my eyes at him, annoyed he's not even remotely jealous. It broke my heart when I heard him whisper *Ray*, and here he is, not caring a single bit that the thoughtful gift I gave him isn't truly his at all.

"You're awfully confident. I wouldn't be, if I were you. If a single memory can make me feel that much love, what would happen if I run into him? I'd probably remember him instantly and fall into his arms, and we'd live happily ever after."

Silas bursts out laughing. "If only, huh?" he mutters, and I push against his chest, glaring at him as I climb off his lap.

"Don't think I won't do it, Silas! Just you wait until I meet the love of my life. You'll regret your indifference!"

He just smirks at me and runs a hand through his hair. I hate that he looks so goddamned sexy sitting there like that, his legs spread, the sleeves of his shirt rolled up so the veins on his forearms are on display.

"Wait," he says. "I thought I was the love of your life?"

I grit my teeth and turn to walk away. "I never said I loved you!"

"Oh, but you did. You said it with the thousand paper cranes, with the way you look at me, and the way you kiss me."

I huff and storm off, Silas's laughter ringing through the

house. "Hey!" he shouts. "I thought I was the one that was supposed to be mad? Weren't you leaving me for your former lover?"

I roll my eyes as I walk into the bedroom, slamming the door closed. He's right. Why am I the one that's so mad?

Chapter Sixty-Five

Alanna

Silas parks the car in his designated spot at the office and turns toward me. "Still mad?"

I glare at him and shake my head. "Nope."

"You sound mad."

"Why would I be mad?"

"If I'm understanding it correctly, you're mad because you're going to leave me for your first love and you two are going to live happily ever after."

I side-eye him and get out of the car. Silas chuckles, and his laughter just grates on me. He's so incredibly annoying. It's maddening enough that he isn't jealous in the slightest, but now he's mocking me, too. "Just wait till it happens," I mutter under my breath. "You won't be laughing then."

"What's that?"

"*Nothing*!"

I walk toward the elevator that leads up to the office, and Silas runs after me. "Alanna," he says, and I pause as I turn back to him, pouting.

He holds up one of my paper cranes and smirks at me. "You know what? I think the thought of you running into your first love's arms and riding off into the sunset does upset me a little, so I'm going to open this one."

"You... why... why are you carrying that around?"

He grins at me as he moves the crane through the air, pretending to make it fly. "This is my new superpower," he informs me. "It's my ammunition against that first love of yours that's going to steal you away."

I walk up to him and reach for it, intending to snatch it out of his hand, but he holds it over my head. "I'm opening it. The more I think about it, the more upset I get, you know?"

"You really don't seem upset."

"I *really* am."

"Si, none of those are appropriate for use outside of the house."

He shrugs. "You said I could use one of these if you upset me. I'm merely following your instructions."

He unfolds it and grins slyly. "Let's see if you can stay mad at me after this."

Silas turns the unfolded piece of paper my way triumphantly. *Kiss for a minute*, it says, and my cheeks flush. What was I thinking, writing that?

"You said it was an IOU," he reminds me. "I'm collecting."

I sigh and step up to him, my hands on his chest, slowly sliding up, until I've got them wrapped around his neck. "I can't give you a full minute, not here in the parking lot. What if someone sees us?"

"I don't care. I'm ready for the world to know you're mine, Alanna. I don't want to hide it."

I shake my head and rise to my tiptoes. "You say that now, but once it happens, the rumors and ridicule will make both of us uncomfortable."

"Kiss," he says, his tone petulant. "I unfolded the crane, so you have to keep your promise."

I smile reluctantly and lean in, my lips brushing over his chastely. Before I can pull away, Silas tangles his hand through my hair and pulls me flush against him roughly, his touch desperate and intoxicating. Every thought falls away as his hands roam over my body, his tongue tangling with mine.

The sound of something falling to the floor near us makes me jump away, my heart racing and my breathing irregular. I turn toward the sound to find Josh staring at us in shock. He bends down to pick up his car keys, his expression tinged with disgust. My heart sinks and I look at Silas in alarm, but he looks calm and unfazed.

"Good morning," Silas says.

"Morning, boss," Josh replies weakly.

I can't even look him in the eye as shame floods me. In the comfort of our home, it was easy to pretend that our happiness wasn't tainted. It was easy to ignore the world around us and the people that'd never understand.

Josh brushes past us looking distraught, and I move to follow him before hesitating, unsure what I'd even say.

"It's fine, baby," Silas says. "They'd find out at some point, anyway. This might not be ideal, but it was unavoidable."

I glance back at him, unsure how to respond or how to even feel. Somehow, I thought he and I could always exist in our little bubble, where our happiness was protected from those that would condemn us, but he's right. This was inevitable.

"Come on," he murmurs. "Let's go face the music. Josh won't keep quiet for long."

He holds his hand out for me, and I hesitate for a moment. Silas smiles at me and nods reassuringly. "Together," he murmurs, "Per aspera ad astra." *Through difficulties to the stars.*

I take his hand, and he entwines our fingers as we walk toward the elevator. I'm so nervous that I feel sick, but Silas's hand in mine grounds me. A small part of me had been waiting for this moment, hoping for it even. When I started folding those cranes, I knew I wanted him forever. I knew I wanted to remove every memory of Ray from his mind. I knew what I was signing up for.

He looks into my eyes as we reach our floor, and I nod. I'm not sure what we're about to face, but I know it won't be support or understanding. They'll judge me harder than they will Silas, and the rumors will be endless.

"What's wrong with you?" I hear Jessica ask Josh as we round the corner.

Silas squeezes my hand and clears his throat. "He saw me kissing Alanna, but he's wondering whether or not he can tell you about it."

Jessica rises from her seat, her eyes wide with disbelief. "What?"

Josh nods and looks away, as though he can't stand to look at us.

"But you two... Alanna... you were dating Ryan, weren't you?" she asks.

I swallow hard and force myself to look into her eyes. "It's true that Ryan and I were dating some time ago, but we broke up before I started at Sinclair Security. Silas and I... we didn't plan this. Neither of us expected to fall for the other, but we did. It wasn't our intention to hide it from you, but we weren't sure you'd understand."

"I *don't*. I don't understand." She walks past us, and I move to follow her before thinking better of it. She put her faith in me when everyone accused me of entering the ψ division through Ryan, enduring ridicule from other colleagues because she stood by me, and in a sense, she must feel betrayed, and I don't know how to make it better.

"Leave her be," Silas says. "Give it a little bit of time."

I nod, and Silas raises our joined hands to his lips, kissing the back of my hand gently before he lets go and walks to his office. I'm tense as I sit down at my desk and pretend not to see the disgusted and shocked looks that are being thrown my way now that Silas is out of sight. It isn't just my own team members that are judging us, it's the other executive employees that are on this floor, too.

Josh swivels his chair toward me and crosses his arms. "So I guess you went after Silas once you realized that everything Ryan owns was actually borrowed from his brother. I was right about you, after all. You got in through nepotism, and you're a gold digger. I don't care if Silas fires me over this, either. You fucking disgust me."

I reel back and steel myself, his words piercing straight through my heart. I knew people wouldn't understand, but I didn't realize how much it'd hurt. "It wasn't like that at all. I have no ulterior motives when it comes to Silas, I swear."

He grits his teeth and stares me down. "Does Ryan even know you're fucking his brother? Or are you leading them both on?"

Ryan. It's only a matter of time before he finds out, and I'm not sure how he'll react. It's one thing for me to deal with the consequences of my actions, but will this destroy the relationship that Silas and Ryan only just rebuilt? And if it does, will Silas forgive me?

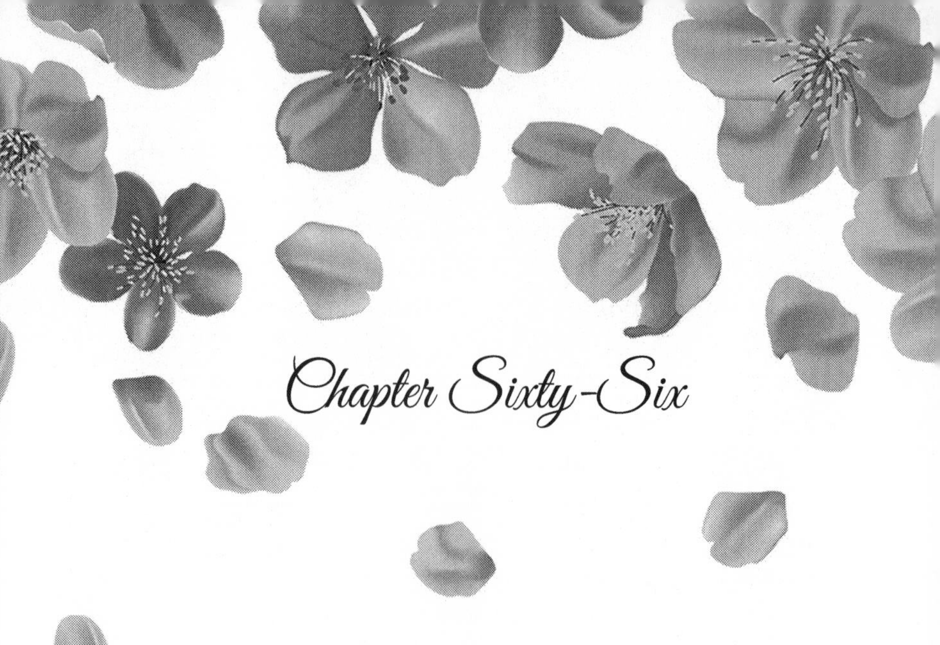

Chapter Sixty-Six

Alanna

"Tell me it isn't true."

I look into Ryan's eyes, his expression tearing straight through my heart. I'm a coward, because I've been avoiding him for as long as I could, using Silas's private elevator whenever I get to work, eating at my desk so he can't intercept me outside and going straight home the moment I finish work. I knew I'd have to face him someday, but I've been delaying this moment for as long as I could. I should've known he'd figure out that the garage is the easiest place to intercept me.

"Tell me they're all just rumors, mindless gossip. Tell me you aren't dating my *brother*."

I look down at my feet and nod. "It's true, Ryan."

He walks up to me and lifts a trembling hand to my face. "*No.* Tell me it's all a joke, Alanna." His voice breaks, and I close my eyes in resignation.

"It isn't. I'm so sorry, Ryan. I didn't... I never meant for it to happen." Except that isn't true, is it? I'm the one who seduced Silas. I was the one who begged for it.

"You're fucking *my brother*?"

"I... it isn't like that."

"What? You're *in love* with him?"

I nod. I've never even told Silas that I love him, so it doesn't feel right to admit it to Ryan, but it's true. I'm hopelessly and irrevocably in love with Silas Sinclair.

"Do you really think he's serious about you, Alanna? He's only with you because he wants to hurt me. Silas can't stand seeing me happy. For years now, he's taken everything I own, leaving both my mother and me penniless, without remorse. You're just another conquest, another part of his plans. You might think he cares about you, but I assure you he doesn't. He'll tire of you eventually, and where will you be? I would've given you everything, Alanna. I *loved* you. I fucking loved you, and you stabbed me in the back, making a fool of me."

"That's *enough*."

I turn at the sound of Silas's voice, my restless heart at ease when he walks toward me. Silas wraps his arm around my shoulder, ignoring the way Ryan flinches. "I told you to wait for my meeting to finish," he admonishes.

I nod and look down at my feet, unsure whether I should shrug his hand off or not. I don't want to hurt Ryan unnecessarily, but I also don't want to lie or hide anything anymore. The lies are eating at me, and though it hurts, I'm glad the truth is out.

"*Why*?" Ryan asks, his voice soft. "Why did you do this to me, Silas? Why her?"

Silas looks at his brother, his expression chilling. "She was never yours to begin with. Didn't you approach her because you knew I'd love her? I do, Ryan. I do love her."

I tense at his words and look up in shock. This isn't how I expected to hear those words for the very first time, but I'm glad to hear them nonetheless.

"You only went after her because you knew she was dating me. Why would you do that? Why, Silas? What have I ever done to deserve this?"

Ryan takes a step back and starts to pace, his hand running through his hair over and over again.

"What went so wrong between us, Silas? I used to look up to you. You were my hero, growing up. You were the big brother all my friends wished they had, but you were mine. I was always so proud to be your brother, even if we didn't share the same mother. Why do you hate me so much? What did I ever do to you? I know you and Mom never got along, but what about me? What did I do to deserve your wrath? You've gone after everything I've ever had, and now you're taking my girl from me?"

Silas frowns, confusion marring his features. "Ryan, I've never hated you. I've done my best to make sure you don't suffer from anything I've done. I bought you an apartment when I took back our family home, and I let you drive any of my cars at any time. I've even given you an allowance without a cap, and I've only questioned your spending *once*. I did all I could to make sure you're minimally affected by my actions."

"You took everything from me and made me live on your terms, at your mercy. Where does it stop, Silas? I've got nothing left for you to take. You've taken every single thing I've ever loved."

"This was never about you, Ryan. Alanna... she isn't one of your possessions. Even if I wanted to, she isn't something I can just *take*. She came to me willingly, and now that she has, I'm never letting her go. Our relationship has nothing to do with you." He tightens his grip on me, his expression pained. "Besides, I wasn't the one who approached her with bad intentions. You set out to use her, and it backfired. Blame me all you want, but if you treated her right and she truly loved you, she never would've looked at me twice. You pushed her away and right into my arms."

Silas pulls me closer and tips his head toward the car. "Let's go," he murmurs.

"This isn't over," Ryan warns. "Don't think that I don't know you've been keeping me away from her. First you took away my access to the top floor, and then you started to make her work over hours whenever I wanted to see her. I know what you've been doing, Silas. I just didn't understand why."

He turns toward me, his gaze torn. "I'm not giving up on you, Alanna. I don't give a fuck that you're with my brother. It won't take you long to see him for the psychopath he is, and when you finally see through him, I'm going to be there for you. I know I fucked up, and now that you have too, we might actually be able to move past this. I'll wait for you."

Silas's grip on me tightens, and he pulls me away from Ryan, his body tense as he leads me to the car. "Are you okay?" I ask as he gets in beside me.

Silas shakes his head, his hands draped over the steering wheel. "I didn't think... I thought... I didn't want to hurt him. Contrary to what he might think, I do care about my little brother. I've done my best to protect him and shield him, but all I've done is make him misunderstand me, and it's too late to make amends now."

I place my hand on his thigh and inhale deeply. "Do you regret it? Us?"

He turns toward me and shakes his head. "Never. I meant what I said, Alanna. I love you. I will always love you. It might take a while, but we'll get through this."

I smile at him. "I love you too, Silas."

He nods as he starts the car. "I know. Our love can withstand more than you could possibly imagine, Alanna. We'll get through this too."

I hope so. I'm terrified he'll end up blaming me for the ruined relationship between Ryan and him. I'm scared Ryan is right, and Silas will eventually tire of me. I'm utterly, entirely, totally, *terrified* that I'm not enough to make the pain worth it.

Chapter Sixty-Seven

Alanna

"These accounts need to be looked at in more detail," Jessica says, her expression sour. It's clear she doesn't want to speak to me, but she can't avoid me within our team.

I hate that I'm making her so uncomfortable. Pretending to be unaffected as our colleagues judge us has been an endless battle. They might not say anything in Silas's presence, but the scathing looks are hard to avoid. The office has been tense lately, each of us doing our job, but without any of the camaraderie that used to exist. Our decision to be together hasn't just affected Ryan, Silas, and me. It's also impacted so many people around us.

"I've got it," I tell her, nodding politely. She grimaces as she walks away, almost as though there's more she wants to say. I'm not sure we'll ever get past this. Her impression of me has changed entirely, and Josh's constant snarky remarks about how he's been right about me all along are only reinforcing her sinking opinion of me.

I straighten my back as I look through the hundreds of social media accounts that have been flagged as suspected foreign interference. Since most companies pride themselves on protecting free speech, removing these becomes our job. We're tasked with hacking accounts to make users lose access, without the platforms having to pull accounts. The backdoors these social media companies leave us, specifically to help us access their systems, are an open secret. Unfortunately, this is all still tedious work. Remove the wrong account, and you'll have media articles throwing blame around, and suspicion will fall on us eventually.

I bite down on my lip as I try to work as fast as I can, fueled by a renewed urge to prove myself. It was bad enough when I started, with everyone accusing me of entering the company through Ryan, but it's undoubtedly worse now.

"Hey."

I look up to find Silas standing by my desk, the office otherwise deserted. How long have I been working? Normally I'd at least have heard people telling each other goodbye, but not today. Then again, they might just have left quietly. Silas and I managed to lose the respect of every single team member, though some are more vocal about it than others.

"Si," I whisper. I walk up to him and slide my hands up his chest and around his neck slowly. This is something I could never do before, and I'm enjoying the feeling of truly being Silas's girlfriend. Though it came at a cost, the freedom we gained will eventually be worth it.

I take in the dark circles underneath his eyes, my heart aching for him. Silas hasn't been himself ever since Ryan found out about us. He might not say it, but he's hurting. We both are. Everything Ryan said to him must still be resounding through his mind. I know he never meant to hurt Ryan. Silas isn't that kind of person.

"Are you okay?"

He looks into my eyes and wraps his arms around my waist. "I'm not sure."

I nod. "Yeah, me neither. It's been strange, because I'm so happy with you, but there isn't a single person that's happy *for* us.

It makes me wonder if we're truly doing something unacceptable. How could a love that feels so right be wrong?"

Si shakes his head and cups my face, his gaze intense. "It isn't. I told you that you and I were inevitable, and I meant it. I don't regret a single thing when it comes to you, not even the pain I've brought my brother."

"But it still hurts, huh?"

He nods. "I didn't expect him to respond the way he did. Ryan… I think he may be more embroiled in his mother's schemes than I realized."

"Mona?"

"Yeah. I suspect she's been using him without him even realizing for much longer than I initially thought. Something just doesn't add up." I frown in confusion, and Silas shakes his head. "Well, never mind. Just like most things with us, this too is bittersweet."

"Bittersweet?"

"Yes. The pain we're causing may be bitter, but underneath it all, at the core of our relationship, sweetness is all I see." He leans in and brushes his lips over mine, kissing me leisurely, openly. We've never been able to do that before. "Sweetness is all I taste," he whispers against my lips.

I smile, unable to help myself. Yeah, we may be coated in despair, but once that washes away, sweetness is all we're left with.

"Come on," Si says. "Let me take you on a date. Everyone who needed to know now knows about us, so there's nothing left for us to fear. I'm ready to publicly claim you as mine. Do you have any idea how I've suffered by not being able to call you mine? I want everyone to know you're officially no longer single."

I burst out laughing and shake my head. "I'm not the one who had women bidding thousands of dollars for a single date with me, you know? Are you going to be okay without all the women around you throwing themselves at you? Is your ego going to survive? Maybe your head will shrink to a normal size. Can you imagine?"

Silas chuckles and taps my nose. "Can't believe this former eligible bachelor is being roasted by his girlfriend in his own damn office."

"Bitter, is it?"

He nods, a fake pout on his face that's far too cute. I rise to my tiptoes and smirk. "Have some sweetness then, boyfriend." I kiss him with everything I've got, every ounce of restrained passion, every bit of sadness and every spark of joy. I give it all to him.

This, right here, is worth everything.

Chapter Sixty-Eight

Silas

I smile to myself as I step out of the shower. Going on a proper date with Alanna was everything I was hoping it'd be. There's something so intoxicating about holding her hand in public. I've never felt anything like it before.

Alanna, a good view and an excellent dinner. It was perfect. Simple, but oh so perfect. It's strange how it's all of these simple things that bring me the most happiness. Putting a smile on her face, treating her to things we could never afford before. It makes it all worth it.

Alanna glances at me through her dresser mirror, pausing midway through combing her hair. I'll never tire of the way she looks at me. She's so honest with her desire, and I don't think I've ever felt more wanted. It isn't just physical between us. This connection… When she disappeared, I tried to convince myself that it wasn't quite what I remember it to be, that I placed her on a pedestal the way we do with lost loved ones, and I suppose I was right. It isn't quite like in my memories. It's better.

I lean back against the wall as her eyes roam over my body,

pausing on the towel wrapped around my hip. "Baby," I murmur, tipping my head to the fist I'm holding up. I uncurl my fingers slowly, showing her the crane in the palm of my hands.

Alanna bursts out laughing, and I grin back at her in return. Yeah, this kind of happiness is something else. It's out of this world, and it was worth waiting for.

"You really have hidden them all over the house, haven't you? Why do these cranes keep popping up out of nowhere?"

I shrug. I absolutely did hide them all over the house without a single ounce of shame. I've got several hidden in every room, ready for me to pull out whenever she's upset. I know she gave them to me to serve as a bridge between us in the event of an argument, but I've found that they're a great way to make Alanna forget all about the worries being with me have caused her.

Even today, as she smiled at me over dinner, the two of us lost in conversation, the light in her eyes would dim occasionally, her thoughts drifting, undoubtedly to the harsh words she's been surrounded with, the ridicule she won't tell me about. One of these paper cranes is exactly what I need to make her forget everything, even if it's only for a few hours.

"I feel kind of upset," I lie. "I'm still thinking about how you said you didn't want fries as a side dish with your steak, and then you ate my fries. *You. Ate. My. Fries.*"

She bursts out laughing, the sound sending a ripple through my heart. Fuck. She's so ridiculously beautiful, and seeing her sitting in our bedroom in nothing but one of my t-shirts... yeah, this is my every dream come true.

"I'm opening this," I tell her. "This paper crane better avenge me. I don't think I'll be able to sleep tonight if I don't get a reward in return for those fries."

She watches as I unfold the origami paper, my heart skipping a beat when I read the word written on it in her handwriting. "Blowjob, huh? You really are my filthy little slut, aren't you?"

She rises from her seat and walks toward me, her steps slow

and measured, an intoxicating smile on her face. "Yes," she tells me. "I am."

Alanna pauses in front of me and grins wickedly before dropping to her knees in front of me. She looks up at me through her lashes and places her hands on my towel, yanking it loose with a hint of impatience. My cock is ready for her. It always is. I don't think I could ever *not* want her.

"I'm sorry," she says, her hand wrapping around the base. "I'm sorry, babe. *So* sorry for eating your fries."

I bite back a smile as she pumps up and down, her eyes on mine as she teases me. I fucking love her. I love every single thing about her.

"I never should've touched them," she says, grinning. "I really deserve to be punished."

"Fucking slut," I whisper as I tangle my hand through her hair. "I love you, little psycho."

She places her lips at the tip of my cock and looks up at me. "I love you too, Si," she says, right before wrapping her lips around me. I tighten my grip on her hair and pull her closer, making her take more of my cock, and she comes willingly, her tongue drawing circles around the parts she knows are most sensitive.

"Look at you taking my cock, baby. I didn't feed you enough at dinner, did I?"

She sucks down hard, and I moan helplessly. She might be the one on her knees, but it's me who's at her mercy.

I ball my hand into a fist, pulling on her hair harder as I move her head back and forth, fucking her face until I'm hitting the back of her throat. Watching my cock slide into her lips is the sexiest thing I've ever seen, and the fucking sight of her has me ready to come.

Every time she moans, the vibrations bring me to the edge. I meant to clear her thoughts, but it's me who can't think straight. "I'm so fucking in love with you," I groan, and she increases the pace, sucking me harder. If she keeps going, I'm going to come all over those pretty lips of hers, but it's her pussy I want.

I pull out of her mouth and yank her to her feet, my hands wrapping around her waist as I lift her up against the wall. Alanna's legs wrap around my hips, and I push her underwear aside roughly, sliding into her in one smooth motion.

"Fuck, Silas," she moans, her head falling back.

I smirk as I tighten my grip on her hips, keeping her pressed against the wall as I thrust into her roughly, taking her hard and fast. "You're so fucking wet, baby. Sucking my cock turned you on, huh? You really are my personal little slut, my own little psycho."

She looks into my eyes, her gaze unfocused as she wraps her arms around my neck, her lips finding mine. She kisses me the same way she just took my cock, her tongue driving me fucking insane. The hold she has over me is unreal.

"This pussy is so good," I murmur against her lips. "I can't fucking take it."

She moans and rotates her hips, ensuring I brush against her clit with every thrust, her own orgasm building.

"You want to come for me, don't you, baby?"

She nods, her movements turning more frenzied. "Please," she begs.

I smirk as I take her harder, giving it to her at the pace she needs to push her over the edge. My eyes fall closed when her pussy contracts, a strong orgasm washing over her and taking me right along with her.

The way her pussy squeezes my cock has me unable to resist. "Oh, fuck, Ray. *Fuck*," I moan, emptying deep inside her.

Alanna tenses and pushes against my chest with considerable strength, and I pull away from her, disoriented. "Let me go," she snaps, her eyes filled with agony that wasn't there seconds before. Her eyes fill with tears, and she sniffs, turning her face away from me.

Fuck. I just called her Ray.

"Babe," I murmur. "It's just a nickname. It's a nickname *for you.*"

"Please," she begs, tears streaming down her face. The look in her eyes fucking guts me. What have I done? How could I have hurt her this way? "Please, just let go of me."

I lower her to the floor gently and draw a shaky breath. How do I explain in a way she'll understand? "I swear, Alanna," I plead. "It's just a nickname for you. You're my ray of sunshine, Alanna. That's all it is."

She looks into my eyes, disappointment mixed with her pain. "Don't," she whispers. "Please don't, Silas."

She walks away, slamming our bedroom door closed with a loud bang, leaving me staring at the door, unsure what to do or say. *Fuck.*

Chapter Sixty-Nine

Alanna

I stare at my screen, my mind replaying the expression on Silas's face when he moaned the name *Ray* while deep inside me. I grit my teeth as pain tears through my heart, leaving me feeling empty.

If that had been the first time I'd heard him say that name, I'd have believed his lies. I would have believed that it's a nickname he gave me, and I'd be none the wiser.

Silas has no idea that he sometimes whispers Ray in his sleep. I've never said a word about it, part of me scared of being confronted with a love so great that it haunts his dreams. The way he's always said her name made it clear he loves her. Who is she? It isn't Raven, of that I'm sure. I've seen the two of them together, and though there's affection between them, it isn't love.

I bite down on my lip as I lean back in my seat. *Ray of sunshine*, he said. I tap my foot anxiously, the pieces slowly falling into place. *Project Sunshine*. It's the firm's most highly encrypted case file, and it appears to be the oldest one in the system. I glance over at Jessica, reluctant to ask her anything, yet unable to push aside my curiosity.

Our friendship is definitely over, but she hasn't completely shut me out. She seems hurt and angry, but she doesn't ignore me like many others do. "Jessica," I murmur, my heart racing.

She looks up and raises her brows in question.

I hesitate and tap my pen on my desk, unsure whether I truly want to know or not. "Do you know what Project Sunshine is about?"

She tenses and glances around furtively before shaking her head. "Not many people know what it's about, but it's the first project the ψ division ever had, and it's still ongoing, though not many people have clearance to access the files. I told you that there's a rumor going around that the boss started this company because of a woman, right? I think Project Sunshine is about her. I'm not sure what that's all about, but the general consensus is that it might be a murder case that's remained unsolved."

Her eyes widen as though she's suddenly remembering my relationship with Silas, and she looks down. "But who knows, right? People always like to speculate. It probably isn't about a woman at all, and if it is, it's in the past."

I nod at her and force my lips into a smile. If it truly was in the past, I wouldn't be so anxious. I'm desperate to remember my past, so I can't fault Silas for having one of his own. I'm just worried that Ray *isn't* in the past. If he truly lost her, there's every chance he'll never get over her. She'll always be the one who got away, the one he'll compare everyone else to. I can't compete with the ghost of a woman, one crafted from only the very best memories of them together.

I glance at Silas's closed office door and clench my jaw. I need to know. I have to find out who she is and what their story is.

I inhale deeply as I start to type, trying my hardest to gain access to the file in every way I can think of, but at each turn, my attempts are blocked and access is denied. I bite down on my lip harshly as I try to circumvent Sinclair Security's encryption software, but it's all to no avail. I should've known it would be impossible. This system was designed by Aria and Grayson Callahan, after all. There won't be any flaws in it that I can exploit. The couple is well-known for the security software they develop, and Sinclair Security works with them almost exclusively to create the encryption systems our firm uses. I won't get anywhere.

"Alanna?"

I jump and close the windows I've got open, my heart aching as I turn toward Silas. I slept in the guest room last night, but when I woke up, he was lying next to me. I'm thankful that he didn't try to make any further excuses, but the continuous guilt in his eyes is just further evidence of his lies, and it kills me. It breaks my heart to think of everything we've gone through, and for what?

Silas stares at me from the doorway to his office, an unreadable expression on his face. I'm worried he was notified of my attempts to breach the system. This could be a fireable offence, but I'm certain I hid my tracks as best as I could.

"Can you come here for a minute? There's something I need to discuss with you."

I nod and rise to my feet slowly, my heart pounding wildly. With the way he loves her, there's no way he'll forgive me for looking into her. I have a lot of faith in my relationship with Silas, but not when it comes to Ray.

I follow Silas into his office, barely able to contain my nerves. I've never felt this way before. I've never loved someone so much that my fear of losing him outweighs the pain of knowing I'm not the woman he truly loves.

Silas turns toward me the moment the door closes behind me, his gaze tender as he cups my cheek. "What were you doing, trying to access restricted files?"

My eyes widen, and I try my hardest to formulate an excuse, but I can't. I can't look him in the eye and lie to him. "Project Sunshine," I tell him. "It's about Ray, isn't it? *Ray of sunshine.*"

"Alanna," he murmurs. "I already told you that Ray is just a nickname for *you*. There's no one else. There's nothing you need to worry about."

I place my hand over his, my heart breaking. "I know you're lying to me," I whisper. "You've been whispering the name Ray in your sleep for months now. Ryan told me about her long before yesterday. Who is she, Silas?"

His eyes fall closed, and he inhales shakily. "Alanna," he whispers. "*Please.*"

I clutch his suit jacket, desperation clawing at me. "Who is she?" I ask again.

"You," he murmurs. "It's you."

Tears gather in my eyes, and I try my hardest to blink them away. "How can you look at me and lie to me with such conviction? Maybe you're just like your brother, after all."

Silas grabs my shoulders and shakes his head. "Oh baby," he whispers. "I don't know how to make you understand, but I swear to you, there's no other woman. There really isn't. You're the one for me, my one and only. You always have been."

I look away and swallow down my grief. "So you won't tell me then?"

Silas looks pained, his expression torn. "There's nothing to tell. There's no one else."

"Then give me access to Project Sunshine."

He buries his hands in my hair, his eyes shimmering with a combination of remorse and desperation. "I can't do that. It's a confidential file, and I can't give you access based on our personal relationship. I have to keep work strictly professional."

"That's an easy excuse for you, isn't it?"

He drops his forehead to mine and inhales shakily. "I know what you're thinking, my love, but please trust me. Trust in us. Can you do that for me?"

I pull away to look at him, unsure what to say. What would happen if one day she walks back into his life? He's asking me for his trust, but can I truly trust him to choose me if it comes down to it? "It's fine if you won't tell me who she is, Silas," I end up saying. "I won't pry into your past any further, but I need you to leave her there. I don't want her name on your lips, not even in your sleep. Not ever."

The way he smiles at me can only be described as *bittersweet*. He's right. Everything between us *is* bittersweet. "Okay," he whispers. "I promise, Alanna."

My shoulders slump in relief, and I nod at him. "I'm going to make you forget all about her, Si. I don't care who she is or what she meant to you. She's your past, but I am your future, you hear me?"

He smiles at me, and the hint of amusement I see in his eyes makes me wonder if he isn't taking my words seriously, but then he nods, his expression sincere. "You *are* my future, Alanna."

I'll let Ray have his past, so long as everything else is mine.

Chapter Seventy

ALANNA

The slight drizzle distracts me enough for me to miss Ryan standing outside of the office at lunchtime, his gaze on me. Our eyes meet, and I freeze. I haven't seen him in a few weeks. He's been avoiding both Silas and me, and I don't blame him.

He walks over to me with an umbrella in his hand and holds it over me, shielding me from the rain. "Alanna," he murmurs.

"Ryan." My voice is tinged with regret, so much standing between us now that the distance can never be breached.

Before everything fell apart for us, before we even fell in love, we were friends. Ryan was one of the only friends I had. He's the only one I felt comfortable around, the only one who shared my interests. Everyone else around me focused on partying so hard that they could barely remember the night before, and I couldn't imagine anything worse. The mere idea of getting so drunk that I'd lose even more of my memories terrified me, and Ryan understood that.

He understood that there were things that were important to me, even if I could never fully comprehend why. He let me follow instincts and sounds, the two of us going on little adventures as we tried to stir my memory, all to no avail. Maybe he did approach me for the wrong reasons, but some space and time allowed me to see clearer. Not everything we had was fake.

"Can we talk?"

I nod, and he leads me to the sandwich store I frequent. We walk in silence, the air surrounding us loaded with regret.

"I love my brother," Ryan says eventually, his voice soft. He turns to face me, the two of us huddled underneath his umbrella. "I really do, Alanna. I love him, but I've also learned to fear him. Hear me out, okay? It's all I ask."

I nod, and Ryan inhales deeply as he looks down for a moment. "Throughout the last few years, Silas has slowly but surely taken everything from my mother and me. You see, my father knew what kind of person Silas is and didn't trust him with our assets or the company. He left everything to my mother, knowing she'd take care of both of us. Silas couldn't accept that and left home."

He runs a hand through his hair, and the pain and sincerity in his eyes tell me he truly believes that his words are true, but every single instinct is telling me that it can't be.

"We didn't hear from him for a few years. Mom tried looking for him, wanting him to come back home, but he wouldn't. Mom tried her hardest to run the company but she struggled, even with the competent staff she had, and the business was at the brink of bankruptcy. Mom told me we had to sell the house, and that she'd found a buyer. That's the first time I saw Silas again. He was standing in front of the door with a suitcase in tow, a sly smile on his face. He told me he was finally home, and in his next breath, he told my mother to pack her bags and get out of his house. Can you imagine that? She raised both of us, yet he threw her out so easily. Turns out he was the one who bought our house. He could've just told us, and we'd have gladly asked for his help and given him the house in return, but he hid his identity as a buyer out of contempt for my mother. He did the same with the company."

Ryan looks into my eyes, his gaze pleading. "Silas is sly and vicious like that. You never truly know what he's thinking or plotting. That is why I'm worried about you. Throughout the years, Silas has taken everything from us, going as far as to quietly buy the company's shares so he could gain control over Dad's company. He didn't even want it. Silas hired a CEO to replace Mom. He's gone after everything we used to have, every car, all of our property, everything. He won't use any of it, but he doesn't want Mom and me to have it. I'm worried it's the same with you. I'm worried you're yet another conquest to him, another way to make me suffer for reasons I cannot understand."

I don't know what to say to him. I'm not even entirely sure what to think at all. I can see the pain in Ryan's eyes, and I don't understand Silas's motivation for doing what he's done, but I'm sure there must be a reason. "Ryan... did you talk to Silas about this? Have you asked him what's going on?"

He nods. "All he says is that he's just righting wrongs of the past, and that he isn't trying to hurt me, but that's all he's doing. He feels wronged for being cut out of the will and is taking that out on us, when everything that happened was Father's wish. I'm not sure where he'll draw the line. Think about it, Alanna. How did you two meet? Was it because I introduced you, or had he been stalking you before that?"

I hesitate, a hint of panic running down my spine. "I... we met at the coffee shop on campus. He'd been coming there for a few weeks before you even introduced us. We never really spoke much, though."

"The coffee shop on campus? Think about it, Alanna. That's nowhere near his office or his house. Do you really think that was a coincidence? He'd been watching you long before I introduced you to him. Why? It's because he's keeping an eye on me, and he no doubt saw how happy we were together."

"No," I murmur weakly. Silas wouldn't do something like

that, would he? And if he did, I played right into his hand when I asked him to take me home.

"I know you live with him," Ryan says softly. "I figured it out the moment I realized you were together. I had my suspicions about you two, but I chose to trust you because I really do love both of you. I ignored every single red flag because I was so scared to lose you, especially to him."

I look away, unable to face him.

"I don't know how long this has been going on, Alanna, but I'm partially to blame. He wouldn't have come after you if not for me. Just think about the way you two got together and truly ask yourself whether or not it's all coincidental, or whether it was carefully orchestrated. You were evicted for no reason, and Silas happened to step in and offer you help? I won't say much more because I truly don't think you'll believe me, but I recommend that you check his financials. See if there was anything suspicious about that eviction, since it's what allowed him to truly win you over. Would you have fallen for him if he didn't have access to you after working hours? If you hadn't moved in together, would you two be dating now? Just think about it."

Ryan stares up at the sky that has finally cleared and pulls the umbrella away, closing it. "I know it's over for us. I know I fucked up and I'll forever pay the price for it, but Silas is doing exactly what I once did to you. You couldn't forgive me for approaching you with ulterior motives and using you, but what he's doing is a thousand times worse. Do you just not see it, or are you refusing to?"

He smiles at me sadly and takes a step away. "Just think about what I've told you, okay?"

Ryan walks away, and I stare at his back, my thoughts in turmoil. I don't know what to believe, and I'm scared there's a thread of truth in Ryan's words. If he's right and everything between Silas and me was a lie, where does that leave us?

Chapter Seventy-One

Alanna

Silas wraps his arm around me as I stir the pasta sauce, his lips brushing over my ear. He's been touching me so much more ever since he called me Ray, almost as though he's scared I'll disappear if he doesn't have his hands on me. It's oddly reassuring, but it's also bittersweet.

"You're quiet today. What's on your mind?"

He presses a kiss to my shoulder and drags his nose up my neck, kissing me right below my ear.

"It's nothing," I murmur, unsure how to bring this up. I'm scared of what his answers will be if I voice the questions I keep within. It's strange to exist in this space where we both feel like we're losing each other, neither of us willing to acknowledge everything that's overshadowing the happiness we fought so hard for.

"Are you sure?"

I turn in his embrace and wrap my arms around his neck. "Si," I whisper. "How come you used to go to the coffee shop on campus? It's nowhere near your office or your home."

He tenses and forces a smile to his face, and my heart sinks. "Someone told me the coffee was really good there."

I stare at him, part of me wanting to press further, but a cowardly part of me wanting to let it go. "Silas," I whisper. "Tell me the truth. Why were you coming to the coffee shop every day? Why did you give me the wrong name?"

He cups my cheek and looks at me pleadingly. "Alanna, it really was because Amy told me to go there. I'd been struggling with some work I needed to complete, so she told me to go there and see if being amongst the students would help. When I was younger, I always used to work in coffee shops, so we thought it would help. I attended Astor college myself, so it's a place I'm familiar with. As for the name, well... do you know how many times I've received a coffee cup with *Silence* written on it? I figured something easier to spell would be better."

I nod slowly, unsure whether I believe him or not. It could be true, but it's one hell of a coincidence, and I'm not sure I believe in coincidence anymore.

"Why are you suddenly asking me this, Alanna?" His tone is strained, his expression harsh. He knows. "Did you see Ryan? Is he the one messing with your mind?"

I hesitate. I've never been able to lie to Silas. "I did see him. I ran into him during my lunch break yesterday."

"So you're now questioning me because of my brother? He's the one who lied to you from the beginning. He's the one who approached you with an agenda. All I've ever done from the very start was look out for you. I've always treated you well, and I've given this relationship all I've got, so why are you letting Ryan take away all the trust we fought to build? Have I ever done anything to make you doubt me?"

Other than calling me by someone else's name? "No," I whisper. "But neither did your brother. If I hadn't overheard him, I'd never have known I was just a pawn to him. How am I supposed to be sure that it's different with you?" Especially now. If Ray is that important to him, why is he with me at all?

Silas grabs my shoulders and inhales shakily. "Don't do this to us, Alanna. I swear to you, I've always loved you. I've never once had bad intentions when it came to you. Never."

"Then why did you tell me to break up with Ryan when we met? If you had good intentions, why didn't you want to see me happy with him?"

"Because I was already in love with you, and you were never supposed to be his. Out of everyone you could've gotten with in this whole goddamn world, Ryan is the one person I couldn't let you be with. Not my brother."

He looks so sincere, but his words can't be true. "Silas, how could you possibly have been in love with me? We hadn't even had a real conversation yet when you told me to break up with Ryan. You say you didn't approach me with ulterior motives, but your actions say otherwise."

"When I walked into that coffee shop and your eyes met mine, I knew you were the one. I knew I had to make you my wife someday. It had nothing to do with Ryan."

"Love at first sight, really? That's what you're going with?"

Silas brushes my hair behind my ear and strokes my cheek with the back of his fingers. "Can you honestly tell me you didn't feel a thing when we first met? When we were standing in that alleyway, did your heart not beat a little faster?"

It did. That one encounter left me feeling flustered for hours, and I didn't dare admit to myself that it was because he'd intrigued me. He'd awakened a part of me that had been missing.

"Alanna, we finally made it. Sure, things aren't perfect and many people around us need some time to get accustomed to us being a couple, but we're finally together with nothing standing in our way. Are you really going to let Ryan tear us apart? Are you going to let him instill doubts? You know exactly what he's doing, and you're letting him get away with it. Can't you see that he's acting out of pain and anger? This is revenge, and you're handing him the knife he's stabbing us in the back with. Please, baby.

Please don't do this to us. Haven't we been through enough already?"

I stare at him, my head throbbing. I close my eyes, a vision of a younger Silas staring back at me in my memory, his expression similar to the one he was wearing just moments ago. "*Get away from me. Just leave me alone,*" I hear myself shout, as though I'm a detached spectator in a memory that doesn't feel like mine.

I open my eyes and look at Silas, who is staring at me with clear concern in his gaze. "Alanna?"

I shake my head, disoriented. "Silas," I ask. "Did we used to know each other?"

He freezes for a moment before shaking his head slowly. If we didn't use to know each other, why does it feel like Silas and I have had an equally painful argument before? Why do I know what he looked like when he was younger? Is my mind playing tricks on me, or is there more to this? I can't help but feel that something isn't right, but for Silas, I'm going to choose to ignore the red flags. I shouldn't, but I can't help myself. Even if our happiness is tainted, I can't let go of it.

Silas seems restless and upset for the rest of the night, and I can't help but feel guilty. He's right. He's always treated me well, and he hasn't done anything to invite my suspicion. It all stems from Ryan, and I can't tell which of the two brothers is messing with me. I'm worried they both are, and I'm walking down the same path I walked with Ryan. I learned the hard way that it only leads to despair.

I pause in the doorway of our bedroom, my eyes roaming over Silas. Tonight is the first night he went to bed without me. He hasn't even kissed me goodnight, and other than the night I spent in the guest room, that hasn't happened once since we started sharing a room.

My guilt is at war with my need to find out the truth, and I inhale deeply as I slip out of the bedroom. It doesn't take me long to find Silas's laptop, and unsurprisingly, his password is the same as the one he had me crack at my first interview.

That too, was an odd coincidence. How could his password have been the same as the tattoo I have on my rib? I bite down on my lip, furtively glancing at the bedroom door as I access his bank statements, unsure what I'm even looking for.

I scroll through the countless transactions, until I find one that makes my heart sink. Silas took $10,000 out of his account on the day I was evicted.

Chapter Seventy-Two

Alanna

I'm only mildly surprised when I see Ryan standing at the corner of the building during my lunch break. It's like he somehow knows when Silas has a meeting and I'll be eating alone. I wouldn't put it past him to have access to his schedule.

"Your expression tells me I was right."

I look up at him and grimace. "I'm not sure what you're talking about."

"Aren't you?"

I shake my head and walk past him, but he falls into step with me.

"So Silas had nothing to do with you being evicted? He didn't orchestrate your entire relationship? You left me after you overheard one single conversation where I said things I didn't mean, but you're going to ignore this?"

I look at him, my heart filled with uncertainty. "I'm not ignoring it. I'm just trying not to jump to conclusions, that's all."

"He's been *stalking* you, Alanna."

I freeze. "What?"

Ryan nods. "After I learned about you two, I started to wonder how that possibly could've happened. You aren't immoral. You aren't the kind of woman who'd date her ex's older brother. It had to be him. So I did some digging and I... I found out he's the reason you lost your memories."

My eyes widen, and my head starts to throb. "What are you talking about?"

"Alanna... Silas had been stalking you, and as you were running away from him, you got into a car accident. He lost track of you for a while, but because of me, he's found you again. He's dangerous, Alanna. I'm not sure why, but he seems obsessed with you. From what my private investigator told me, you were rich, and you'd been volunteering at a shelter Silas stayed at when he left home. He realized you were an opportunity to change his life, so he pursued you, but you weren't having any of it. You had a boyfriend, but Silas didn't care. He wouldn't give up, and in the end, he caused you to be in that accident. In many ways, it probably saved your life. Who knows how far he would've gone if he hadn't lost track of you?"

Fragments of memories flash through my mind. Me driving a Porsche. Packing food for a homeless shelter. Screaming at Silas to leave me alone. Every memory I've recalled but couldn't place now fits. The big room with bunk beds that I've seen before must have been while I was volunteering. Me shouting at a younger looking Silas... was it because he'd been stalking me?

I begin to feel sick, my head pounding so wildly that I feel like it might burst. Did Silas approach me because he knew me in the past, or did he approach me because of Ryan? Was it a combination of both? Either way, he's lying to me. He lied when I asked him if we knew each other in the past, and he lied about his reason for coming to the coffee shop. What else did he lie about? "The information you found, can you email it to me, please? I want to see it for myself."

Ryan nods and wraps his arm around me. "Are you okay, Alanna? I didn't mean to upset you. I just felt like you needed to know. It kills me to watch you fall for his schemes. I don't know what his intentions are, and I'm worried about you. I'm worried you're in danger."

"Hey, take your hands off her!" My head snaps up at the sound of Silas's voice, a sharp throbbing pain blinding me.

Silas pulls me into his arms and holds me tightly, my pulse racing. "What's going on?" he asks. "I told you to stay away from her, Ryan. Mess with me all you want, but she's off-limits."

The sound of Ryan's laughter grates on me, and I instinctively bury my face deeper against Silas's neck. "I'm leaving," Ryan says. "Think about what I said, Alanna."

Silas gently walks me back to the office, supporting me with his arm. "What did he tell you, Alanna?"

I look up at him, taking in the clear panic in his gaze. "What do you think he said? You've been keeping so much from me, it could be anything."

He tenses against me, falling silent as we walk into his office. He closes the door behind us and turns toward me. "I won't keep anything from you anymore, Alanna. Tell me what he said to you. Give me a chance to defend myself."

"Silas, I'll ask you one last time. Did we use to know each other? Before I lost my memories?"

He grits his teeth and nods.

"Why did you lie to me? When I asked you if we knew each other before I lost my memories, why did you lie?"

Silas runs a hand through his hair and sighs. "Because amnesia is tricky. If I tell you about your past, it'll distort your memories, and you might never regain them. Besides, you seem happy now, and the past mostly holds pain. Why would I want that for you? If your brain decided that you're better off without those memories, who I am to then force you to remember something that might harm you? Alanna, every time you even try to recall your memories, you suffer from blinding headaches and nausea. Nothing good comes from trying to remember."

"That's a convenient excuse."

"It's the truth."

"The truth... something that should be factual but seems increasingly subjective. Tell me, Silas. Were you the reason I was evicted?"

He looks into my eyes and crosses his arms. "No."

"Is that the truth?"

"It is."

"Then why did you take out 10k on the day I was evicted?"

"I didn't. *Ryan* did."

I laugh humorlessly. "I can't trust either of you. You just keep throwing blame around. I can't even ask you about our past because I can't trust you to tell me the full truth. All I know for now is that you've been lying to me every step of the way. I don't trust you. I can't tell whether your intentions toward me are pure, or if anything we had was real at all. I can't tell if you're playing some type of sick game, and it scares me. *You* scare me, Silas."

"Alanna—"

I hold my hand up and shake my head. "No. I can't do this. You knew about my past. You saw me struggling to remember, and you still didn't say a word. Would you really do that if you are the man I see in my dreams? If that were the case, wouldn't you want me to remember you?"

"It's not that simple, Alanna. I was trying to protect you."

"From what? Because from where I'm standing, the one I need protecting from is *you*."

I shake my head and turn to walk out of his office. "I can't do this, Silas. I need some space and time to think. I don't know what to believe, but I do know I *don't* believe *you*."

Chapter Seventy-Three

SILAS

I unlock the door to the apartment I bought for my brother and walk in uninvited. The smile on his face tells me he was expecting me. Ryan leans back on the sofa, his arms wide. "Took you longer than I expected."

I look into his eyes, seeing more of his mother in them with each passing day. For years I've given him the benefit of the doubt, telling myself he's a victim in the battle between his mother and me, but in reality I failed to realize that my attempts to protect him instead gave him the ammunition he hurt me with.

"Do you love her?" I ask, my voice soft. "Have you ever loved her?"

The smile melts off his face, and he nods. "Yes. I admit that I wasn't planning on falling for her, but I did. I fell hard, and by the time I realized it, it was too late."

"Then why do you continue to hurt her? Why are you messing with her memories? Isn't it enough for you to see her happy?"

"It wasn't enough for *you*," he says. "So why would it be enough for me?"

I shake my head. "It would have been. If she'd truly been happy with you, I'd have left her alone. We both know she wasn't. She was content with you, but she wasn't happy. You know that as well as I do."

Ryan rises to his feet and clenches his jaw. "That's bullshit. If not for you, I'd have won her back and made her happy."

"So, what? If you can't have her, she can't be happy at all?"

Ryan looks away. "Not with you, Silas. Not after the way you've been lying to her. I know what you've done. I know she got hurt because of you."

"No," I tell him. "You don't. You think you know what happened between the two of us, but you weren't there, so where are you getting your information from? Where are you hearing the lies that you're whispering into Alanna's ears?" His eyes flicker with a hint of uncertainty, and I sigh. "I read the report you sent to Alanna, and none of it is true. I don't know where you got that information, but someone has been lying to you."

I run a hand through my hair and inhale deeply as I take my wallet out of my pocket and carefully take out an old photo of Alanna and me. "Here," I murmur as I hand it to him. I'm kissing Alanna's cheek in that photo, the two of us so young and so clearly in love. "Alanna is the only woman I've ever loved, and contrary to what you seem to think, she loved me too. She might not remember me, but she still dreams of me."

Ryan's eyes widen, a hint of confusion flashing through them. As expected, whatever it is Mona has been telling him isn't true.

"The only reason I'm telling you this is because I need you to stop. There's only so much I can overlook, and you're hurting her. You're messing with her memories and the sense of security I've fought to give her. I'm not using her, and I never approached her with ulterior motives. I didn't take her from you, Ryan. She's always been mine."

Ryan stares at me for a moment, as though he's trying to

assess the truthfulness of my words, and I stand in silence as he tries to make up his mind.

"Ryan," I say, my voice soft. "She *is* Ray. She's the girl I've mentioned before, the love of my life, the one who got away. When we were younger, I nicknamed her Ray, because she's my ray of sunshine. It's always been her."

I run a hand through my hair and stare up at the ceiling. "Do you have any idea how it killed me to watch her with you? You think you're in pain, but take a moment to consider what it must have been like for me. I spent years searching for her, only to find her in your arms. My younger brother, the very same one I vowed to protect, with the love of my life. Do you have any idea why she was interested in you in the first place?"

Ryan shakes his head, and I smile bitterly. "Your eyes. We both have Dad's unique green eyes. She recognized them but couldn't understand why. The only reason I've stayed silent was because she left you willingly, and I didn't want to force her to be with me through knowledge of our past. I wanted to win her over fair and square, all over again. And I did. She came back to me, and that's all that mattered to me. I didn't want to burden you with knowledge of our past, and I didn't want to risk you telling her that she and I have history together, because there's a good reason she still hasn't regained her memory. Her past is filled with pain, Ryan. Recovering her memories will wreck her, and I won't put her through that for my own selfish desires."

He stares at me as though he's struggling to comprehend what I'm telling him, and I pray I'm getting through to him. I once vowed to protect him, to take care of him in my father's stead, but I'm at the end of my tether. I can't do this much longer. I can't keep destroying myself in an attempt to keep the promise I made my father. "You meeting Alanna wasn't a coincidence," I tell him. "But then you know that, don't you? Your mother never does anything without reason. You told me you met Alanna when your mother took you to volunteer at the beach, but is that something she's ever done before? Didn't she specifically point out

Alanna as a way to get into my good graces? Why do you think that is?"

Ryan looks away, closing up at the mention of his mother. He's blind to her shortcomings, and nothing I do or say will ever change that. He feels protective of her, but he doesn't realize the love he has for her is what's slowly destroying him.

"There's nothing I can do or say that will make you understand why your mother and I don't get along, but you aren't stupid, Ryan. Surely you can see you're being manipulated? I don't know what she's telling you, but look at the photo in your hands. Does it look like Alanna feared me? If you're doing this to protect her, then stop. All you're accomplishing is hurting her, and some of the damage may be irreparable. Some of her memories could be distorted and lost forever."

"I'm not just doing it to protect her, Silas. I don't give a fuck about your history with her. It doesn't matter, because she can't remember it, anyway. As far as she knows, *I'm* her first kiss. *I'm* the first person she slept with. *I'm* her first boyfriend. With you out of the way, who do you think she'll want to lean on?"

I smile humorlessly. "You won't win her back this way. You can't keep up the lies you're telling her. What do you think she'll do once she realizes you're lying to her all over again?"

He looks away, the desperation in his eyes hitting me hard. He knows he won't get away with his lies, but it's worth it to him so long as he doesn't have to see her with *me*.

"What is it going to take for you to stay away from her?" I ask, my tone defeated.

Ryan glances at me, a calculative look in his eyes. "What is she worth?"

I look away, my heart heavy. "Everything."

He chuckles, the sound grating. "Then give me everything. Give me everything you took from us and I'll tell Alanna that everything I've told her was a lie. I'll confess, and I'll never appear in front of her again."

I look at him in disbelief. "Ryan, everything I took from your mother should've been mine in the first place."

"Dad never wanted you to have the house or the company. That's why he didn't leave it to you, Silas. I'll give you a week to think about it. If you decline, I'm going to see Alanna, and I'll tell her you threatened me."

He smiles as he walks away, leaving me standing in his empty living room. For so long, I've been holding onto the little boy who cried at our father's funeral, the child that needed me so desperately. I've forgiven him for so much that he's done, and in doing so I condemned myself.

Chapter Seventy-Four

Silas

I walk into our bedroom to find Alanna pulling her clothes off the racks in our wardrobe, and panic runs down my spine. "What are you doing?"

She whirls around, her eyes wide. "Si-Silas," she stammers. "I thought you had a meeting that'd be running late?"

I stare at her in disbelief. "What are you doing, Alanna? Were you seriously just going to disappear without saying a word? Again?"

I walk up to her and grab her shoulders, my thoughts whirling. Does she have any idea what it'd do to me to have her disappear again? I nearly lost my mind looking for her. I'm not sure I can survive it twice.

"Alanna, no matter what happens, please don't ever just disappear without a word. Please don't make me worry like that. If nothing else, I need to know that you're safe. Do you understand?"

She nods, her face marred with regret. "I wasn't planning on disappearing, Si. I was going to call you after I left. I just... I didn't... I wasn't sure if you'd let me go."

I pull my hands back and look away, my heart shattering. "You're scared? *Of me*?"

She shakes her head and holds her hands up. "Silas, I'm really confused, and I... I really do need some space. I need to think. I feel like I've been immersed in a world that isn't real. First with Ryan, and now with you. Most of my memories are based on lies. Do you know how that feels? Do you have any idea what it feels like to find out that every memory you cherish is at least partially a lie? Do you understand how much it hurts to know that the one person I trusted most lied to me and kept things from me the entire time?" She runs a hand through her hair and inhales shakily. "It isn't just that I'm confused by everything Ryan told me, and despite the compelling arguments he made and my shifty memory, I still... I still love you. What hurts the most is that you've been deceiving me when you knew how much it hurt me when Ryan did the same thing to me. I get that you have your reasons, and you seem to think you had my best interests at heart, but you had no right. I just, I'm not sure I can trust you. I don't know what's real and what isn't, and I don't know how you're entangled in my past and whether you're someone I should fear. I don't know, and it kills me that I can't trust you to tell me the truth. Even if you want to tell me everything now, I no longer want to hear it, because I don't trust you."

Looking at her makes me feel like I'm losing her all over again. It hurts just as much as it did the first time. "Alanna," I say, my voice soft. "I asked you once if you wanted to know about you past if it came at the risk of your memories being distorted, and you told me you didn't want to know. I knew I didn't have the right to keep it from you, so I gave you a choice, and your choice resulted in my silence. I really am the man you dream of, and I wanted you to remember it yourself. Everything you and I have gone through... you have no idea, do you? You're the reason I am the person I am today. You're the reason I worked as hard as I did.

Everything I've done was for you. When I told you that you *are* Ray, I meant it. It's always been you."

She stares at me with such longing in her eyes that I struggle to stay away from her. I close the distance between us and cup her face tenderly. "I've waited for you for five years, Alanna. I'll wait another five years if I need to. I just hope you won't put us through that. There's nothing I can say that'll prove my innocence, not now that my brother has already distorted your memories. All I can do is hope you'll regain your memories and that they'll lead you back to me."

"Si... I don't want to hurt you, but I don't know what to believe." Her voice breaks, and I drop my forehead to hers, trying my hardest to hide my pain from her. The last thing I want to do is keep her from doing what is right for her, even if that means leaving me.

"I know," I whisper. "It's okay, Alanna. I know you're struggling to figure out what to believe, and I did keep things from you. I know I've hurt you, and I broke your trust. I may have good intentions, but that doesn't make it hurt any less. I get that, and I'm willing to give you all the space you need... but please, baby. Please don't let Ryan influence you any further. Please keep an open mind and assess his intentions the way you have mine. Please think about everything I've done, and what I stand to gain or lose by being with you. Please, Alanna. Please forgive me."

She nods and pulls away to look at me. "I want to," she whispers.

"Then that's enough for me for now."

Alanna looks into my eyes, her gaze searching. "Silas, do you love me?"

"I love you. Without a doubt. Without reason. I have always loved you, even when you weren't with me. I never wavered, and I never will."

She rises to her tiptoes, her lips brushing past mine softly. I inhale sharply, scared to move for a moment, scared that this is the last time I'll ever feel her lips against mine. Alanna kisses me, her hands moving into my hair, a sense of desperation in her touch.

I pull her flush against me, needing more of her but not wanting this to be goodbye. "I love you," I whisper in between kisses. "I love you so fucking much, baby." She moans against my lips, and I deepen our kiss, my touch turning rougher, more urgent. "Please remember me. *Please.*"

"Si," she groans, and I lift her into my arms, her legs wrapping around my hips as I push her against the wall, kissing her harder. Just as I'm about to carry her to our bed, she pulls away. "Si... I..."

I carefully put her down, wishing I could just tie her to me instead. I wish I was capable of everything I'm being accused of, because if any of it was true, I'd never let her go, no matter what her wishes are.

Instead, I watch as she walks to our bed and zips up her suitcase. I watch as she walks out of the room, the door falling closed behind her. The sound of the front door closing follows soon after, and I sink down to the floor, my heart breaking in a way it never has before. Perhaps part of it had healed throughout the years, so the pain had dulled, or perhaps I love her more now than I ever did before.

I inhale shakily and reach into my suit jacket, pulling out one of her paper cranes. "Grant her wish," I whisper. Alanna wished for my happiness, and my happiness is *her*.

Chapter Seventy-Five

Silas

"Silas?" I snap out of my thoughts at the sound of Amy's voice and find her standing in front of my desk. How long has she been trying to get my attention?

"What is it?"

I haven't been able to focus on anything at all since Alanna left. She requested holiday leave from work, so I haven't seen her in over a week now. The security team told me she's safely checked into a bed-and-breakfast nearby, but I'm still restless. I'm worried I'm truly losing her, and it's killing me to give her the space she asked for. All I want to do is call her so I get to hear her voice.

"We found your father's lawyer. He entered the country this morning, and I instructed our interception team to pick him up. He's being transported to our interrogation room as we speak."

I sit up in shock. "We've been looking for him for years."

Amy smiles excitedly. "He must have thought it'd be safe to return now. I think we'll get him to talk quite easily. If he's back, he either needs more money, or he wants his life back. Whichever it is, cooperating with us will be his best bet. Mona has nothing left to offer him."

I nod. "Let's go. Send someone to collect Ryan for me. I want him to see this. If we get the answers we're after, then this might finally show him his mother's true colors. And if we don't, then he equally has a right to know that too."

Amy nods and walks out of my office, a determined look on her face. She's one of very few people who know how tough the last couple of years have been. I know she must share the satisfaction I'm feeling right now. Even if we don't get the answers we seek, at least we found him.

I'm tense as I walk into the control room, making sure the cameras are on. I don't want to miss anything today.

"Why did you bring me here?" Ryan asks the moment Amy leads him into the interrogation room's backroom. I turn toward him, feeling torn. With everything he's done lately, I no longer see him as the cute kid I wanted to protect. But at the same time, I can't let go of the obligation I feel. I can't help but wish that he's only this way because of his mother, and that the truth will change him.

"You'll see."

I watch as Michael is led in by the interception team, his eyes filled with panic. I let him sit in the room by himself for a moment, his thoughts undoubtedly going wild. If he truly did what I think he did, then I can't be the only person he screwed over.

I inhale deeply as I open the door to the room and walk in, his eyes widening when he sees me.

"Silas."

"Michael," I nod. "Long time no see."

He looks older, the calculating look in his eyes long gone. "It must have been exhausting looking over your shoulder for so many years, only to still get caught in the end."

He looks away and shakes his head. "I don't know what you're talking about."

I sit down opposite him and entwine my fingers as I stare him down. "I'm not the little boy you betrayed anymore," I tell him, my voice soft. "In the time you've been gone, I built Sinclair Security. It's one of the biggest security firms in the world, covering everything from private investigation, bodyguard services and even cybersecurity. Turns out I wasn't the only one that's been looking for you," I bluff. "I wonder how much money I stand to make if I hand you over."

His eyes widen, true fear finally filling his eyes. "You can't do that to me, Silas. They'll kill me."

"I know." I glance at my hands and lean back in my seat. "To be honest, I don't need the money Mona and you took from me. It took some time, but I've got enough of my own. What I want is the truth. Why did you forge my father's will? How did you do it?"

He rocks back and forth in his chair, contemplating his next move. "If I tell you, I want protection. I want the bodyguard services your firm offers in exchange for the full truth."

I nod. "Very well. That's easy enough. Talk."

"I want it in writing."

I rise from my seat and chuckle. "You're insane if you think I'm going to wait for my lawyers to draw up a contract. I don't have time for that. This is a take it or leave it deal. Either you talk right now, or I'm handing you over to someone who'll make you. What is it going to be?"

He grits his teeth and nods, his expression haunted. I have no idea who is after him, but fear has always been a strong motivator.

"It was all Mona's idea. She offered to pay me a ten percent cut of the entire estate if I forged your father's will and left everything to her."

I nod and sit down at the table, wondering what Ryan must be feeling right now, if he even believes Michael at all. He's been making excuses for his mother all his life.

"What was in the original will?"

"75% went to you to account for your mother's stake in the

business, and the other 25% went to Ryan. Mona didn't get anything. She was worried about it mostly because the will determined that you would hold Ryan's share too, until he turned 25. She'd be left with nothing and no access to any funds, either."

I nod, my thoughts reeling. "My father died unexpectedly, yet it was ruled to be a natural death. She had him cremated as soon as she possibly could to prevent me from doing a second autopsy. Did she have anything to do with my father's death?"

Michael shakes his head. "I don't know. All I know is that he'd asked me to start divorce proceedings, and a few weeks later, he was dead. If she did do it, I wasn't involved."

I run a hand through my hair and look up at the ceiling. I can't prove that she killed him, but I'm certain she did. "Okay," I tell him. "Thank you for your time. My men will see you out."

"What about my bodyguard services?"

I frown at him. "What are you talking about?"

"S-silas, you promised me. If you could find me this easily, they will too."

"You can't outrun your bad deeds, Michael. You'll pay for what you've done, and I won't even need to dirty my hands."

"You lied to me."

I rise to my feet and smile at him. "Isn't that exactly what you once did to me?"

I walk away without looking back, not a single ounce of remorse nagging at my conscience. He deserves whatever it is that's coming for him.

"Did you hear that?" I ask Ryan.

He's staring at the window, his face as white as a sheet. "How much did you pay him to say all of that?"

My heart sinks and I look away. "Ryan, if after all this, you still can't see the truth, then you truly are a lost cause."

He looks at me, his eyes flashing with anger. "I'm not retracting my offer. I'm still going after Alanna if you don't give me what I'm owed. You've got three days left, Silas. Make them count."

I stare at him in disbelief as he walks out of the room, my heart sinking as I think back to the little boy who cried his heart out at our father's funeral. It's that image of him that made me weak, and it's that same image that's now going to cost me everything.

Chapter Seventy-Six

ALANNA

"Are you sure you want to try this?" my psychologist asks. "Hypnotherapy could help, but it could also generate even more false memories if it works at all. It isn't like in the movies, where you'll just magically remember everything. Because your amnesia has lasted for so many years, the chances of full recovery are slim."

I nod without hesitation. "I want to try. Recently I've been told a lot of things about my past, and while they don't feel right, I can suddenly remember those exact scenes. I can't tell what is true and what isn't. I want at least a hint of my own memories, something that's mine, not something I'm being told is true."

"I understand," the doctor says. "Let's give it a try then, shall we?"

She leads me to the sofa and tells me to make myself comfortable. I'm nervous, scared of what I might see, but I close my eyes nonetheless.

"Let's start with controlling your breathing, okay?"

I follow her steps, counting my breaths until my thoughts still, going through the motions with her. I try my best to imagine the serene landscape she's describing, the sun shining on my face. It takes a while, but eventually, I sink into the fantasy she laid out. She takes her time, slowly adding some of the details I told her about into the scenario, until it all starts to feel real.

"That man you keep dreaming of, he's smiling at you and grabs your hand."

I never used to be able to see his face, but this time I picture him as Silas, the younger version of him I saw in my memories. Could it truly be him?

"He pulls you along, the two of you walking hand in hand."

My imagination follows the scenario and I just watch as the scene becomes more and more familiar, until we're standing underneath a large blossom tree. One I've seen before. I gasp and sit up, my hands wrapping around myself.

"What is it? What did you see?"

I shake my head, a sad smile on my face. "Nothing. It was just a place I went to recently. It isn't something from my past."

She nods and smiles in understanding. "We can try it again soon, if you want, but your case is tricky. I'm not sure it'll work."

I rise to my feet and nod. "I get it. Thank you for trying nonetheless."

I'm absentminded as I leave her office, something not feeling quite right. There's something about the blossom tree that feels like it was a *sign*.

I hesitate for a moment before flagging down a taxi, trying my hardest to recall the directions to the place Silas took me to on my birthday. It was that very same tree, I'm sure of it.

I stare up at the *no trespassing* sign as I push the taxi door closed, a strange sense of belonging washing over me. I know this place, and it isn't just because Silas took me here recently.

I walk up to the tree, my head throbbing, almost as though it wants me to remember, but can't push past the blocks containing it.

I place my hand against the tree trunk and inhale shakily. "Tell me your secrets," I whisper. "Tell me mine."

I look around, unsure what for, until my eyes land on a small shovel hidden behind the tree. It looks old, rust eating at the handles, but the moment I see it, I just know that's what I was after. I grab it with both hands and stare at it for a moment, trying to figure out why it feels so familiar to me. I must have used this before.

My knees hit the floor as I start to dig, unsure why but certain that's what I'm here for. Before long, the shovel hits something hard, and I dig out a glass bottle. I brush the dirt off and hold it up to the light. There's something in there. I open the bottle carefully and take out the paper inside it, my hands trembling as I uncurl it.

It's a drawing of me. Or rather, it's a handmade birthday card, similar to the one Silas gave me this year. This one too, was no doubt drawn by him. It's an image of a younger me sitting underneath the blossom tree, my ankles crossed and my face tipped up toward the sun, a happy smile on my face.

I open it hesitantly, my eyes widening at the date written on the top right corner. It's a birthday card for last year, back when I'd just started dating Ryan.

Alanna, my ray of sunshine

It's been over four years since you went missing, and I still come here every year on your birthday. No matter how much time passes, I can't let go. I can't give up hope that someday I'll run into you somewhere, and you'll explain to me why you disappeared without a word.

I keep dreaming that you and I grow old together, and the years we spent apart are one of those things we'll tell our grandchildren about. The epic love story of their grandparents.

The more time passes, the more I wonder if maybe I'm wrong, and nothing happened to you at all. Maybe you just had enough of the life we lived. Maybe being with me was too hard. Maybe hope wasn't enough to live on. Maybe that last argument we had made you realize that you can do better, and you left to create a better life for yourself than what I could've given you.

Who knows... maybe you're out there, happy with someone else. If you are, I'll wish you the best and quietly cheer you on. The only thing I've ever wanted for you was happiness, even if it isn't with me.

I love you, Alanna. Even after all these years. I loved you long before I first uttered those words, and I'll love you until I draw my last breath. I hope you're out there somewhere, so I'll get to tell you this in person someday: Happy birthday, Ray.

Ψ

The letter is signed with the ψ symbol, and hot tears stream down my cheeks. *ψ* is a *person*. It's Silas. He's the one I've been looking for.

I hate that I can't remember anything about him, about us. I bite down on my lip and move to fill the hole I just dug, but just before I throw on some dirt, I see something else buried. Another bottle.

I pull that out too and continue to dig, unearthing a total of four bottles, including the one I've already opened. There seems to be one for every year since I woke up in the hospital, all of them containing a handmade birthday card.

It can't be that I ran away because Silas stalked me. These bottles prove that he loved me more than anything, holding onto our relationship even as I went missing.

But if we were dating, then why do I remember us arguing? Why do I remember screaming at him to stay away from me? Was it just an argument, or was there more to it?

I draw my knees to my chest as tears flow down my face. I need to know the full truth, and no one but me can give me that.

Chapter Seventy-Seven

Alanna

I look up at the building I've come to consider home. It's strange how quickly I felt at home with Silas when I've always felt so out of place everywhere else. Or maybe it isn't strange at all. Maybe it was fate.

I'm a coward for coming home when I know he's at work. I'm not even sure what I'm doing here, but I can't stay away. I keep telling myself that I'm only here to pick up the few things I forgot to pack, but I can't even convince myself of that. I can't fight the urge to be near Silas, but I also can't call him, not while my thoughts are still such a mess. I'm even more confused now than I was before. I wish I could see the full picture, but I'm not even holding all the pieces. Each time I feel like I'm making progress, I suddenly find myself back at the start.

I walk into the living room, my mind replaying the way Silas and I worked together, the way he kissed me on the sofa. My gaze shifts to the closed bedroom door and I take a hesitant step forward. My heart aches at the mere sight of the bed we used to share. He told me he'd never brought another woman here before, and I believe him. I truly believe this place was ours. Maybe it has been for longer than I even realized. My eyes drop to the note left on top of the bed, and I pick it up with a frown.

Alanna,

I'm sure that you'll find your way back home sooner or later, whether it be for a few minutes or forever. I'm giving you all the space you asked for, but in return, please make sure you stay safe.

Please, baby, take one of the cars when you leave. The thought of you taking public transportation late at night worries me. I won't ask more of you. I won't ask you to call me, nor will I ask you to come back to work. I won't ask anything of you that you're not ready to give.

All I ask is that you stay safe.

All my love,

Silas

Has he been putting this note on the bed every morning, knowing one day I'd walk in here and find it? My heart starts to ache at the thought of him waiting for me. If he truly is the man I've been dreaming of, then he must've been waiting for me for years. Could a love like that truly exist?

With each passing day, I'm more sure that he never posed a

threat to me, no matter what Ryan might be saying. What I can't figure out is if Silas truly loves me, or if he's in love with the person in his memories. I'm undoubtedly in love with him, but can I be with a person who knows more about me than I know about myself? Someone who's been keeping things from me throughout our relationship?

I'm worried that I'm making the same mistake that I made with Ryan. Am I ignoring red flags because I so desperately want to belong somewhere? My willingness to forgive Silas for anything at all scares me. I've never felt a love so great that I'd willingly turn a blind eye to lies and deception, just so I don't lose him. It isn't healthy, and I can't put myself through this again. Not even for Silas. Not when there's so much about him that I still don't know.

My heart feels heavy as I head to the door, hesitating for a moment before pressing the floor for the garage. Somehow, I can't deny such an earnest request. I don't think Silas has ever asked anything of me that harmed me. Despite what Ryan might lead me to believe, he hasn't ever done anything that wasn't in my best interests. He might have lied to me, but I don't think he did it maliciously. The only question is where that leaves us. How do I date a man who holds the answers to all of my questions, but who might lie to me to protect me?

I'm lost in thought as I head to the garage, my heart leading me one way while my brain points toward a different road. I walk past the row of Silas's cars, my eyes dropping to the one in the corner.

It's just an old car, he'd told me. In hindsight, he seemed somewhat nervous when I asked about it. Is it yet another part of my past?

For a moment, I'm terrified that I'll find the car that hit me, and that Ryan's warnings are all true. I bite down on my lip harshly as I lift the cover up, pulling at it until it comes undone. I yank it off, finding an old blue truck hiding underneath.

I stare at it, irrational devastation suddenly washing over me as a sharp pain has me clutching my head. Memories of this car driving away flood my mind, slowly getting further and further away. There's no further context to the memory, but the pain I feel is real. Staring at this car makes me feel like all hope is lost, like I've truly lost everything.

I drop down to my knees and massage my temples as more memories come flooding back. An older man behind the wheel, a proud and loving look on his face. The two of us standing in a graveyard together, stricken with grief.

Dad.

I start to feel sick as memories of the hospital come to mind, followed by a police officer and a man in a black suit standing in front of my house.

Insurance fraud.

Assisted suicide.

Memories of Silas and me in his small bedroom at the shelter come to mind, all of the memories I'd blocked suddenly rushing back, along with the pain of losing my parents and the homelessness that followed.

My vision starts to blur as I recall volunteering, the phone calls with Silas that made me fall for him. My eighteenth birthday underneath the tree, and the promises he made me.

Silas, my Si.

I try my hardest to climb to my feet, but no matter how hard I fight, I can't escape the darkness.

"Silas," I whisper, and then my vision goes black.

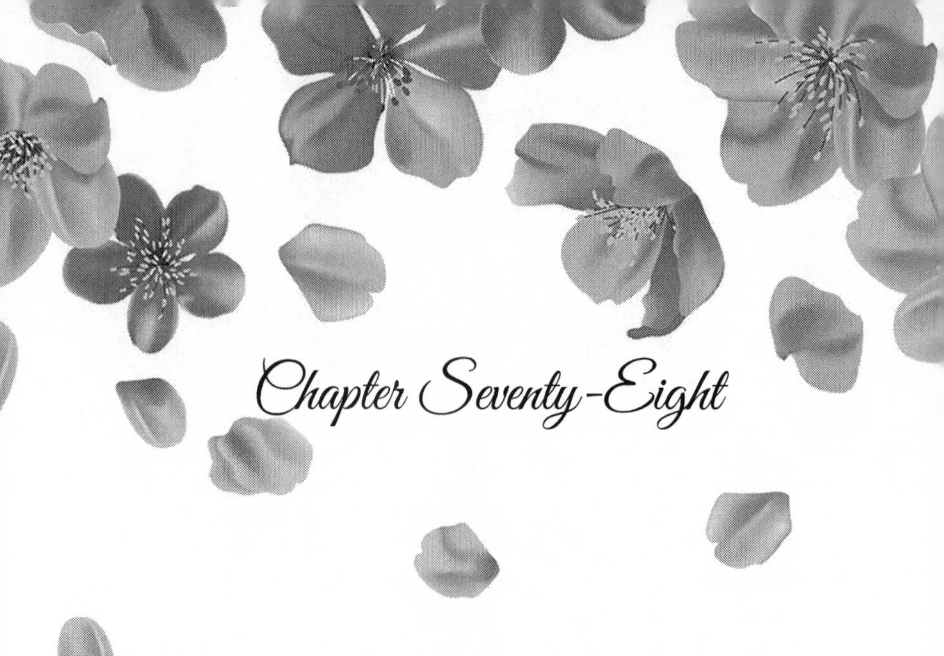

Chapter Seventy-Eight

Silas

I stare at the paperwork in front of me, unsure what to do. Everything I've fought to regain, gone with a single signature. It hits me even harder now that I know that my father truly intended for me to have everything I now own.

"You can't do this," Amy says, her tone pleading.

I shake my head and look away. "I don't have a choice. Everything I've done has been for her. I've done everything within my power to protect her from the pain of her past, but I've reached the limit of what I can do. If I don't put a stop to what Ryan is doing, I'll lose her forever. With each lie he tells her, he distorts her memories, solidifying a false image of me. I can't lose her again, Amy. I don't think I can survive it. Besides, I can't let this happen to her. I can't let him take something so precious from her."

"Silas, it'll cost you everything. Is she really worth everything you spent years building? Please be rational. If she were to regain her memory, do you really think she'd want you to do this?"

I shake my head. "She wouldn't, but what choice do I have?"

"We can always handle Ryan the way we've handled others."

I chuckle, not in the least surprised at her ruthlessness. "We can't. He's my *brother*. While this document definitely ensures the end of any relationship between us, I won't harm him."

She nods, her expression dissatisfied. Amy glances at her watch and grimaces. "He'll be here soon."

Moments later, a knock sounds on my office door, and Ryan walks in. I look up at him, a strange kind of pain tugging at my heart. He's my last remaining family member, and in the end, he betrayed me just like his mother did. I tried so hard to put him on the right path, shielding him from his mother's intentions as best as I could, and all it earned me was a knife in the back.

Ryan sits down opposite me, his eyes on the documents. "Everything I've ever wanted in return for everything you've always wanted," I murmur.

He looks up then, his expression unreadable. "You'd truly give up everything for her?"

I nod. "Without a second thought. Nothing I have is worth having, if I don't get to share it with her. I'll sign, but the moment it's done, this is also the end of any relationship between you and me. I'm done, Ryan."

I pick up the papers and straighten them, placing them in front of me before I pick up my pen, the very same one Alanna once gave me for my birthday, many years ago. Heartbreak of a different kind fills me as I sign on every single page, dropping the pen when it's done.

This doesn't just sign away all of my assets. It also cuts my little brother out of my life, once and for all. It's the end of everything I've tried to do for him, every effort I've made to shield him from the feud between his mother and me. It's proof that it was all in vain.

I push the papers toward him, and Ryan stares at them in shock, almost as though he truly didn't believe I'd sign them. As if there's anything I wouldn't do for Alanna. She and I have already proven that we can live without worldly belongings. So long as

I've got her, there's nothing else I need. I just hope she feels the same way.

A commotion outside my office grabs my attention, and before I realize what's going on, Alanna comes storming into my office, her hair a mess and tear marks marring her face.

"Si," she says, her voice breaking. The look in her eyes has me freezing. She hasn't looked at me quite in the same way in years.

"Oh God, *Si*."

She bursts into tears and I jump out of my seat, rushing toward her just as her legs give in. I catch her before she falls, and Alanna reaches for me, her fingers tracing over my face.

"Baby, what's going on? Are you okay? What happened?"

"I'm s-so sorry," she sobs. "Si… I *remember*."

I stare at her wide-eyed, certain my ears are deceiving me, but then she smiles at me in that way she used to.

"Really," she promises. "I remember everything. The two of us living together in the shelter. The way you always used to tell me not to put myself into dangerous situations. You giving me that handkerchief on the day I buried my mother, and you buried your father. The way you drew the ψ symbol onto my rib. I remember the day you took my first kiss, and every first you've taken since. I remember it all. I'm sorry I didn't recognize you straight away. I'm so sorry for everything I've put you through. I'm sorry, Si. I'm so sorry."

I tighten my grip on her and hold her tightly. "You remember."

She nods, her body heaving with the force of her sobs. "I'm sorry I made you worry so much throughout the years, Si. When we had that argument about me moving into college dorms, I was so upset that I wasn't thinking straight. I got into a car accident, and when I woke up, I couldn't remember anything. I never would've stayed away from you otherwise. Never."

"It's okay," I promise her. "It's okay, Ray. All that matters is that you found your way back to me."

She nods, and I rub her back gently. If she remembers me, she must also remember her father. She's cried so many bitter tears over him, and I'm worried that the pain feels fresh for her all over.

"Are you okay, my love? If you remember everything..."

She pulls away to look at me and nods. "I will be. I got through the pain once, thanks to you. I'll do it again."

I cup her face and wipe her tears away, my forehead dropping to hers. Alanna's arms wrap around my neck, her lips pressing against mine with a years-old urgency.

This kiss hits differently. It's filled with a thousand promises and a thousand apologies. "I love you so much, Silas," she whispers against my lips. I groan and thread my hand through her hair, fisting it in my hand to bring her closer. Alanna comes willingly, and I deepen the kiss, needing all of her. This. So long as I've got this, I don't need anything else.

The sounds of ripping paper pulls us apart, and we turn toward my desk to find Ryan ripping up the contract I just signed. He throws the shreds onto my desk and turns toward us with remorse brimming in his eyes.

I pull away from Alanna and take a step toward him, but before I can say a word, he walks out of my office, the door closing behind him.

I glance back at Alanna and gently brush her hair out of her face. The way she's looking at me breaks my heart.

"I'm so sorry, Silas," she whispers, her voice breaking.

"Don't be," I tell her. "All that matters is that you're here with me now. The past doesn't matter as much as the future does."

She nods, and I take a step closer to her, grinning from ear to ear. I thought I'd lost her forever, yet the woman staring back at me with love shining through her eyes is undoubtedly my Ray.

Chapter Seventy-Nine

Silas

"Si," Alanna says as we walk into the house, the two of us pausing in front of the mirror in the hallway. "I never truly forgot you." Her voice is soft and apologetic, as though she wants to reassure me but doesn't know how to.

I turn toward her and wrap my hands around her shoulders. "I know, Ray," I whisper. I can't lie to her and say that her treating me like a stranger hasn't hurt me, but it was bearable because even though she didn't realize it, our love shone through. "I saw it in the thousand cranes you folded for me, the tattoo on your rib and the handkerchief you carry with you. It was in the way you kissed me, the way you couldn't resist me, even though you fought this thing between us so hard. Even when I couldn't call you mine, I knew your heart still belonged to me."

She nods and takes a step closer to me, her arms wrapping around my neck. "You never stopped searching for me, did you?"

I shake my head. "How could I? I knew you were out there somewhere, and I refused to believe you simply left me. We may have had an argument, but it wasn't the kind that would have you walking away from everything we had."

"*Silas*," she says, her voice pained. "What if I'd died? What if you'd never found me? Were you just going to waste away your entire life because of me? That's not what I wanted for you."

I lean in and press a lingering kiss to her forehead. "If you'd died, I'd avenge you and spend the rest of my life mourning you. I once promised you that you'd be my last love, and I meant it. If one day I found out that you'd been buried, I'd bury my heart right alongside you and count down the days until I see you again."

"You're crazy," she says, tears filling her eyes.

"I know." I drop my head to hers and inhale shakily. "Maybe I really am crazy, Alanna, because I knew you were still out there. I could feel it in my soul. I knew you were waiting for me to find you, so I never stopped searching. I'm sorry it took me so long, baby."

Alanna sniffs, and I wrap my arms around her fully, hugging her tightly as she bursts into tears. "I'm sorry it took me so long to come back to you. I'm sorry I hurt you so much, Si. I'm so sorry."

I wrap my hand over the back of her head, her face nestled against my neck. "All that matters is that you found your way back home, baby."

She rises to her tiptoes, her lips finding mine. The way she kisses me is different. It's tinged with regret, and I lift her into my arms. Alanna wraps her legs around my hips as I carry her to our bedroom, her lips never leaving mine. "Do you have any idea how scared I was?" I whisper against her lips. "When you went missing, Ricardo and other residents went searching for you, but you were nowhere to be found. I nearly went crazy trying to find you."

"I'm sorry," she whispers. "I'm here now, Si. I'm here, and I'm never leaving you again. You'll never be alone again, I promise."

I lay her down on our bed and climb on top of her, covering her body with mine. "You can't," I tell her. "You can't ever leave me again, Alanna. I barely survived it the first time, and my heart took another beating when I walked in here to find you packing your bags."

She cups my cheek and looks into my eyes. "I didn't know what to believe, Si. Ryan..."

I tense, and she looks away, guilt marring her beautiful face. I thread my hand through her hair and tilt her face back toward mine. "It's okay, baby. Your heart was always mine, whether you wanted to admit it or not."

She looks into my eyes, a tear rolling down her face. "Forgive me," she whispers. "Please forgive me, Si. I was chasing the closest thing to you I could find, and meeting you again was the start of the end for Ryan and I. You're the only one I've ever loved, Si."

I smile at her, the feeling bittersweet. "There's nothing to forgive, Ray. If you dating him truly changed anything for me, I'd have let you go the moment I found out about the two of you."

I turn us over so we're both on our side, facing each other. It's strange, because she's been here all along, yet the way she looks at me today is different. It truly is *her* now.

"I'm so proud of you," she tells me, her gaze roaming over my face. She traces the contours of my face with the tip of her fingers, and the way she smiles at me has my heart skipping a beat. "This home, everything you've built. You did everything you told me you would. Si, you even kept some of the promises you once made me, all without me even realizing. Buying me a dress to change into before a date? The diamond necklace you gave me on my birthday? Even the bedroom we're in now is so similar to all of my Pinterest inspiration boards. You've made both of our dreams come true, and I couldn't be more proud. I'm so sorry I wasn't by your side throughout the years, Si."

It's so surreal to have my Ray lying here with me. Until now, I didn't even realize just how much I still missed her, even when she was here with me. "I did it for us," I admit. "I did it because I knew that someday you'd be here with me."

"When you told me you were the man of my dreams, you meant it, huh?"

I chuckle, my nose brushing past hers. "In more ways than one."

She bursts out laughing and pushes against my shoulder, making me roll onto my back before she climbs on top of me. "I have so many questions about the last couple of years, and there's so much that still doesn't make sense to me, but it can wait."

I smile at her, my hands wrapping around her waist. "Is that so? Well, you did find your first love. I suppose this is the part where you ride off into the sunset with the man of your dreams, leaving me heartbroken?"

She narrows her eyes at me and shakes her head. "I can't believe you teased me like that when you knew it was you all along!"

I burst out laughing, my heart overflowing with happiness. This, right here, right now. This is the future I always envisioned.

"I'm not one for riding into the sunset, Si," Alanna says, a teasing smirk on her face. "But I'm definitely up for riding you until sunrise."

My cock hardens at her words, and I tighten my grip on her waist. "Then ride me, Ray."

Chapter Eighty

ALANNA

Silas holds my hand in his as we walk into the cemetery where both our parents have been laid to rest. "Remember the day we first met?" I ask.

He glances at me and nods. "Even then, you were a ray of sunshine on a cloudy day. You were just a child, and you still managed to make me smile. I wonder if it was destiny, you know?"

I nod and tighten my grip on his hand. "I used to think about this a lot, back when we were in the shelter. I wondered about fate and destiny, and how things could've turned out the way they did for you and I. I think of it even more now. The way we fell apart, the way we found our way back to each other. How could that be anything short of destiny?"

"Maybe I'm crazy, but I'd like to think it was our parents," he says, his voice soft. "I didn't even used to believe in this kind of stuff, but over the years I've come to wonder if perhaps they're watching over us, gently guiding us along our way, supporting us in the only way they can. It can't be a coincidence that I met you that day, and that we met again at the shelter."

I look up at him, my heart heavy. "The way we keep finding our way back to each other… I think it's fate, Silas. Maybe I'm a little bit of a hopeless romantic, but if soulmates exist, then you are mine. I have no doubt."

He smiles at me as we walk over to my parents' graves. I'm oddly nervous as we round the corner. The last couple of days have been tough. I've had the worst headaches as I tried my best to make sense of all the memories I lost, grief hitting me as though it was fresh all over again. It's hard to grieve a person the world seems to have forgotten, but at least Silas was there for me, holding me each time it got too hard. I spent many nights crying myself to sleep, my heart breaking not just over the loss of my father and the choice he made, but also everything Silas and I lost, everything I put him through. The guilt has been hard to stomach, and though he's tried his best to reassure me, I can't shake the remorse I feel.

"Mom, Dad," I murmur, my eyes roaming over their spotless tombstones. "This is Silas, and you would have really loved him. I'd introduce him to you as my boyfriend, but that doesn't seem like quite enough to describe what he means to me."

Silas wraps his arms around me, his touch comforting. I lean into him, my heart breaking all over again.

"I suppose you've seen him throughout the years, haven't you? He's taken better care of you than I could at the time." Silas maintained my parents' graves in my absence, ensuring the tombstones were kept clean and going as far as having flowers delivered weekly. I don't know what I did to deserve him, but I'm going to spend the rest of my life repaying him for everything he's done for me.

"Dad," I whisper. "He's the one who saved your truck. Remember when I told you that I had to sell it? Silas bought it back for you, and he's taken really good care of it. If not for that beloved truck of yours, I might still be living as a shell of myself, feeling like I'm incomplete. In the end, it was both Silas and you that saved me, in more ways than one."

I stare at the tombstones in front of me, feeling conflicted. "I'm still mad at both of you. Every day, I still wonder if there's anything I could've done, or something I should have said. Some days I wonder if maybe I just wasn't enough for you, Mom. And Dad? I still feel like I failed you. Doing what you did, making me give you up in return for *money*? The fact that you even considered it at all makes me wonder how terrible of a daughter I must have been for you to think that's something I could live with." I sniff as fresh tears roll down my face. I've been crying most days since I regained my memories, but it's been bittersweet. The past might hold a lot of pain, but it holds just as much love. "The man you hired... he upheld his end of the bargain as best as he could, even after all of your plans fell apart. He paid for my education, Dad. If not for Silas, I'd never have known, and I figured... I figured telling you that would help you rest easier. I wish you'd never done it, but you should know it wasn't all in vain." I inhale shakily and run a hand through my hair. "I'm hurt, and I'm angry, but I still love you. I still miss you, and there still isn't anything I wouldn't do to see both of you one more time."

Silas raises our joined hands to his lips and kisses the back of my hand, his expression pained. "Per aspera ad astra," he tells me. "I know it hurts, and you don't have to forgive them immediately, but don't let the pain poison you, Ray. This, too, is one of the hardships that turned you into the person you are today. You and I have been immersed in misery, but because of and *despite* it, we've come as far as we did. Through adversity, we reached the stars."

I nod and smile up at him. He's right, of course. He always is. "I'm not sure who I would be without you, Si. Adversity may have shaped us, but love did, too. I love you, Silas Sinclair. Today, and every day to come."

The way he smiles at me has my heart racing as we walk over to his parents' tombstones. "I had my father's ashes buried next to mother," he tells me as we pause in front of them. "So they could be together at last. A few years ago, I found out that my father had purchased the plot next to mother, much like your father did. This was my way of honoring the wish he never voiced."

I hold his hand as Silas greets his parents before turning to me. "This is the woman I'm going to marry," he says, and my heart skips a beat. "I've already asked her to marry me, but she thought I was joking. I wasn't. It's okay though, I'll try again, and again, until she says yes. Her name is Alanna, but I call her Ray. Sometimes, when she's acting a little crazy, I call her *my little psycho*. She's sweet and smart and beautiful, and you would have loved her so much."

I lean into him, the biggest smile on my face. It's strange to be here, in the same place we met, so many years later. Life nearly tore us apart, but we made it. Through adversity, we made it.

"Dad," Silas says, his tone regretful. "When you passed away, I made you a promise. I told you that I'd take care of Ryan in your stead, that I'd protect him from Mona, and that no harm would come to him." He inhales shakily and runs a hand through his hair. "I'm going to have to break that promise. I hope you'll forgive me. I've done my best, Dad. I've given him as many chances as I could, but I'm done. I can't save him when he's the one that's knowingly and willingly walking down this path. I'm sorry."

Silas wraps his arm around me, and I look up at him. The pain I see in his gaze tears me apart, even more so because I know I played a part in it too. I'm not sure I'll ever be able to make up for everything he's had to endure. That's the tricky thing about memories. The ones we most want to forget will forever haunt us, and the ones we want to hang onto fade day by day.

"What are you going to do?"

Silas inhales deeply and tucks a strand of my hair behind my ear. "What I should have done long ago."

Chapter Eighty-One

Silas

I suspected this day would come, but I've done everything in my power to keep it from happening. I was even willing to overlook the harm his mother did me, letting the lawyer walk instead of detaining him, but I should have known better.

I should have realized that Ryan needs to learn how to handle the consequences of his actions, the way I had to. Shielding him from everything the way I did only allowed his mother to bury her claws into him that much deeper, taking him beyond salvation.

I stand by the choice I'm making today, but that doesn't make it any easier. I glance at the police officer next to me and nod, standing back as he knocks on Mona's door.

Ryan opens the door, and regret hits me hard. I know this is going to hurt him, but I'm done burying the truth for his benefit. "Silas? What is the meaning of this?"

Mona appears behind him and Officer Davis glances at me. He and I have worked together on cases Sinclair Security has provided consultancy services for, but today is more of a personal favor. I nod at him, and he straightens.

"Mona Wright, you are under arrest on account of forgery of your husband's will." Ryan's eyes widen as Officer Davis reads out her rights to her, and she sends her son a panicked look, but Ryan is looking at me.

"It's really true?" he asks, his voice breaking.

I nod. "You know it is."

"Ryan! Do something! Please, tell your brother to stop this. It's all part of his vendetta against us. He's just doing this to hurt us, Ry. This is what he's like. Please, talk some sense into him. Don't let him do this to me."

He glances at his mother and takes a step back. Mona freezes in surprise, her gaze moving toward me. "What did you tell him?" she asks, her tone harsh.

"Nothing. I didn't have to, Mona. You did this all by yourself. I would've let it go, you know? For Ryan, I would have spared you. You fucked up when you touched Alanna. Even then, I let it go, knowing Ryan wasn't in on it. You should've counted your lucky stars and let it be once she came back to me. You never should have tried to use her to get to my assets. If you'd stayed away from her, you'd have been left with the money I paid you to acquire what you lost. Now? Now you'll lose everything, the way I once did."

Officer Davis leads her away, and Ryan watches her without a word. "We have the lawyer's taped confession, but he's told me he kept evidence too, in case she didn't pay him his share after the deed was done. He's willing to turn it in to lessen his own forgery sentence. She's going to jail, Ryan."

He nods and looks down at his feet. "I'm sorry, Silas. I didn't see it at the time. I didn't realize that my own mother was manipulating me to hurt you. Even when you pointed it out, I refused to acknowledge it and continued to hurt you. I know what I've done to you, to Alanna." He runs a hand through his hair and stares up at the sky. "After I ripped up the papers you signed, I confronted my mother, and she told me the report she'd given me was false. I should've known then that she must have lied about more than just that. It doesn't make anything right, but I truly thought I was protecting Alanna by warning her against you. The reports were just so... I guess it was convenient for me to believe it. It was easier than believing that she simply chose you over me, that I'd lost the one girl I've ever loved. But you were right when you told me that she was never mine. I see it now, and nothing I do or say will ever make up for the pain I've caused."

I look away, a small part of me still struggling to cut ties with my brother. "No," I tell him. "Nothing ever will." I take a step away from him. "I told you that the moment I signed those papers, I'd also be cutting my ties with you. Those words still hold true, Ryan. I understand that your mother fed you elaborate lies, but you aren't a child anymore. When I showed you that picture of Alanna and me and asked you to stop hurting her, to stop messing with her memories, you should have listened to me. I've let you do whatever you wanted, giving you chance after chance. I did it because I made Dad a promise, and I stuck to it until you gave me no other choice, even at my own expense."

I look away and inhale deeply. "I need you to hand in the keys of the apartment I gave you, Ryan. I've already blocked your access to all of my accounts, and I'm taking my cars back, too. Everything I've done for you stops here. The only thing I'll let you keep is your job."

He looks down at his feet and nods, his expression somber. Ryan hands me his keys without putting up a fight, and I breathe a sigh of relief. I don't have it in me to keep arguing with him. I'm just done with it all.

"Someday, Silas... do you think you and I can be like we used to be?"

I look at my little brother, wondering the same. "I don't know," I tell him honestly. "I'd like to think that that's possible, but as it stands, I don't trust you around my family. I can't forgive you for the way you hurt Alanna, even if she does."

"Your family," he repeats, his voice soft. "I suppose that's what she's always been, huh? But what I am?"

I shake my head. "Nothing," I tell him. "From today onward, you're nothing to me."

Ryan straightens, remorse leaving his eyes lowered. "I'm sorry, Silas. I realized it the moment Alanna walked into your office with tears in her eyes. She looked at you, and it's like I didn't even exist. That's when I realized that there's no way that photo of you two could have been fake. I realized that I'd hurt you both, and I walked away hoping it wasn't too late to right my wrongs."

"But it was," I say.

Ryan nods. "You were there for me throughout the years, doing more than you needed to, trying your hardest to make up for the time you missed. You tried to protect me from my mother, and I thanked you by hitting you where it hurt most. I really am sorry, Silas. Despite everything I put you through, you never gave up on me, and I'll do the same. It may not have felt like it to you recently, but you've always been my hero. Maybe someday, you'll believe that again. Until then, I'll do what you've wanted me to do all along. I'll work on becoming the person Dad would have wanted me to be."

I nod at him, hoping he means his words. Maybe someday he and I can be on speaking terms again, but I don't see myself forgiving him for the way he hurt Alanna. There is a lot I can forgive, but not that.

No one hurts my girl and walks away unscathed.

Chapter Eighty-Two

ALANNA

"Do you know why the boss called this meeting?" Jessica asks, her tone concerned. "He's never called for such a large-scale meeting before."

It took a while, but Jessica and I are on better terms now. It isn't like before, where we'd grab coffees together and joke around, but at least things aren't awkward between us anymore.

I shake my head as I follow her to the rooftop. Silas requested that every single Sinclair Security employee attend this meeting, but didn't disclose what it'd be about. "I'm as clueless as you are."

Jessica and I both frown when we see Silas standing in front of a large white screen, a microphone in his hands. His eyes find mine, and he smiles at me. What is going on? Normally he mentions even mundane work things to me, but this is catching me by surprise.

"Most of you must be curious about why you're here, so let me address that first," he says, his gaze roaming over the large crowd that has gathered. There must be hundreds of people standing here, all of us focused on Silas. "The prime purpose of this meeting is to address some rumors that have been spreading."

He turns toward the screen and points a small remote at it, the screen lighten up with the words *Project Sunshine*.

"Ever since I founded this company, I've heard rumors about me starting this company because of a woman." The crowd falls silent, and Silas looks around for a moment, as though he's ensuring he's got everyone's attention. "Those rumors are true."

Whispers erupt around us, excitement spreading across the crowd. Jessica looks at me with concern in her gaze, but I merely smile at her reassuringly before turning back to Silas.

Silas waits for the noise to die down before he speaks again. "Project Sunshine was Sinclair Security's first official project, and as of today, I'm officially closing it."

The slide behind him changes, revealing a photo of the two of us a few years ago, Silas's arm wrapped around me. This photo must have been taken at the shelter shortly after we started dating. I can feel people turn toward me, whispering and pointing. It's what they've done from the moment they found out about Silas and me, and it never gets any easier, but today it feels a little less malicious.

"Those of you who suspected that Project Sunshine was about a woman were right. The girl in this photo was the reason Sinclair Security was founded. She is the reason you all have a job today. Project Sunshine was named after *Ray of Sunshine*, a nickname I gave Alanna Jones many years ago. Five years ago, Alanna was in a car accident that resulted in her losing her memory. For five years, I searched for her. Last year, I finally found her. I haven't spoken up about this before, because Alanna only recently regained her memory, but it's time I put all the rumors to rest. That includes rumors about Alanna and me."

He holds his hand out, and I hesitate before walking toward him, my heart racing as I place my hand in his. Silas entwines our fingers and holds onto me tightly, and I look up at him, unsure what he's doing, and *why*. Why did he call this meeting?

"Most of you are aware that Alanna and I are dating, but none of you knew our story. Now, let me be clear, our private life is none of your business. The only reason I'm telling you about our past is so you have all the facts as you decide what to do next."

Silas wraps his arm around me, his grip tight. "I'm aware some of you have been slandering my girlfriend, spreading rumors and subjecting her to workplace harassment. It seems you have forgotten that you work for a security firm, one filled with high-tech cameras and microphones. The only reason I've remained quiet as long as I have was so I could identify those of you who failed to adhere to our company's policies."

I watch as half the crowd reaches for their phones, several gasps breaking the silence.

"If we have identified you as slandering Alanna, you'll have received a termination notice. You will not get a recommendation from me, and I strongly recommend you seek employment outside of the industry, because no company will take you after being fired from Sinclair Security."

My stomach drops, and I look up at him wide-eyed. "Are you crazy?" I whisper.

Silas tips his head toward mine and smiles. "Yes," he tells me. "So what?"

"You can't do this, Silas. You can't just fire people!"

"I knew you'd say that," he tells me, sighing. "The world doesn't deserve you, Alanna. These people hurt you and slandered you, and you still want to advocate for their jobs?"

I send him a pleading look. This will just alienate so many of his employees, and I suspect it'll also tarnish his reputation in the industry. He'll just be known as the guy who fired people because of his girlfriend. "I don't care about them, Si. Please don't do this, okay? This is unnecessary, and it's crazy. You cannot just fire people over something like this. You'd better take back your words."

Silas shakes his head as he turns back to the crowd. "At Alanna's request, I'll tell you that these termination notices aren't final.

I will allow you to make amends for your mistakes. Those of you who, based on the story I just shared with you, wish to apologize for their actions, may submit a formal letter of apology to Alanna by the end of the day. She may, at her sole discretion, choose to recall my termination notice."

He makes it sound like he's doing them a favor, but in reality, he's just making matters worse. Apology letters? Is he insane? He's just humiliating anyone who offended or hurt me.

"Yes," Amy says. "That sounds fair."

I shake my head at her in disbelief. She's worked for Silas for far too long. He's influencing her in the worst way. Before long, she too, will be a complete nut job.

"You're dismissed. Get back to work and think long and hard about your actions. You had the guts to speak the words you did, so you'd better handle the consequences with the same vigor."

The crowd disperses, most of them sending me pleading looks as they walk away. "You truly are insane," I tell Silas. "You can't just do stuff like that!"

He wraps his arms around me, his gaze intense. "I can, and I will. Did you really think I'd make you suffer in silence? I was just biding my time. I will never ever let any harm come to you again, Alanna. Anyone who so much as harms a hair on your head is going to pay ten times the price. I'm done being lenient. I won't compromise on anything relating to you."

"You're crazy," I tell him, "but I love you."

He grins at me and cups my face, leaning in. "I love you more, Ray," he whispers, his lips brushing past mine, once, twice, before he kisses me.

"Hey, you know what?" he whispers against my lips.

I pull back to look at him. "What?"

"I think that wish of yours has been granted. This. This is true happiness, the kind we've always wanted."

I grin at him, my heart overflowing with the exact happiness he's describing. This really is it. This moment, right now. It's all of our dreams come true.

Chapter Eighty-Three

Alanna

I lean against the kitchen counter and quietly watch Silas. He's been acting weird all week, and I'm not sure what's going on. He's been coming home late every day, not returning until I'm fast asleep, and I'm not sure why. I checked with Amy, and he truly is staying at the office late, but what is keeping him so busy? Even now, he's on his phone instead of spending his morning with me. Our mornings used to be my favorite part of the day, but lately I've been feeling lonely even though Silas is right here with me.

I'm worried he's hurting because of Ryan, but I'm not sure how to make it better. I don't even want to mention Ryan to him, because I don't want him to be reminded of my past with Ryan. I've hurt Silas more than I realized at the time, and I'm scared he's finally realizing that the past can't be undone, that he can't live with my unknowing betrayal.

"Si," I murmur. "Are you okay?"

He looks up from his phone, startled. It's almost like he forgot I'm even here. "Yeah," he tells me, his gaze roaming over my face. I can't decipher the way he's looking at me. Why do his eyes appear to be filled with such longing when I'm standing right here?

"There's somewhere I want to take you today," Silas says.

I nod, my heart racing. There's something about the tone of his voice that makes me uneasy. Lately I've found myself overthinking everything, wondering how I can make up for the pain I put him through, and whether I'll ever be good enough for him.

Silas offers me his hand, and I hold on to him tightly as he leads the way to the garage. He seems absentminded as he starts the car, and I'm too nervous to ask him where we're going. He seems so distant lately, and I can't help the way my heart aches.

I tense when the roads become more and more familiar. "The blossom tree," I whisper.

Silas nods and turns to me as he parks the car. "This used to be where I went when I missed my mother. It's where some of my most precious memories were created when I was younger, and as I grew older, you became the center of them."

He gets out of the car and walks around it, offering me his hand. I look up at him nervously and place my hand in his. I can't tell what's going on, and his expression unnerves me. He can't be here to end things, can he? In the same place we started?

Silas chuckles and pulls me closer. "You're wearing your overthinking face, little psycho."

I tear my gaze away in embarrassment, and Silas laughs, surprising me. This is the first time I've heard him laugh all week.

"Come on," he says, bending down. "I've got something to show you."

Silas lifts me into his arms and grins at me, setting my restless heart at ease. "Keep your eyes on me until I tell you otherwise," he orders, and I nod in agreement. That's an easy enough request. I'll never get enough of looking at him. I thought he was handsome when we were younger, but nothing could've prepared me for Silas as he is now. Everything about him is better than it was in my memories. The way he loves me is fiercer, the way he kisses me leaves me breathless, and then there's the way he touches me, as though each time could be our last. I thought I loved him before, but with each day, my feelings for him grow. I've never been this scared of losing someone. I don't think I even know who I'd be without Silas. He completes me, in every way that matters.

"Ready?"

I nod, and Silas puts me down, his arm wrapping around me as he turns me toward the tree. A soft gasp escapes my lips as I stare at the tree in disbelief, paper cranes hanging from some of the branches and fairy lights threaded through them. It looks magical, and my doubts fall away. He isn't trying to break up with me. This is something else altogether, isn't it?

"You weren't working overtime," I say, my tone accusatory even though I can't keep the smile off my face.

Si takes a step away and grabs the small shovel I once bought, rust coating its edges. "No, Ray. I wasn't working overtime. Those paper cranes? Yeah, they're no joke. I can't believe how long it took to fold a thousand of them. It astounds me that you did that for me."

He hands me the shovel, and I take it from him. "Do they have wishes written on them, too?"

He nods and reaches for one of the cranes, pulling it off the tree. "They do," he tells me. "Each of these cranes carries the same wish. I buried the same wish underneath this tree, too. Do you want to guess what it is? If you get it right, I'll owe you a wish, anything you want at all."

I don't dare to voice my thoughts. I'm scared I'm misreading him, and this isn't what I think it is. "I'll pass today," I tell him, my voice trembling. "Let me dig it up without guessing."

Silas chuckles and nods at me. "Fine, but I have a feeling you'd have guessed right."

I smirk as I sink down on my knees and retrieve the glass bottle impatiently. I have a feeling I know what's hidden within, and I've waited for this longer than I dare to admit.

Silas is smiling at me as I jump back to my feet, my hands trembling as I open the bottle. I glance up at him, his eyes filled with love as he watches me. I'm so nervous I nearly drop the bottle as I take out the rolled-up sheet of paper inside.

"Open it," Si says, his voice laced with urgency, as though he wants this as much as I do.

I bite down on my lip as I do as I'm told, finding a drawing of Silas and me, underneath this tree. Fairy lights in the trees and cranes hanging on the branches, just like today. Except... in the drawing, Silas is down on one knee, a ring in his hand.

"Alanna," he says, dropping down to one knee, the paper crane still in the palm of his hand, except, I realize now that the crane in his hands isn't made of paper. It's a white ring box in the shape of a crane. Silas opens it and holds it up for me, his hand trembling ever so slightly.

"Each of the paper cranes hanging on this tree carries the same wish. For years now, there's only been one thing I've wanted. You, by my side, for the rest of our lives. I know you're regretful about the way things went down, and I see the pain in your eyes, my love. I swear to you that we're fine. Now, and in the future, too. I won't let what happened stand between us. I won't ever punish you for living your life when I couldn't be part of it. You loved me when I had nothing, Alanna. You loved me when you couldn't even *remember* me. That is enough for me. Per aspera ad astra, baby. The adversity we faced was part of our journey, and we only came out stronger in the end. From today onwards, let's leave the past where it belongs. Let's focus on our future together, you and I. Let's build the life we've always dreamed of, together. Make my wish come true, baby. Marry me, Alanna."

I sniff as tears run down my face, nodding at Silas as I smile through the tears. "Yes," I tell him. "*Yes*."

Silas slides a huge diamond ring onto my finger and rises to his feet. "Thank God," he murmurs, taking me into his arms. His lips brush over mine, and I rise to my tiptoes. "I don't know what I would've done if you'd said no. I would've had to kidnap you and shit. My backup plans weren't very solid."

I burst out laughing and kiss him. “You’re crazy,” I whisper against his lips.

“Only for you,” he murmurs before threading his hand through my hair, kissing me until everything but him fades away.

If there’s one thing I’ve learned, it’s that the future is uncertain. No matter how much we plan, no matter how hard we work, everything can change at the blink of an eye. The one thing I’m certain of is that no matter what, Silas and I will always find our way back to each other.

CHAPTER 84
Epilogue

ALANNA

"You look beautiful, Ray," Silas tells me as he offers me his hand.

I narrow my eyes at him and press my index finger against his chest. "You'd better think I'm prettier than the bride, Si. If I catch you looking at her a second too long, we're going to have a problem."

He bursts out laughing and nods. "Yes, my little psycho. I won't look at Raven for more than a second. How about that?"

I nod in satisfaction and take his hand, enjoying the way his wedding ring looks on him. Married life has been more fun than I thought it'd be. It's given both of us a sense of security we've never had before, but it didn't change the core of who we are. We still have fun together, and we still joke around together. Marriage has been everything I hoped it'd be and more.

"I can't believe she's marrying the guy who was supposed to marry her sister," I murmur. "It's crazy."

Silas nods and wraps his arm around me as we head to the venue. "She's always loved him. The only reason she and I were together at all is because she knew about you, and I always knew her heart belonged to someone else, too."

I nod. "I know that, but I'm still worried about her." Oddly enough, Raven and I became friends after Silas and I got engaged. I ran into her while dress shopping at a fashion brand that I didn't realize she owns, and her sincere kindness won me over. She offered to help me plan our wedding, and we've been friends ever since. The press had a field day with us, but neither she nor I cared. Raven is probably one of my only real friends, and I think it's the same for her.

"You know what she's like," Silas says as we walk into the wedding hall. "She isn't just going to let him break her heart. If she agreed to marry him, it's because she hasn't given up on winning him over."

I look up at him, annoyed he isn't more concerned about her. She's one of *his* friends too. This has been a somewhat strange side effect of marriage. We're both so confident in our relationship. Silas will never cheat on me, so though I might joke about Raven, I know he genuinely isn't interested. I'm the center of his world, and he is mine. He always will be.

"Do you know why he's marrying her instead of her sister? Raven told me her sister and this Windsor dude were in love."

Si nods as we take our seats, his arm wrapped around me. "Ares Windsor," he reminds me. "His engagement with Raven's sister was originally due to a merger. I can only assume she backed out, and Raven was asked to take her place."

"That's some bullshit."

Silas and I both sit up as our friends walk toward us. Adrian and Leia Astor sit down next to us, big grins on their faces. Adrian is one of Silas's very few friends, and though they don't see each other often, they're surprisingly close. Every once in a while, they go on cute dates together, probably to bitch about Leia and me.

"You didn't bring the kids?" I ask, disappointed. While Silas and I aren't ready to have kids of our own, I love playing with Leia and Adrian's kids. They're just so cute and well-behaved, and they're always teaching me things about Bollywood and Hindi slang.

"No, they're with their grandparents. I'm so excited to have a day off. I just love weddings!" Leia says, and I smile at her enthusiasm. I should be more excited for Raven, too. After all, she's marrying the man she's always wanted.

"Hey, Silas," Adrian murmurs. "Can Ley and I borrow your truck again?"

My lips fall open as I stare at him. "My father's truck?" I glance between the two of them, noting Leia's flaming cheeks. "What have you two done in my father's precious truck?"

Adrian's eyes widen and he looks so apologetic that I burst out laughing. "Of course you can borrow it." Dad would probably find it funny and endearing, knowing his truck seems to mean a lot to Leia and Adrian.

Si leans into me, his lip brushing over my ear. "You just had to tease him, didn't you?"

I shrug and nod. Of course, I already knew Leia and Adrian love borrowing Dad's truck. There's nothing Silas doesn't tell me.

Music starts to play, and we all rise to our feet as Ares enters, taking his place at the altar, all four of his brothers by his side. He looks stone-faced, but I'll admit that he's handsome. I can see why Raven fell so hard, I just hope he ends up falling just as hard.

Raven walks in, and his eyes widen, a hint of emotion flickering in his gaze. Hmm… maybe this marriage isn't as doomed as I thought it was. The way he looks at her isn't the way he'd be looking at her if he didn't feel a thing for her.

I watch them closely throughout the ceremony, unable to put my worries to rest.

"Question for your thoughts?" Silas whispers.

Ares tenses when he's asked to kiss the bride, but then he leans in and wraps his hand around the back of her neck, kissing her in a way that seems entirely inappropriate considering that until recently, Raven was nothing more than his fiancée's sister. Hmm… good for her.

I glance at my husband and smile. "I'm thinking that Raven's marriage isn't as doomed as I thought it was. I'm glad we attended the ceremony. I feel a lot better now that I've seen them together."

Silas nods, his gaze searching. Sometimes, he looks at me suspiciously. Si always thinks I'm up to some kind of trouble, but this time I'm really not. "Ask your question," he says.

"When we got married, you told me that everything you own is mine now too, right? Does that include Sinclair Security?"

Silas hesitates. "It does… but you cannot send men after Ares Windsor without reason, little psycho. His family is one of our biggest clients, and you really shouldn't interfere with their marriage."

I nod. "Fine, but promise me this. If he hurts her, I get to drag him into an interrogation room and beat him up."

Silas runs a hand through his hair and sighs. "Okay, fine."

I grin at him and lean in to kiss his cheek. "I knew you loved me."

The way he looks at me with such love and exasperation has me giggling. I've never been this happy before, and I know he feels the same way. Silas and I had to fight for everything we've got, including each other. In the end, it was all worth it.

We both rise to our feet as the ceremony wraps up. "You're leaving already?" Leia asks. "You won't stay for the reception?"

I shake my head and place my hand on her shoulder. "We can't. Silas's brother is coming over for dinner tonight. We only really see him every few months, so we didn't want to reschedule. Let's have a picnic with the kids soon, okay? I have the perfect place in mind."

Leia nods and Silas greets Adrian before we head out, our car already waiting for us on the curb. Silas turns to me and narrows his eyes. "You'd better not look at Ryan for more than a second," he warns me, and I burst out laughing. It took us a while, but over time, Ryan and Silas's relationship recovered somewhat. It'll never be what it used to be, but at least they're on speaking terms again. I suppose it helped that Ryan started dating Amy, surprising us all. That, combined with how hard he's been working at Sinclair Security, convinced Silas to give him one final chance. I'm glad he did, because cutting Ryan out of his life made him unhappier than he'd ever admit.

"Fine, but you do know you're crazy, right?"

"Only for you, Ray."

Want a little more of Silas and Alanna? Download the contents of the other three bottles Alanna dug up when she tried to regain her memories. Three more birthday cards from Silas. There's a link available on my website.

Raven & Ares's story, The Wrong Bride, is coming soon

The Off-Limits Series

Have you read the other books in the off-limits series? If not, you can check them out below.

1. Until You

After breaking up with her cheating boyfriend, Aria gets her dream job and a place to stay with her brother's best friend, hotshot software CEO Grayson. But neither knows their online selves have been flirting for months...

2. Dr. Grant

Amara Astor is the one woman Dr. Noah Grant vowed to stay away from, but when she walks into his office with a sex toy stuck inside her, all bets are off.

3. Professor Astor

Leia thought she would never see the man of her dreams again, but two years later, he shows up — as her new professor. And if that weren't enough, Adrian is also the mysterious billionaire that just hired her as a nanny...

Made in the USA
Las Vegas, NV
07 August 2023